Maureen Child writes for [...] can't imagine a better job. A [...] ious Romance Writers of A [...] an author of more than on [...] books regularly appear on bestseller lists and have won several awards, including a Prism Award, a National Readers' Choice Award, a Colorado Romance Writers Award of Excellence and a Golden Quill Award. She is a native Californian but has recently moved to the mountains of Utah.

Cat Schield has been reading and writing romance since high school. Although she graduated from college with a BA in Business, her idea of a perfect career was writing books for Mills & Boon. And now, after winning the Romance Writers of America 2010 Golden Heart® Award for Best Contemporary Series Romance, that dream has come true. Cat lives in Minnesota with her daughter, Emily, and their Burmese cat. When she's not writing sexy, romantic stories for Mills & Boon Desire, she can be found sailing with friends on the St. Croix River, or in more exotic locales, like the Caribbean and Europe. She loves to hear from readers. Find her at www.catschield.com and follow her on Twitter, @catschield.

Sara Orwig is an Oklahoman whose life revolves around family, flowers, dogs and books. Books are like her children: she usually knows where they are, they delight her and she doesn't want to be without them. With a master's degree in English, Sara has written mainstream fiction, and historical and contemporary romance. She has one hundred published novels translated in over twenty-six languages. You can visit her website at www.saraorwig.com

Seductive Revenge

MAUREEN CHILD
CAT SCHIELD
SARA ORWIG

MILLS & BOON

First Published in Great Britain 2019
by Mills & Boon, an imprint of HarperCollins*Publishers*
1 London Bridge Street, London, SE1 9GF

SEDUCTIVE REVENGE © 2019 Harlequin Books S. A.

The Tycoon's Secret Child © 2017 Harlequin Books S.A.
Two-Week Texas Seduction © 2017 Harlequin Books S.A.
Reunited With The Rancher © 2017 Harlequin Books S.A.

Special thanks and acknowledgement are given to Maureen Child, Cat Schield and Sara Orwig for their contribution to the *Texas Cattleman's Club: Blackmail* series.

ISBN: 978-0-263-27656-5

0619

MIX
Paper from
responsible sources
FSC™ C007454

This book is produced from independently certified FSC™ paper to ensure responsible forest management.

For more information visit: www.harpercollins.co.uk/green

Printed and bound in Spain
by CPI, Barcelona

THE TYCOON'S SECRET CHILD

MAUREEN CHILD

To the world's greatest editors,
Stacy Boyd and Charles Griemsman—
in the world of writers and editors,
you two shine. Writing isn't always easy
but you guys bring out the best in all of us.

One

Wesley Jackson sat in his corporate office in Houston, riding herd on the department heads attending the meeting he'd called. It had been a long two hours, and he was about done. Thankfully, things were winding down now and he could get out of the city. He didn't mind coming into town once in a while, but he always seemed to breathe deeper and easier back home in Royal.

Didn't appear to matter how successful he became, he'd always be a small-town guy at the heart of it. Just as, he thought with an inner smile as he set one booted foot on his knee, you couldn't take Texas out of the businessman.

"Am I keeping you from something important?" Wes asked suddenly when he noticed Mike Stein, the youngest man on his PR team, staring out a window from the other side of his wide mahogany desk.

Mike flinched. He was energetic, usually eager, but

a little distracted today. Not hard to understand, Wes thought, considering it was January 2 and everyone in the office was probably nursing the dregs of a hangover from various New Year's parties. And Wes could cut the kid a small break, but that was done now.

"What?" Mike blurted. "No, absolutely not. Sorry."

Tony Danvers snorted, then hid the sound behind a cough.

Wes's gaze slid to him, then to the woman sitting on the other side of him. Mike was new, but talented and driven. Tony knew his way around the company blind-folded, and Donna Higgs had her finger on the pulse of every department in the building. The three of them exemplified exactly what he expected from his employees. Dedication. Determination. Results.

Since everything else he'd wanted discussed had been covered in the last two hours, Wes finally brought up the most important item on his agenda.

"The Just Like Me line," he said, flicking a glance at Tony Danvers. "Any problems? We on track for spring delivery to outlets?"

This new doll was destined to be the biggest thing in the country. At least, he told himself, that was the plan. There were dolls that could be specially ordered to look like a child, of course. But Wes's company had the jump on even them. With the accessories available and the quick turnaround, the Just Like Me doll was going to smash all sales record previously set for...*anything.* He smiled to himself just thinking about it. A line of dolls that looked like their owners. Parents could find a doll that resembled their child, either online or at retail locations. Or they could special order one with accessories to make it even more like the child in question.

Wes once considered bringing the doll out early, to

catch the Christmas shopping frenzy. But he'd decided against it, banking on the fact that by February children would already be tired of their Christmas toys and looking for something new.

He was counting on making such an impact that by *next* Christmas, the dolls would be on every kid's wish list. And every child who had already received one would be looking for another. Maybe one in the image of a best friend or a sibling.

The possibilities were endless.

Tony sat back in his brown leather chair, hooked one ankle on a knee. "We're right on schedule, boss. We've got dozens of different designs of dolls. Every ethnicity, every hair type I've ever heard of, and a few that were news to me."

"You're so male," Donna Higgs, the marketing director, muttered with a shake of her head.

Tony winked at her. "Thanks for noticing."

Wes grinned but not at the two friends' byplay. His company, Texas Toy Goods Inc., was going to be the most talked-about toy company in the country once these dolls hit. Marketing, under Donna's steady hand, was already set for a huge campaign, he had the PR department set to flood social media, and a test group of kids had already proclaimed the doll a winner. After ten years of steady growth, Wes's company was poised for a jump that would change Wes from a multimillionaire to a billionaire practically overnight.

He'd started his company on not much more than a shoestring. He had had ideas, a partner he'd managed to buy out several years ago and a small inheritance from his father. With that, and his own driving ambition, Wes built a reputation for coming up with new ways of doing things in a centuries-old industry. He was known for his innovation and creativity. Thanks to him, and the best employees in the business, they'd built on their early successes until TTG was a presence in the toy industry. And the Just Like Me doll was going to give them that one last push over the top.

Each doll was unique in its own way and was going to appeal to every child on the planet. He had visions of European distribution as well, and knew that soon Texas Toy Goods was going to be an unstoppable force in the industry. And that wasn't even counting the upcoming merger he was working on with Teddy Bradford, the current CEO of PlayCo, or his other ventures under the Texas brand umbrella.

"So," Wes said, bringing them back on topic, "if the parent doesn't find exactly what they're looking for, we're set up for them to order specifics."

"Absolutely." Tony straightened up then leaned forward, bracing his forearms on his knees. "There'll be a kiosk in every toy department. The computer will link them to us and they can put in an order for any specific detail they need. Say, if the child has a prosthetic, we can match it. If the child has a specific disability, we're prepared for everything. From wheelchairs to braces, we can give every child out there the feeling of being special. Having a doll in their own image. Naturally, specific orders would take a little longer…"

Wes frowned. "How much longer?"

"Negligible," Donna put in. She checked something on her iPad and looked up at him. "I know Tony's production, but in marketing, we've been working with turnaround time so we can advertise it. With the wide array of dolls already available, we can put out a special order in a couple of days."

"That works." Nodding now, Wes leaned back in his

own chair. "Make sure the factory floor is up to speed on this, and I want a centralized area devoted *only* to this project."

"Uh, boss?" Mike Stein held up one hand as if he were in class. But then, he was young and enthusiastic and would eventually get used to the more wide-open discussions Wes preferred during meetings.

"What is it?"

Mike glanced at the others before looking back at Wes. "We've got the ads lined up and the social media blast is ready to roll on the day."

"Good."

"But," Mike added, "I know it's not my department—"

"Doesn't matter," Wes told him. He liked his people being interested in *all* departments, not just their specialties.

"Okay. I was thinking, having a dedicated area at the factory could be problematic."

Tony actually leaned a little toward the left, putting some distance between himself and the new guy. At least the others knew better than to tell Wes something couldn't be done.

"Why's that?" Wes asked calmly.

"Well, it means pulling people off the line and setting them up to handle *only* these special orders."

"And?"

"Well," Mike continued, clearly unwilling to back off the track he found himself on. Wes could give him points for having guts. "That means we have people who are standing there *waiting* for something to do instead of working on the line and getting actual work done."

"What changes would you suggest?" Wes asked coolly.

Tony cleared his throat and gave a barely there shake

of his head, trying to tell the kid in code to just shut up and let this one go. But Mike had the bit in his teeth now and wouldn't drop it.

"I would leave them working on the line and pull them out when a special order came in and then—"

"I appreciate your idea," Wes said, tapping his fingers against the gray leather blotter on his desk. "I want my people to feel free to speak up. But you're new here, Mike, and you need to learn that at TTG, we do things a little differently. Here, the customer is always number one. We design toys and the delivery system to facilitate the people who buy our toys. So if that means we have a separate crew waiting for the special orders to come in, then that's what we do. We're the best. That's what breeds success."

"Right." Mike nodded, swallowed hard and nodded again. "Absolutely. Sorry."

"No problem." Wes waved the apology away. He'd either learn from this and pick up on the way things were done at TTG, or the kid would leave and find a job somewhere else.

But damn, when did he start thinking of guys in their twenties as *kids*? When did Wes get ancient? He squashed that thought immediately. Hell, at thirty-four, he wasn't old. He was just *busy*. Running his company ate up every moment of every damn day. He was so busy, his social life was a joke. He couldn't even remember the last time he'd been with a woman. But that would come. Eventually. Right now, TTG demanded and deserved his full concentration.

Of course, his brain whispered, it hadn't always been that way. There'd been one woman—

Wes cut all thoughts of her off at the pass. That was done. Over. He hadn't been interested in long-term and she'd all but had *marriage and children* tattooed across her forehead. He'd had to end it and he wasn't sorry. Most of the time.

Having a relationship with one of his employees hadn't been a particularly smart move on his part. And sure, there'd been gossip and even resentment from some of his staff. But Wes hadn't been able to resist Belle. What the two of them had shared was like nothing he'd ever known. For a time, Wes had been willing to put up with whispers at work for the pleasure of being with Belle.

But it was over. The past.

"We've got the accessories covered, I think," Donna said. "When the special orders come in, we'll be able to turn them around in a flash."

"Good to hear. And if you don't have it?" Wes asked.

"We'll get it." Donna nodded sharply. "No problem on this, boss. It's going to work as smoothly as you expect it to. And it's going to be the biggest doll to hit the market since the vegetable patch babies back in the '80s."

"That's what I want to hear." Wes stood up, shoved both hands into his pockets and said, "That's all for now. Keep me in the loop."

Tony laughed. "Boss, everybody runs everything by you."

One corner of Wes's mouth quirked. "Yeah. Just the way I like it. Okay, back to work."

He watched them go, then told his assistant, Robin, to get him some fresh coffee. He'd need it once he started going through business emails. Inevitably, there were problems to walk through with suppliers, manufacturers, bankers and everyone else who either had a piece—or wanted one—of the Texas Toy Goods pie. But instead of taking a seat behind his desk, he walked across the wide office to the corner windows. The view of Houston was familiar, impressive. High-rises, glass walls reflecting sunlight that could blind a man. Thick white clouds sailing across a sky so blue it hurt the eyes.

He liked the city fine, but it wasn't somewhere he wanted to spend too much time. At least twice a week, he made the drive in from Royal, Texas, and his home office, to oversee accounts personally and on-site. He believed in having his employees used to seeing him there. People tended to get complacent when there was an absentee boss in the picture. But if he had a choice, he'd pick Royal over Houston.

His hometown had less traffic, less noise and the best burgers in Texas at the Royal Diner. Not to mention the fact that the memories in Royal were easier to live with than the ones centered here, in his office. Just being here, he remembered late-night work sessions with the woman he refused to think about. All-night sessions that had become a blistering-hot affair that had crashed and burned the minute she whispered those three deadly words—*I love you*. Even after all this time, that moment infuriated him. And despite—maybe *because* of—how it ended, that one woman stayed in his mind, always at the edges of his thoughts.

"What is it with women?" he asked the empty room. "Everything was going fine and then she just had to ruin it."

Of course, a boss/employee relationship wasn't going to work for the long haul anyway, and he'd known that going in. And even with the way things had ended, he couldn't completely regret any of it. What bothered him was that even now, five years later, thoughts of Belle kept cropping up as if his mind just couldn't let go.

A brisk knock on the door had him shaking his head

and pushing thoughts of her to the back of his mind, where, hopefully, they would stay. "Come in."

Robin entered, carrying a tray with a single cup, a thermal carafe of coffee and a plate of cookies. He smiled. "What would I do without you?"

"Starve to death, probably," she said. Robin was in her forties, happily married and the proud mother of four. She loved her job, was damn good at it and kept him apprised of everything going on down here when he was in Royal. If she ever threatened to quit, Wes was prepared to offer her whatever she needed to stay.

"You scared the kid today."

Snorting a laugh as he remembered the look of sheer panic on Mike's face, Wes sat down at his desk and poured the first of what would be several cups of coffee. "He'll survive."

"Yeah, he will. A little fear's good. Builds character."

One eyebrow lifted as Wes laughed. "Your kids must be terrified of you."

"Me?" she asked. "Nope. I raise them tougher than that."

Wes chuckled.

"Harry called. He's headed into that meeting in New York. Said he'd call when he had it wrapped up."

Harry Baker, his vice president, was currently doing all the traveling around the country, arranging for the expedited shipping the new doll line would require. "That's good. Thanks."

After she left, Wes sipped at his coffee, took a cookie, had a bite, then scrolled to his email account. Idly, he scanned the forty latest messages, deleting the crap. He scanned the subject lines ruthlessly, until he spotted Your secret is out.

"What the hell?" Even while a part of his mind was

thinking *virus or an ad for timeshares in Belize,* he clicked on the message and read it. Everything in him went cold and still. The cookie turned to ash in his mouth and he drank the coffee only to wash it down.

Look where your dallying has gotten you, the email read.

Check your Twitter account. Your new handle is Deadbeatdad. So you want to be the face of a new toy empire? Family friendly? Think again.

It was signed, Maverick.

"Who the hell is Maverick and what the hell is he talking about?" There was an attachment with the email, and even though Wes had a bad feeling about all of this, he opened it. The photograph popped onto his computer screen.

He shot to his feet, the legs of his chair scraping against the polished wooden floor like a screech. Staring down at the screen, his gaze locked on the image of the little girl staring back at him. "What the—"

She looked just like him. The child had Wes's eyes and a familiar smile and if that wasn't enough to convince him, which it was, he focused on the necklace the girl was wearing. Before he and Belle broke up, Wes had given her a red plastic heart on a chain of plastic beads. At the time, he'd used it as a joke gift right before giving her a pair of diamond earrings.

And the little girl in the photo was wearing that red heart necklace while she smiled into the camera.

Panic and fury tangled up inside him and tightened into a knot that made him feel like he was choking. He couldn't tear his gaze from the photo of the smiling little girl. "How does a man have a daughter and not know it?"

A daughter? How? What? Why? *Who?* He had a *child.* Judging by the picture, she looked to be four or five years old, so unless it was an old photo, there was only one woman who could be the girl's mother. And just like that, *the* woman was back, front and center in his mind.

How the hell had this happened? Stupid. He knew *how* it had happened. What he didn't know was why he hadn't been told. Wes rubbed one hand along the back of his neck and didn't even touch the tension building there. Still staring at the smiling girl on the screen, he felt the email batter away at his brain until he was forced to sit, open a new window and go to Twitter.

Somebody had hacked his account. His new handle was, as promised, Deadbeatdad. If he didn't get this stopped fast, it would go viral and might start interfering with his business.

Instantly, Wes made some calls, reporting that his account had been hacked, then turned the mess over to his IT guys to figure out. He reported the hack and had the account shuttered, hoping to buy time. Meanwhile, he was too late to stop #Deadbeatdad from spreading. The Twitterverse was already moving on it. Now he had a child he had to find and a reputation he had to repair. Snatching up the phone, he stabbed the button for his assistant's desk. "Robin," he snapped. "Get Mike from PR back in here *now.*"

He didn't even wait to hear her response, just slammed the phone down and went back to his computer. He brought up the image of the little girl—his *daughter*—again and stared at her. What was her name? Where did she live? Then thoughts of the woman who had to be the girl's mother settled into his brain. Isabelle Gray. She'd disappeared from his life years ago—apparently with his child. Jaw tight, eyes narrowed, Wes promised himself he was going to get to the bottom of all of this and when he did…

For the next hour, everyone in PR and IT worked the situation. There was no stopping the flood of retweets, so Wes had Mike and his crew focused on finding a way to spin it. IT was tasked with tracking down this mysterious Maverick so that Wes could deal with him head-on.

Meanwhile, Wes had another problem to worry about. The merger with PlayCo, a major player in the toy industry, was something Wes had been carefully maneuvering his way toward for months. But the CEO there, Teddy Bradford, was a good old boy with rock-solid claims to family values. He'd been married to the same woman forever, had several kids and prided himself on being the flag bearer for the all-American, apple pie lifestyle.

This was going to throw a wrench of gigantic proportions into the mix. And so far, Teddy wasn't taking any of Wes's calls. Not a good sign.

"Uh, boss?"

"Yeah?" Wes spun around to look at one of the PR grunts. What the hell was her name? Stacy? Tracy? "What is it?"

"Teddy Bradford is holding a press conference. The news channel's website is running it live."

He stalked to her desk and only vaguely noticed that the others in the room had formed a half circle behind him. They were all watching as Bradford stepped up to a microphone and held his hands out in a settle-down gesture. As soon as he had quiet, he said, "After the disturbing revelations on social media this afternoon, I'm here to announce that I will be taking a step back to re-evaluate my options before going through with the much anticipated merger."

Wes ground his teeth together and fisted his hands at his sides. Teddy could play it any way he wanted to for the press, but it was easy to see the merger was, at the moment, dead. All around him, his employees took a collective breath that sounded like a gasp.

But Teddy wasn't finished. The older man looked somber, sad, but Wes was pretty sure he caught a gleam of satisfaction in the other man's eyes. Hell, he was probably enjoying this. Nothing the man liked better than sitting high on his righteous horse. Teddy hadn't even bothered to take his call, preferring instead to call a damn press conference. Bastard.

"Here at PlayCo," Teddy was saying, "we put a high priority on family values. In fact, you could say that's the dominant trademark of my company and it always will be. A man's family is all important—or should be. After this morning's revelations, I have to say that clearly, Wes Jackson is not the man I'd believed him to be, and so I have some thinking to do in the next few days. As things stand now, it would take a miracle to persuade me to believe otherwise." Questions were fired at him, cameras chattered as shutters clicked over and over again. But Teddy was done.

"That's it. That's all I've got to say." He looked out over the crowd. "You have more questions, I suggest you throw them at Wes Jackson. Good day." He left the podium in the midst of a media circus and Wes rubbed his eyes, trying to ease the headache crouched behind them.

Stacy/Tracy turned the sound off on the computer, and silence dropped over everyone in the room like a damn shroud. Inside Wes, irritation bubbled into anger and then morphed quickly into helpless rage. There was nowhere to turn it. Nowhere to focus it and get any kind of satisfaction.

As of now, the merger was in the toilet. And yeah, he was concentrating on the business aspect of this nightmare because he didn't have enough information to concentrate on the personal. Furious, Wes watched his PR team scramble to somehow mitigate the growing disaster. His assistant was already fielding calls from the media and this story seemed to be growing by the minute. Nothing people liked better than a scandal, and whoever this Maverick was, they obviously knew it.

For the first time ever, Wes felt helpless, and he didn't like it. Not only was his company taking a hit, but somewhere out there, he had a child he'd known nothing about. How the hell had this Maverick discovered the girl? Was Isabelle in on all of this? Or was someone close to her hoping for a giant payout along with pay-*back*? Whatever the reason, this attack was deliberate. Someone had arranged a deliberate assault on him and his company. That someone was out to ruin him, and his brain worked feverishly trying to figure out just who was behind it all.

Running a successful business meant that you would naturally make enemies. But until today he wouldn't have thought that any of them would stoop to something like this. So he went deeper, beyond business and into the personal, looking for anyone who might have set him up for a fall like this. And only one name rose up in his mind. His ex-girlfriend, Cecelia Morgan.

She and Belle had been friendly for a while back in the day. Maybe Cecelia had known about the baby. Maybe she was the one who had started all this. Hell, she might even be Maverick herself. Cecelia hadn't taken it well when he broke up with her, and God knew she had a vicious temper. But if she was behind it all, *why*? Her company, To the Moon, sold upscale merchandise for kids. They weren't in direct competition, but she was as devoted to her business as Wes was to his, and maybe that was the main reason the two of them hadn't worked out. Or, he told himself, maybe it was the mean streak he'd witnessed whenever Cecelia was with her two best friends, Simone Parker and Naomi Price. He knew for a fact that people in Royal called the three women the Mean Girls. They were rich, beautiful, entitled and sometimes not real careful about the things they said to and about people.

He didn't know if she'd had anything to do with what was happening, but there was one sure way to find out. Leaving his employees scrambling, Wes drove home to Royal to confront his ex and, just maybe, get some answers. The drive did nothing to calm him down, since his brain kept focusing on the photo of that little girl. His daughter, for God's sake.

He needed answers. The only one who could give them to him was Belle, so finding her was priority one. His IT staff was now focused on not only mitigating his business disaster, but also in finding Isabelle Gray. But until he did locate Belle, Wes told himself, at least he could do *something.* Knowing Cecelia could always be found at the Texas Cattleman's Club for lunch, he headed there the moment he hit town.

Cecelia was in the middle of what looked like a lunch meeting with a few of her employees. And though breaking it up would only encourage gossip, Wes wasn't interested in waiting for her to finish. The TCC was a legend in Royal, Texas. A members-only club, it had been around forever and only in the last several years had started accepting women as members—quite a few of the old guard still weren't happy about it. The dining room was elegant, understated and quiet but for the hush of conversation and the subtle clink of silverware against china.

On the drive from Houston, Wes's mind had raced with the implications of everything that had happened. A child he didn't know about. A merger in the toilet. His reputation shattered. And at the bottom of it all, maybe a vengeful ex. By the time he stood outside that dining room, he was ready for a battle.

"Mr. Jackson." The maître d' stepped up. "May I show you to a table? Are you alone for lunch or expecting guests?"

"Neither, thanks," Wes said, ignoring the man after a brief, polite nod. Wes speared Cecelia with a cold, hard gaze that caught her attention even from across the room. "I just need a word with Ms. Morgan."

Once she met his cool stare, she frowned slightly, then excused herself from the table and walked toward him. She was a gorgeous woman, and in a purely male response, Wes had to admire her even as his anger bubbled and churned inside. Her long, wavy blond hair lay across her shoulders and her gray-green eyes fixed on him, curiosity shining there. She wasn't very tall, but her generous figure and signature pout had brought more than one man in Texas to his knees.

She gave him a smile, then leaned in as if to kiss his cheek, but Wes pulled back out of reach. He caught the surprise and the insult in her eyes, but he only said, "We need to talk."

There were already enough people talking about his

business today, so he took her forearm in a tight grip and led her away from the dining room to a quiet corner, hoping for at least a semblance of privacy. Cecelia pulled free as soon as he stopped and hissed, "What is going on with you?"

"You know damn well what," he said in a gravelly whisper. "That email you sent."

Those big, beautiful eyes clouded with confusion. "I have zero idea what you're talking about."

He studied her for a long minute, deciding whether she was lying or not. God knew he couldn't be sure, but he was going with instinct here. She didn't look satisfied with a mission accomplished. She looked irritated and baffled.

"Fine," he said grimly and dug his cell phone out of a pocket. Pulling up his email, he handed the phone to her and waited while she read it.

"Maverick? Who the heck is Maverick?"

Her expression read confusion and a part of him eased back a little. But if she wasn't Maverick, who was?

"Good question. I got an email this morning from a stranger. They sent me a picture of a daughter I never knew existed." He opened the attachment and showed her the picture of the smiling little girl. That's when he saw the flash of recognition in her eyes and he realized that Cecelia knew more than she was saying. Her face was too easy to read. His daughter's existence hadn't surprised her a bit.

"You knew about the girl." It wasn't a question. His chest felt tight.

Taking a deep breath, Cecelia blew out a breath and said, "I knew she was pregnant when she left. I didn't know she'd had a girl."

"She?"

Cecelia huffed out a breath. "Isabelle."

He swayed in place. He'd known it. Seeing that neck-lace on a little girl with his eyes had been impossible to deny. Isabelle. The woman he'd been involved with for almost a year had been pregnant with *his* daughter and hadn't bothered to tell him. More than that, though, was the fact that apparently Cecelia had known about his child, too, and kept the secret. Belle had left town. Cecelia had been right here in Royal. Seeing him all the damn time. And never once had she let on that he had a child out there. He couldn't rage at Belle. Yet. So it was the woman in front of him who got the full blast of what he was feeling. Every time she'd seen him for the last five years, she'd lied to him by not saying anything. She'd *known* he was a father and never said a damn word. What the hell? And who was Maverick and how did he know?

"You knew and didn't say anything?" His voice was low and tight.

She tossed a glance over her shoulder toward the table where she'd left her friends, then looked back at him. "No, I didn't. What would have been the point?"

He glared at her. "The point? My kid would be the point. And the fact that I didn't even know she existed."

"Please, Wes. How many times have you said you don't want kids or a family or anything remotely resem-bling commitment?"

"Not important."

"Yeah, it is." She was getting defensive—he heard it in her voice. "She was pretty sure you wouldn't be happy about the baby and I agreed. I just told her what you'd said so many times—that you weren't interested in families or forever."

Having his own words thrown back at him stung, but worse was the fact that *two* women he'd been with had conspired to keep his child from him. No, he'd never planned on kids or a wife, but that didn't mean he wouldn't want to know.

"Then what?" he asked, his voice sounding as if it was scraping along shattered glass. "You wait a few years, find this Maverick and tell *him*? Help him slam me across social media? For what? Payback?"

Her head snapped back and her eyes went even wider. "I would never do that to you, Wes," she said, and damned if he didn't almost believe her. "I wouldn't hurt you like that."

"Yeah?" he countered. "Your rep says otherwise."

She flushed and took a deep breath. "Believe what you want, but it wasn't me."

"Fine. Then where is Isabelle?"

"I don't know. She only said she was going home. A small town in Colorado. Swan...something. I forget. Honestly, we haven't stayed in touch." Tentatively, she reached out one hand and laid it on his forearm. "But I'll help you look for her."

"You helped enough five years ago," Wes ground out, and saw her reaction to the harsh tone flash in her eyes.

Too bad. He didn't have time to worry about insulting a woman who very well might be at the heart of this Maverick business. Sure, she claimed innocence, but he'd be a fool to take her word for it. When he rushed out, he barely noticed the waiter hovering nearby.

Wes's entire IT department was working on this problem, but he should be researching himself. His own tech skills were more than decent. He could have found Isabelle years ago, if he'd been looking. Yeah, he'd have to sift through a lot of information on the web, but he'd find her.

And when he did, heaven better help her, because hell would be dropping onto her doorstep.

Isabelle Graystone sat at the kitchen table working with a pad and pen while her daughter enjoyed her post-preschool snack.

"Mommy," Caroline said, her fingers dancing as she spoke, "can I have more cookies?"

Isabelle looked at the tiny love of her life and smiled. At four years old, Caroline was beautiful, bright, curious and quite the con artist when it came to getting more cookies. That sly smile and shy glance did it every time.

Isabelle's hands moved in sign language as she said, "Two more and that's it."

Caroline grinned and helped herself. Her heels tapped against the rungs of the kitchen chair as she cupped both hands around her glass of milk to take a sip.

Watching her, Isabelle smiled thoughtfully. It wasn't easy for a child to be different, but Caroline had such a strong personality that wearing hearing aids didn't bother her in the least. And learning to sign had opened up her conversational skills. Progressive hearing loss would march on, though, Isabelle knew, and one day her daughter would be completely deaf.

So Isabelle was determined to do everything she could to make her little girl's life as normal as possible. Which might also include a cochlear implant at some point. She wasn't there yet, but she was considering all of her options. There was simply nothing she wouldn't do for Caroline.

"After lunch," Isabelle said, "I have to go into town. See some people about the fund-raiser party I'm planning. Do you want to come with me, or stay here with Edna?"

Chewing enthusiastically, Caroline didn't speak, just used sign language to say, "I'll come with you. Can we have ice cream, too?"

Laughing, Isabelle shook her head. "Where are you putting all of this food?"

A shrug and a grin were her only answers. Then the doorbell rang and Isabelle said, "Someone's at the door. You finish your cookies."

She walked through the house, hearing the soft click of her own heels against the polished wood floors. There were landscapes hanging on the walls, and watery winter sunlight filtering through the skylight positioned over the hallway. It was an elegant but homey place, in spite of its size. The restored Victorian stood on three acres outside the small town of Swan Hollow, Colorado.

Isabelle had been born and raised there, and when she'd found herself alone and pregnant, she'd come running back to the place that held her heart. She hadn't regretted it, either. It was good to be in a familiar place, nice knowing that her daughter would have the same memories of growing up in the forest that she did, and then there was the added plus of having her three older brothers nearby. Chance, Eli and Tyler were terrific uncles to Caroline and always there for Isabelle when she needed them—and sometimes when she didn't. The three of them were still as protective as they'd been when she was just a girl—and though it could get annoying on occasion, she was grateful for them, too.

Shaking her long, blond hair back from her face, she opened the door with a welcoming smile on her face—only to have it freeze up and die. A ball of ice dropped into the pit of her stomach even as her heartbeat jumped into overdrive.

Wes Jackson. The one man she'd never thought to see

again. The one man she still dreamed of almost every night. The one man she could never forget.

"Hello, Belle," he said, his eyes as cold and distant as the moon. "Aren't you going to invite me in?"

Two

Isabelle felt her heart lurch to a stop then kick to life again in a hard thump. *Invite him in?* What she wanted to do was step back inside, slam the door and lock it. Too bad she couldn't seem to move. She did manage to choke out a single word. "Wes?"

"So you do remember me. Good to know." He moved in closer and Isabelle instinctively took a step back, pulling the half-open door closer, like a shield.

Panic nibbled at her, and Isabelle knew that in a couple more seconds it would start taking huge, gobbling bites. As unexpected as it was to find Wes Jackson standing on her front porch, there was a part of her that wasn't the least bit surprised to see him. Somehow, she'd half expected that one day, her past would catch up to her.

It had been five long years since she'd seen him, yet looking at him now, it could have been yesterday. Even in this situation, with his eyes flashing fury, she felt that bone-deep stir of something hot and needy and oh, so tempting. What was *wrong* with her? Hadn't she learned her lesson?

Isabelle had loved working for Texas Toys. They were open to new ideas and Wes had been the kind of boss everyone should have. He encouraged his employees to try new and different things and rewarded hard work. He was always hands-on when it came to introducing fresh products to his established line. So he and Isabelle had worked closely together as she came up with new toys, new designs. When she'd given in to temptation, surrendered to the heat simmering between them, Isabelle had known that it wouldn't end well. Boss/employee flings were practically a cliché after all. But the more time she spent with him, the more she'd felt for him until she'd made the mistake of falling in love with him.

That's when everything had ended. When he'd told her that he wasn't interested in more than an affair. He'd broken her heart, and when she left Texas, she'd vowed to never go back.

It seemed though, she hadn't had to. Texas had come to *her*.

"We have to talk." His voice was clipped, cold.

"No, we really don't." Isabelle wasn't going to give an inch. She wasn't even sure why he was here, and if he didn't know the whole truth, she wasn't going to give him any information. The only important thing was getting rid of him before he could see Caroline.

"That's not gonna fly," he said and moved in, putting both hands on her shoulders to ease her back and out of the way.

The move caught her so off guard, Isabelle didn't even try to hold her ground. He was already walking into the house before she could stop him. And even as she opened her mouth to protest, his arm brushed against her breast and she shivered. It wasn't fear stirring inside her, not even panic. It was desire.

The same flush of need had happened to her years ago whenever Wes was near. Almost from the first minute she'd met him, that jolt of something *more* had erupted between them. She'd never felt anything like it before Wes—or since. Of course, since she came back home to Swan Hollow, she hadn't exactly been drowning in men.

After Wes, she'd made the decision to step back from relationships entirely. Instead, she had focused on building a new life for her and her daughter. And especially during the last year or so, that focus had shut out everything else. Isabelle had her brothers, her daughter, and she didn't need anything else. Least of all the man who'd stolen her heart only to crush it underfoot.

With those thoughts racing through her mind, she closed the door and turned to face her past.

"I think I deserve an explanation," he said tightly.

"You *deserve*?" she repeated, in little more than a hiss. She shot a quick look down the hall toward the kitchen where Caroline was. "Really? That's what you want to lead with?"

"You should have told me about our daughter."

Shock slapped at her. But at the same time, a tiny voice in the back of Isabelle's mind whispered, *Of course he knows. Why else would he be here?* But how had he found out?

One dark eyebrow lifted. "Surprised? Yeah, I can see that. Since you've spent *five years* hiding the truth from me."

Hard to argue with that, since he was absolutely right. But on the other hand… "Wes—"

He held up one hand and she instantly fell into silence

even though she was infuriated at herself for reacting as he expected her to.

"Spare me your excuses. There *is* no excuse for this. Damn it, Isabelle, I had a right to know."

Okay, that was enough to jolt her out of whatever fugue state he'd thrown her into. Keeping her voice low, she argued, "A right? I should have told you about *my* daughter when you made it perfectly clear you had no interest in being a father?"

Wanting to get him out of the hall where Caroline might see him, she walked past him into the living room. It was washed with pale sunlight, even on this gloomy winter day. The walls were a pale green and dotted with paintings of forests and sunsets and oceans. There were books lining the waist-high bookcases that ran the perimeter of the room and several comfortable oversize chairs and couches.

Oak tables were scattered throughout and a blue marble-tiled hearth was filled with a simmering fire. This room—heck, this *house*—was her haven. She'd made a home here for her and Caroline. It was warm and cozy in spite of its enormous size, and she loved everything about it. So why was it, she wondered, that with Wes Jackson standing in the cavernous room, she suddenly felt claustrophobic?

He came up right behind her and she felt as if she couldn't draw a breath. She wanted him out. Now. Before Caroline could come in and start asking questions Isabelle didn't want to answer. She whipped around to face him, to finish this, to allow him to satisfy whatever egotistical motive had brought him here so he could leave.

His aqua eyes were still so deep. So mesmerizing. Even with banked anger glittering there, she felt drawn to him. And that was just…sad. His collar-length blond hair was ruffled, as if he'd been impatiently driving his fingers through it. His jaw was set and his mouth a firm, grim line. This was the face he regularly showed the world. The cool, hard businessman with an extremely low threshold for lies.

But she'd known the real man. At least, she'd told herself at the time that the man she talked, laughed and slept with was the real Wes Jackson. When they were alone, his guard was relaxed, though even then, she'd had to admit that he'd held a part of himself back. Behind a wall of caution she hadn't been able to completely breach. She'd known even then that Wes would continue to keep her at a safe distance and though it had broken her heart to acknowledge it, for her own sake, and the sake of her unborn child, she'd had to walk away.

"That was a hypothetical child," he ground out, and every word sounded harsh, as if it was scraping against his throat. "I never said I wouldn't want a child who was already *here*."

A tiny flicker of guilt jumped into life in the center of her chest, but Isabelle instantly smothered it. Five years ago, Wes had made it clear he wasn't interested in a family. He'd told her in no uncertain terms that he didn't want a wife. Children. *Love.* She'd left. Come home. Had her baby alone, with her three older brothers there to support her. Now Caroline was happy, loved, settled. How was Isabelle supposed to feel guilty about doing the best thing for her child?

So she stiffened her spine, lifted her chin and met Wes's angry glare with one of her own. "You won't make me feel bad about a decision I made in the best interests of my daughter."

"*Our* daughter, and you had no right to keep her from me." He shoved both hands into the pockets of his black leather jacket, then pulled them free again. "Damn it, Isabelle, you didn't make that baby on your own."

"No, I didn't," she said, nodding. "But I've taken care of her on my own. Raised her on my own. You don't get to storm into my life and start throwing orders around, Wes. I don't work for you anymore, and this is *my* home."

His beautiful eyes narrowed on her. "You lied to me. For five years, you lied to me."

"I haven't even spoken to you."

"A lie of omission is still a lie," he snapped.

He was right, but she had to wonder. Was he here because of the child he'd just discovered or because she'd wounded his pride? She tipped her head to one side and studied him. "You haven't even asked where she is, or how she is. Or even what her name is. This isn't about her for you, Wes. This is about *you*. Your ego."

"Her name is Caroline," he said softly. He choked out a laugh that never reached his eyes. "I'm pretty good at research myself. You know, you're something else." Shaking his head he glanced around the room before skewering her with another hard look. "You think this is about ego? You took off. With *my* kid—and never bothered to tell me."

Was it just outrage she was hearing? Or was there pain in his voice as well? Hard to tell when Wes spent his life hiding what he was feeling, what he was thinking. Even when she had been closest to him, she'd had to guess what was going through his mind at any given moment. Now was no different.

She threw another worried glance toward the open doorway. Time was ticking past, and soon Caroline would come looking for her. Edna, the housekeeper, would be home from the grocery store soon, and frankly,

Isabelle wanted Wes gone before she was forced to answer any questions about him.

"How did you find out?" she asked abruptly, pushing aside the guilt he kept trying to pile on her.

He scraped one hand across his face then pushed that hand through his hair, letting her know that whatever he was feeling was in turmoil. Isabelle hadn't known he was capable of this kind of emotion. She didn't know whether she was pleased or worried.

"You haven't seen the internet headlines today?"

"No." Worry curled into a ball in the pit of her stomach and twisted tightly. "What's happened?"

"Someone knew about our daughter. And they've been hammering me with that knowledge."

"How?" She glanced at her laptop and thought briefly about turning it on, catching up with what was happening. But the easiest way to discover what she needed to know was to hear it directly from Wes.

"I got an email yesterday from someone calling themselves Maverick. Sent me a picture of my daughter."

"How did you know she was yours?"

He gave her a cool look. "She was wearing the princess heart necklace I once gave you."

Isabelle sighed a little and closed her eyes briefly. "She loves that necklace." Caro had appropriated the plastic piece of jewelry, and seeing it on her daughter helped Belle push the memory of receiving it from Wes into the background.

"You liked it once too, as I remember."

Her gaze shot up to his. "I used to like a lot of things."

Nodding at that jab, Wes said, "The same person who sent me the picture also let me know my Twitter account had been hacked. Whoever it was gave me a new handle. Real catchy. Deadbeatdad."

"Oh, God."

"Yeah, that pretty much sums it up." He shook his head again. "That new hashtag went viral so fast my IT department couldn't contain it. Before long, reporters were calling, digging for information. Then Teddy Bradford at PlayCo called a press conference to announce the merger we had planned was now up in the air because, apparently," he muttered darkly, "I'm too unsavory a character to be aligned with his family values company."

"Oh, no…" Isabelle's mind was racing. Press conferences. Reporters. Wes Jackson was big news. Not just because of his toy company, but because he was rich, handsome, a larger-than-life Texas tycoon who made news wherever he went. And with the interest in him, that meant that his personal life was fodder for stories. Reporters would be combing through Wes's past. They would find Caroline. They would do stories, take pictures and, in general, open her life up to the world. This was fast becoming a nightmare.

"The media's been hounding me since this broke. I've got Robin fielding calls—she'll stonewall them for as long as she can."

Wes's assistant was fierce enough to hold the hordes at bay—but it wouldn't last. They would eventually find her. Find Caroline. But even as threads of panic unwound and spiraled through her veins, Isabelle was already trying to figure out ways to protect her daughter from the inevitable media onslaught.

"So." Wes got her attention again. "More lies. You're not Isabelle *Gray*. Your real last name is Graystone. Imagine my surprise when I discovered *that*. Isabelle Gray didn't leave much of a mark on the world—but while typing in the name you gave me, up popped Isabelle *Graystone*. And a picture of you. So yeah. Surprised. Even more surprised to find out your family is all over the business world. As in Graystone shipping. Graystone hotels. Graystone every damn thing.

"You didn't tell me you were rich. Didn't tell me your family has their fingers into every known pie in the damn country. You didn't even tell me your damn name. You lied," he continued wryly. "But then, you seem to be pretty good at that."

She flushed in spite of everything as she watched his gaze slide around the room before turning back to her. Fine, she had lied. But she'd done what she'd had to, so she wouldn't apologize for it. And while that thought settled firmly into her brain, Isabelle ignored the niggle of guilt that continued to ping inside her.

"Why'd you hide who you were when you were working for me?"

Isabelle blew out a breath and said, "Because I wanted to be hired for *me*, for what I could do. Not because of who my family is."

Irritation, then grudging respect flashed across his face. "Okay. I can give you that one."

"Well," she said, sarcasm dripping in her tone. "Thank you so much."

He went on as if she hadn't said a word. "But once you had the job, you kept up the lie." His eyes narrowed on her. "When we were sleeping together, you were still lying to me."

"Only about my name." She wrapped her arms around her middle and held on. "I couldn't tell you my real name without admitting that I'd lied to get the job."

"A series of lies, then," he mused darkly. "And the hits just keep on coming."

"Why are you even here, Wes?" She was on marked time here and she knew it. Though it felt as if time was crawling past, she and Wes had already been talking for at least ten minutes. Caroline could come into the room any second. And Isabelle wasn't ready to have *that* conversation with her little girl.

"You can even ask me that?" he said, astonishment clear in his tone. "I just found out I'm a father. I'm here to see my daughter."

Damn it. "That's not a good idea."

"Didn't think you'd like it." He nodded sharply. "Good thing it's not up to you."

"Oh, yes, it is," Isabelle said, lifting her chin to meet his quiet fury with some of her own.

Funny, she'd thought about what this moment might be like over the years. How she would handle it if and when Wes discovered he had a child. She'd wondered if he'd even *care*. Well, that question had been answered. At least, partially. He cared. But what was it that bothered him most? That he had a child he didn't know? Or that Isabelle had lied to him? At the moment, it didn't matter.

"You don't want to fight me on this, Belle." He took a step closer and stopped. "She's my daughter, isn't she?"

No point in trying to deny it, since once he saw Caroline, all doubts would disappear. The girl looked so much like her dad, it was remarkable. "Yes."

He nodded, as if absorbing a blow. "Thanks for not lying about it this time."

"Wes…"

"I have the right to meet her. To get to know her. To let her know me." He stalked to the fireplace, laid one hand on the mantel and stared into the flames. "What does she know about me?" He turned his head to look at her. "What did you tell her?"

His eyes were gleaming, his jaw was set and every

line of his body radiated tension and barely controlled anger.

"I told her that her father couldn't be with us but that he loved her."

He snorted. "Well, thanks for that much, anyway."

"It wasn't for your benefit," she said flatly. "I don't want my daughter guessing that her father didn't want her."

"I would have," he argued, pushing away from the mantel to face her again. "If I'd known."

"Easy enough to say now."

"Well, I guess we'll never know if things would have been different, will we?" he said tightly. "But from here on out, Belle, things are going to change. I'm not going anywhere. I'm in this. She's mine and I want to be part of her life."

Isabelle was so caught up in the tension strung between them, she almost didn't notice Caroline walk quietly into the room to stand beside her. Her first instinct was to stand in front of her. To somehow hide the little girl from the father who had finally found her. But it was far too late for that.

Instantly, Wes's gaze dropped to the girl, and his features softened, the ice melted from his eyes and a look of wonder crossed his face briefly. Of course he could see the resemblance. Isabelle saw it every time she looked at her daughter. She was a tiny, feminine version of Wes Jackson and there was just no way he could miss it.

"Hi," he said, his voice filled with a warmth that had been lacking since the moment he arrived.

"Hi," Caroline said, as her fingers flew. "Who are you?"

Before he could say anything, Isabelle said, "This is Mr. Jackson, sweetie. He's just leaving in a minute."

He shot her one quick, hard look, as Isabelle dropped one hand protectively on her daughter's shoulder.

"We're not done talking." His gaze was hard and cold, his voice hardly more than a hush of sound.

"I guess not," she said, then looked down at her baby girl. Using her hands as well as her voice, she said, "I heard Edna's car pull into the driveway a minute ago. Why don't you go help her with the groceries? Then you can go upstairs and play while Mommy talks to the man."

"What about the ice cream?" Caro asked.

"Later," she signed. Sighing a little, she watched Caroline smile and wave at Wes before turning to head back to the kitchen.

Once the little girl had hurried out of the room, Wes looked at Isabelle. "She's deaf?"

"Good catch," she said and instantly regretted the sarcasm. No point in antagonizing the man any further than he already was. "Yes. She has progressive hearing loss."

"And what does that mean exactly? For her?"

"That's a long conversation better suited to another time," Isabelle said, in no mood whatsoever to get into this with Wes right this minute.

She wouldn't have thought it possible, but his features went even icier. "Fine. We'll put that aside for now." He lowered his voice. "You should have told me. About her. About everything."

Fresh guilt rushed through her like floodwaters spilling over a dam, but she fought it back. Yes, she remembered what it had been like to discover that Caroline was losing her hearing. The panic. The fear. The completely helpless feelings that had swamped her for days. Now she could look into Wes's eyes and see the same reactions she'd once lived through. He had been hit with a lot of information in a very short time, and if it had been her, she probably wouldn't have been as controlled as he was managing to be.

For some reason, that really irritated her.

Isabelle was willing to live with the consequences of the decision she'd made so long ago. Besides, in spite of being faced with Wes now, she was still sure that not telling him had been the right choice. "I did what I thought was right, Wes. You more than anyone should appreciate that."

"What's that supposed to mean?"

"Oh, please." She laughed shortly and wished tears weren't starting to pool behind her eyes. "You go through life making split-second decisions. You trust your gut. And you go with it. That's all I did, and I'm not going to apologize for it now."

He moved in on her until she swore she could feel heat radiating from his body and reaching out to hers. She caught his scent and helplessly dragged it into her lungs, savoring the taste of him even as she knew that going down this road again would lead to nothing but misery.

Besides, she reminded herself wryly, that wasn't passion glittering in his eyes. It was fury.

"We're not done here, Belle."

She gulped a breath, but it didn't help the sudden jolt to her heart. No one but Wes had ever called her Belle, and just hearing him say it again brought her back to long nights on silk sheets, wrapped in his arms. Why was it that she could still feel the rush of desire after so long? And why *now*, for heaven's sake?

It had taken her years to get past those memories, to train herself to never relive them. To push her time in Texas so far back in her mind that she could almost believe it never happened. Until she looked into her baby girl's face and saw the man she couldn't forget.

"I can't talk about this now. Not with Caroline here. I don't want her—"

"Informed?" he asked. "Can't take the chance of her finding out her father is here and wants to be with her?"

"It's a lot to put on a little girl, Wes, and I'm not going to dump it all on her until you and I come to some sort of agreement."

"What kind of agreement?" His tone was cautious. Suspicious.

"Like I said, not here." She took a breath to steady herself and wasn't even surprised when it didn't work. How could she find her balance when staring into the aqua eyes that had haunted her dreams for years? "Once you get back to Texas, call me and we'll talk everything out."

A half smile curved his mouth then disappeared, leaving no trace behind. "I'm not going back to Texas. Not yet."

"What? Why? What?" Her brain short-circuited. It was the only explanation for the way she was stumbling for words and coming up empty.

"I've got a room at the Swan Hollow Palace hotel," he said. "I'm not going anywhere until I get some time with my daughter. So that agreement you want to work on? We'll be doing it here. Up close and personal."

Her heart was racing, and breathing was becoming an issue. As if he could read exactly what she was thinking, feeling, he gave her that cold, calculated smile again, and this time, Isabelle's stomach sank.

"What time does she go to bed?"

"What?" God, she sounded like an idiot. "Eight o'clock. Why?"

"Because I'll be here at eight thirty." He headed out of the room, but paused at the threshold and looked back at her. Eyes fixed on hers he said, "Be ready to talk. I'm staying, Belle. For as long as this takes, I'm staying. I'm going to get to know my daughter. I'm going to catch up on everything I've missed. And there's not a damn thing you can do about it."

Swan Hollow, Colorado, was about thirty miles southwest of Denver and as different from that bustling city as it was possible to be. The small town was upscale but still clearly proud of its Western roots.

Tourists, skiers and snowboarders visited and shopped at the boutiques, antique stores and art galleries. Main Street was crowded with cafés, restaurants, bars and a couple of B&Bs, along with the shops. There was even a small mom-and-pop grocery store for those who didn't want to make the drive to the city.

The buildings on Main Street were huddled close together, some with brick facades, others with wood fronts deliberately made to look weather-beaten. Tall iron streetlamps lined the sidewalks and gave the impression of old-fashioned gas lights. Baskets of winter pines with tiny white lights strung through their branches hung from every lamppost. Every parking spot along the street was taken, and hordes of people hustled along the sidewalks, moving in and out of shops, juggling bags and exhaling tiny fogs of vapor into the air.

If he were here on vacation, Wes might have been charmed by the place. As it was, though, his mind was too busy to pay much attention to his surroundings. Amazing how a man's world could crash and burn within forty-eight hours.

The Palace hotel stood on a corner of Main Street, its brick facade, verdigris-tinged copper trim and shining windows making a hell of a statement. He'd already been told by the hotel clerk that the place had been in business since 1870. It had had plenty of face-lifts over the years, of course, but still managed to hold onto its historic character, so that stepping into the hotel was like moving into a time warp.

He walked into the lobby, with its scarlet rugs spread out across gleaming wood floors. Cream-colored walls were decorated with paintings by local artists, celebrating the town's mining history and the splendor of the mountains that encircled Swan Hollow on three sides. The lobby was wide and warm, with wood trim, a roaring fire in the stone hearth and dark red leather sofas and chairs sprinkled around the room, encouraging people to sit and enjoy themselves. He was greeted by muted conversations and the soft chime of an elevator bell as the car arrived. The quiet, soothing atmosphere did nothing to ease the roiling tension within him.

He avoided eye contact with everyone else as he walked past the check-in desk, a long, shining slab of oak that looked as if it had been standing in that spot since the hotel first opened. Wes took the elevator to the top floor, then walked down the hall to his suite. After letting himself in, he shrugged out of his jacket, tossed it onto the dark blue couch and walked across the room to the French doors. He threw them open, stepped out onto his balcony and let the icy wind slap some damn sense into him.

January in Colorado was freezing. Probably beautiful, too, if you didn't have too much on your mind. There was snow everywhere and the pines looked like paintings, dripping with layers of snow that bowed their branches. People streamed up and down the sidewalks, but Wes ignored all that activity and lifted his gaze to the mountains beyond the town limits. Tall enough to scrape the sky, the tips of the mountains had low-hanging gray clouds hovering over them like fog.

Wes's hands fisted around the black iron railing in front of him, and the bite of cold gave him a hard jolt. Maybe he needed it. God knew he needed something.

He had a *daughter*. There was no denying the truth even if he wanted to—which he didn't. The little girl looked so much like him, anyone would see the resemblance. His child. His little girl.

His stomach twisted into knots as the enormity of this situation hit him. He huffed out a breath and watched the cloud of it dissipate in the cold air. That beautiful little girl was *his*. And she was deaf.

He should have *known*.

He should have been a part of all of this. He might have been able to do something—anything—to help. And even if he couldn't have, it was his *right* to be a part of it. To do his share of worrying. But his daughter's mother hadn't bothered to clue him in.

As furious as he was with Isabelle, as stunned as he was at being faced with a *daughter*, he couldn't deny it wasn't only anger he'd felt when he was in that house.

"She looks even better now than she did five years ago," he muttered. Isabelle had always had a great body, but now, since having a child, she was softer, rounder and damn near irresistible.

Instantly, her image appeared in his mind and the grip he had on the icy railing tightened until his knuckles went white. That long, blond hair, those eyes that were caught somewhere between blue and green, the mouth that could tempt a dead man. He hadn't seen her in five years and his body was burning for her.

"Which just goes to prove," he mumbled, "your brain's not getting enough of the blood flow."

He shivered as the wind slapped at him, and he finally gave up and walked back into his suite. With everything else going on, he didn't need a case of pneumonia. Closing the doors behind him, he went to the fireplace and flipped a switch to turn on the gas-powered flames.

It was quiet. Too damn quiet. He stared at the fire for a minute or two, then dropped onto the couch, propping his boots up on the sturdy coffee table. Late afternoon sunlight came through the windows in a pale stream, the fire burned, and his brain just shut down. He needed to think, but how the hell could he when he was distracted by his own body's reaction to the woman who'd lied to him since the moment he met her?

"Isabelle Gray." How had she managed to get hired under a false name? Didn't his damn personnel department do a better job of checking résumés than that? "And she's rich," he exclaimed to the empty room. "Why the hell was she working for me anyway?"

But the "rich" part probably explained how she'd gotten away with changing her name to get a job. She'd been able to pay for whatever she'd needed to adopt a different name. Closing his eyes, Wes remembered the slap of shock he'd felt when looking for Isabelle Gray online only to find Isabelle *Graystone*. The names were enough alike that the search engine had hooked onto her real identity. Seeing her picture, reading about who she really was had been yet another shock in a day already filled with them.

He had no explanation for any of this, and checking his watch, Wes saw that he had several hours before he could go back and demand she give him the answers he needed. What was he supposed to do until then?

He dragged his cell phone out of his pocket and turned it back on. He'd had it off during his visit to Belle's house since he hadn't needed yet another distraction. Now, the message light blinked crazily and he scrolled through the list of missed calls.

Starting at the top, he hit speed dial and waited while his assistant's phone rang.

"Hi, boss," Robin said.

"Yeah, you called. Anything new?" He got up and walked to the bar in the far corner of the room. He opened the fridge, saw the complimentary cheese plate and helped himself before grabbing a beer. Twisting off the cap, he took a long drink to wash the cheese down and gave Robin his attention.

"IT department reports they're no closer to discovering who this Maverick is or even where he sent that email from."

"I thought they were supposed to be the best," he complained.

"Yeah, well, IT's pretty impressed with Maverick," she said wryly. "Seems he bounced his signal all over hell and back, so they're having a time pinning it down." She took a breath and said, "You already know that email account's been closed, so the guys here say there isn't much hope of running him to ground."

Perfect. He had his own computer experts and they couldn't give him a direction to focus the fury still clawing at his throat.

"What else?" Another swallow of beer as he plopped back onto the couch and stared at the flames dancing in the hearth.

"Personnel did a deeper check on the name you gave them, and turns out Isabelle Gray's name is really Graystone. Her family's got holdings in pretty much everything. She's an heiress."

He sighed. "Yeah, I know that."

"Oh. Well, that was anticlimactic. Okay. Moving on."

She forced cheer into her voice. "On the upside, IT says the Twitter trend is dying off. Apparently you're down to number ten today instead of number one."

"Great." Wes made a mental note to check with his IT guys on the status of his Twitter account when he got off the phone. What he really needed was for some celebrity to do something shocking that would be enough to push him off the stage entirely.

"And the warehouses are set up for delivery of the doll. Everything's ready to roll out on time."

"Good." He set the beer on the coffee table and rubbed his eyes in a futile attempt to ease the headache pounding there. "Keep on top of this stuff, Robin, and make sure I'm in the loop."

"Boss," she said, "you *are* the loop."

He had to smile and he was grateful for it. "Right. Did you hear from Harry today?"

"Yep, he's on it. He's working with PR to put a spin on all this, and when he's got the ideas together, he says he'll call you to discuss it."

"Okay. Look, I'm going to be staying in Colorado for a while."

"How long?"

"Not sure yet." However long it took to make sure the mother of his child understood that she was living in a new reality. "You can always get me on my cell. I'm at the Swan Hollow Palace hotel—"

"Swan Hollow?" she asked.

"Yeah." He smiled to himself again. "Weird name, but nice town from what I've seen."

"Good to know. I still can't believe you made the reservations yourself rather than let me handle it as always."

"I was in a hurry," Wes said and wondered why he was almost apologizing to his assistant for usurping her job.

She paused, then went on. "Fine, fine. When the final drawings on the PR campaign are turned in, I'll overnight them to you at the hotel. If you need anything else, let me know and I'll take care of it."

"Robin," he said with feeling, "you are the one bright spot in a fairly miserable couple of days."

"Thanks, boss," she said, and he heard the smile in her voice. "I'll remind you of that when I want a raise."

"I know you will," he said and was still smiling when he hung up.

Alone again, he drank his beer, and still facing hours to kill before speaking to Isabelle again, Wes had an idea. Grabbing the remote that worked both the flat-screen television and the computer, he turned the latter on. In a few minutes, he was watching an online video to learn ASL.

American Sign Language.

Three

Wes could have walked to Isabelle's house, since it was just outside town, but at night, the temperature dropped even farther and he figured he'd be an icicle by the time he arrived. The five-minute drive brought him to the long, winding road that stretched at least a half mile before ending in front of the stately Victorian. His headlights swept the front of the place and he took a moment to look it over.

The big house was painted forest green and boasted black shutters and white gingerbread trim. Surrounded as it was by snow-covered pines, the old house looked almost magical. Lamplight glowed from behind window glass, throwing golden shadows into the night. Porch lights shone from what used to be brass carriage lanterns and signaled welcome—though Wes was fairly certain that welcome wasn't something Belle was feeling for him.

"Doesn't matter," he told himself. He turned off the

engine and just sat there for a minute, looking up at the house. He'd been thinking about nothing but this moment for hours now, and he knew that this conversation would be the most important of his life. He had a child.

A daughter.

Just that thought alone was enough to make his insides jitter with nerves. He didn't even *know* her, yet he felt a connection to this child. There were so many different feelings running through him, he couldn't separate them all. Panic, of course—who could blame him for being terrified at the thought of being responsible for such a small human being? And whether Belle wanted to admit it or not, he *was* as responsible for Caroline as she was.

But there was more. There was…wonder. He'd helped to create a person. Okay, he hadn't had a clue, but that child was here. In the world. Because of *him*. He smiled to himself even as a fresh wave of trepidation rose up inside him.

Nothing in his life had worried him before this, but at least internally, Wes had to admit that being a father was a damn scary proposition. What the hell did he know about being a parent?

His own mother had died when Wes was six months old. His father, Henry Jackson, had raised him single-handedly. Henry had done a good job, but he'd also managed to let his son know in countless different ways that allowing a woman into your life was a sure path to misery. Though he'd made it clear it wasn't *having* a woman that was the problem—it was losing her.

He'd loved Wes's mother and was lost when she died. Once when Wes was sixteen, Henry had finally talked to him, warning him to guard his heart.

"Wes, you listen good. A woman's a fine thing for a man," Henry had mused, staring up at the wide, Texas sky on a warm summer night. "And finding one you can love more than your own life is a gift and a curse all at once."

"Why's that?" Wes held a sweating bottle of Coke between his palms and leaned back in the lawn chair beside his father. It had been a long, backbreaking day of work on the ranch, and Wes was exhausted. But he and his dad always ended the day like this, sitting out in the dark, talking, and it didn't even occur to him to give it up just because he was tired.

"Because once you give your heart to a woman, she can take it with her when she leaves." Henry turned and looked his son dead in the eye. "Your mama took mine when she died, and I've lived like half a man ever since."

Wes knew that to be true, since he'd seen the sorrow in his father's eyes ever since he was old enough to identify it.

"Love is a hard thing, Wes, and you just remember that, now that you're old enough to go sniffing around the females." He sighed and focused on the stars as if, Wes thought, the old man believed if he looked at the sky hard enough, he might be able to peer through the blackness and into Heaven itself.

"I'm not saying I regret a minute of loving your mother," Henry said on a heavy sigh. "Can't bring myself to say that, no matter how deep the loss of her cut me. Without her, I wouldn't have you, and I don't like the thought of that at all. What I'm trying to tell you, boy, is that it's better to not love too hard or too permanent. Easier to live your life when you're not worried about having the rug pulled out from under your feet." He stared into Wes's eyes. "Guard your heart, Wes. That's what I'm telling you."

Wes had listened well to his father's advice. Oh, he

loved women. All women. But he kept them at arm's length, never letting them close enough to get beyond the wall he so carefully constructed around his heart. All through school, he'd been single-mindedly focused on building a business he started with his college roommate.

Together, they'd bought up hundreds of tiny, aerodynamically perfect toy planes at auction, then sold them at a profit to bored college students at UT. Within a week, planes had been flying from dorm windows, classrooms, down staircases. The students set up contests for flight, distance and accuracy. Seeing how quickly they'd sold out of their only product, Wes and his friend had put the money they made back into their growing business. Soon, they were the go-to guys for toys to help fight boredom and mental fatigue. By the time they graduated, Wes had found his life's path. He bought out his friend, allowing him to finance his way through medical school, and Wes took Texas Toy Goods Inc. to the top.

Along the way, there had been more women, but none of them had left a mark on him—until Belle. And he'd fought against that connection with everything he had. He wasn't looking for love. He'd seen his own father wallow in his sorrow until the day he died and was able to finally rejoin the woman he'd mourned for more than twenty years. Wes had no intention of allowing his life to be turned upside down for something as ephemeral as *love*.

Yet now here he was, out in front of Belle's house, where his *daughter* slept. The world as he knew it was over. The new world was undiscovered country. And, he told himself, there was no time like the present to start exploring it.

He got out of the car, turned the collar of his black leather jacket up against the wind, closed the car door and headed up the brick walk that had been shoveled clear. Funny to think about all the times he'd avoided the very complication he was now insisting on. Still, he thought as he climbed the steps to the porch, he could take the easy way out, go along with what Belle wanted and simply disappear. His daughter wouldn't miss him because she wasn't even aware of his existence.

And that was what gnawed at him. His little girl didn't know him. She'd looked up at him today and hadn't realized who the hell he was. Who would have thought that the simple action would have hit him so hard? So yeah, he could walk away, but what would that make him?

"A coward, that's what," he grumbled as he stood before the front door. Well, Wes Jackson was many things, but no one had ever accused him of cowardice, and that wasn't going to change now.

He might not have wanted children, but he had one now, and damned if he'd pretend otherwise. With that thought firmly in mind, he rapped his knuckles against the door and waited impatiently for it to open.

A second later, Belle was there, haloed in light, her blond hair shining, her eyes worried. She wore faded jeans and a long-sleeved, dark rose T-shirt. Her feet were bare and boasted bloodred polish on her nails.

Why he found that incredibly sexy, he couldn't have said and didn't want to consider.

"Is she asleep?" he asked.

"She's in bed," Belle answered. "Sleep is a separate issue." Stepping back to allow him to enter, she closed the door, locked it and said, "Usually, she lies awake for a while, talking to herself or to Lizzie."

Wes stopped in the act of shrugging out of his jacket and looked at her. "Who's Lizzie?"

"Her stuffed dog."

"Oh." Nodding, he took his jacket off and hung it on the coat tree beside the door. For a minute there he'd actually thought maybe he was the father of twins or something. Looking at Belle, he said, "I half expected you to not open the door to me tonight."

"I thought about it," she admitted, sliding her hands into the pockets of her jeans. "Heck, I thought about snatching Caro up and flying to Europe. Just not being here when you showed up."

He hadn't considered that possibility. Now Wes realized he should have. He'd done his research and knew that Belle was wealthy enough to have disappeared if she'd wanted to, and he'd have spent years trying to find her and their daughter. Anger bubbled but was smoothed over by the fact that she hadn't run. That she was here. To give him the answers he needed.

"I would have found you."

"Yeah, I know." She pulled her hands free, then folded her arms across her chest and rubbed her upper arms briskly, as if she were cold. But the house was warm in spite of the frigid temperatures outside. So it must be nerves, he told himself and could almost sympathize. "That's just one of the reasons I didn't go."

Curious, he asked, "What're the others?"

Sighing a little, she looked up at him. "Believe it or not, you showing up here like this isn't the only thing I have to think about. My daughter comes first. I couldn't tear Caro away from her home. She has friends here. The uncles who love her are here. Secondly, this is my place, and I won't run. Not even from you."

He looked down into her eyes and saw pride and determination. He could understand that. Hell, he could *use* it. Her pride would demand that she listen to him whether she wanted to or not. Her pride would make sure she caved to his demands if only to prove she didn't fear him becoming a part of their daughter's life.

Belle had always been more complicated than any other woman he'd ever known. She was smart, funny, driven, and her personality was strong enough that she'd never had any trouble standing up for herself. Which meant that though he'd get his way in the end, it wouldn't be an easy road.

As they stood together in the quiet entryway, iron-clad pendant lights hung from the ceiling and cast shadows across her face that seemed to settle in her eyes. She looked…*vulnerable* for a second, and Wes steeled himself against feeling sympathy for her. Hell, she'd cheated him for five long years. He'd missed her pregnancy, missed the birth of his daughter, missed every damn thing. If anyone deserved some sympathy around here, it was *him*.

As if she could sense his thoughts, that vulnerability she'd inadvertently shown faded fast. "Do you want some coffee?"

"I want answers."

"Over coffee," she said. "Come on. We can sit in the kitchen."

He followed her down the hall, glancing around him as he went. The house was beautiful. There were brightly colored rugs spread everywhere on the oak floors so that the sound of his footsteps went from harsh to muffled as he navigated through the house. The dining room was big, but not formal. There was a huge pedestal table with six chairs drawn up to it. Pine branches jutted up from a tall porcelain vase and spilled that rich fragrance into the air.

He couldn't help comparing her home to his own back

in Royal. Though Wes's house was big and luxurious, it lacked the warmth he found here. Not surprising, he supposed, since he was only there to sleep and eat. The only other person who spent time in his house besides himself was his housekeeper, and she kept the place sparkling clean but couldn't do a thing about the impersonal feel. Frowning a little, he pushed those thoughts aside and focused on the moment at hand.

Isabelle didn't speak until they were in the kitchen, then it was only to say, "You still take your coffee black?"

"Yeah," he said, surprised she remembered. The kitchen had slate-blue walls, white cabinets, black granite on the counters and a long center island that boasted four stools. There was a small table with four chairs in a bay window, and Isabelle waved him toward it.

"Go sit down, this'll take a minute."

He took a chair that afforded him a view of her, and damned if he didn't enjoy it. He could be as angry as ever and still have a purely male appreciation for a woman who could look *that* good in jeans. Hell, maybe it was the Texan in him, but a woman who filled out denim like she did was the stuff dreams were made of. But he'd already had that dream and let it go, so there was no point in thinking about it again now.

He narrowed his gaze on her. She was nervous. He could see that, too.

Well, she had a right to be.

"So," he said abruptly, "how long have you lived here?"

She jolted a little at the sound of his voice reverberating through the big kitchen, but recovered quickly enough. Throwing him a quick glance, she set several cookies on a plate, then said, "In Swan Hollow? I grew up here."

He already knew that, thanks to the internet. "So you've always lived in this house?"

She took one mug out of the machine, reset it and set the next mug in place. "No, my brother Chance lives in the family home now."

One eyebrow lifted. Truth be told, as soon as he'd discovered who Belle was and where she lived, he hadn't looked any deeper. "You have a brother? Wait. Yeah. You said *uncles* earlier."

She gave him a wry smile. "I have three older brothers. Chance, Eli and Tyler. Fair warning, you'll probably be meeting them once they find out you're here."

Fine. He could handle her brothers. "They don't worry me."

"Okay. The three of them live just up the road. My parents had a big tract of land, and when they died, Chance moved into the big house and Eli and Tyler built homes for themselves on the land."

"Why didn't you? Why live here and not closer to your family?"

She laughed shortly. "In summer it takes about five minutes to walk to any of their houses. It's not like I'm far away." She carried a plate of cookies to the table and set them down. Homemade chocolate chip. When she turned to go back for the coffee, she said, "I wanted to live closer to town, with Caroline. She has school and friends…" Her voice trailed off as she set his coffee in front of him and then took her own cup and sat down in the chair opposite him.

"Big house for just the two of you," he mused, though even as he said it, he thought again about his own home. It was bigger than this place and only he and his housekeeper lived there.

"It's big, but when I was a girl, I loved this house."

She looked around the kitchen and he knew she was seeing the character, the charm of the building, not the sleek appliances or the updated tile floor. "I used to walk past it all the time and wonder about what it was like inside. When it went up for sale, I had to have it. I had it remodeled and brought it back to life, and sometimes I think the house is grateful for it." She looked at him and shrugged. "Sounds silly, but…anyway, my house-keeper, Edna, and her husband, Marco, my gardener, live in the guest house out back. So Caro and I have the main house to ourselves."

Outside, the dark pressed against the windows, but the light in the room kept it at bay. Wes had a sip of coffee, more to take a moment to gather his thoughts than for anything else. He was at home in any situation, yet here and now, he felt a little off balance. It had started with his first look at Belle after five long years. Then seeing Caroline had just pushed him over the edge. He really hadn't taken in yet just how completely his life had been forever altered. All he knew for sure was that things were different now. And he had to forge a path through uncharted territory.

When he set the mug back on the table, he looked into her eyes and asked, "Did you tell Caroline who I am?"

She bit at her bottom lip. "No."

"Good."

"What?" Clearly surprised, she stared at him, questions in her eyes.

"I want her to get to know me before we spring it on her," Wes said. He'd had some time to think about this, during his long day of waiting, and though he wanted nothing more than to go upstairs and claim his daughter, it wasn't the smart plan. He wanted Caroline to get used to him, to come to like him before she found out he was her father.

"Okay," she said. "That makes sense, I guess."

She looked relieved and Wes spoke up fast to end whatever delusion she was playing out in her head. "Don't take this to mean I might change my mind about all of this. I'm not going anywhere. Caroline is *my* daughter, Belle. And I want her to know that. I'm going to be a part of her life, whether you like the idea or not."

Irritation flashed on her features briefly, then faded as she took a gulp of her coffee and set the mug down again. "I understand. But you have to understand something, too, Wes. I won't let Caroline be hurt."

Insult slapped at him. What was he, a monster? He wasn't looking to cause Caroline pain, for God's sake. He was her father and he wanted her to know that. "I'm not going to hurt her."

"Not intentionally. I know that," she said quickly. "But she's a little girl. She doesn't know how to guard her heart or to keep from becoming attached. If she gets used to having you around, having you be a part of her world, and then you back off, it will hurt her."

He was used to responsibility, but suddenly that feeling inched up several notches. Wes couldn't have a child and ignore her. But at the same time, he was about to break every rule he'd ever had about getting involved with someone. There was danger inherent in caring about anyone, and he knew it. But she was his daughter, and that single fact trumped everything else.

"I'm here because I want to be," he said, then tipped his head to one side and stared at her. "I'm not dropping in to get a look at her before I disappear. Yes, I have an important product launch coming up and I'll have to return to Texas, but I plan on being a permanent part of Caroline's life, which you don't seem to understand. It's interesting to me, though, that suddenly I'm the one defending myself when it's *you* who has all the explaining to do."

"I didn't mean that as an attack on your motives," she said quietly. "I just want to make sure you understand exactly what's going to happen here. Once Caroline gives her heart, it's gone forever. You'll hold it and you could crush it without meaning to."

"You're still assuming I'm just passing through."

"No, I'm not." She laughed shortly, but it was a painful sound. "I know you well enough to know that arguing with you is like trying to talk a wall into falling down on its own. Pointless."

He nodded, though the analogy, correct or not, bothered him more than a little. Was he really so implacable all the damn time? "Then we understand each other."

"We do."

"So," he said, with another sip of coffee he really didn't want. "Tell me."

"I'm not sure where to start."

"How about the beginning?" Wes set the coffee down and folded his arms across his chest as he leaned back in his chair. "If you have family money, why the hell did you come to work for me?"

"Rich people can't have jobs?" Offended, she narrowed her eyes on him. "You have money, but you go into the office four days a week. Even when you're at home in Royal, you spend most of your free time on the phone with PR or marketing or whatever. That's okay?"

He squirmed a little in his chair. Maybe she had a point, but he wouldn't concede that easily. "It's my company."

She shook her head. "That's not the only reason.

You're rich. You could hire someone to run the company and you know it. But you *enjoy* your job. Well, so did I."

Hard to argue with the truth. "Okay, I give you that."

"Thank you so much," she muttered.

"But why did you lie to get the job? Why use a fake name?" He cupped his hands around the steaming mug of coffee and watched her.

"Because I wanted to make it on my own." She sighed and sat back, idly spinning the cup in front of her in slow circles. "Being a Graystone always meant that I had roads paved for me. My parents liked to help my brothers and I along the way until finally, I wanted to get out from under my own name. Prove myself, I guess."

"To who?"

She looked at him. "Me."

He could understand and even admire that, Wes realized. Too many people in her position *enjoyed* using the power of their names to get what they wanted whenever they wanted it. Hell, he saw it all the time in business—even in Royal, where the town's matriarchs ruled on the strength of tradition and their family's legacies. The admiration he felt for her irritated hell out of him, because he didn't *want* to like anything about her.

She'd lied to him for years. Hidden his child from him deliberately. So he preferred to hold onto the anger simmering quietly in the pit of his stomach. Though he was willing to cut her a break on how she'd gotten a job at his company, there was *no* excuse for not telling him she was pregnant.

Holding onto the outrage, he demanded, "When you quit your job and left Texas, you didn't bother to tell me you were pregnant. Why?"

"You know why, Wes," she said, shaking her head

slowly. "We had that *what if* conversation a few weeks before I found out. Remember?"

"Vaguely." He seemed to recall that one night she'd talked about the future—what they each wanted. She'd talked about kids. Family.

"You do remember," she said softly, gaze on his face. "We were in bed, talking, and you told me that I shouldn't start getting any idea about there being anything permanent between us."

He scowled as that night and the conversation drifted back into his mind.

"You said you weren't interested in getting married," she said, "had no intention of *ever* being a father, and if that's what I was looking for, I should just leave."

It wasn't easy hearing his own words thrown back at him, especially when they sounded so damn cold. Now that she'd brought it all up again, he remembered lying in the dark, Belle curled against his side, her breath brushing his skin as she wove fantasies he hadn't wanted to hear about.

He scraped one hand across his face but couldn't argue with the past. Couldn't pretend now that he hadn't meant every word of it. But still, she should have said something.

"So you're saying it's my fault you said nothing."

"No, but you can see why I didn't rush to confess my pregnancy to a man who'd already told me he had no interest in being a father." She rubbed the spot between her eyes and sighed a little. "You didn't want a child. I did."

"I didn't want a hypothetical child. You didn't give me a choice about Caroline."

"And here we go," she murmured with a shake of her head, "back on the carousel of never-ending accusations.

I say something, you say something and we never really *talk*, so nothing gets settled. Perfect."

She had a point. Rehashing old hurts wasn't going to get him the answers he was most interested in. He wanted to know all about his little girl. "Fine. You want settled? Start talking, I'll listen. Tell me about Caroline. Was she born deaf?"

"No." Taking a sip of coffee, she cradled the mug between her palms. "She had normal hearing until the summer she was two."

Outside, the wind blew snow against the window and it hit the glass with a whispering tap. Wes watched her and saw the play of emotions on her face in the soft glow of the overhead lights. He felt a tightness in his own chest in response as he waited for her to speak.

"We spent a lot of time at the lake that summer, and she eventually got an ear infection." Her fingers continued to turn the mug in front of her. "Apparently, it was a bad one, but she was so good, hardly cried ever, and I didn't know anything was wrong with her until she started running a fever.

"I should have known," she muttered, and he could see just how angry she still was at herself for not realizing her child was sick. "Maybe if I'd taken her to the doctor sooner..." She shook her head again and he felt the sense of helplessness that was wrapped around her like a thick blanket.

Wes felt the same way. The story she told had taken place nearly three years ago. He couldn't change it. Couldn't go back in time to be there to help. All he could do now was listen and not say anything to interrupt the flow of words.

She took a breath and blew it out. "Anyway. Her fever

suddenly spiked so high one night, I was terrified. We took her to the emergency room—"

"We?" Was she dating some guy? Some strange man had been there for his child when Wes wasn't?

She lifted her gaze to his. "My brother Chance drove us there, stayed with us. The doctors brought her temperature down, gave her antibiotics, and she seemed fine after."

"What happened?"

She sighed and sat back in her chair, folding her arms across her chest as if comforting herself. "When she healed, she had hearing loss. We didn't even notice at first. If there were hints or signs, we didn't see them. It wasn't until the following summer that I realized she couldn't hear the ice cream truck." She smiled sadly. "Silly way to discover something so elemental about your own child, but oh, she used to light up at the sound of those bells."

She took a breath and sighed a little. "The doctors weren't sure exactly what caused it. Could have been the infection itself, the buildup of water in her ears or the effects of the antibiotics. There was just no way to know for sure."

"Wasn't your fault." He met her gaze squarely.

"What?"

"It sounds to me like you couldn't have done anything differently, so it wasn't your fault."

Horrified, he watched her eyes fill with tears. "Hey, hey."

"Sorry." She laughed a little, wiped her eyes and said, "That was just…unexpected. Thank you."

Wes nodded, relieved to see she wasn't going to burst into tears on him. "Will her hearing get worse?"

"Yes." A single word that hit like a blow to the chest.

"It's progressive hearing loss. She can still hear now, and will probably for a few more years thanks to the hearing aids, but eventually..."

"What can we do?"

Her eyebrows lifted. "As much as I appreciate you being kind before, there is no *we*, Wes. I am doing everything I can. She wears hearing aids. She's using sign language to expand her conversational skills, and get familiar with it before she actually has to count on it. And I'm considering a cochlear implant."

"I read about those." He leaned his forearms on the table. He'd been doing a lot of reading over the last several hours. There were dozens of different theories and outlooks, but it seemed to him that the cochlear implants were the way to go. Best for everyone. "They're supposed to be amazing. And she's old enough to get one now."

"Yes, I know she is." Belle looked at him and said, "You know, her doctor and I do discuss all of this. He's given me all of the information I need, but it's not critical to arrange surgery for Caro right this minute. It's something I have to think about. To talk about with Caro herself."

Astonished, he blurted, "She's only four."

"I didn't say she'd be making the decision, only that I owe it to her to at least discuss it with her. She's very smart, and whatever decision I make she'll have to live with." She pushed up from the table and carried her unfinished coffee to the sink to pour out. "I'm not foolish enough to let a little girl decide on her own. But she should have a say in it."

"Seriously?" He stood up, too, and walked over to dump his own coffee. He hadn't really wanted it in the first place. "You want to wait when this could help her now? You want to give a four-year-old a vote in what happens to her medically?" Shaking his head, he reached for his cell phone. "I know the best doctors in Texas. They can give me the name of the top guy in this field. We can have Caro in to see the guy by next week, latest."

She snatched the phone right out of his hand and set it down on the counter. "What do you think you're doing?"

"What you're too cautious to do," he said shortly. "Seeing to it that Caro has the best doctor and the best treatment."

Both hands on her hips, she tipped her head back to glare up into his eyes. "You have known about her existence for two days and you really think you have the right to come in here and start giving orders?"

Those green-blue eyes of hers were flashing with indignation and the kind of protective gleam he'd once seen in the eyes of a mother black bear he'd come across in the woods. He'd known then that it wasn't smart to appear threatening to that bear's cubs. And he realized now that maybe trying to jump in and take over was obviously the wrong move. But how the hell could he be blamed for wanting to do *something* for the kid he hadn't even known he had?

"All right." Wes deliberately kept his voice cool, using the reasonable tone he wielded like a finely honed blade in board meetings. "We can talk about it first—"

"*Very* generous," she said as barely repressed fury seemed to shimmer around her in waves. "You're not listening to me, Wes. You don't have a say here. My daughter's name is Caroline *Graystone*. Not Jackson. I make the decisions where she's concerned."

His temper spiked, but he choked it back down. What

the hell good would it do for the two of them to keep butting heads? "Do I really have to get a DNA test done to prove I'm now a part of this?"

Her mouth worked as if she were biting back a sharp comeback. And she really looked as if she were trying to find a way to cut him out of the whole thing. But after a few seconds, she took a breath and said, "No. Not necessary."

"Good." Something occurred to him then. "Am I named as her father on the birth certificate?"

"Yes, of course you are." She rinsed out her coffee cup, then turned the water off again. "I want Caro to know who you are—I'd just rather have been the one to pick the time she found out."

"Yeah, well." He leaned against the counter. At least the instant burst of anger had drained away as quickly as it came. "Neither of us got a vote on that one."

The problem of Maverick rose up in his mind again, and he made a mental note to call home again. Find out how the search for the mystery man was going. And it seriously bugged him that he had no idea who it might be. Briefly, he even wondered again if Cecelia and her friends were behind it, in spite of Cecelia's claim of innocence. But for now, he had other things to think about.

"Why does anyone care if you have a child or not? Why is this trending on Twitter?" She sounded as exasperated as he felt, and somehow that eased some of the tension inside him.

"Hell if I know," he muttered and shoved one hand though his hair. "But we live in a celebrity culture now. People are more interested in what some rock star had for dinner than who their damn congressman is."

She laughed a little, surprising him. "I missed that. Who knew?"

"Missed what?" Wes watched the slightest curve of her mouth, and it tugged at something inside him.

"Those mini rants of yours. They last like ten seconds, then you're done and you've moved on. Of course, people around you are shell-shocked for a lot longer…"

"I don't rant." He prided himself on being calm and controlled in nearly all aspects of his life.

"Yeah, you do," she said. "I've seen a few really spectacular ones. But in your defense, you don't do it often."

He frowned as his mind tripped back, looking for other instances of what she called rants. And surprisingly enough, he found a couple. His frown deepened.

"You've got your answers, Wes," she said quietly. "What else do you want here?"

"Some answers," he corrected. "As for what I want, I've already told you. I can't just walk away from my own kid."

"And what do you expect from fatherhood? Specifically."

"I don't know," he admitted. "I just know I have to be here. Have to be a part of her life."

She looked into his eyes for a long second or two before nodding. "Okay. We'll try this. But you have to dial it back a little, too. You're the one trying to fit yourself into *our* lives—not the other way around."

He hated that she had a point. Hated more that as confident as he was in every damn thing, he had no clue how to get to know a kid. And he *really* didn't like the fact that he was standing this close to Belle and could be moved just by her scent—vanilla, which made him think of cozying up in front of the fire with her on his lap and his hands on her—damn it, this was *not* the way he wanted this to go.

"If you can't agree to that," she said, when he was silent for too long, "then you'll just have to go, Wes."

Fighting his way past his hormones, Wes narrowed his eyes, took a step closer and was silently pleased when she backed up so fast she hit the granite counter. Bracing one hand on either side of her on that cold, black surface, he leaned in, enjoying the fact that he'd effectively caged her, giving her no room to evade him.

"No," he said, his gaze fixed with hers. "You don't want to take orders from me? Well, I sure as hell don't take them from you. I'll stay as long as I want to, and there's not a damn thing you can do about it."

She took a breath, and something flashed in her eyes. Anger, he was guessing, and could only think *join the club*. But it wasn't temper alone sparking in her eyes— there was something more. Something that held far more heat than anger.

"You lied to me for years, Belle. Now I know the truth and until I'm satisfied, until I have everything I want out of this situation, I'm sticking."

She planted both hands flat on his chest and pushed. He let her move him back a step.

"And what is it you want, Wes? What do you expect to find here?"

"Whatever I need."

Four

Whatever I need.

Wes's words echoed in her mind all night long. Even when she finally fell asleep, he was there, in her dreams, taunting her. It was as if the last five years had disappeared. All of the old feelings she'd had for him and had tried so desperately to bury had come rushing back at her the moment she saw him again.

She had three older brothers, so she was used to dealing with overbearing men and knew how to handle them. Isabelle wasn't easily intimidated, and she wasn't afraid to show her own temper or to stand up for herself, either. But what she wasn't prepared for was the rush of desire she felt just being around Wes again.

He was the same force of nature she remembered him being, and when his focus was directed solely at her, he wasn't an easy man to ignore. Old feelings stirred inside her even though she didn't want them and the only thing that was keeping her sane at the moment was the fact that it wasn't just her own heart in danger, it was Caroline's. And that Isabelle just couldn't risk. She had to find a way to appease Wes, avoid acting on what she was feeling for him and protect Caroline at the same time. She just didn't know yet how she would pull it off.

"Well," Edna said when Isabelle walked into the kitchen. "You look terrible."

Isabelle sighed. Makeup, it seemed, couldn't perform the miracles all the TV commercials promised. "Thanks. Just what I needed to hear."

Edna was in her sixties, with short silver hair that stood up in tufted spikes. Her brown eyes were warm and kind and a little too knowing sometimes. Today she wore her favored black jeans, black sneakers and a red sweatshirt that proclaimed, *For Most of History, Anonymous Was a Woman.—Virginia Woolf.*

"Seriously, did you get *any* sleep?" Edna pulled a mug from under the single-serve coffeemaker and handed it over.

It was gray and cold outside, typical January weather in Colorado. But the kitchen was bright and warm and filled with the scents of coffee and the breakfast Edna insisted on making fresh every morning.

Grateful for the ready coffee, Isabelle took the cup and had her first glorious sip. As the hot caffeine slid into her system, she looked at her housekeeper and gave her a wry smile. "Not much."

Sipping her own coffee, Edna gave her a hard look. "Because of Wes?"

She jolted and stared at the other woman. "How do you know about him?"

"Caro told us this morning. She says he's pretty and that you said he's a friend." Edna tipped her head to one side. "Marco told me to butt out, but who listens to husbands? So, Wes is more than a friend, isn't he?"

Before answering that question, Isabelle looked around and then asked, "Where's Caro?"

"Outside with Marco. She wanted to make sure the snowman they made last weekend was still standing." She paused. "So? Who is he?"

"We've known each other way too long."

Edna laughed. "That's what happens when you grow up in a town of twelve hundred people. We all know too much about each other. Probably keeps us all on the up and up. Can't do a damn thing wrong around here and get away with it." She narrowed her eyes. "And you're stalling."

"I know." Pulling out a stool at the island counter, Isabelle dropped onto it and reached out to grab a biscuit she knew would be stuffed with ham and scrambled eggs. It was Caroline's favorite breakfast, so naturally the indulgent Edna made them a lot. Taking a bite she chewed and said, "He's Caro's father."

"Whoa." Edna's eyebrows shot up. "Wasn't expecting that." She leaned on the countertop. "What does he want?"

"Caro." She took another bite and chewed glumly.

The other woman straightened up in a blink. "Well, he can't have her."

It was good to have friends, Isabelle told herself with a quiet sigh. She'd known Edna and Marco her whole life. They'd both worked for her family since Isabelle was a child. And at an age when they could have retired, instead, they'd come to work for Isabelle, to help raise Caro. And she knew that she would never be able to pay them back for their friendship or their loyalty.

Smiling, Isabelle said, "No, he can't. But to be fair,

he doesn't want to take her away, he just wants to be a part of her life."

"That's a bad thing?" Edna pushed the plate of biscuits closer to Isabelle. "Talk and eat. You're too thin."

Isabelle knew it was useless to argue, so she dutifully took another one. "It's not bad necessarily," she said, breaking off a piece of biscuit and egg to pop into her mouth. "But it's…complicated. Caro doesn't know who he is and I don't know how much he's going to push for. Plus, he's so angry that I never told him about her that he's not even trying to be reasonable…"

"Are you?"

Isabelle's gaze shot to Edna's. "Hey. Whose side are you on, anyway?"

"Yours. Absolutely." Reaching over for a dishcloth, Edna wiped up a few crumbs. "But come on, sweetie. The man's a father and you never told him. Most men like to know if their sperm scores a goal."

She snorted a laugh even while she nodded. "True. But he said he didn't want kids."

"That's before he had one." Edna sighed and leaned on the counter again so she could look directly into Isabelle's eyes. "Even Marco didn't want kids till we had our first one."

"That's hard to believe." Frowning, Isabelle remembered how Marco had devoted himself to Edna and their three kids. Even now, he spent most of his free time with their grandchildren. A more family-based man she'd never known.

"Well, it's true." Edna shook her head and grinned. "When I told him I was pregnant the first time, the man went pale—and with that Italian olive complexion of his, it wasn't easy."

Isabelle laughed a little. True.

"My point is, he completely freaked," Edna admitted. "I think he was scared, though God knows a man will never admit to *that*. But once he came around to the idea of being somebody's daddy, he was all for it, and the man is the best father in the world."

"He is," Isabelle murmured.

"So why not cut this Wes guy a break and see what happens?" Edna shrugged. "You two might find a way to work through this."

"Anything's possible, I suppose." But at the moment, Isabelle was having a hard time believing that. She could remember, so clearly, how it had felt to have him looming close to her last night. She'd felt the heat of him reaching for her. And when she'd pushed him away, she'd come very close to grabbing him instead and pulling him closer.

Really irritating that she could be furious with him and *still* want him so badly.

"Is there more going on here than just worry for Caro?" Edna asked quietly.

Isabelle looked at the other woman. "Too much and not enough all at the same time."

Edna took a sip of coffee. "I hate when that happens."

Room service brought him coffee and toast. Wes ate and drank while he ran through the latest stream of emails clogging up his inbox. Deleting as he went, he kept expecting to see another message from Maverick. Why, he didn't know. The damage had already been done. But wouldn't he want to gloat? Wes really hoped so, because just one more email from the mystery man might be enough to help Wes's IT department nail the bastard.

Until that happy day, Wes focused on what he *could*

do. The TV was on, the local news channel a constant murmur of sound in the room. One part of Wes's mind paid attention to the reporters, wondering if he'd hear more about this Maverick mess. Meanwhile, he concentrated on answering business emails, then made a call to his VP. When Harry answered, Wes smiled. Good to know his employees were up and working as early as he was.

"Morning, Wes," Harry said. "Sorry to say, if you're calling for an update on Maverick, I don't have one for you yet."

Scowling, Wes rubbed his forehead and walked to the French doors of his suite. It was too damned cold to throw them open, so he settled for holding back the drapes and staring out at Swan Hollow as the small town woke up. The clouds were low and gray—no surprise, and yet more snow was forecasted for today.

"How is it no one can nail this guy—or woman?" Wes grumbled, not really expecting an answer. "Is Maverick some kind of technical ninja or something?"

Harry laughed shortly. "No. So far, he's just been lucky. He got in and out of your account so fast, the IT guys couldn't track him. But Jones in IT tells me he's rigged it to let him know if anyone tries to breach again."

"Well, that's something." It was a lot, really, just not enough. Wes didn't function well with helplessness. Because he'd never accepted it before. Always, he'd been able to do *something*. He'd never been in the position of standing on the sidelines, watching other players make moves he couldn't.

And he didn't like it.

"Not enough, I know," Harry said, as if he knew exactly what Wes was thinking. "But we're still working it. On the downside, Teddy Bradford won't take my call, so if you want to try to do CPR on that merger, you'll have to reach out to him yourself."

"Yeah, I tried before I left Texas. He blew me off, too."

"It may just be over, boss."

"No, I won't accept that," Wes said. "We spent nearly two years putting that merger on the table and I'll be damned before I let some cowardly rumormonger ruin it. There's a way to save us taking over PlayCo, and I'll find it."

"If you say so," Harry told him, but disbelief was clear in his tone.

Fine, he'd proved people wrong before, and he could do it again. Turning away from the view, Wes voiced a suspicion that had occurred to him only late last night. "You think maybe Teddy's working this from both angles?"

A pause while Harry thought about it. "What exactly do you mean?"

Wes had been turning this over in his mind for hours now, and though it sounded twisted, he thought it could just be true. "Well, we had a deal and he's backed out—what if he and Maverick were in on it together?"

"For what reason?" Harry asked, not shooting down the theory right away.

Any number of reasons, really, Wes told himself, but the most likely one had slipped into his mind last night and refused to leave. "Maybe he's lined up a deal with a different toy company and needed a way to get out of our merger without looking bad."

There was a long pause as Harry considered the idea. "Anything's possible," he said, his voice slow and thoughtful. "I'll put some feelers out. I've got some friends over at Toy America. I'll talk to them. See what I can find out."

"Good. Let me know ASAP if you discover anything." Wes picked up the coffee carafe from the dining table and poured himself another cup. If Bradford was working with Maverick to try to ruin Wes and his company's reputation, heads were going to roll. "I'm going to be here at least a few more days—"

"Yeah." Harry sighed. "Okay, I promised myself I wouldn't ask why you were in Duck Springs, Colorado…"

Unexpectedly, Wes laughed. "Swan Hollow."

"What's the difference?" Harry asked. Then before Wes could speak, he said, "Just tell me. Is everything all right?"

Wes's smile faded slowly. Things were as far from all right as they could get, he thought, but he didn't bother to say anything. Harry and the rest of the company had probably figured out that Maverick's email about Wes's daughter had been nothing but the truth. But that didn't mean he was ready to discuss it with everyone. Not even his friend Harry.

"Yeah," he said, gulping coffee. "Everything's fine. I just have a few…personal issues to work out."

Understatement of the century. There was so much rushing through his mind, he hadn't gotten more than a couple of hours of sleep all night. And this morning, Wes felt like his eyeballs had been rolled around in sand. In those long sleepless hours, his brain had raced with images, ideas. A daughter. The dead merger. A saboteur— perhaps even his ex—trying to take down his business. And then there was Belle. A woman he should know better than to want—yet apparently his body hadn't gotten that memo.

"If you say so." Harry didn't sound convinced, but

then he added, "When you're ready to talk about it, I'm here. And if I can do something, let me know."

"Find Maverick," Wes said. "That's what I need you to do. Keep everyone on it. I want to know who and where this guy is."

"We're working it, boss. Do what you have to do and don't worry about what's going on back in Houston. We'll find him. I'll be in touch."

After Harry hung up, Wes tossed his phone onto the couch and grabbed the remote when he saw the stock report flash onto the television screen. Draining his coffee cup, he punched up the volume and then cursed as the anchor started speaking.

"Things are not looking good for TTG Inc.," the man said in a low, deep voice. "Texas Toy Goods' stock has taken a hard dip over the last couple of days. CEO Wes Jackson has not yet commented on the short-lived scandal that apparently was behind Teddy Bradford of PlayCo announcing the end of their much-anticipated merger."

The stocks reporter then turned to the digital screen behind him and tracked the TTG stock on a downward slide. Meanwhile Wes's temper inched up in an opposite trajectory.

"TTG Inc.," the man said, "is down five points, and my sources say there are no immediate plans to put the merger back in play. PlayCo, the anticipated merger partner, on the other hand, has ticked up two points in the last twenty-four hours."

Disgusted, Wes hit the mute button and wished fervently that his thoughts were as easy to silence. One thing he knew for sure. Once a stock started slipping, the whole thing took on a life of its own. People would worry and sell off their stock and his price would dip even lower.

He had to put a stop to this before he lost everything he'd worked for. Stalking to the carafe of coffee, he refilled his cup and carried it with him to the door when a knock sounded.

Who the hell could that be? Room service had already come and gone. He doubted very much that Belle would be dropping in for a visit. And he was in no mood to talk to anybody else. Riding on temper, he yanked the door open and demanded, "What?"

A tall man in a heavy brown coat with a sheepskin collar stood on the threshold. He had narrowed blue eyes, short, light brown hair and a neatly trimmed beard. Two men with a slight resemblance to the first man stood right behind him, and not one of them looked happy to be there. Wes braced himself for whatever was coming.

"You Wes Jackson?" The first man spoke while the other two continued to glare at Wes.

"Yeah, I am." He met that flat cool stare with one of his own. "Who're you?"

"Chance Graystone."

Damn it. Well, Belle had warned him about her older brothers. Looked like he was going to meet the family whether he wanted to or not.

Chance jerked a thumb over his shoulder. "My brothers, Eli and Tyler. We're here to talk to you."

"That's great." They didn't give Wes an opportunity to shut the door on them. Instead, all three of them pushed past him into the room. Each of them somehow managing to give Wes an accidental shove as they did.

"Well, sure," he said. "Come on in."

All three men stood in the living room of the suite, waiting for him. Their stances were identical. Feet braced wide apart, arms across their chests, features cold, mouths tight. They could have stepped right out of an old Western movie—three sheriffs ready to face the outlaw. Who would, he told himself, be *him*.

There was no avoiding this. Slowly, Wes closed the door then glanced down into the cup he held. "This is not gonna be enough coffee."

Still, he took a sip to steel himself then deliberately took his time as he strolled out to meet Belle's brothers. He had no idea what was coming. Did they want to talk? Fight? Ride him out of town on a rail? Who the hell knew? Setting his coffee cup down on the closest table, he faced the three men. Wes guessed Chance was the oldest, since he took the lead in the conversation.

"We're here to set you straight on a few things."

"Is that right?" Wes wasn't intimidated, though he had the feeling the Graystone brothers were used to putting the fear of God into whoever happened to be standing against them at the time. Well, they were going to have a hard time with him. He didn't scare easily, and he *never* backed down when he knew he was right.

"That's about it," Chance said in a flat, dark voice. "Isabelle's our sister. Caro's our niece. You do anything to hurt either one of them and we're going to have a problem."

Wes shifted his stance to mock the three men facing him. Arms across his chest, he glared at each of them in turn before settling his gaze back on Chance. "I'd say that what happens between Belle and me is our business."

Chance took a single step forward. "Then you'd be wrong. You made your choice. You let her walk out of your life five years ago."

Though he might have a point, Wes didn't acknowledge it. "She didn't tell me about our daughter."

The two brothers behind Chance exchanged a quick look. "He's right about that," one of them said.

Chance nodded. "Yeah, she should have told you. I give you that."

"Thanks," Wes said wryly.

"We told her so when she first came home. It wasn't right, her keeping it from you."

"Agreed."

"But Isabelle does things her way. Always has. She doesn't take advice well."

"Yeah," Wes said. "Me neither. Who knew she and I would have that in common?" One of the brothers—Eli or Tyler, he didn't know which was which—smiled at that. "Just how did you guys know I was here? Did Belle send you to scare me off?"

"This is a small town, man. Word started spreading the minute you drove up to Isabelle's house, and the talk hasn't slowed down since." Chance laughed shortly. "Besides, there is no way Isabelle would have come running to us. Our little sister doesn't need a man to protect her."

Wes waved one hand at the three of them. "And yet…"

Chance smiled slightly. "Just because she doesn't need it doesn't mean she won't get it."

He could understand that. Family standing for family. But knowing that didn't mean he liked being warned off or threatened.

"Fine." Wes nodded and met Chance's steady gaze with his own. "I'm not here to hurt Belle. I'm here to connect with my daughter. And," he added, "there's no way you can stop me."

A long, tension-filled silence followed as the men took each other's measure. Wes didn't flinch. He'd faced down adversaries before. He'd been in his share of fistfights growing up, and he'd won them all. He'd looked across boardroom tables at competitors aching to take him down, and he hadn't folded to anyone. Damned if he'd start now. A part of him admired Belle's brothers. Loyalty was everything to him, and maybe that's why Belle's lies had cut so deeply. But he could understand these men standing up for their sister even as he knew it wouldn't stop him from doing what he'd come to Swan Hollow to do.

Finally, Chance nodded. "Can't say that I blame you for coming here. Actually, under other circumstances, I might even like you for it."

Wes laughed.

"But we'll be watching," Chance promised. "You make Isabelle or Caroline unhappy—it won't be pretty."

"Seems fair," Wes agreed. "As long as you three understand I'll be staying in town as long as I please. I'll see my daughter and your sister as often as I can manage it, and I don't want any of you interfering. This is between Belle and I."

Chance's gaze locked with Wes's for a long moment. Then he nodded. "I think we have an understanding."

"And you're not going to have an easy time of it," one of the other brothers quipped, a half smile on his face. "Isabelle's got a head like a rock when her mind's made up. And she's probably not real happy that you're here."

Wes frowned, and Chance laughed at his expression.

"Yeah," the man said a second later. "I'm thinking Tyler's right and you've got bigger problems with Isabelle than you do dealing with us."

Belle's brothers silently filed out of the room. Wes stayed where he was and didn't watch them go.

He'd been alone since his father's death a few years earlier. No siblings, no extended family, and since he'd never known anything different, he hadn't really missed it, either. Until just now. But even he could see that the Graystone siblings were tight. Close-knit. And a part of him he hadn't even been aware of was almost jealous of it.

Then his mind started clicking. Thoughts, ideas, possible plans flashed through his brain so quickly he couldn't separate them all. But somewhere in the chaos of his thoughts there was a single notion that began to shine brightly. If he could make it work, it might solve everything.

Yes, he wanted Maverick caught. Dealt with. The man—or whoever—had cost him a merger Wes had spent two years setting up. On the other hand, if not for Maverick, he might never have known about his daughter's existence. Wes didn't want another relationship with Belle—she'd lied to him for five years. But he did want to be a part of Caroline's life.

And as his mind worked, he realized there might be a way to salvage that merger after all. As long as he was here, in Colorado, spending time with Caro and Belle anyway, he might be able to use this time to convince the CEO of PlayCo that he, Belle and Caroline were a happy little family. Teddy Bradford wanted family values? Well, Wes might be in a position to offer that. *If* Bradford wasn't behind the Maverick mess himself.

It was a thought. Something to look at, maybe plan for. Making the best of a situation was what Wes did. And that damn merger meant too much to just walk away from it.

The key to all of this came down to one word. A word Wes had avoided for years, but now it had caught him, held him and wouldn't let go.

Family.

Five

An hour later, after leaving Caro in her pre-K classroom, Belle found Wes waiting for her in the parking lot. He was leaning against a huge black SUV, watching her, and he looked…dangerous. Okay, maybe that was just her. The day was bright and freezing, with high clouds studding a deep blue sky. Pine trees were layered with snow, and high barriers of the white stuff lined the parking lot where it had been pushed by the maintenance crew.

She'd like to think Wes looked out of place at the school in his black jeans, forest green sweater and black leather jacket. The truth was, he fit in everywhere. His blond hair ruffled in the wind, and as he pulled his sunglasses off to look at her, she noted his eyes were narrowed against the glint of the sun off the snow.

He looked dark, edgy, and her heart gave a hard thump she couldn't deny. Having Wes come back into her life was throwing everything off balance. Thoughts of him had kept her awake all night as her brain replayed memories she'd tried to bury for the past five years.

Working with him had been challenging, but fun. As focused as he was on his own vision, Wes had always been the kind of boss to welcome other ideas besides his own. That made for a great working environment, and Isabelle had loved being a part of it—until she fell in love with the boss. Then, everything had changed for her.

She'd let herself believe that the partnership she felt with him at work could extend to the personal, too. But even when they were alone together, at their most intimate, Isabelle had felt Wes pulling back. And the harder she tried to reach him, the more elusive he became. Finally, she'd had to realize that he wouldn't change. Would never be able to love her as she loved him and that waiting and hoping would slowly wear her heart away like waves against rock, until there was nothing left.

Now, he was back. Pushing himself into her life whether she liked it or not. Refusing to go away. It seemed, she thought, that Wes would always do the opposite of what she wanted him to.

All around her, the sidewalk and parking lot was alive with people. Parents soothing toddlers, folks starting cars, rushing off to the rest of their days. But all she could see was Wes.

She headed toward him. "What are you doing here?"

"Wanted to see her school." He pushed away from what was probably a rental. "Wanted to see you."

Just five years ago, those words would have turned her heart inside out. Now, she was worried. Why did he want to see her? Before she could find out, someone called her name.

"Isabelle!" She turned and smiled tightly at the woman hurrying toward her.

"Hi, Kim. What's up?" From the corner of her eye, Isabelle saw Wes approaching. Kim's reaction was instantaneous and completely predictable. The woman's eyes widened in appreciation, and a soft, speculative curve lifted her mouth.

Typical.

"What can I do for you?" Isabelle asked, drawing the woman's attention back to her.

"Oh. Right." She smiled at Wes again as he walked up to stand beside Isabelle. "Sorry. I just wanted to remind you that you volunteered to provide refreshments for the girls' dance recital next week."

"Sure. Thanks for the reminder," Isabelle said, "I've been so…busy, I'd forgotten."

"I don't blame you for being…*busy*," Kim said, shifting her gaze to Wes again. "Hello. I'm Kim Roberts."

He took her hand in his. "Wes Jackson."

She never took her eyes from his as she said, "Isabelle, you've been keeping this gorgeous man all to yourself? Selfish."

Kim was doing everything but drooling, and Isabelle had to squelch a flash of irritation. Just like the old days, she told herself. Even when Isabelle was standing right beside him, women would coo and practically purr at him, completely ignoring Isabelle's presence.

"Wes is an old…friend of mine from Texas," she said and scowled when he smiled at her explanation. "He's here visiting."

"Well," Kim said, her smile brightening enough that she looked like an actress in a toothpaste commercial, "maybe we could get together while you're in town. I'd love to show you around."

"Thanks," Wes said, "but I think Isabelle's got that covered." He turned his back on Kim and asked Isabelle, "Are you ready to go?"

"What? Oh. Yes." Surprised that he had turned down Kim's oh-so-generous offer, Isabelle looked up at him and wondered, not for the first time, what he was thinking. He tugged at her arm and she'd actually started walking with him until she realized he was escorting her to his car. Then she stopped. "My car's here."

"We'll come back for it later." He helped her into the oversize Suburban, then closed the door.

Kim was staring after them, a look of shock on her features. It had probably been years since a man had shown such a lack of interest in her. Sadly, Isabelle knew that Kim would only react to his response as a challenge. She liked Kim, but the woman was always on the prowl for her next ex-husband.

"She's interested in you, you know," Isabelle said as Wes drove through the parking lot and out onto the street.

He snorted. "That type's interested in everything male."

"That was rude," Isabelle muttered. "True, but rude. Anyway, where are we going?"

"I don't know," he said, aiming the car for Main Street. "Why don't you tell me? What do you usually do after dropping Caroline at school?"

Frowning, she half turned in her seat to look at him. Even his profile looked hard, implacable. Why was it she liked that about him even as it drove her crazy? Okay, fine, he was here to see Caroline. But why was he spending time with *her*? "What's this about, Wes? Do you plan to just follow me around town?"

He shrugged. "Would you rather we go back to your place and talk?"

"No." Being alone with him wasn't a good idea. Even knowing better, she might be tempted to—nope.

"There you go. So where are we headed?"

She sighed. The man was nothing if not determined. Rather than argue with him, she surrendered. "Business supply store," she said. "I need a new laser printer and some other supplies."

One eyebrow winged up. "Still working? What do you do now?"

"What I always did. I design toys, only now I free-lance," she said, turning her face to look out the window at Swan Hollow as it flashed past.

"For who?"

She thought about not telling him, but the minute she considered it, she let it go. The man could find out the truth easily enough if he did a little digging online. So really, it was pointless to try to keep it a secret even though she didn't love the idea of allowing him even deeper into her life.

"Myself," she said, keeping her gaze focused out the side window so she didn't have to look at him.

"Right," he said wryly, "because rich people can work, too."

She whipped her head around to glare at him. "Why is it when *you* have your own company that's okay, but when I do, I'm a rich dilettante just killing time?"

"I didn't say that."

"You didn't have to." She took a breath and let it out again. "Besides, my life is not your business."

"If that life concerns Caro, then you're wrong. It is."

"Where is this coming from?" She squirmed in her seat and wished she were on her feet so she could pace off the nervous energy pulsing inside her. "You never wanted kids, so why are you so fixated on involving yourself with Caro?"

"Because she's *mine*," he said and stepped on the brake for a red light. Turning to meet her eyes, he said, "I protect what's *mine*."

"So it's just a pride thing?" she asked, trying to read his features, his eyes, hoping she'd see something that would reassure her. That would let her know they'd find a way to work all this out. But as usual, Wes hid what he was thinking, feeling, locking it all down behind an impenetrable wall.

"You hid my daughter from me, Belle. That's not a pride thing, that's a damn fact."

His eyes flashed, a muscle in his jaw flexed and his hands fisted on the steering wheel. Staring into those intense eyes of his, Isabelle knew that he would be a formidable enemy. But was that really what they'd come to? Were they so obviously on opposite sides of this one issue that there would be no way to reach some kind of accord?

He couldn't use his money against her, because she had plenty of her own. But she couldn't use hers against him for the same reason—there, at least, they were on equal ground.

But what would a court say, she suddenly wondered. If he got a lawyer and sued for custody, would the judge punish her for keeping Caroline from him for years? Would he order her daughter turned over to her father? A way to make up to him for all the time he'd lost with Caro? God, that thought opened up a hole inside her.

"I did what I thought was the best thing for me," she said softly. "For Caroline."

"Well," he snapped as the light turned green and he stepped on the gas again, "you were wrong."

But she hadn't been wrong at all, Belle thought. The only thing she'd done wrong was get caught.

"Your brothers came to see me this morning."

"They what?" The change in subject was so startling, it completely threw her off. But a second later, Isabelle gritted her teeth and rolled her eyes. This was her own fault. She had planned to tell her brothers today about Wes being in town. She should have known that they would hear the town grapevine buzzing long before that. Rubbing her fingers against her forehead, trying to fight a headache that seemed to have settled in permanently, Isabelle reminded herself that Chance, Eli and Tyler loved her. They were just being protective. They were looking out for Caroline.

Nope, trying to calm herself down wasn't working, she thought. She was still furious. "What did they do?"

One corner of his mouth quirked in response to the tone of her voice.

"You think this is amusing?" she asked, stunned at the sudden shift in his attitude.

"I didn't this morning," he admitted. "When they pushed their way into my hotel room, my first instinct was to go a few rounds with them. But now, seeing how them interfering really frosts you, yeah. It's amusing."

"That's great," she said, nodding as her world tipped even farther off balance. "You're bonding with my brothers. I should have expected that. You're all so much alike."

"Excuse me?"

She glanced at him. "Now you're offended. That's what I find funny." Shaking her head, she said, "You don't even see it. You, Chance, Eli and Tyler are all pushy, domineering, know-it-alls. You think you know what's best for *everyone* and none of you are willing to listen to reason."

"Reason?" he repeated. "I think I've been pretty damn reasonable so far."

"Ah," she said, lifting one hand. "*So far* being the key words in that sentence. How do I know you're not going to suddenly decide to sue me for custody of Caro?" she asked, blurting out her deepest fear. "How do I know you're not already planning to take her away from me?"

"Because I just found out about her two days ago?" he asked. "I'm good, but even I need more time than that."

He parked the car in the lot and shut off the engine, and Isabelle shifted in her seat to look at him. "How much time, Wes? How long do I have before you come after me with all of your lawyers?"

Wes shifted in his seat, too, until they faced each other in the closed-off silence of the big car. Outside, people wandered in and out of the store and a few more clouds filled the sky, threatening more of the snow that still covered the parking lot. "Who said anything about lawyers?"

"I've been waiting for *you* to say it," she admitted. "But just know, if you bring lawyers into it, so will I."

"Yeah, I know." He nodded grimly. "So no lawyers. We do this between us."

Isabelle released a breath she hadn't realized she'd been holding. For now, at least, she didn't have to worry about Wes taking her to court. He might change his mind later, but she'd be grateful for today. "Okay, good. So how do we settle this?"

"To start? You get used to me being here. Being with Caroline. I'll jet back and forth to Texas as needed for business, but I plan on being here. A lot. Don't fight me on it, Belle," he warned. "We'll figure the rest out as we go."

She didn't like it. But why would she? Still, she liked

this better than the idea of a protracted courtroom drama where they ended up at each other's throats. That wouldn't be good for Caro—or for any of them. It went against every instinct she had to let him into her and her daughter's lives. But the way she saw it, she just didn't have a choice.

Staring into those beautiful eyes of his, she felt that near magnetic pull that she'd always experienced around him. That was dangerous, but only to her. Isabelle knew she would have to be on guard—and never let him know what he could do to her with just a look. Her reawakened feelings aside, it would be easier all the way around if she could just get through this situation with Wes without slipping back into dangerous feelings.

Wes hadn't wanted a family—kids. Finding out that she had kept Caroline from him had hit him in his pride, so naturally he'd had to come here. Had to get answers. But it wouldn't last, she told herself. He'd spend some time here and then he'd go back to his real life and she could return to normal. All she had to do was hang on until Wes remembered that he liked being unencumbered by a family.

"So are we good?" he demanded.

He was watching her, waiting.

"Yes," she said. "We're good. For now." And that was the best she could give him.

"That's a start," he said and opened the car door.

Much later, bedtime was a little crazier than usual. Caroline was fascinated with Wes, and Isabelle couldn't blame her. When Wes smiled, the female heart melted. Didn't matter if you were four or eighty-four, the man had a power. For the last five years, Isabelle had assured herself that she was immune to Wes's charms.

It was a hard thing to discover that she'd been lying to herself, too.

"Another story!" Caroline said, grinning up at Wes. The two of them were sitting on the floor in front of her bed.

Isabelle leaned one shoulder against the doorjamb and folded her arms across her chest. She couldn't tear her eyes off the man and his daughter. Just like she couldn't help wondering where they would all be right now if she had told Wes about Caroline from the beginning. Would he have changed? Would he have wanted the three of them to be a family?

Had she cheated all of them out of what they might have had? God, that was a terrible thought and one that couldn't do the slightest bit of good. What she had to do now was concentrate on the moment at hand and not get lost in memories or dreams of *what if*.

Wes had a book on his lap, and while he read the story out loud, he also tried to use sign language. The movements were a little clumsy, and he got quite a few of the hand signs completely wrong. Isabelle noticed Caroline giggling a little when Wes read the word *bear* and signed something entirely different. But making mistakes wasn't important. The fact that he was trying, that he was going to the trouble to learn ASL tugged at Isabelle's heart.

"Wes," Caro said and signed, "read the one about Christmas."

He feigned dramatic shock. "Christmas is over."

"Not *next* Christmas," Caro argued, with a little giggle that rippled through Isabelle's heart.

"Three stories is enough, Caroline," Isabelle said from the doorway, and the girl and her father both turned to look at her. Two sets of eyes the color of the sea in the

Caribbean studied her. She saw Wes in her daughter every day, but seeing the two of them together like this, the resemblance was heartbreaking.

She wasn't blind here. Not only was Wes enjoying this time with Caroline, but her little girl already adored him. Once she found out Wes was her father, that affection would be sealed forever. And again, Isabelle felt that twinge of guilt for keeping them apart.

"Mommy..." Caro dipped her head, looked up and let her bottom lip jut out just enough for a really good pout.

Isabelle laughed in spite of herself. "Not a chance, kiddo. Now get into bed and I'll tuck you in."

Dragging herself to her feet, Caro sighed heavily, turned and crawled under the covers, tugging them up to her chin. "Can Wes tuck me in tonight?"

Wow. Arrow to her heart. Shifting a glance to Wes, she saw the pleasure shining in his eyes, and that actually took a bit of the sting out of Caro's request. She'd never had to share her daughter with another parent before. The joys, the worries, the sleepless nights had all been for her alone. But standing in the bedroom with Wes, both of them looking at the child they'd created together, Isabelle could almost see what she'd been missing. It was more than sharing the responsibilities. It was sharing those secret looks of pride and understanding when their child did something cute. Or silly. Or tender.

So Isabelle took a step forward, into that joint custody world. Bending down, she gave Caro a kiss and whispered, "Sleep tight. I love you."

Then she stepped aside and let Wes be the one to smooth the sheet and blanket, to sweep soft, silky hair back off their girl's forehead. He kissed her cheek and said, "Good night, Caroline."

"G'night," she said on a yawn. "Will I see you some more tomorrow?"

Wes straightened up and glanced at Isabelle meaningfully before looking back at his daughter. "You sure will."

For the next week, Isabelle felt like a caged tiger in the zoo. Someone was always watching her—and that someone was Wes. Every time she turned around, there he was. At the grocery store. At Caro's school—where he'd charmed the little girl's teacher until the woman was practically a puddle of goo in front of him.

He showed up at her house nearly every evening, bringing dinner with him—which endeared him to Edna, who enjoyed the time off from cooking. He helped Marco pull a tree stump from the backyard, and now Isabelle had to listen to Marco's glowing remarks about a "city man" who knew how to put in a real day's work.

But the worst, she thought, as she pulled into the school parking lot, was Caro herself. The little girl was completely in love with her father.

Wes had plenty of charm when he wanted to use it, as Belle was in a position to know. But she'd never really stood back and watched as he made a conquest. The women in town, Edna, they were one thing, but seeing Caro respond to her father's determination to win her over had been both touching and worrisome. The harder Caro fell for Wes, the easier it would be for him to eventually break the girl's heart. Though to be honest, she hadn't really seen any sign of Wes pulling away. Instead, he seemed focused on being an integral part of Caro's life.

And all of it worried Isabelle. Sooner or later, he would return to Texas. What then? Would he want to take Caroline back with him? Would they end up in a bitter custody fight after all? Or would he have his fill of playing daddy and just leave—breaking Caroline's heart? Even a best-case scenario was filled with possible misery. Say she and Wes worked it out together and he didn't get tired of being a father? Wouldn't he want Caro with him in Texas for at least part of the year?

Isabelle's head hurt, and she didn't see any relief in her near future. So she pushed all of those thoughts out of her mind and tried instead to focus on her work.

She went over the last of her digital drawings, adding a touch of color here, smoothing a sharp line there, until she was completely satisfied. Well, *completely* was a stretch. She was never truly satisfied with her work, and invariably, once she'd sent the drawings off, she would think of dozens of things she could have done differently.

But the most important thing here was getting her latest designs to the manufacturer who could get started on production. Isabelle sent off a quick email, attaching the designs, and then shifted her attention to the paperwork that had been mounting over the last few days.

"You work from home?"

Isabelle jolted in her chair, glanced at the open doorway to her home office and slapped one hand to her chest when she saw Wes standing there. "How did you get in?"

"Edna let me in. Told me you were up here."

Traitor, Isabelle thought. Her housekeeper was clearly indulging her inner matchmaker. Too bad the woman didn't know that Wes wasn't interested in a match of any kind. Isabelle's heart ached a little at that internal reminder. It would be so much easier for her if she could just get past the feelings for him that kept resurfacing.

He strolled into the room, hands in his pockets, and wandered the perimeter, invading her space, looking at everything. She bit her tongue, because telling him to get out of her office would only make him that much more determined to look around. He took long, slow strides, moving with a sort of stealthy grace that made her insides quiver completely against her will.

Taking a deep breath, Isabelle watched as he checked out the full-color digital printouts of her latest sketches she had taped to a wall and the easel where one of her charcoal sketches was on display. Then he moved onto the dry erase board, with her schedule laid out, and finally to the corkboard where she'd affixed dozens of pictures of children holding toys.

Her office was at the front of the house on the second floor. Caroline called it the tower room. The windows looked out over a landscape that included the woods full of snow-covered pines, a lake, and in the distance, mountains that looked tall enough to scrape the sky.

The room wasn't very big, but she didn't need a massive office since there was no one to impress. She had a desk with a computer, an easel and paints, and space enough to pace when she needed to think. But right now, Isabelle wished for a much bigger space, because her office seemed to have shrunk the moment Wes walked into it.

"What is all this?" he asked quietly, turning at last to look at her.

"My work. It's what I do now," she told him and stood up from behind her desk. She didn't want to be seated while he loomed over her. "I set up a nonprofit that provides toys to hospitalized children. I call it Caro's Toybox."

She didn't look at him, instead focusing on the pictures of the smiling kids she kept in her office as inspiration. "I do the design work and the manufacturer produces the toys, then we distribute them."

He looked at those smiling faces in the photographs, too, and asked, "How'd you get into this?"

Isabelle walked up to stand beside him so that both of them were looking at those happy faces staring back at them. "When Caro was so sick, and then diagnosed, we spent a lot of time in the local hospital. We saw ill, scared children, and I realized that stuffed animals, or dolls, or even a toy plane could bring comfort to those kids when no one was around."

She sighed as memories rushed into her mind—sharing waiting rooms with other worried mothers, hearing the muffled cries of children, punctuated by an occasional wail of pain.

"I held Caro on my lap as doctors poked and prodded her. She was scared, but she had me there to try to comfort her," she said sadly. "But there were a lot of kids on the ward who spent too much time alone in their beds. Their moms and dads had other kids to take care of, and jobs, too. Nurses are amazingly great, but they're frantically busy and can't always take the time to try to ease a child's fear."

"I wish I'd been there. For Caro. For you." His voice was low, soft and tinged with regret.

Isabelle looked at him and saw his features soften and felt closer to him than she ever had. Whether he'd been there or not, he was Caroline's father, and only the two of them could really understand what it was like to have a sick child you couldn't help.

"I wish you had been, too." She looked up at him. "I know it's my fault that you weren't, and for that, I'm really sorry."

He looked down at her, and his clear aqua eyes shone with emotion that he couldn't hide. "Thanks. For saying that. For meaning it."

Isabelle's heart thumped hard in her chest. Her stomach swirled with anticipation, expectation and a jolt of nerves that only increased with every breath she drew. "I do, Wes," she said. "If I could do it all over…"

He shook his head, reached out and laid one hand on her shoulder. "We can't do any of it over. But we can do it differently from here on."

The heat of his touch drifted down, sliding into her chest and filling her with a kind of warmth she hadn't known in five years. Staring into his eyes, she was drawn in by that magnetic pull she'd always felt around him. It took everything she had to keep from moving into him, wrapping her arms around his neck and kissing him. But that would only make this moment even more confusing than it already was.

So she only reached up to cover his hand with her own. "We can do that."

He released her as his eyes warmed and a half smile curved his mouth. "Good." He shifted his gaze back to the faces on her board. "So you decided to try to take care of all of those kids," he said.

"To do what I could, yes." She too looked at the board where smiling children were caught in a moment of time. "We set up a toy room on the pediatric floor—" She broke off and chuckled. "Nothing fabulous, of course, usually a maintenance closet that we take over. We add shelves, paint and stock it with toys. Then every new patient gets to choose a toy for themselves."

She smiled a little, remembering the excitement of the kids when they were given the chance to go toy shopping right in the hospital. "It's a good feeling, watching children go into the room and inspect everything there before making their choice."

"Yeah," he said softly, "I bet it is."

She felt him looking at her, and she turned her head to meet his gaze. He was giving her a quizzical look, as if he was trying to figure her out. "What is it?"

He shook his head. "Nothing. I'm just...impressed."

"And surprised?"

"No, not really," he said, tipping his head to one side to look at her more deeply. "You always had a big heart."

Now *she* was the one shocked. And a little off balance. These few moments with Wes had fundamentally changed how they were dealing with each other. Which was good for Caroline, but dangerous for Isabelle. Old feelings were awakened and new ones were jolting into life. "Well, it's getting late, and I need to pick up Caro at school."

"Yeah," he said. "I'll go with you. But first..." He paused, looked down at her and said, "I'd like to help you. With this."

"What?"

"If you had more toys available, you could get into more hospitals, right?" He studied each smiling face on the board as if committing them each to memory.

"Well, yes," she said, watching him. "We've been moving slowly, running on donations and what we can produce. It's taking longer than I'd like."

"Then let me help," he said, and this time he turned to her and reached out to hold her upper arms in a soft, firm grip. "What you're doing is something special. Something important, and it makes me proud that you started it all. So let me in, Belle. Let me be a part of what you do."

Her heart jumped into a fast, heavy rhythm. His eyes on hers, she saw his sincerity. Saw how much he wanted this and what it meant to him. She was touched more deeply than she'd expected. With Wes's help she could grow her program faster than ever before. They could reach more children. Offer more comfort. That he wanted to do this meant more to her than anything else he could have done.

"I'd like that very much," she said.

A slow, satisfied smile curved his mouth, and his eyes gleamed. He rubbed his hands up and down her arms, creating a friction that kindled the heat already building inside her.

"Thanks for that," he said. "I think we'll make a great team."

Isabelle smiled, but her heart hurt a little, since five years ago, she'd thought the same thing.

Six

If anyone had told Wes a month ago that he'd be sitting front row center at a four-year-old's dance recital, he would have called them crazy. Yet, here he was. And most amazing of all, he was having a good time.

Isabelle sat beside him, and next to her were Edna and Marco. On Wes's right, Chance, Eli and Tyler sprawled in the too-small chairs, trying to get comfortable. The elementary school auditorium was packed with parents, grandparents and kids of all ages. The room was big, the chairs were uncomfortable and in the corner beside the stage, an elderly woman was playing a piano that looked as if it could have been one of the first ones ever made.

Smiling to himself, he shook his head and leaned in when Isabelle whispered, "Look over there."

He followed her gaze and spotted Caro, standing in the wings, peeking around the stage curtain. When she saw him, she grinned and her little face brightened. She waved, then made the sign for *thank you*. His heart did a slow, hard roll in his chest as he signed back *you're welcome*.

Of course she didn't have to thank him for coming. There was literally nowhere else he'd rather be than here, waiting to see his little girl take part in a dance recital. With the help of the hearing aids she wore, Caro could hear the music well enough to participate in the dancing she loved. Wes frowned thoughtfully to himself as Caro ducked back behind the curtain to join her class.

How long, he wondered, would the hearing aids work? How long before she entered a completely silent world? He'd been doing research on the cochlear implant, and the more he read the more certain he was that he wanted to get Caroline to a specialist as soon as possible. Yes, he knew that there were many, many happy, healthy deaf people and he knew that Caro would no doubt have a fulfilled life no matter which path she took. But was it so wrong for a father to do everything he could to try to make his child's life a little easier?

He glanced at Isabelle, who had the look of a nervous mom. Her blond hair waved and curled across her shoulders, and as she listened to Edna, she laughed quietly and her greenish-blue eyes shone. She wore a red silk shirt and black slacks, and just looking at her sent a jolt of desire whipping through Wes that he fought like hell to tamp down.

Ever since their talk in her office a couple of days ago, the tension between them had eased in one way and tightened in another. Though there was less anger, more understanding now, the sexual buzz they shared was stronger than ever. Hell, it had been five years since he'd been with her, and sitting beside her now, it was all he could think about.

But he had to move carefully. Slowly. He couldn't give

in to what he wanted if his desires were going to make everything else harder. He needed to get his daughter to a specialist. He needed to save the merger, though right now that looked impossible. And soon, he was going to have to be back in Texas to take care of the business he couldn't handle over the phone. And he wanted Belle and Caroline to go with him. Sex would just complicate everything.

Damn it.

"Oh, hell," Chance muttered from beside him. "Hide me."

Frowning, Wes looked up and saw Kim Roberts headed their way, her gaze fixed on the oldest Graystone brother. Wes was so pleased her laser focus was on someone other than *him*, he couldn't even feel sorry for Chance.

"They're starting!" Isabelle reached over, grabbed Wes's hand and squeezed as the piano music got louder and the lights in the hall were dimmed.

"Thank God," Chance mumbled as Kim had to retreat and find a seat. "Saved by tiny dancers."

Wes grinned, then everything in the room faded away but his daughter, one of a dozen little girls dressed as butterflies as they pranced across the stage. Brightly colored tissue paper wings fluttered, pigtails bounced and nervous giggles erupted in more than a few of the performers. In the darkness, he and Isabelle held hands, linked together by one beautiful little girl and the heat threatening to engulf them both.

After the performance, Wes stood apart from the group of parents, siblings and relatives. He was watching them all as his mind raced. His gaze fixed on Belle, behind the refreshment counter, laughing, talking and serving punch, cookies and cupcakes. And he thought he'd never seen anything more beautiful.

Wes wasn't kidding himself. He had no more interest in love than he ever had. But he could admit he wanted Belle. And that he needed her. In more ways than one. If he could convince Teddy Bradford that he, Belle and Caroline were really a happy little family, then he might be able to salvage the merger that meant so much to his company.

If he felt a twinge of something that could have been guilt, he denied it. He wasn't planning to use Belle and Caroline. But it was hardly his fault if being with his daughter and Belle helped solve a major problem.

He wandered toward the table and stepped up in time to listen in as Caro began a step-by-step description of the performance they'd just seen. Words rushing, fingers flying, his little girl was quivering with excitement, and Wes loved every second of it. Seeing his daughter with her blond hair in pigtails, big aqua eyes wide with happiness, made him smile. She was so small that her butterfly wings really did look as if they could lift her into the sky, but it was her tiny pink ballet shoes that for some reason struck his heart like an arrow.

She'd gotten to him, he realized. In little more than a week, Caroline had become so important to him, he couldn't imagine a life without his daughter. He'd never expected, or wanted, to be a parent, and now he couldn't imagine why. He wanted to tell Caroline he was her father. But he wasn't going to do that then disappear back to Texas and only be involved in her life in the most peripheral way.

He wanted more. Wanted to be there every damn day to watch her grow up. To be a part of her world. But Belle and Caro were a package deal—so he had to somehow convince Belle that the three of them belonged together.

He glanced at Belle, standing behind the refreshment

counter, helping Caro take the paper off her cupcake. He smiled to himself. The two of them were so beautiful it was hard not to look. The buzz of conversations, the ripples of laughter seemed to drift away. He was so caught up in watching them, he didn't even notice Chance walking up alongside him.

"You're making plans, aren't you?" he asked.

"What?" Caught, Wes looked at him.

"It's all right," Chance said, shoving his hands into his pockets. "See, there's a look in your eye when you look at my sister that tells me I should back off. Let you two figure this out. So that's what I'm going to do."

"Glad to hear it," Wes said wryly, though he hadn't been the least bit worried about Chance Graystone or his brothers.

"Don't make me sorry." The man wandered over to Caro, scooped the girl up in his arms and gave her a spin that had giggles erupting and floating in the air like soap bubbles.

Wes watched and continued to plan. That little girl was his. Her mother was his, too. She just didn't know it yet.

But she would, soon.

By the time they got back to Belle's house, Caro was wired on sugar and excitement and getting her ready for bed was a challenge Wes was happy to leave to Belle. While they were upstairs, he went out to his car to get the surprise he'd had sent in from Texas. He'd called his company three days ago to order it, and tonight was the perfect time to give it to Caroline.

The now familiar house was quiet when he went back inside and headed up the stairs to his daughter's bedroom. But as he approached the open door, he heard

Belle and the little girl talking. Shadows thrown from the night-lights plugged in at intervals along the hall crouched in corners. The old house sighed in the cold wind whipping under the eaves. Moving quietly, he stopped in the doorway and blatantly eavesdropped.

"Is Wes gonna kiss me good-night?"

"He'll be here in a minute, sweetie."

"He's nice," Caro said, and though he couldn't see her, he imagined her small hands moving with every word, and his heart swelled.

"Yes, he is nice," Belle said, and Wes couldn't help but wonder if it had cost her to agree with her daughter.

"He's funny, too, and pretty and I think he should stay here now."

"Here?" Belle asked. "In Swan Hollow?"

"Here with us, Mommy," Caro answered and Wes went perfectly still, waiting to hear the rest. "He likes me and he should be here so we can play some more."

"Wes lives in Texas, honey," Belle said gently. "He's just visiting us."

"He's gonna *leave*?" There was a catch in Caro's throat that Wes felt as well.

"Not right away," Belle reassured her daughter, "but yes, he'll have to go home soon."

"But he can be home here, Mommy."

"It's not that easy, baby."

"Why?"

"Because…" She paused, clearly searching for an explanation that would make sense to a little girl. "…because his house is in Texas."

"Why?"

"Because that's where he lives."

"But *why*?"

He muffled a snort. He really shouldn't be enjoying

so much how Belle squirmed, Wes thought. Still, he couldn't help the deep pang of regret he felt at making his little girl unhappy. It only strengthened his resolve to stay in her life permanently.

"Can we go to Texas?" Caro asked, trying a new tack.

Another long pause, and Wes imagined that Belle was wishing he would hurry and show up to dig her out of the conversation.

"No, we really can't."

"Why?"

He heard Isabelle sigh.

"What about your uncles? They all live here. Wouldn't you miss them?"

"Yes. But they could come, too!"

Wes felt a surge of pride. It seemed his daughter was as hardheaded as he was.

"Baby girl," Belle said, "how about we just enjoy Wes while he's here, okay?"

"But I don't want him to leave."

Wes's heart filled and he had to gulp in a breath to steady himself.

"I know, sweetie," Belle said softly. "Neither do I."

And he smiled. There it was. She didn't want him to leave any more than Caro did. So maybe it wouldn't be hard to convince Belle to come back to Texas with him. To try being together—not just for the sake of their daughter.

And on that happy thought, he stepped into Caroline's room. It was a little girl's dream, he imagined. Everything from a canopy bed to a play table and chairs and bookcases filled with stories to be read over and over again. There were stuffed animals, a child's learning computer and, in the corner, a dollhouse as tall as Caro herself.

"Wes!" Caroline scooted out of bed, ran to him and threw her arms around his legs.

There went that twist to his heart again. While he hugged his daughter, his gaze caught Belle's, and he knew she was wondering how much of their conversation he'd overheard.

"Did you bring a present?" Caro squealed, her fingers moving as fast her voice. "For me?"

"It's a present for the best dancer in the whole show," he said, tapping his finger against his mouth. "Now who was that?"

"Me!" Caroline shouted. "It was me. Wasn't it me?" she asked, now sounding a little less confident.

"You bet it was you," Wes told her and handed her the red ribbon–wrapped white box.

"Mommy, look!" Caro staggered toward her mother, balancing the box awkwardly but refusing to put it down.

"I see," Belle said, laughing. "Why don't you put the box down so you can open it?"

"I will!" Caro set it on the floor, plopped down beside it and yanked at the ribbon until it fell away. Then she lifted the lid, pushed back the white tissue and said, "Ooh…"

One small word drawn out into a sigh of pleasure so rich and deep. Wes had to grin. She liked it.

"Mommy, *look*!" Caroline pulled the doll out of the box and inspected every inch of her. "She's like me, Mommy. Her hair and her eyes and, Mommy, she gots *hearing aids* like me!"

"You like her?" Wes asked unnecessarily.

"I *love* her," Caro said and handed the doll to her mother so she could run at Wes again. This time, he scooped her up and held her so she could throw her small arms around his neck and hang on. He'd never felt anything as wonderful as a freely given hug from his child. Her warm, soft weight in his arms, the scent of her shampoo, her grip on his neck and her whisper of "Thank you, Wes" made his heart fill to bursting.

Then he looked at Belle and saw her beautiful eyes shining with unshed tears and he was lost completely. He felt the ground beneath his feet shift as if he were standing in an earthquake. These two females had shattered him without even trying. And he wasn't entirely sure it bothered him.

Once Caroline was tucked in with her new doll clutched tightly to her chest, Isabelle led Wes from the room and pulled the door almost closed behind them.

In the dimly lit hallway, she turned to look up at Wes and said softly, "She loves that doll. Thank you."

"You don't have to thank me. But I'm glad she loves it." He smiled and threw a quick glance at the door separating them from their daughter. He looked back at Isabelle. "It's from our new Just Like Me line. We're set to launch in a few weeks, so Caro got one of the very first."

The fact that he'd thought of it, arranged to have the doll sent here, touched Isabelle so deeply, her heart ached. "It meant so much to her. To me, too. You could have told her then. That you're her father."

He shook his head slowly. "No. I don't want to give her a present and a responsibility all at once. When I tell her who I am, I want it to be the right time."

Tears still brimmed in her eyes, remembering her daughter's excitement and the wonder on her face when she realized the doll had hearing aids just like she did. Wes could not have given her anything that would have meant more. It was hard on a child, being different from all of the other kids, but Caro was so much a force of nature, that even at four, she was completely sure of herself. And yet, having a doll with hearing aids had suddenly given Caro a boost of even more self-confidence.

Wes had given their daughter more than a doll. He'd given her acceptance. Now, with his simple truth that he wanted to wait for the right time to admit to Caroline who he was, Isabelle's heart was lost. Again.

She took a breath, grabbed Wes's hand, pulled him along the hallway and said, "Come with me."

"Where we going?"

"Where we were always headed," she said and tugged him into her bedroom. No point in lying to herself, Isabelle thought. This had been inevitable from the moment he arrived in Colorado. She'd known it, felt it. As if seeing him again had fanned every ember inside her into life, now that banked fire was a raging inferno and she didn't want to try to quench it anymore.

Moonlight on snow reflected into the room through the wide windows, giving the bedroom a soft, pale glow. She took a quick glance around the familiar space, the mountains of pillows stacked against the curved brass headboard, the thick, dark green comforter, the cozy chairs in front of the bay window and the brightly flowered rug across the gleaming wood floors. Reaching out, she flipped a wall switch and the gas fireplace in the sky blue–tiled hearth leaped to life.

This was her sanctuary. She'd never invited a man into this space before—not only because she hadn't been interested, but because she hadn't wanted Caroline to watch men coming and going. Not that there would have been a parade of men or anything. Yet tonight, it somehow seemed inevitable that Wes would be the first. Isabelle wasn't nervous, because it felt too right to her to second-guess herself. She'd made her decision and wouldn't back down now.

"Belle?" Wes looked down at her, desire warring with questions in his eyes.

"No talking," she said and went up on her toes. She hooked her arms around his neck, tipped her head to one side and kissed him with everything she had.

Surprised, it took him a second to react, but then he was kissing her back, making Isabelle's head spin when he deepened that kiss, stealing her breath. He parted her lips with his tongue, dipping into her mouth to taste, explore with a hunger that matched her own.

His arms came around her, pressing her body tightly to his. Isabelle felt like she was on a roller coaster. Her stomach pitched wildly, her heartbeat thundered in her chest and everywhere he touched her, her skin burned.

One of his big hands caught the back of her head and his fingers speared through her hair, holding her still for the wild plundering of her mouth. She felt every inch of his body along hers and moaned at the hard length of him pushing against her abdomen. She wanted him, maybe more now than she ever had before.

She hadn't been with a man since Wes. Isabelle had told herself that she simply wasn't ready. That one day she would be and then she would move on. Find a life. But the simple truth was, she hadn't been able to be with another man because it was always Wes that she wanted. Everything she'd once felt for him came rushing back in an undeniable wave, knocking her sideways while she struggled to find balance.

Wes walked her forward a few steps, eased her onto the bed and then followed her down. He never let go of her, only adjusting his grip so that his hands could slide over her body with a fierce possessiveness that thrilled

Isabelle. Finally, he tore his mouth from hers and she gasped and gulped for air.

Tipping her head back into the mattress, she felt him tugging at the buttons of her shirt and wished wildly for Velcro closing. It would be so much faster. At that last thought, the fabric parted and his hand came down on one of her breasts. Even through the silky lace of her bra, she felt the heat of him, and when his thumb rubbed across her nipple, she whimpered.

"Wes…"

"No talking," he whispered. "Remember?"

"Right. No talking. All I'll say is…*more*."

"Right there with you," he muttered and flicked open the front clasp of her bra, freeing her breasts so that he could lower his head and take first one nipple and then the other into his mouth.

Everything inside her exploded. Isabelle arched into him as his lips, tongue and teeth pulled at her sensitive nipples. A kaleidoscope of sensation shattered inside her mind. While he tortured her with his mouth, he slid one hand down her body to the waistband of her slacks, and in seconds he had the button and zipper undone. His fingers slipped beneath her panties to stroke her center.

And just like that, she was wearing too many clothes. Isabelle's mind struggled for clarity, even as her body shrieked at her to stop thinking and just feel. But she needed more of him. The hot slide of skin to skin, the feel of his hard, muscular body pressed to hers. The amazing sensation of him pushing into her depths and filling her completely.

"I want to feel you," she whispered.

He lifted his head and grinned. "You are."

She laughed a little and felt it tremble through her. "Funny. But take your clothes off."

"Yes, ma'am," he said, bending down to plant another long, hard kiss on her mouth.

She loved the taste of him, the feel of him. And when he moved away from her to peel off his clothes, she missed his warmth, the heat of their bodies wrapped together. He stood up, and she shrugged out of her clothes, kicked her pants off and lay on the comforter, watching him. When he stopped dead, with his hands at his belt, she managed to ask, "What's wrong?"

"We can't do this."

"What?"

He pushed both hands through his hair in frustration. "No protection, Belle. I haven't kept a condom in my wallet since I was in college."

She was glad to hear it. But she laughed a little and said, "Oh. For a second there, I thought you were changing your mind."

"Not a chance," he said, "but unless you—"

"In the bedside table drawer," she said, wanting to cut this conversation short and get back to shivering and trembling.

He pulled the drawer open, then looked at her, eyebrows arched. "Quite the supply," he said. "Been busy?"

She shook her head, licked her lips and choked out a short chuckle. "No. I think of that drawer as my hope chest. I figured it's better to have them and not need them—"

"Than to need them and not have them," he finished for her.

"Exactly."

He grabbed one of the foil packets, stripped out of his clothes and said, "I do like a woman who's prepared."

"Show me."

He didn't need another invitation. He came to her,

covering her body with his, and Isabelle sighed at the first soft, warm contact of his skin to hers. She'd missed this so much. His scent, his taste, his strength. He was a businessman, but his big hands still carried the calluses he'd earned as a young man. And the scrape of his rough palms along her body created a new and even more exciting layer of sensation.

He rolled over, bringing her on top of him, and she loved looking down into those sea-colored crystal eyes. His hands cupped and kneaded her behind and she writhed on top of him in response. She kissed him hard, fast, then raised her head to watch him as she shifted, rising up, moving to straddle him.

In the moonlit room, even the air felt like magic. This moment was one she'd been thinking and dreaming of since she'd first opened her door and seen him on her porch. Slowly sitting up, she dragged the palms of her hands across his chest and loved the flash of something hot and dark that shot through his eyes.

Isabelle felt a rush of sexual power that ratcheted higher and higher inside her as she went up on her knees and slowly, slowly, lowered herself onto him. She took his hard, thick length inside, inch by glorious inch, and when he was filling her completely, she sighed and reveled in everything she was feeling.

He reached up, covering her breasts with his hands, tweaking and tugging at her nipples until she groaned and twisted her body in response. That movement sent shock waves rippling through her system and made her want to feel more, to feel it all.

Unable to wait a moment longer to experience the release clamoring inside her, Isabelle moved on him, rocking up and down in a slow, rhythmic dance that created tingles that rose up and burst and rose up again. She lifted her arms high over her head, giving herself over to what was happening, and the feel of his hands on her breasts only fed the fire that burned brightly inside her.

Then his hands dropped to her hips and guided her into a faster pace. His gaze locked on hers, they stared into each other's eyes as they claimed each other in the most intimate way possible. The tingle at her core became an incessant burn that ached and ached, pushing her toward the release she needed. And when Isabelle felt she couldn't take it a moment more, the needing, the desire, he shifted one hand to her center and rubbed that sensitive nub at her core.

"Wes!" She cried his name but kept moving on him, kept rocking, twisting her hips in a blind effort to take him higher, deeper. That bone-deep ache intensified as they moved together in a dance as ancient as time, and when her body exploded, shattering into a fusillade of color and sensation, Isabelle clung to his forearms and rode the wave to the end.

Only then, when she was shaking and shivering, did Wes let himself follow. She stared into his eyes and watched as he surrendered himself to her. Gave himself to her.

And she wished, from the bottom of her heart, that that surrender was complete.

Seven

An hour later, they were lying wrapped together beneath the comforter. There was a bottle of wine on the nightstand, thanks to Wes making a trip down to the kitchen. He'd had to wait until he was sure his legs would work—but he'd needed those few minutes away from Belle. Away from what they'd shared, to try to think. Hopeless, though, since there wasn't enough blood flow to fuel his brain. All he knew was that what he'd just shared with Belle had been so much more than he'd expected. So much more than he'd been ready for. He'd have to take the time—later—to examine it all from every possible angle. But for now, he was only hoping to experience it all again. Soon.

Outside, snow fell again in soft, white puffs that danced against the window and slid down the glass. Inside, the room was warm, the wine was cold and firelight tossed dancing shadows across the walls.

"Well," Belle said on a sigh, "that was…"

Wes smiled to himself, then took a sip of his wine. "Yeah, it was."

Belle tugged the edge of the comforter up to cover her breasts as she leaned back on the pillows propped against the brass headboard. Then she pushed one hand through her hair and sipped at her own wine. "So, do we need to talk about this?"

Why did women always want to *talk*? He grinned and shrugged. "We're both naked, lying here drinking wine, and I don't know about you, but I'm already thinking about round two. What is there to talk about?"

She shifted, sliding one leg over his. "Well, I thought I should try to explain why we had round one."

He ran his hand over her thigh and smiled when she shivered. Wes didn't want her thinking too much about any of this. Better that they simply accept what happened and build on it. Why ask too many questions? The answers might not be what either of them wanted to hear.

"Oh, no explanation necessary." He winked and said, "I understand completely. You couldn't fight off your desire for me any longer, and in a rush of lust, you surrendered to the urge to fling yourself into my manly arms."

She blinked at him, then smiled, then laughed as she shook her head. "You're crazy."

"That's been said before," he told her and moved, taking her wineglass and setting it on the table beside his. He wanted her off balance with no time to think, to consider, to second-guess the decision she'd already made. Because there was more that he wanted and now that he'd made this much headway, he didn't want to backslide.

He cupped her face in his palm, stared into her eyes and said, "I have to go back to Texas, Belle. Tomorrow. The day after, at the latest."

Surprise flickered in her eyes. She covered his hand with hers. "You're leaving?"

"I have to get back." That was true. His company was trying to fight its way out of a scandal. He had to try to save that merger. And they were getting ready for the big toy launch. And that was just dealing with TTG. He had any number of other companies he had to check on. "There are things I have to be on-site to handle. I've already stayed longer than I should have—not that I'm sorry about that. But I've got to get back."

Her eyes mirrored what she was thinking. They always had. That's why he had known five years ago that she was falling for him. Why he'd let her go. And why right now, he knew she didn't want him to leave.

"Caro will miss you."

He kissed her. "Only Caro?"

She sighed. "I will, too, damn it."

He laughed, enjoying the irritation on her face. "I can fix that. Come with me."

She blinked at him. "To *Texas*?"

"Why not?"

"How many reasons do you need?" She inched away from him, scooted higher on the pillows and pushed her hair back from her face again.

"Come for a week, Belle." He talked fast, knowing he had to drive his point home and make it count. "Come home with me. Let me show Caroline where I live, let her see some of Texas."

"I can't just pick up and go, Wes."

She wasn't saying no outright, so that gave him some wiggle room. He'd take it. "Give me a reason why not. One good one. We'll start there."

"Caro's school."

He almost laughed. "Pre-K, Belle," he said, shaking

his head at the sad attempt at an excuse. "It's not like she's in med school. You could pull her out for a week. Call it an extended field trip."

She scowled at him, clearly realizing that she hadn't offered much of a reason. A second later, she tried again. "Fine. Then there's my work. I have donations to line up, plans to finalize…"

He was prepared for that argument, too. Wes had been thinking about this for a few days now, and tonight had sealed it all in his mind. He had to go back home, and he wasn't going to leave alone.

"And in Texas, you can visit the company, meet with the PR team, and they'll help you come up with ways to drum up more donations."

"I don't need help—"

"And," he interrupted, "you can go through the toy catalog at the company and choose which toys of ours you want to add to your project."

"I hate when you interrupt me."

"I know. Maybe that's why I do it." He gave her another smile and she rolled her eyes.

Then she bit her lip and her gaze slid from his as if she didn't want him to see what she was thinking. He knew she was considering it, and he also knew enough to let his adversary work through everything without another interruption. *Adversary.* That word stuck in his brain until he mentally erased it. She wasn't an enemy. She was—hell, he wasn't completely sure what Belle was to him. He only knew that he wasn't ready to be without her.

"Say we do go with you. Then what?" she finally asked, her voice little more than a whisper.

"What do you mean?"

She half turned on the bed to meet his gaze. Firelight

played over her skin and flickered in her eyes. "I mean, say we spend the week together, all of us. What happens after that? Caro and I come back home, you stay in Texas and we all go on with our lives like before?"

He smoothed her hair back, more because he couldn't stop himself from touching her than for any other reason. His fingertips traced along her jawline then dropped to where her hand lay on the comforter. He took it in his and held on. He thought about it for a second, considered his options, then went with honesty.

"I don't know, Belle. Neither of us *can* know. All I'm sure of is that I want you and Caro to come with me. To be with me. Give me that week, Belle."

Her gaze never wavered. She looked at him for several long, tense seconds as if trying to see past his reserve to what he was really thinking. If she knew, he told himself, she would never come with him.

He wanted her in Texas not only because he wanted more time with Caro. Not only because he wanted Belle in his bed. But because if the three of them presented a united front, the scandal driven by Maverick might disappear entirely and Teddy Bradford could get back on board with the merger.

His people were no closer to finding the mysterious Maverick, but he had learned that Bradford wasn't in talks with anyone else. So the odds of him being in on the scandal eruption were really low. And that meant that the merger might still be salvageable. If he worked this right.

He swallowed his impatience and let Belle see only what he wanted her to see. A man unwilling to let go just yet.

Finally, she nodded. "Okay. A week. After that, we'll talk about what comes next."

He squeezed her hand and smiled. "We'll work something out," he promised her and meant it. No matter what else happened in his life, he knew he'd find a way to keep Caro, and maybe her mother, in his life.

She smiled, but it was barely more than a slight lifting of her lips. Wes knew she wasn't sure of this decision, but he wasn't going to give her a chance to change her mind, either.

"Good," he said, leaning in to kiss her. "Now that that's settled…" He pushed the comforter down and cupped her breast, thumb and forefinger rubbing her hardened nipple until her eyes glazed over and she gave a soft sigh. Smiling down into her eyes, he quipped, "I think it's time to think about round two. I'm feeling the need to fling myself at you. How do you feel about that?"

She held his hand to her breast and with her free hand she reached up and drew his face to hers. "Fling when ready."

He grinned. Damned if he hadn't missed her. He hadn't allowed himself to acknowledge it before now. He remembered all the nights they'd stayed awake talking, laughing, making love. He'd never had that in his life until Belle, and when she left Texas, she'd taken all of it with her.

No other woman had given him what she had. Now she was back in his life, and he wasn't going to let her go anytime soon.

He bent his head to kiss her and instantly lost all thought under the rising tide of need. Tomorrow could take care of itself. For tonight, all he wanted was *this*.

Two days later, the three of them were on Wes's private jet. Edna had urged her to go, to see where this thing with Wes would lead, and with that tiny bit of encouragement, Isabelle was going to give it a try. Of course, it didn't help anything to know that Chance, Eli and Tyler were less than thrilled at her going off with Wes. Though they'd changed their initial opinion of him mainly because of the way he was with Caro, Isabelle's brothers were still not ready to trust him not to hurt her or her daughter.

Neither was she, when it came right down to it. But if she didn't try, she'd never forgive herself. Still, Isabelle knew she had to approach this time with Wes carefully. If not to protect her own heart—then at least to guard Caroline's.

Because her little girl was thrilled with this new adventure. Caro loved the plane, loved flying above the clouds and loved the limo ride from the airport to Wes's home just west of Royal, Texas.

Five years ago, Wes had been in the process of building his home. Isabelle had seen the blueprints, they'd talked about different design features and she'd suggested quite a few changes to the original plan. Now, seeing it finished, Isabelle thought it was breathtaking.

Under the soft Texas winter sun, the massive two-story house sprawled across a beautifully landscaped property. There was a tidy lawn that seemed wider than a football field. Young trees ran the perimeter of the property with a few older live oak trees that had been left standing during construction. Flowers in wildly bright and cheerful colors hugged the base of the house and lined the brick walk that led to the long, inviting porch.

The house itself was a gorgeous blend of wood and stone and glass. Tall windows lined the front of the house and glinted in the sunlight. Stone walls made the house look as if it had been standing in that spot for decades. The porch was filled with rocking chairs and a swing that hung by thick chains from the overhead beams. A white wood railing completed that picture, along with the baskets of flowers that stood at either side of the double front doors.

Isabelle was used to seeing mountains, and the land here was flat, but for a few rolling hills in the distance. And still, it was beautiful.

It seemed strange, Isabelle thought. They'd left Colorado in the middle of the latest snowstorm. There were snowdrifts four feet high all over Swan Hollow. And here in Texas, there were winter flowers blooming under a mild sun. Kind of a culture shock for Isabelle, but Caroline didn't seem to have a problem with it.

The little girl, clutching her new favorite doll, bolted from the limo onto the grass. She spun in a circle, holding her head back and laughing. When she stopped, she looked at her mother, wide-eyed. "There's no snow, Mommy!"

"I know, baby." Isabelle tossed a glance at Wes to see him smiling indulgently. Looking back to Caro, she asked, "Do you like it?"

"I like making snowmen," she said thoughtfully, taking another slow spin to look all around her. "But I like this, too."

"I'm glad you do," Wes said, using sign language as well as speaking. "We don't have snow, but we have other fun stuff."

"Like what?" Caroline asked, eyes bright and interested.

Put on the spot, he seemed to flounder for a minute and Isabelle waited, curious to see how he'd recover. She shouldn't have doubted him.

"Oh, we've got a big zoo that has a carousel and we've got lakes. We can go out on a boat—"

"I like boats!" Caroline grinned. "Uncle Chance has a boat and it's fun!"

"Good to know," Wes said wryly. "There's an amusement park in Houston where we can go on rides, and there's a trampoline park, too." He reached out and gently tugged one of her pigtails. "Texas has a lot of great stuff."

"But no snow."

He shook his head. "Not usually."

She thought about that for a second then shrugged. "It's okay. Home has snow, so it's okay you don't."

"Well, thanks," Wes said, slanting a look at Isabelle. "You know, your mom used to live in Texas."

"Really?" She looked up at her mother. "Did you have fun with Wes, too?"

Before she answered, she saw the speculative expression on Wes's face and smiled to herself. The man was impossible. "I sure did, honey. So will you."

At least, Isabelle really hoped so. Looking at her little girl's excitement right now, she could only pray that nothing happened to dampen that enthusiasm. Shifting her gaze to Wes, Isabelle tried to see beyond the facade to the man beneath. What did this trip mean to him? Was it simply to get a little extra time with his daughter? Was he considering a future for all of them? Or was there another reason for this trip altogether? Impossible to know.

"Why don't we go inside," Wes said to Caroline. "Then you can see your room."

"*My* room?" Caro asked, her mouth wide-open in pleased surprise.

"Yep, and it's special just for you." He took Caroline's hand, winked at Isabelle, then walked to the front door, the little girl skipping and chattering happily alongside him.

Isabelle followed, shaking her head. The man never

ceased to surprise her. Of course he had a room for Caroline. He'd had two days, after all. No doubt he'd made a few calls and had everything taken care of just the way he wanted it. It probably should have bothered her that he was so obviously planning on more than just a week with Caroline. You didn't go to that kind of trouble for a child who would only be spending a few days there. But on the other hand, how could she be upset with a man who went the extra mile to make their daughter feel special?

"A dog! You gots a dog!"

Caroline's squeal of delight reached Isabelle as she stepped up onto the porch, and she couldn't quite hold back a sigh of defeat. Caro had been asking for a dog for months, and Isabelle had kept putting her off. Now Caroline would be even more determined than ever.

Isabelle stepped into the entryway and immediately noted the warm oak floors, the pale misty-green walls and the thick oak trim everywhere. There was a table near the stairs where a vase of flowers stood and several doors leading off a long hallway that stretched to the back of the house. Later, she'd have time to explore. But for right now, Isabelle's gaze was fixed on her daughter and the golden retriever currently adoring each other.

"What's his name?" Caro demanded as she buried her face in all that soft, golden fur.

"Her name is Abbey," Wes said, signing as well as speaking.

Isabelle had to admit that his signing had really come a long way in a week. Clearly he was practicing a lot.

Abbey, reacting to her name, abandoned Caroline briefly to welcome Wes home, her nails clicking on the hardwood floor. Then the big dog shifted her attention to Isabelle, coming up to her and leaning against her, giving Isabelle the opportunity to stroke that sleek golden head.

But when the hellos were done, the dog shot straight back to Caroline. She plopped to the floor in front of the little girl and rolled over to her back to allow for a good belly rub. Caro complied with a delighted laugh.

"I like dogs," Caro shouted over her own laughter when Abbey sprang up to lick the girl's face.

"She likes you, too," Wes said, then as an older woman approached, said, "I'm home, Bobbi."

"So I see." Bobbi had long, gray-streaked black hair, currently in a thick braid that hung over one shoulder. She wore jeans, a long-sleeved blue T-shirt and dark red cowboy boots. "You brought me a little girl to spoil, too, I see."

"Hi," the girl announced. "I'm Caroline."

"Nice to meet you," Bobbi said. Then, holding out a hand, she said, "You must be Isabelle."

"I am, it's nice to meet you, too." Isabelle looked around, then back to the woman who was so clearly in charge. "It's a gorgeous house."

"Needs some life in it," Bobbi pointed out with a slanted look at Wes. "But looks like it'll be a little livelier for a while anyway."

"All right," Wes said, tossing a knowing look at the older woman. "Caro, you want to see your room? It's upstairs."

Bobbi's eyebrows lifted at the sign language he used, but then she nodded as if pleased to see it.

"I do! Come on, Abbey!" Caroline headed for the stairs at a run, and the dog was only a pace behind her.

Isabelle and Wes followed, and when he took her hand, she held on, pleased at the warmth. The connection. This was a big step for her. Coming back to Royal with the man she had once run from. Odd that she'd never planned on it, but she'd ended up coming full circle. If it all worked out somehow, great. If it didn't, would she pay for this decision for the rest of her life? For her own sake, as well as Caroline's, she hoped not.

At the top of the stairs, they turned left and Wes led the way to a door halfway down the hall. When he threw it open, Caroline raced inside, then stopped dead and sighed, "Oh, boy."

Isabelle had to agree. Wes had gone all out. The room was a pale, dreamy blue, with white curtains at the windows and a blue-and-white coverlet on the bed. There was a table and chairs in one corner, bookshelves filled with books and a child-size blue couch covered in white pillows, just made for curling up and daydreaming. There was a mural on the wall of butterflies, fairies and storybook castles and a thick blue rug spread across the wood floors.

How he'd managed all of this in just a couple of days was amazing. Unless, Isabelle thought with a sideways glance at him, he'd been planning to get her and Caro to Texas all along. Good thing? Bad? She couldn't be sure yet.

Caroline whipped around, still clutching her doll in the crook of one arm, and threw her free arm around Wes's knees. Tipping her head back, she said, softly, "Thank you, Wes."

He cupped the back of her head and smiled down at her with a gentleness that touched Isabelle's heart. There were so many layers to the man that she doubted she would ever learn them all. But this man, the gentle, loving man, was the one she'd fallen so deeply in love with years ago. It was a side of him she'd rarely seen, and it was all the more beautiful now because of it.

And Isabelle was forced to admit, at least to herself, that she *still* loved him. Watching him with their daughter had only solidified the feelings that had never faded away. She'd known five years ago, even when she left him, that she wouldn't be able to run far enough to outdistance what she felt for him. She'd tried. She'd buried herself in work she believed in, in caring for her daughter and in being a part of her town and her family.

But in spite of everything, for five long years, Wes had remained in the back of her mind, in a corner of her heart. And even as she tried to fool herself, she'd known somehow that what she felt for him was still alive and well. Today just proved that.

As her heart ached and her throat tightened, he lifted his head, catching her eye, and everything inside her melted. Isabelle had risked a lot by coming here with him, staying with him. But it was too late to back out now. She had to see this through. See where it would take her. Love didn't disappear just because it was inconvenient. But if she walked away a second time with a broken heart, Isabelle wasn't sure she'd survive it.

"You're welcome," he said to the little girl still beaming at him as if he were a superhero.

Caroline gave him another quick grin, then climbed onto her couch to try it out and Abbey crawled up right beside her, laying her big head in the little girl's lap. Clearly, a mutual adoration society had been born.

"Now," Wes said to Isabelle, "I'll show you your room." He took her hand again to lead her directly across the hall.

The moment he opened the door, she knew it was the master bedroom. It was massive. Far bigger than her own bedroom at home, this one boasted a stone fireplace on one wall, with a flat-screen TV mounted over the mantel. There were two comfy high-back chairs and a small table in front of the hearth, and on either side of the fireplace, floor-to-ceiling bookcases. A bank of windows on the far wall was bare of curtains and displayed a view of the trees, grass, a swimming pool and those hills she'd spotted before, off in the distance. There was also what looked like a barn. Or a stable.

She wondered idly how many acres he owned, but then her thoughts were scattered by a glance at his bed. It was *huge*. A dark blue duvet lay atop the mattress, and the head and footboard were heavy golden oak. Dark red rugs were tossed across the shining floor, and all in all, it was a beautiful, masculine space. But it was the bed that kept drawing her gaze. Finally she forced herself to look away, to meet Wes's gaze.

In his eyes, she saw the glint of desire and the determination of a man who knew what he wanted and had no trouble going after it. "You don't have another guest room?"

He gave her a half smile, reached out and stroked one hand down her back. Isabelle took a breath, then steeled herself against her reaction. The ripple of goose bumps along her arms, mixed with the heat building at her core, was enough to shatter any woman's defenses.

"Sure," he said, voice a low rumble of need, "but we can't pretend we didn't sleep together. Can't go back, Belle." His gaze locked on hers. "And I wouldn't even if we could. Don't think you would, either."

She shook her head. No point in denying it.

"Do you really want us to be sneaking up and down the hallway in the middle of the night?"

The image his words painted was both pitiful and funny. She sighed. "With Caro right across the hall…"

Wes chuckled. "She won't think anything of it, Belle. Heck, with Abbey around, she probably won't *notice*." He moved in and wrapped both arms around her. "We already crossed this bridge back in Colorado, you know. You're not going to try to tell me you're sorry about it, are you?"

No, she really wasn't. Maybe she should have been, but she wasn't. Five years without him had been long and lonely. Having him back in her life might be dangerous to her heart, but Isabelle knew that loving him was no longer a choice for her. It just *was*.

As for sharing his bed here… Isabelle would be going to bed long after Caro. And she'd be up before her daughter in the morning, so her little girl would probably never realize where her mother was spending the night. And honestly, Isabelle admitted silently, she wanted to stay with Wes. She was here for a week. Why not enjoy what she had while she had it? Risk be damned. If this time with him was destined to end, Isabelle at least wanted *now*.

"No," she said, "I'm not sorry." She watched pleasure dart across his eyes, then she lifted one hand and cupped his cheek, just because she wanted to. "I'll stay here. With you."

"Good." He caught her hand and held onto it. "Now that we've got that settled…come on."

Frowning at his abrupt shift, she asked, "Where are we going?"

"Outside. Let's find out if Caro likes her pony."

"What?" She laughed as he pulled her along behind him and wondered how she'd ever made it through the last five years without him.

Eight

"**B**oss?" Robin's voice was a little loud, which made Wes think this wasn't the first time she'd spoken to him.

Whatever the situation going on at home, he had to focus here at work. "Sorry. Yeah. What were you saying?"

She frowned at him. "Everything all right?"

"Sure." He pushed up from his desk, stood straight and shoved his hands into his pockets. "So what's going on?"

She didn't look like she believed him, but since he was the boss, she went with it. "Okay, the news from Texas Tech is good," she said. "They've got the next line of tablets ready to roll before summer, with the new bells and whistles you ordered."

"Good." He moved out from behind his desk and walked to the window overlooking the city of Houston. While the PR and IT teams were still working on uncovering the mysterious Maverick, Wes was concentrating on the other arms of Jackson Inc. He had majority interest in Texas Tech; Texas Jets, a charter jet service; and a few other smaller yet growing companies. He'd been building his empire for decades, and getting to the bottom of Maverick's deliberate sabotage of Texas Toy Goods was important. He couldn't risk the man going after any of his other companies as well.

"I want to talk to Sam Holloway at Texas Jets sometime today," he said, never taking his gaze from the cityscape sprawled out below him. "And then get me Andy at Texas Tech. I want to hear details on those bells and whistles."

"Got it."

He half turned from the window. "Are Belle and Caroline still in the PR department?"

"Isabelle is, yes," Robin told him. "But Maggie from PR took Caroline down to the cafeteria for a chocolate shake." She sighed and smiled. "That little girl is just adorable, boss. I gotta say, makes me miss my own kids' younger days."

"Yeah, she's pretty great," he said, thinking, as he had been for days now, about how Caroline had wormed her way straight into his heart, and no matter what happened between him and Isabelle, nothing for him would ever be the same again.

"She showed me how to say hello in sign language." Robin shook her head. "Smart kid. Just like her daddy."

His eyebrows lifted.

"Please." Robin waved one hand at him. "No, you didn't make some grand announcement, but I'd have to be blind to not notice the child has your eyes. Right down to the unusual color."

"It's not a secret," he said, then half laughed at himself. "At least, not since Maverick blasted it all over the internet. But I haven't told Caro who I am yet."

"For heaven's sake, *why*?" Robin asked.

She sounded completely exasperated, and Wes realized that for some reason, his assistant and his housekeeper shared the same attitude. Neither of them was intimidated by him and both of them continually seemed to forget just who was really in charge. "You know, I could fire you," he pointed out wryly.

She waved that away with a flick of her hand. "That'll never happen and we both know it. So why haven't you told that child you're her father?"

"Because I want her to know me. To—" it was humiliating to admit "—*like* me."

Robin gave him an understanding smile. "She already does, boss. You can see it in the way her face lights up when you walk into the room."

He pushed his hand through his hair. Robin was right. He'd seen that look. It had made him feel ten feet tall. So why then was he waiting to tell his daughter who he really was? He hated to think it was fear. Hell, nothing had scared Wes in…well, ever. But the thought of that little girl turning from him could bring him to his knees.

"Robin," he said abruptly, "I'm taking the rest of the day off."

"I'm sorry. I think I must have had a stroke. What was that?"

"Surrounded by sarcasm," he said with a nod. "I'm taking the day off."

"Yesterday, you took Caroline to the aquarium, the day before it was ice-skating and the day before that you and Isabelle had her riding roller coasters." Robin tipped her head to one side and looked at him. "I'm beginning to think you might be looking for a life, boss."

"I'm beginning to think you may be right." He grinned

and shrugged into his jacket. "Just forward my calls to my cell. I'll check messages later."

He caught up to Isabelle in PR. The room was bustling, people typing on keyboards, sketching on whiteboards and huddled around desks, arguing and discussing. The noise level was high, so Wes decided to try out some sign language. He caught her eye and from across the room, she smiled at him. Then she flushed and chuckled when he started signing.

At another desk, a guy named Drake laughed, too, then ducked his head and pretended he hadn't.

"Something funny?" Wes asked him.

"Um, no, sir," the kid answered quickly, his gaze darting from side to side to avoid making direct contact with Wes's. "It's just that, um, my mother's deaf. I speak sign language, and, well..."

"Perfect." Wes sighed and shook his head. "What were the odds," he muttered. Then he bent low and whispered, "I expect you to forget everything you just saw."

"Didn't see a thing," Drake assured him and deliberately went back to work with a frenzied attack on his keyboard.

Nodding, Wes was satisfied that the kid wouldn't be telling anyone that the boss had just signed, *You look incredible. I want you in bed. Now.*

Isabelle walked toward him, still smiling. He took her hand and led her from the room. Out in the hall, he said, "Well, that was unexpected. I didn't think there'd be someone here who understands sign language."

She squeezed his hand and let him see her smile grow. "It's okay. I don't think he's going to be telling anyone that you want me in bad."

He stopped. *"Bad?"*

Laughing, she nodded. "You're getting better at signing every day, but it's pretty tricky."

No wonder the kid had laughed. "Still, having you wrapped up in bed and bad on top of it isn't a bad idea, either. I could eat my way down to you and then just keep going."

Her eyes flashed and she licked her lips, sending a jolt of heat straight down to the one area of his body that hadn't relaxed since he'd first seen her. Shaking his head, he murmured, "I came to get you so we could take Caro to the zoo. But now..."

She tipped her head to his shoulder briefly, then looked up at him. "Zoo first. Bad later."

"Deal."

They must have walked for miles, Isabelle thought. She and Wes and Caroline had spent hours at the zoo, and she wouldn't have thought that Wes would enjoy it. But he had. Just as much as he'd enjoyed the amusement park and the ice-skating. Maybe it was the magic of seeing things through the eyes of a child, but he'd been more relaxed and happy in the last few days than she'd ever seen him. In a gray suit, now minus the red power tie, he should have looked out of place at the zoo. But she'd learned that Wes wasn't a man easily defined. Despite the suit, he carried Caro on his shoulders and didn't seem to mind when her ice cream cone dripped all over him. On the ride home to Royal, it took only seconds for Caro to be sound asleep in her car seat. After checking on her, Isabelle sat back and turned her head to look at Wes. Her heart did a quick tumble as she stared at his profile. "Caro had a wonderful time today."

He glanced at her and gave her a half smile. "So did I.

Until this week, I hadn't taken a day off in years. I think Robin is shell-shocked."

Isabelle laughed. She'd always liked Wes's no-non-sense assistant. "She'll recover."

"How did it go in the PR department?" He paused. "You know, before I got there. You get anything you can use?"

"Absolutely." In the couple of hours she'd been with PR that morning, Isabelle had found new and clever ways to hit people up for donations. "Mike actually suggested that I sort of adopt out hospitals."

"You lost me." He steered the car into the passing lane to go around a truck.

"Well—" she turned in her seat to face him even though he had to keep his eyes on the road "—it's like, I print up information on specific hospitals. The kids—first names only—their health issues, how long they'll be there in that sterile environment. Let potential donors see these kids as real people rather than just another random charity."

"Good idea." He nodded. "And you'd send these fly-ers or newsletters or whatever out to your mailing list?"

"To start, yes, but I could also make more of a splash on my Facebook page. And get more involved in social media. Honestly, I get so busy with the actual work that I forget I also have to get out there and promote what the charity does, too. Social media is so hot right now—"

"Believe me," Wes said with a tight groan, "I know."

"Right." She winced, remembering suddenly that it had been a Twitter attack that had brought them back together. "Sorry. Sore spot."

"It's okay," he said, shaking his head. "Go ahead."

"All right. So Mike suggested I start a public Face-book page detailing what the nonprofit is about. Pictures of the toys we give to these kids. Maybe pictures of the toy closets in the hospitals themselves. I'd like to add pictures of the kids with their toys, but I'd have to get their parents to sign releases..."

"They probably would," he said.

"You think so?"

"You should know better than me what a parent of a sick kid would be feeling. What would you have done if someone had given Caro a brand-new doll or stuffed animal when she was miserable in the hospital?" He looked at her briefly.

"I'd have kissed them," she admitted. "So, okay, maybe you're right about that. I can check with some of the parents at the hospital when we go home next week and—"

"About that..."

She looked at him for a long second or two before saying, "What?"

"Well," he said, shifting position slightly in his seat, "I was just thinking that maybe one week here won't be enough time. I mean, for Caroline. To get to know me, my place—hell, Texas."

Isabelle frowned, and her stomach jumped with a sudden eruption of nerves. "We agreed on a week, Wes. I have work. Caro has school. We don't live here."

"You could."

"What are you saying?" Her heart jumped into her throat and the hard, rapid beat thundered in her ears. Was he saying what she thought he might be saying, because if he was, driving down the freeway doing eighty miles an hour was an odd time to be saying it. "You want us to *live* here?"

"Sure. The house is huge, plenty of room, Caro could go to school in Royal and—"

He kept talking, but Isabelle had stopped listening. There was no mention of love or commitment or anything else in that little speech. He wanted them in his house, her in his bed, but he was no closer to intimacy than he had been five years ago, so Isabelle did them both a favor and interrupted him. "Wes, it's really not the time to talk about this."

His mouth worked as if he were biting back words clamoring to get out. Finally though, he said, "Okay. But you can think about it."

She could practically guarantee she wouldn't be thinking about anything else. The fact that he could just bring up the idea so casually, though, told Isabelle more than she wanted to know. He wasn't looking for family. For love. He wanted her and Caro to be a part of his life without strings. Without the ties that would make them a unit.

Maybe she'd been fooling herself from the beginning.

"Okay," he said, still frowning, "we'll table that discussion for now. Instead, you can tell me if you got a chance to look through the toy catalog I gave you yesterday."

He went from frowning to facile in the blink of an eye. She'd forgotten he could do that. Isabelle used to be fascinated by the way he could switch gears so easily. If he saw himself losing one argument, he'd immediately change tacks and come at it from a completely different direction, and pretty soon, he had exactly what he'd wanted all along.

Now, he was doing it to *her*. Isabelle was going to keep her guard up around him, because he was her weakness. She couldn't let him see that she loved him, because one of two things would happen—he'd either back off as he had five years ago. Or, worse yet, he'd look at her with pity.

She wasn't interested in either.

"I did," she said, deliberately cheerful. "You've got some great things, Wes. If you're serious about donating, we'd love to add anything you can spare."

He reached over and took her hand, holding it in his much larger one. The heat of him swept up her arm to puddle in the center of her chest, wrapping her heart in the warmth of him. God, she wasn't going to be able to protect her heart, because it was already his.

"Just tell Robin what you need. She'll take care of it."

"Thanks." She couldn't stop looking at him. Maybe she was storing up memories, Isabelle thought. Maybe a part of her knew that this couldn't last and was instinctively etching him into her mind so that years from now, when she was still missing him, she could pull these images out and remember.

She only hoped it would be enough.

The following evening, Wes realized that he was in the middle of the very situation he'd been avoiding for years. He had a woman and a child in his home, and instead of feeling trapped, he felt…good.

But then, this wasn't permanent, was it? That thought didn't bring him the rush of happiness he would have expected. When he'd suggested to Belle that she and Caroline could stay with him, she hadn't jumped at it, had she? So he was still looking at saying goodbye to them all too soon. His guts twisted into knots. Isabelle had only agreed to be here for a week, and four of those days were already gone.

And instead of being at home with them right now, he was here at the Texas Cattleman's Club for a meeting. Shaking his head, he lifted the crystal tumbler in front of him and took a small sip of his scotch. Usually, he enjoyed coming into town, sitting in the lounge, talking with friends, joining in on plans for the future of the club. But tonight, he knew Isabelle and Caroline were back at the house, and he caught himself constantly wondering what they were up to while he was stuck here.

"Your head's not in this meeting," an amused voice noted.

Wes looked at Clay Everett and gave him a nod. "Good catch." Clay was a local rancher with brown hair, green eyes and a permanent limp due to a bull-riding accident. Like Wes, Clay was a driven, stubborn man.

"So what's more fascinating than painting the club restrooms?" Tom Knox asked.

"Oh, I don't know," Toby McKittrick said wryly. "*Everything*, maybe?"

Wes grinned and gazed at each of the men in turn. Tom looked the part of the ex-soldier he was, with broad shoulders, lots of tattoos and the scars he carried as a badge of honor. He was a man to be counted on.

Toby was taller, leaner and just as stubborn as the rest of them. A rancher, he was loyal to his friends, tough on his enemies and didn't take crap from anyone.

"Yeah, got better things to do than sit here and listen to a lot of nonsense," Wes said, idly turning the scotch glass in damp circles on the tabletop.

"So I heard," Tom said with a knowing smile. "Isabelle's back. How's that going?"

"The word is," Clay offered slyly, "our boy Wes here is practically domesticated."

"No way," Toby put in with a laugh. "The woman who could put a leash on this man hasn't been born yet."

"Not what I hear," Clay said, taking a sip of his beer.

Great. Even his friends were talking about him, wondering about what was going on. He supposed bringing

Isabelle and Caro back to Royal had been inviting the gossip, but what the hell else could he have done? Eventually, he knew, the talk in Royal would move on to some fresh meat and he and his problems would fade away. All he had to do was make it that long without popping someone in the mouth.

And he didn't have a damn leash around his neck.

Wes nodded as he lifted his glass to the other men. "Good to be with friends who know just how to aim their shots."

They all took a drink and Toby said, "Damn straight. What're friends for, after all? And since we're such good friends, maybe we should go back to your place with you. Let Isabelle know that when she gets tired of dealing with you, we stand at the ready."

Giving him a smile, Wes shook his head. "Yeah. That'll happen. I don't think so."

Clay grinned. "Worth a try. When do we meet your daughter, then?"

Wes shot him a look. He shouldn't have been surprised, since half the country had been talking about him, thanks to Maverick and Twitter. Still, it seemed weird to have someone ask about his *daughter* so easily.

"Soon," he said. "Hopefully. Her mother and I have some things to work out first. Which I could be at home doing if I wasn't here listening to the old-timers gripe about too many changes."

"The girl's a cutie," Clay told him. "Saw pictures of you three in the grocery store."

"What?" Wes just looked at his friend and waited.

"Yeah, those tabloids by the cash registers? There you all were at the ice-skating rink." Clay shrugged. "Headline was something like hashtag Deadbeatdad No More."

"Great. That's terrific."

"Hey," Toby said, "it's better than saying you're *still* a crappy father."

"I didn't know I was a father," Wes pointed out.

"Yeah, we know," Tom said, holding both hands up in mock surrender. "We're just saying that everybody else seeing the three of you looking like a family is going to take the sting out of that whole Twitter nonsense."

He had a point, Wes told himself. And if the pictures were in the tabloids, they'd be showing up other places, too. Magazines, newspapers, online. Teddy Bradford would see them and maybe rethink his position on the merger. One of the reasons Wes had brought Isabelle and Caroline back to Texas with him was to take the pressure off the scandal.

So why was he feeling a little guilty about all of this now?

Wes scanned the room, noting the members who were here and wondering about those who weren't. Hell, it was a pain in the butt to have to come to redecorating meetings, but if you were a member you should damn well show up and do what needed doing.

The club had been the same for more than a hundred years. Typical of the wealthy, men-only clubs of the day, the TCC had mostly been decorated with masculine comfort in mind. Hunting trophies along with historical Texas documents and pictures dotted the walls. Dark beams crossed the ceilings, which were higher now, thanks to the renovations done after damage incurred by the last tornado. The furniture was dark leather, a blaze burned in the stone fireplace and the thick rugs that were spread across the gleaming wood floor were a deep red.

Of course, since female members were admitted to the club several years ago, there'd been some changes, too. The child care facility was the most monumental, but there were smaller, less obvious changes as well. The walls were a lighter color, there were fresh flowers in the meeting rooms and the quiet hush that used to define the old place had been replaced with an abundance of feminine voices.

Wes had no problem with female members and neither did his friends. But the old guard still wasn't happy and usually fought the women on every change they tried to institute. Even something as stupid as what they were dealing with tonight—the color of the restrooms.

Wes focused on a trio of women across the room who were even now arguing with two older men whose faces were practically purple with suppressed rage. Shaking his head, Wes looked at his ex, Cecelia Morgan, and her pals Simone Parker and Naomi Price. The three of them together were surely annoying, but he'd always thought of them as benign, somehow. Now though, he had to wonder if the trio of Mean Girls were behind the Maverick business. Yet even as he thought it, Cecelia spouted off about the color of the walls in the women's restroom as if deciding on Springtime Peach was the most important thing in the world. Could she really be behind the devious attack on him?

While she propped her hands on her hips and glared at the older man in the leather chair, Wes could hardly believe that once upon a time, he'd been involved with Cecelia. What the hell had he ever seen in her? Sure, she was gorgeous, but she and her friends still seemed to be locked into high-school behavior, living up to their nickname, the Mean Girls.

As he watched, Simone Parker, with her bold blue eyes, long black hair and body built to wake the dead, leaned into old man McGuire, shaking her finger in his face. Right beside her was stunning Naomi Price, with brown eyes and long reddish-brown hair. Naomi had a self-satisfied look on her face as she watched Simone battle with the old man. Cecelia, though, gave a glance around as if she were looking for a way out.

Briefly, her gaze met Wes's, and she must have read the disgust on his face, because damned if she didn't look embarrassed to be a part of the scene playing out in front of her. But thankfully, Cecelia was no longer Wes's problem.

As if he could read Wes's mind, Toby sighed and said, "Those three should have grown out of that nonsense after high school." He paused, then added, "Especially Naomi. That's just not who she is. Not really."

"I don't know," Tom put in. "The three of them have been bothering people in Royal for years. Maybe it's just become a habit for all of them."

"Then it's one they should break," Wes said, taking another sip of scotch.

"Agreed," Toby muttered darkly.

"All right now." Parker Reese, pediatrician at Royal Memorial hospital, spoke up loudly enough to be heard over everyone else. "Can we cut to the chase here? Let's get the decisions done so we can get out of here."

Normally, Parker was quiet, approachable, but not overly friendly. The crowd quieted, the club's president, Case Baxter, took over and the Mean Girls subsided into silence.

"Well, damn," Wes muttered. He might actually get out of this meeting in time to tuck Caroline in and read her a story. "It's a miracle."

"Yeah," Toby said, "I'm thinking we owe Parker a beer."

A couple hours later, he was home in bed, waiting for the woman he couldn't get enough of. When the bedroom door opened and Belle slipped inside, he smiled. "Caro asleep?"

"Out like a light," she said, "still clutching her doll to her chest. She hasn't come up with the right name for her yet, but she's working on it." Belle eased under the covers and moved in close to Wes, laying her head on his shoulder.

The big bed faced the fireplace, where a nice blaze was going, sending out flickering light and shadow around the room. He tucked his arm around her and held her close, thinking this just couldn't get much better.

A shame he had to shatter it. Holding on to her, just in case she tried to pull away, Wes said, "I spoke to a specialist in Houston today."

She stiffened in his arms, but only tipped her head back to look at him. "About…?"

Wes scowled. "You know what about. Caroline."

"Wes, we agreed that we'd decide on specialists *together*."

"I just talked to him, Belle," Wes said, stroking one hand up and down her back. "I didn't sign our girl up for surgery."

Seconds ticked past, and he watched as anger drained away to frustration, then to simple curiosity. "Okay, fine. What did he say?"

"That he couldn't tell me anything without examining Caro," Wes admitted, "which I knew already. I was just asking some general questions. To satisfy my own curiosity."

"And did you?"

"Yeah." He smoothed one hand through her hair, letting the silky tendrils slide through his fingers. "I wondered, what do you think about getting her a cochlear implant in only one ear?"

She frowned up at him and waited, so he continued.

"We could start out with one, let her go for a few years, see if there are more advancements made in the meantime, and then later on we can include her in the decision making. If she wants to get a second one, then we do that. If not, we don't."

He looked into her eyes and hoped she saw that he was only trying to figure out the best thing for Caroline. It wasn't easy to know what to do, and he figured all parents felt the same. Different issues, maybe, but no one had a game plan that would let them see the future. To *know* which path was the right one to take.

"When she's older, Caroline can tell us what she wants to do. But meanwhile, we make sure she doesn't lose too much ground."

Isabelle was quiet for so long, Wes half wondered if she'd just zoned out. But then she reached up and ran the tip of her finger across his lips. "You surprise me, Wes."

"Yeah?" He kissed her fingertip. "How?"

"That's an excellent compromise from a man not known for making them."

He gave her a wink. "I'm a great businessman. I know how to make deals that everyone can live with. Ask anyone."

"I don't have to ask." She gave him a wry smile. "I've seen you convince people to do things they had no intention of doing, and it looks like you've done it again."

"Yeah?" He smiled. Wes wasn't trying to fast-talk Belle into anything, but he couldn't pretend he wasn't going to do everything he could to help his child, either.

"Yeah," she repeated, and turned, bracing one arm across his chest as she looked at him. "I don't know why I didn't think of it myself. Somehow I convinced myself it was all or nothing, but it's not. We can ease into the implant situation and see how Caro responds."

"Exactly." Wes pulled her over to lie on top of him and skimmed his hands down her back to her behind. She sighed and briefly closed her eyes before looking at him again, and he thought he'd never seen anything as beautiful as this woman.

"We can't get into the specialist until next week." He stared up into her eyes and watched as a layer of frost dazzled their surface. Belle never had been an easy woman, and he could see clearly that she was willing to dig her heels in.

"We won't be here next week," she said quietly.

"You could be. Stay." His hands gripped her hips to hold her in place, because he could tell she wanted to slide off him. Hard to argue with a man when you were both naked and pressed together. Which was exactly why he was keeping her right where she was.

"We've been through this already, Wes," she said. "Why should we stay?"

He watched those eyes of hers, felt himself drowning in them, and every instinct he possessed warned him to take a huge mental step back. To ease away. Let her slide off his body and put some distance between them. But he couldn't do it.

He knew he had to give her a reason to stay, and so he offered the only one he had. "I'm not ready for you to go."

She went still, her hands on his shoulders, her mouth no more than a breath away from his. He waited what felt like forever for her to speak. When she did, he released a breath he hadn't realized had been caught in his chest.

"Okay," she said softly. "We'll stay a few more days. To see the specialist."

A few more days wasn't forever, but it would do for now.

"Deal," he said, then rolled over, taking her with him, holding her body beneath his as he bent to take her nipple into his mouth.

She trembled and he felt like a damn king. She sighed and it was like music. Night after night, they came together, and it was always good. Always right. Always better than the time before. He couldn't get enough of her and didn't think he ever would.

Five long years without her had taught him that no other woman could compare to her. And he wasn't ready to lose her again just yet.

Her hands slid from his shoulders down his arms, and Wes felt every stroke like a line of fire dissolving into his bones. Sliding his hands along her body, he laid claim to her in the most intimate, ancient way. Every line and curve of her body became his as he tasted, touched, caressed.

Moonlight speared through the windows, bathing the room in a pale, silvery light. Her eyes caught that light, reflected it and shone like beacons, drawing Wes in closer, deeper. He felt himself falling and couldn't seem to stop it. Didn't know if he *wanted* to stop it.

At this moment, all he knew was that he needed to lose himself in the woman with him. She brought him confusion, laughter, warmth and the near constant need to be inside her. Wes ached for her night and day. The longer he was with her, the more that need intensified. That alone should have worried him, he knew. But the simple fact was, he didn't care what, if anything, it meant. All he could think about was *her*.

She arched into him, and Wes smiled against her skin. She moved against him, shifting her hips, letting him know that the ache inside was building. He loved that she felt what he did, that she wanted as desperately as he did. *Loved.* He blanked his mind at that wayward thought and gave himself up to the moment.

Wes skimmed one hand down to her core and cupped the heat nestled there. Instantly, she lifted her hips, rocking helplessly beneath his touch.

"Wes," she said on a sigh, "don't tease me…"

"Teasing's half the fun," he murmured and took first one nipple then the other into his mouth, tugging, suckling, relishing the tiny gasps and groans she made. He dipped one finger into her center, then another. He stroked her inside and out, while his thumb traced lazy, relentless circles over that most sensitive bud at the heart of her. She twisted in his grasp, moving her hips, arching her back, as her breath came faster, faster. He suckled at her breast, felt her tremble and knew it wasn't enough. He wanted her mindless, defenseless.

Sliding down the length of her body, he knelt between her thighs, scooped his hands beneath her bottom and raised her high off the mattress.

"Wes—" Her eyes were burning. Her hands fisted in the sheet beneath her as her legs dangled off the bed.

Keeping his gaze locked with hers, he bent his head to her center and covered her with his mouth. Instantly, her head tipped back into the bank of pillows behind her and her grip on the sheets tightened until her knuckles went white.

He smiled to himself as he used his lips, tongue and teeth to drive her to the brink, only to keep her from going over. He held her on the edge deliberately, feeling her shake and shiver, knowing what her body wanted, knowing how she craved it, because he did, too.

Again and again, his tongue laid claim to her and Wes

knew he'd never hear anything more beautiful than the whimpering sighs sliding from her throat.

"Wes, please. Please."

He laid her down and reached for the bedside drawer. Grabbing a condom, he sheathed himself, then leaned over her to sheathe himself again…inside her. He entered her on a whisper, and she sighed at the sense of completion when he filled her. Wes closed his eyes and stayed perfectly still for a long moment, savoring the sensation of being held inside her body. The heat, the slick feel of her surrounding him. Then he opened his eyes, looked down into hers and murmured, "Enough."

"Now, Wes," she said, gripping his hips even as she lifted her legs to wrap them around him. *"Now."*

"Yes," he murmured and lowered his head to kiss her. His body rocked into hers, and he fell into a frantic rhythm, his hips pounding against hers, pushing them both faster, higher until release hung just within reach in the darkness. They lunged for it together and together they shattered, holding onto each other as they took the fall.

And with her wrapped in his arms, Wes closed his eyes and held her tight.

Nine

The following night, they left Caroline in Bobbi's care and went to dinner at the Texas Cattleman's Club. Isabelle had always loved the place, for its history, its meaning to the town of Royal. It had never bothered her that it had traditionally been an all-male private club. Heck, she figured women liked time to themselves, too. But now that women were welcome as members, she loved the changes that had only been started the last time she was in Royal.

There was a different feeling to the place. Not exactly feminine, but at least a few of the rough edges seemed to have been smoothed over.

"It's been a while since you've been here," Wes said, tucking her hand through the crook of his arm.

"Five years," she said, glancing up at him. He looked gorgeous, of course, but then Wes Jackson would have to work at looking anything less than amazing. His black suit was elegantly tailored, and the deep red tie against the white dress shirt looked great. His hair was ruffled—she didn't suppose it would ever look anything but. And she liked it that way.

She was wearing a long-sleeved navy blue dress with a full skirt and a scooped neckline that just hinted at the cleavage beneath. Her black heels added three inches to her height, and she still had to look up to meet Wes's gaze. But she saw approval and desire in his eyes, so it was worth it. "Do you still come here for lunch every week?"

"Usually." He nodded to the waiter and headed for his favorite table. Wes seated Isabelle then sat down opposite her. "It's a good spot to get together and talk business."

Wine was served after a moment or two, and Isabelle's eyebrows arched. "Ordered ahead of time, did you? Think you know me that well?"

"Yes, I do." He leaned across the table and smiled. "Your favorite here is the chicken marsala and a side salad, blue cheese dressing."

"I don't know whether to be flattered that you remembered or appalled that I'm so predictable."

"Be flattered," he said. "You've never been predictable, Belle. You always did keep me guessing. Still do."

"I'm glad to know that," she said and took a sip of her wine. Setting the glass back down again, she looked at him, sitting there with all the quiet confidence of a king. He was in his element here, and she was on his turf. She'd have done well to remember that, but sadly, it was too late now. Isabelle had tumbled right back into love with the man, and there didn't seem to be a way out that didn't include a lot of pain.

"Thank you," he said, throwing her off balance again.

"For what?"

"For agreeing to stay into next week. To talk to the specialist with Caro."

They hadn't spoken about that since the night before, but then really, what was there to say? He'd caught her in a weak moment, Isabelle told herself. Naked and wrapped up in his arms, she might have agreed to anything. So she could hardly be blamed for putting off leaving for a few more days. Besides, Caroline loved it here.

Her little girl spent hours in the stable with the head groom, Davey. He was teaching her about horses and had already taught her how to brush her pony, Sid, named after her favorite character in the *Ice Age* movies, and feed him. Caroline was thriving, with both of her parents at her side, with Bobbi and Tony. Not to mention Robin and everyone at the Houston office.

She was a sweet girl and people responded to that, making Caroline feel like a princess wherever she went. In fact, Caro hadn't once asked about going home. Which should, Isabelle thought, worry her. When they did eventually leave, it would be a hard thing for Caroline. It was going to be nearly impossible for Isabelle.

"You're welcome," she said, shoving those dark thoughts down into a corner of her mind. "I'm interested in what the specialist has to say, too."

"Good." He lifted his glass, looked past her and sighed. "Damn it."

"What is it?" She made to turn around, but he stopped her.

"Don't look. It's Cecelia Morgan, and it looks like she's coming over here."

Wes's ex-girlfriend. When she was in Royal before, Isabelle and Cecelia had been friendly, but never friends. The last time she'd spoken to Cecelia, the woman had happened upon her while Isabelle was indulging in a good cry. After hearing her out, Cecelia had urged Isabelle to leave Royal, insisting that Wes would never be interested in a child or commitment or any of the other things that Isabelle had wanted so badly.

"Hi, Wes," the woman said with a cautious smile as she stopped at their table. "Isabelle."

"Hello, Cecelia," Isabelle said, wondering why the woman looked so uncomfortable. "It's nice to see you again."

The other woman smiled wryly, clearly not believing the platitude.

Cecelia was beautiful, with her blond hair, long legs and a figure that would make most women incredibly jealous. But right now her green eyes were filled with regret that had Isabelle curious.

"Look," Cecelia said softly, giving a quick look around the room to make sure she wasn't being overheard. "I don't mean to interrupt, so I won't be long. I just had to stop and say something to both of you."

"What is it, Cecelia?" Wes asked, his deep, curt voice anything but welcoming.

The other woman heard the ice in his voice and stiffened in response. "I just wanted to apologize to you. Both of you. I should have told you about your daughter, Wes. And Isabelle, I never should have said that Wes wouldn't want his child. I feel terrible for my part in all of this and I just wanted to say I'm really sorry."

"Cecelia—I don't blame you for that." Isabelle reached out to her, but the other woman shook her head and held up one hand for quiet.

"It's okay. I just saw you both here and I wanted to say that I've got some regrets over things I did in the past.

That's all." She took a step back. "So, just...enjoy your dinner." And she was gone.

"That was weird," Wes said. "I don't think I've ever seen her so thoughtful."

"It was unexpected," Isabelle agreed. She wouldn't have believed that Cecelia would ever apologize like that. The woman had never been concerned with anyone beyond herself and her two best friends. But maybe, Isabelle thought, as her gaze settled on Wes, people really could change.

The next morning, Wes was at the Houston office for a few hours before heading home to take Belle and Caroline to a park. He laughed to himself at the thought. Hell, even with the upcoming launch, he'd taken more time off lately than he had in years. And though he'd never been one to delegate important duties, he'd been doing just that more and more lately—and feeling his priorities shift as if they'd taken on a life of their own. Business had always been his joy. His passion. Growing his companies had been the focus of his life—until he'd discovered he was a father. One little girl—and her mother—had changed everything for Wes.

He leaned back in his desk chair and stared out the window at the steel-gray winter sky. January in Texas didn't mean snow like Colorado, but the weather could change on a dime and usually did. The park might not be the best destination for today.

"Boss?"

He turned his head to Robin in the open doorway. "What is it?"

"You're not going to believe this," she said, worrying her bottom lip, "but Teddy Bradford is on video call for you."

Frowning, Wes straightened up. Teddy hadn't taken Wes's calls since all of this started. Granted, Wes had been focused more on damage control than in trying to reach out to Teddy—especially after the press conference the man had held. Still, the CEO of PlayCo had been silent up until now, so what had changed?

"Put him through." Wes turned to the monitor on his desk and waited. Teddy's face appeared on the screen moments later.

The older man was in his sixties, with salt-and-pepper hair and shrewd green eyes. He was in good shape and in person was an imposing figure. But Wes wasn't so easily intimidated.

"Bradford," he said, with a nod of greeting.

"Jackson." Teddy gave him a benevolent smile and folded his hands together, laying the tips of his index fingers against his chin. "I thought it was time we talked."

"Why now?" Best to play his cards close to the vest. Wes had learned early on when people were caught up in casual conversation, they made slips. So he watched what he said and tried to make the other man give away his secrets instead.

Teddy leaned back in his oversize maroon leather chair. "I've seen the pictures of you with your daughter and her mother. You're making quite the splash, publicity-wise."

Understanding dawned. Hell, this was just what Wes had originally hoped for. He'd known that photographers would be following him around hoping to get more dirt to feed the scandal that had erupted almost two weeks ago. Instead, the pictures were of him, Belle and Caro together. Happy. Enjoying each other. And he had known that people would assume they were the family they appeared to be.

The plan had worked great. Except that Wes no longer felt as if he were pretending. Things had changed for him, he realized. It wasn't a subterfuge anymore. The situation felt real to him, and he couldn't imagine living without Belle and Caro. That was an unsettling thought for a man who'd spent his entire life avoiding commitment, love and any semblance of family.

Putting all of that aside for the moment, he asked, "Why exactly are you calling, Teddy?"

The older man's face creased in an avuncular smile that instantly rubbed Wes the wrong way.

"That takeover could be back on the table for you," Teddy said, dropping his hands to rest on his desktop. "As a family man myself, I can appreciate when a man makes a mistake and sets it right. You getting things straight with the mother of your child has made me look at you in a new light."

Pompous old bastard. What Wes really wanted to do was hang up. Teddy Bradford as the arbiter of family values was annoying enough. Knowing that he had somehow gotten the old goat's approval really stuck in his craw.

"You should know, though," Teddy continued, in that oh-so-confidential tone, "that we've had another offer for the company. I wanted to give you a heads-up before I make any decisions. Maybe we can still work something out on the merger."

Wes's expression didn't give away what he was thinking. Mainly because he wasn't sure how he felt about any of this. Taking over PlayCo, blending it into his own company had been his purpose for a couple of years now. A part of him was eager at the chance to seal the very deal that had been shattered so completely by the mysterious Maverick. Yet there was another part of Wes that was standing back, wary of this sudden magnanimous burst from the other man.

"Shame about that little gal of yours," Teddy was saying with a sad shake of his head. "Saw she's got a set of hearing aids. Looks like she'll have some challenges ahead."

Wes gritted his teeth. Caroline was the most amazing kid he'd ever met. Hearing or not, she was way better than this man's version of *challenged*.

"I appreciate the phone call," Wes said, somehow managing to hide the guilt nearly choking him. "But like you said in that press conference, I've got a lot of thinking to do."

"Is that right?"

"Teddy," Wes said, "there's a lot going on right now, so I'll have to get back to you on this."

"See that you do," Teddy said, then stabbed a finger at the disconnect button and the screen went dark.

For a second or two, Wes just sat at his desk as fury ebbed and flowed inside him. At Bradford. At the situation he'd found himself in. At himself for dragging Belle and Caro into this mess. The merger with PlayCo was huge. He was being offered the very merger he'd been working toward for two years. But taking it, he might have to swallow more than he was willing to. And Wes didn't know if he could do it. Or even if he was interested in trying.

Still, there was more to think about here than just himself. Expanding the company meant hiring more people, and that was good for everyone. And hadn't this been exactly what he'd been aiming for all along? So what was he waiting for? Why was he easing back from the very thing he'd been counting on?

He scrubbed both hands over his face. "Robin!"

Seconds later, his assistant appeared in the doorway.

"Gather the heads of every department," he said. "I want them here in an hour, discussing that call from Bradford."

"Yes, boss."

When she left, Wes was alone with his thoughts again. And he didn't much like them.

Isabelle stopped by the Royal Diner to pick up the lunch she'd ordered. Amanda Battle, the diner's owner, was at the counter, waiting with Isabelle's takeout bag. Inside that bag were Wes's favorites—grilled ham-and-cheese sandwiches and fresh onion rings. Not the healthiest lunch in the world, Isabelle thought, but a spontaneous office picnic required more than raw veggies and a salad.

Wes was supposed to come home early and take her and Caro out for the afternoon. But Isabelle had received such great news from home, she hadn't wanted to wait to see him. So an office picnic sounded like fun. Besides, Wes had been devoting so much time to her and Caro, Isabelle knew he had a lot of work to catch up on. The new toy launch was still a few weeks away, but he had to be on-site to handle any problems that might crop up.

She couldn't wait to tell him that the toys she'd selected from Wes's company had already arrived in Swan Hollow. And they'd sent so much more than she'd expected, Isabelle was sure she could supply two or three children's wards with those toys alone.

But as good as the news was, it also meant she had to leave for home soon. The distribution of toys was always a logistical nightmare, and she had to be there to supervise it all. She hated the thought of leaving, which was silly since that had been the plan all along. But things had changed, hadn't they? Wes had changed. So maybe after the work was done in Swan Hollow, she and Caro could come back. Maybe.

"Well, it's about time you came in to see me."

Isabelle cleared her mind, slid onto one of the counter stools and smiled at Amanda. "Sorry, I've been busy."

"So I heard." Amanda slid a cup of coffee toward her. "In fact, the whole town's been talking about you and Wes and your daughter almost nonstop. And you know the diner is the unofficial clearinghouse for information."

Isabelle winced, knowing that she was the subject of gossip and speculation. But honestly, she'd expected nothing less. Royal's lifeblood was gossip, and if you wanted to find out the latest news, you came to the Royal Diner.

"Bobbi had your daughter in here yesterday for a milkshake," Amanda said. "She's a cutie."

"Thanks." Isabelle glanced around the familiar diner and was glad to see it hadn't changed. Black-and-white floors, red vinyl booths, and the delicious scent of cheeseburgers cooking on the grill. She was also happy to see there weren't many customers this early in the day.

"How's Wes taking being an instant daddy?" Amanda asked, leaning against the counter.

Back when Isabelle was living in Texas, she'd spent a lot of time in Royal. She and Amanda had become friends, and it was really good to see her again. Actually, she'd enjoyed a lot about being back in Royal and hadn't really expected to, since she'd left Texas so abruptly, thinking to put it all behind her.

"It's been a little iffy," Isabelle said honestly. "He's crazy about Caroline and the feeling's mutual."

"But...?"

She smiled and sighed. Amanda always had been too intuitive. "But I have the same problem I did five years ago," she admitted. "I love him and he likes me. And just how fifth grade does that sound?" She sighed and gave in to her inner worries. "I just don't know if this is going to work or not."

"Sweetie," Amanda said softly, "nobody ever knows that going in. With Nathan and I, it was touch and go from the beginning. But it was worth it. So don't give up. Just ride it out and hope for the best."

Good advice, she thought, and if it was just *her*, maybe she would. But she had Caroline to worry about now, too. And she couldn't justify risking her little girl's heart on the off chance that Wes would see how good they all were together and want it to be permanent.

Although... "Wes has been...different," Isabelle said, keeping her voice low, confidential, just in case there were any big ears listening in. "He's warmer than he was. More reachable somehow. Less obsessed with his business. Sometimes I look at him and I think, it could work. And then I worry that I'm seeing what I want to see. Basically," she said on a choked laugh, "I'm going a little crazy."

Amanda laughed and patted her hand. "Isabelle, we're *all* a little crazy."

Smiling ruefully, she admitted, "I hate that I'm getting pulled in, but Amanda, I keep thinking that this time Wes and I might have the chance to build something."

Amanda sighed in commiseration. "Sweetie, if he has a brain in his head, he won't mess this up."

"I hope you're right."

When Isabelle reached the office in Houston, Robin wasn't at her desk, but the door to Wes's inner sanctum was partially open. Thinking he and Robin were going over some work, she approached quietly and listened, not wanting to interrupt.

"It worked perfectly." A man's voice spoke up. "Bradford was so impressed seeing pictures of you, Isabelle and Caroline together, he's giving you everything you wanted."

Isabelle took a breath and held it as she stood, rooted to the spot.

Another man spoke up. "Maybe Maverick did you a favor, bringing this all out into the open."

Isabelle sucked in a breath.

"Maverick, whoever he or she is, wasn't trying to help me. And I still want the IT department working on finding out just who the hell he or she is."

"Right. Sorry, boss."

Isabelle's throat was tight and her stomach was alive with nerves.

"Back to Bradford," Wes said. "He's still talking about another offer on the table."

"Yes," a woman answered, "but he called you. Clearly he prefers selling out to us."

The man spoke up again, and Isabelle was pretty sure she recognized the voice as Mike from the PR department. "If you can just make the whole family thing work for another couple of weeks, we could seal the deal."

Family thing. Had it all been an act? A performance for Teddy Bradford? Had any of what she'd felt in the last week or more been real?

"I'm not waiting two weeks to give Bradford my decision," Wes said.

Heart dropping to her feet, Isabelle backed away from the door. No, she told herself. Nothing was real. It was all for show. All to help Wes nail down the merger that was, in spite of what she'd believed, still all important to him. Clutching the takeout bag, she bumped into the edge of Robin's desk and staggered. She felt as though the world was tipping beneath her feet. Everything she'd thought, hoped for, was a lie. How could she have been so stupid?

Wes had only been using her and Caroline to fight back against that Twitter attack and the crashing of his business plans. How could she have believed even for a second that he'd meant any of it? That he'd suddenly learned how to love?

Furious with him but even more with herself, Isabelle turned to leave, then stopped at Robin's voice. "Oh, hi, Isabelle. Are you here to see the boss?"

Panicked, desperate to escape, she forced a smile and shook her head. "It's not important. He's busy. Here." She handed the bag of food to the other woman and left, this time at a sprint.

Robin came back into the office carrying a Royal Diner takeout bag, and Wes frowned. "You called in for takeout from *Royal*?"

"Nope," she said. "Isabelle was in the outer office. She brought this for you, but she left because she could see you're busy."

Busy. Wes's brain raced, going back over everything that had been said in the last few minutes. Had Isabelle heard it? Was that why she left? *Damn it.* He jumped up from behind his desk and hit the door at a dead run. "I'll be back."

He didn't bother with the elevator—it would have taken too long. Why the hell had she chosen *today* to surprise him? If she'd heard any of what was being said in his office, she had to be furious. But she'd calm down once he explained. He bolted down the stairs and hit the parking garage just as the elevator arrived and Isabelle stepped out. She took one look at him and her features iced over.

Explaining wasn't going to be as easy as he'd hoped. "Belle—"

"Don't." She hurried past him. "I don't want to talk to you right now."

He took hold of her upper arm and didn't let go when her gaze shifted meaningfully to his hand on her. The parking garage was cold, dark, and their voices were echoing through the structure. Overhead lights fought the darkness and squares of watery sunlight speared in through the entrance and exits.

"Damn it, you don't understand."

"I understand everything," she countered, yanking her arm free. "Maverick messed up your plans."

"Damn right he did."

"And everything with me, with Caro, was all a lie. You *used* us to get that stupid merger that's so important to you."

Insulted, mostly because her accusation held a hell of a lot of truth, Wes swallowed his own anger before speaking again. "That merger was important. Something I've been working toward for years. But I wasn't using you. Either of you."

"Sure." She nodded sharply, her eyes narrowed on him. "I believe you."

"Yeah, I can see that." Helplessness rose up in him and nearly choked his air off. Wes hated this feeling and could honestly say that until he'd met Isabelle, he'd never really experienced it. "I don't know what you heard—"

She sneered at him. "I heard all I needed to."

He thought back fast, recalling what everyone was saying in the minutes before he'd found out she'd run off. Gritting his teeth at the memory, he said, "It was out of context."

"Right."

His anger burst free. "Are you going to listen to me about this or just keep agreeing with me to shut me up?"

"Which will get me out of here the fastest?" She folded her arms over her chest and tapped the toe of her shoe against the concrete in a staccato beat.

Irritating, fascinating, infuriating woman.

Scowling, he said, "Did it hurt that pictures of the three of us were in the news? No. But did I arrange it? No. I didn't lie to you, Belle."

"Really." She tipped her head to one side. "Explain Caro's bedroom."

"What?"

"Murals on the wall. Rugs. Chairs. New bed. Toys." She ticked them all off, then said, "You started preparing for our arrival long before you asked me to come to Texas. This was all a plan from the beginning."

"Yeah," he said, refusing to deny this much, at least. "When I found out I had a daughter—after her mother had lied to me about it for five years—I had a room set up for her. That makes me a bad guy?"

She shook her head. "You don't get it. But then, you never did." She started walking again.

"What the hell? You don't finish an argument? You just walk off."

"This argument *is* finished," she called back, and the click of her heels on concrete sounded out like beats of a drum.

He let her go. No point chasing her down to keep

arguing here. He'd give her time to calm down. Let her get back home, think everything through.

Wes listened to her car door slam and the engine fire up. "Once she settles a bit, it'll be fine," he told himself. "I'll fix all of it tonight."

Ten

Belle wasn't there when he got home.

At first, he couldn't believe it. He'd expected to find her in the great room, quietly stewing. Wes had arrived, flowers in hand, ready to smooth out every rut between them and charm her into seeing things his way. The reasonable way.

Now, he stood in the empty room, a bouquet of lavender peonies gripped in one tight fist. There was no sign of either his wife or his daughter.

Wife?

That word had popped into his head from God knew where, and Wes rubbed his forehead as if trying to erase it. But it wouldn't go. When had he started thinking of Belle as a wife? About the time, he figured, that he'd realized he had no interest in living his life without the two people who meant everything to him. Staggered, he shook his head and kept looking around the room.

None of Caroline's toys were lying abandoned in the middle of the floor. Belle's electronic tablet wasn't on the coffee table, and the house *felt* empty.

His heart fisted in his chest, and a soul-deep ache settled over him. Why the hell would she leave? He pushed one hand through his hair and turned a fast circle, checking every damn corner of the empty room as if somehow expecting Isabelle and Caroline to simply appear out of thin air. "She was supposed to *be* here," he muttered. "We're supposed to straighten this out. She's supposed to *listen* to me, damn it."

Refusing to believe that she would simply leave without a word, without even a damn note, he headed for the stairs and was stopped halfway across the hall.

"They're gone."

He stared at Bobbi and ground out, "When?"

"A few hours ago." She leaned one shoulder against the doorjamb and crossed her arms over her chest.

Hours? They'd left hours ago?

"Why the hell didn't you call me at work?" he demanded. "Let me know?"

"Because she asked me not to," Bobbi snapped, her gaze drilling into his.

Looked like Belle wasn't the only woman he'd pissed off today. His housekeeper was clearly disgusted with him. But that didn't excuse her keeping this from him.

"You realize that you don't work for Belle, right?"

"And you realize that I'm on her side in this, right?"

When had he lost complete control of his world? This kind of thing just didn't happen to Wes Jackson. "You're fired," he said tightly.

"No, I'm not," she retorted and pushed off the wall. Wagging one finger at him, she added, "You can't fire me, because you *need* me. Just like you need Isabelle and your daughter."

He felt the punch of those words as he would have a fist. She was right. He was alone and she was right. He did need them. Wes scowled more fiercely, not knowing whom he was more angry with. Bobbi? Or himself?

"That little girl was *crying* when they left."

Himself, he thought. He was definitely most angry at himself. And yet, Belle hadn't had to leave. She should have stayed. Talked this out. Wes swallowed back a fresh tide of anger rising up from the pit of his belly. Sure, he'd screwed up. But Belle had walked out. Caro had been crying. Had Belle cried, too? Regret shattered the anger, and guilt buried what was left. So many emotions were charging around inside him, it was a wonder Wes could draw a breath at all.

"You should have called me." Turning his back on Bobbi, he took the stairs three at a time and headed straight to the master bedroom.

No sign of Belle there, either. Somehow, he'd wanted to believe that his housekeeper had been lying to him. That she was trying to make him wise up before facing Isabelle. But she hadn't lied. He threw the walk-in closet door open and stared at the empty rack where Belle's clothes had been hanging only that morning.

Hell, her scent was still there, lingering in the still air. Haunting him until her face rose up in his mind and he couldn't see anything else. But she was gone.

He left his bedroom, stalked across the hall to Caro's room and felt his heart rip when he found it as empty as the rest of the house. A soft whining sound caught his ear and he looked around the door to the child-size couch. Abbey was stretched out, as if waiting for Caro to come back. The dog lifted her head when he entered, then seeing him alone, whined again and dropped her head to her paws.

Wes knew just how she felt.

He glanced down at the peonies he still held in his clenched fist. Then he dropped them to the floor and stepped on the fragile petals on the way out of the room.

Grabbing his cell phone, Wes walked across his bedroom until he was staring out over the yard. He hit speed dial, and while he waited, he looked at the stables, then the corral, where Caro's pony was wandering alone. His daughter should be there right now. Waving at him. Signing to him. But no, her mother had taken her away. *Again.*

He was so wrapped up in his own thoughts, it startled him when a voice came on the line and said, "She doesn't want to speak to you."

"What?" Wes yanked the phone from his ear and glanced at the number he'd dialed, making sure it was Belle's. But there was no mistake.

"Edna?" he asked, realizing Belle's housekeeper was running interference for her. She couldn't even talk to him on the *phone*? "Where's Belle?"

"She's here at home where she belongs," Belle's housekeeper informed him. "And she asked me to tell you she's got nothing more to say to you. She says that everything that needed saying was said this morning."

He held the phone so tight, it should have shattered in his grasp. Taking one long, deep breath, Wes reached down deep for patience and came up empty-handed. He couldn't believe that she was going to such lengths to avoid him.

"So her answer is to run away?" he countered.

"She didn't run. She flew."

Was he paying off some terrible karma from a past life? Why else would every woman he knew be giving him such a hard time? Couldn't they all see that there were two sides to this?

"Damn it, Edna, put her on the phone."

"Don't you curse at me. And I don't take orders from you."

He was beginning to wonder if *anyone* did. Taking another deep breath, he held it for a second, then released it to calmly ask, "Can I speak to my daughter then?"

"Nope."

A fresh rush of anger surged through him at the nonchalant attitude. He'd never been more frustrated in his life. Separated from his family by hundreds of miles and an emotional chasm that appeared too deep to cross. "You can't keep her from me."

"I can't, no," she said flatly. "But Isabelle can, and good for her, I say. You had a chance at something wonderful and you threw it away. You threw *them* away. I know what you did, so if you're looking for understanding, you dialed the wrong damn number."

Then she hung up.

Stunned, Wes stared at his phone for a long second. *Nobody* hung up on him! "What the hell is wrong with everybody?"

There was no answer to his strangled question. His cell didn't ring; the blank screen taunted him. So he threw his window open, pitched the phone into the yard, then slammed the sash down again.

And he still didn't feel better.

"What did he say?" Isabelle looked at Edna.

"I think it's fair to say that his cookies are completely frosted." Handing the phone back, Edna picked up a plate of brownies and set it in front of Isabelle. "He's mad, of course, and I think a little hurt."

"I doubt it." Edna was too nice, too optimistic. Wes wasn't hurt—just frustrated that she hadn't fallen in line with his plan. You couldn't hurt Wes Jackson with a sledgehammer. A person had to *care* to be hurt.

Like her daughter cared. Just as Isabelle had feared, leaving Texas had been a misery for Caroline. The drama from earlier that day was still playing through her mind.

"But I don't want to go," the little girl had wailed, bottom lip jutting out in a warning sign of a meltdown approaching.

"I know you don't," Isabelle told her. "But it's time we left. We have things to do at home, baby girl."

She sniffled dramatically. "Like what?"

"School."

"I can go to school here. Wes says so."

Oh, thanks so much for that, Isabelle thought with a new burst of anger at the infuriating man. "You already have a school. And Edna and Marco and your uncles miss us."

"But I will miss Wes. And Abbey! Abbey sleeps with me, Mommy. She'll be sad if I go away."

Isabelle sighed. "The dog is not supposed to be sleeping in your bed."

"We sleep on my couch."

"Perfect," she muttered and threw the rest of Caro's clothes into the suitcase. A cab would be there to pick them up in twenty minutes, and the charter jet was waiting on the tarmac. Sometimes, she thought, it was good to be rich. At least she didn't have to wait for a commercial flight and chance having to deal with Wes again. "Go get your doll, sweetie."

"I don't want to leave Wes. And Abbey. And Tony. And Bobbi. And Sid."

Isabelle sighed. She hated putting Caro through this.

Hated even more that it was all her fault for coming to Texas in the first place. For risking so much. For wanting to believe that she and Wes could share a future as well as a past. She should have known better. But apparently, one heartbreak in a lifetime just wasn't enough for her.

"Mommy, I don't wanna go!" Hands were flying and Isabelle wondered how her daughter managed to shout in sign language.

"We have to go." My God, Isabelle could actually feel her patience dissolving. She understood what Caro felt, but there was nothing she could do to ease any of it. The best thing for all of them was to leave Texas as quickly as possible. Get back to normal. So she stooped to what all parents eventually surrendered to. Bribery. "When we get home, we'll get you the puppy you wanted, okay?"

Caro's little hands flashed like mad as her features twisted and her eyes narrowed. "Don't want another dog. Want Abbey."

Things had not improved from there. Caro had cried and pleaded and begged, then at last had resorted to not speaking to her mother at all. By that point, Isabelle had been grateful for the respite. But she knew that tomorrow morning when her darling daughter woke up, there was still going to be trouble.

"God, I'm an idiot," she muttered and sipped at the tea Edna had made for her. Not only was her daughter miserable, but Isabelle's own heart was breaking. How could she have been so stupid to love Wes again? To hope again?

"Oh, honey, you're in love," Edna said with a wave of her hand. "That makes idiots of all of us."

She lifted her gaze to the other woman. "I never should have let Caro's heart get involved. How could I have done that to my daughter?"

"She's *his* daughter, too, honey." Sighing, Edna added, "I know you don't want to hear it right now, but the fact is, he has a right to know her and a right for Caro to know him."

Disgusted with herself, Isabelle muttered, "Well, if you're going to use logic…"

Laughing now, her old friend said, "Take the tea up to your room. A couple brownies wouldn't hurt, either. Get a good night's sleep. There'll be plenty of time tomorrow to worry yourself sick over all this."

"Maybe I will," Isabelle said and stood up. She'd go to her room, but she knew she wouldn't be sleeping. Instead, she'd be lying awake, remembering the last time she'd seen Wes and the flicker of guilt she'd read in his eyes.

"Where the hell did it all go sideways?" he asked the empty room and then actually paused to see if the universe would provide an answer.

But there was nothing. Just his own circling thoughts and the relentless silence in the house. He'd never minded it before. Hell, he'd relished it. Having this big place all to himself—but for Bobbi—had been like an island of peace.

Now it was more like a prison.

And he paced the confines of it all night as any good prisoner should. He went from room to room, staring out windows, listening to his own footsteps on the wood floor. He let Abbey out and stood in the cold January night, tipping his head back to look at the ink-black sky with the bright pinpoints of stars glittering down at him. Then he and the dog, who was yet another female ignoring him, went back into the house and were stuck with each other.

And in the quiet, Wes remembered the meeting that morning. Remembered everyone talking about the merger and how the pictures of him and his family had saved the situation with PlayCo. Recalled that even he had talked about it.

Mostly though, he remembered the look on Belle's face when he caught up with her in the parking garage. The hurt. The betrayal. He took a breath, looked around his empty bedroom and knew what he had to do. Dawn was just streaking the sky when he picked up the phone.

"More news out of Texas this morning," the stock reporter on the TV said. "Renewed talks of a merger between Texas Toy Goods Inc. and PlayCo have ended. Again." The reporter smiled, checked her notes and continued. "This time though, it's Wes Jackson, CEO of Texas Toy Goods, who's backing away. Mr. Jackson confirmed the news earlier today. So far, Teddy Bradford hasn't been available for a comment."

Isabelle stared at the television as if she couldn't believe what she'd just heard. "Why would he do that? Why would he call off the merger?"

Chance stood in the middle of the room and shrugged. "Maybe he finally realized there are other things more important."

She looked at her oldest brother and wondered. About this time yesterday, she'd walked into Wes's office for a surprise picnic only to have the world fall out from beneath her feet. Now, it felt like it was happening all over again. What was she supposed to think? Why did he stop a merger that he'd been so determined to pull off? Did he expect her to see that report and come running back to him? Oh, God, what did it say about her that she *wanted* to?

The doorbell rang, and since Chance was up already, he said, "I'll get it. You stay here."

Her brothers had circled the wagons as soon as she came home. While Chance kept her company, Eli and Tyler were with Caro in the kitchen while she had lunch. It was good to have family. Especially when everything seemed to be going so wrong.

"Okay, thanks," she said, curling up on the couch to watch the financial reports, hoping for more of a clue as to what Wes was up to.

When she heard the argument from the front hallway, though, Isabelle jolted to her feet, one hand slapped to her chest, as though she could soothe her suddenly galloping heart. Two voices, raised.

"What're you doing here?" Chance demanded.

"I'm here to see Belle. And my daughter."

Wes's voice. Hard. Implacable. Her heart jumped again, and the pit of her stomach came alive with what felt like thousands of butterflies. She couldn't believe he was here. He'd come to her. Why? Isabelle turned to the doorway and stood completely still. Waiting.

"Get out of my way, Chance," Wes grumbled.

"I warned you once what would happen to you if you made either my sister or my niece cry."

"Don't try to stop me."

"You don't deserve them, you know."

"You're probably right," Wes said. "But they're my family and no one can keep me from them."

For a moment, Isabelle held her breath, shocked to the bone by what Wes had said.

"Don't blow this again," Chance warned.

A moment or two later, Wes was there, staring at her, and what she saw in his eyes stunned her. He'd always been so locked down. So emotionally distant that he was practically unreadable. But today, everything she'd ever dreamed of seeing was there, in his beautiful sea-green eyes.

Drawn by the loud argument, Eli and Tyler marched into the room, too, and Isabelle's three brothers formed a half circle behind Wes. Supportive? Threatening? She couldn't be sure, and at the moment, she didn't care. All she could see was Wes and all she felt was a rising sense of hope that fluttered to life in the center of her chest.

Wes didn't care about her brothers, either. He'd known before he arrived that he'd have to force his way past the Graystone wall of protection, and he'd been prepared for it. The brothers had given him a welcome as icy as the Colorado weather, but it didn't matter. He'd been willing to face anything to reach Isabelle.

Looking at her now, his heart thrummed in his chest and he took his first easy breath since the night before, when he'd found her gone and the world as he'd known it had ended. He crossed the room to her in a few long strides and stopped when he was within touching distance. God, he wanted to reach out to her, but there were things he had to say first. Things she needed to hear. Ignoring her brothers, he focused on the only woman he'd ever loved and started talking.

"I was wrong."

She blinked at him, and he read the surprise on her face.

Smiling sadly, he went on in a rush. "I know. I don't say that often. But I was stupid. Shortsighted. Stubborn. I never should have let you leave me five years ago. And I can't let you go now."

"Wes—"

"No," he said, quickly interrupting her. "Let me say this, Belle. Say what's needed saying for way too long."

She nodded, and he felt a wild flicker of optimism in his chest. He couldn't stop looking at her. Her beautiful eyes were wide with a mixture of disbelief and expectation. Her blond hair fell loose to her shoulders and the blue sweater she wore over jeans made her eyes look deeper, as if they held every secret in the universe.

Shaking his head, he began, "See, when my mother died, my father lived the rest of his life in misery. He never recovered, because he'd loved her too much." He reached out, laid both hands on her shoulders and smiled because he was there, with her again. This was the most important speech he'd ever make and he hoped to hell he'd find the right words. "I promised myself I'd never let a woman mean that much to me. It was a kid's reaction. A kid's vow—and it guided me most of my life. Yesterday though, I realized that I had never looked beyond my Dad's pain. But now I see that the happiness my father had before he lost my mom was worth the risk. Worth everything."

God, it sounded pitiful, even to him. He'd lived his life in fear. Love had had him running for years. And he'd never realized that by evading it, he'd been missing out on the best part of life. Well, no more.

"I love you, Isabelle," he said. "I loved you five years ago. I love you now. I will always love you."

She took a breath and swayed slightly in place, lifting one hand to her mouth. Absently, Wes heard her brothers leave the room, and he was grateful. He wanted privacy for this. For the most important moment of his life.

"I want to believe," she said, and he could see the truth of that in her eyes. "But how can I risk Caro's heart? She was devastated when we left yesterday. She cried herself to sleep last night."

He closed his eyes briefly and silently cursed. If he

hadn't been so stupid, he never would have hurt his child. Hurt the woman he loved. Created such a damn mess out of everything.

"It tears at me to hear that," he said. "But you can trust me, Belle." He looked into her eyes and willed her to see the truth. "You'll never be rid of me again. Even if you tell me to go away today, I'll just come back. I'll keep trying for however long it takes to convince you that you're all I want. All I need."

She bit her bottom lip, and tears welled in her eyes. Feeling hope lift like a helium balloon in his chest, Wes kept talking. "I called off the merger."

"I know. I saw it on the news. I couldn't believe it."

"Yes, you can. I put Teddy off. None of that matters to me anymore. The only merger I'm interested in is the one between us. Marry me, Belle. You and Caroline come home with me. Build a future and a family with me."

"Oh, Wes…"

He smiled now, because he could see that she believed. That she was going to say yes. "You can design toys for the company, and together, we'll make sure Caro's Toybox is big enough that every child around the world has a toy to play with and a stuffed animal to cuddle."

A short, choked laugh shot from her throat.

Now that he was on a roll, he just kept building on the future he could see so clearly. "I want more kids, Belle. Brothers, sisters for Caroline. I want us to build a family so strong, not even your hardheaded brothers could tear it down."

She laughed again, louder this time, and reached up to cup his face between her palms. He closed his eyes briefly and released the last of his worries. The heat of her touch sank into him, reaching down into the darkest, loneliest corners of his heart, and left him breathless.

"It's not my brothers you have to worry about, Wes," she said, with a slow shake of her head. "It's *me*. Because once I say yes, I'm never letting you go."

Wes grinned. "That is the best news I've ever heard. So are you saying yes?"

"How could I not? I love you, Wes. I always have. So yes, I'll marry you and have babies with you and build a future filled with family."

"Thank God," he whispered, then reached into his pocket. Showing her the small blue velvet box, he opened it to reveal a square-cut emerald surrounded by diamonds.

"It's beautiful," she whispered.

He slid it onto her finger. "*Now* it's beautiful."

Then he kissed her, and she melted against him while Wes gave silent thanks for whatever gods had blessed him with a second chance at the love of a lifetime.

"Hey, you two," Eli called out. "Come up for air. There's a little girl here who wants to say hi."

They broke apart, and Wes looked down into the shining face of his daughter. Caro was staring up at him with pleasure in her eyes and a delighted smile on her face. She wore the red plastic heart that had first started him out on the journey that had led him here to this amazing moment. Shooting a quick look at Belle, he grinned. "I can't believe you saved that necklace."

Her smile was soft, tender. "It was the first thing you ever gave me. And Caro loves it. She loves you too, Wes. It's time she knows who you are."

Nodding, Wes went down on one knee in front of his daughter. Weirdly, nerves rattled the pit of his stomach. "I missed you," he said and signed.

"Me too," she answered, then threw her arms around his neck.

The force of that hug freely given shook Wes to his

soul. Tears burned his eyes, so he closed them, reveling in the knowledge that he would never lose Belle and his daughter again. Then he pulled back, looked into her eyes and said softly, "I'm your father, Caro, and I love you very much."

Her eyes went wide and her mouth dropped open. She shifted her gaze to her mother and asked, "Really?"

"Really, baby," Belle said through her tears.

The little girl looked at Wes again and gave him a bright, happy smile. Her fingers flying along with the words pouring from her, she asked, "You're my daddy?"

"Yes," Wes said and signed.

"I wished that you were," she said, grinning now. "And my wish came true! I love you, Wes. I mean, *Daddy*."

His heart burst in a sweet blast of love and joy as Wes reached out to scoop her up and stand, still holding her close. Balancing his daughter on one arm he draped the other around Belle's shoulders and knew he'd never been more complete.

Completely shattered still as his daughter's simple words made him feel like the luckiest man on the face of the planet, he paid no attention to Belle's grinning brothers, still watching. He simply handed Caroline to her mother to free his hands and then he carefully signed, "I love you, too, baby girl."

Caroline clapped, Belle laughed and sighed all at once, and the Graystone brothers were applauding.

Wes wrapped his arms around his girls and told himself he was never letting go.

Back in Royal...

Brandee Lawless left her foreman in charge of the mare and her new foal and walked through her ranch house with a smile on her face. Though the birth had gone well, she wanted to email her vet, Scarlett McKittrick, to come give the new mother and baby a once-over.

She snatched her Stetson off, letting her long, wavy blond hair tumble free to the middle of her back. Shrugging out of her jacket as she walked toward her ranch office, Brandee grinned to herself. How could she not?

Everything was going great for her. After the tornado that had caused so much damage to the town of Royal and so many ranches—including her own—things were looking up. She'd rebuilt and now was bigger and better than ever, with plans for even more.

"Basically," she said aloud as she walked into her office and hit the light switch, "everything's coming up Brandee."

She laughed a little, sat down behind her desk and booted up the computer. A couple minutes later, she had her email open and scanned her inbox. But one particular email had her frowning as she read the subject line.

ARE YOU READY TO PLAY?

Wary, because she didn't recognize the sender—who the heck was Maverick? She opened the email and read the brief, yet somehow threatening missive.

You're next.

* * * * *

TWO-WEEK TEXAS SEDUCTION

CAT SCHIELD

For everyone trying to make ends
meet while keeping your dreams alive.
Never give up, never surrender.

One

Before she'd moved to Royal, Texas, few people had ever done Brandee Lawless any favors. If this had left her with an attitude of "you're damned right I can," she wasn't going to apologize. She spoke her mind and sometimes that ruffled feathers. Lately those feathers belonged to a trio of women new to the Texas Cattleman's Club. Cecelia Morgan, Simone Parker and Naomi Price had begun making waves as soon as they'd been accepted as members and Brandee had opposed them at every turn.

Her long legs made short work of the clubhouse foyer and the hallway leading to the high-ceilinged dining room where she and her best friend, Chelsea Hunt, were having lunch. At five feet five inches, she wasn't exactly an imposing figure, but she knew how to make an entrance.

Instead of her usual denim, boots, work shirt and cowboy hat, Brandee wore a gray fit-and-flare sweater dress with lace inset cuffs over a layered tulle slip, also in gray.

She'd braided sections of her long blond hair and fastened them with rhinestone-encrusted bobby pins. She noted three pair of eyes watching her progress across the room and imagined the women assessing her outfit. To let them know she wasn't the least bit bothered, Brandee made sure she took her time winding through the diners on her way to the table by the window.

Chelsea looked up from the menu as she neared. Her green eyes widened. "Wow, you look great."

Delighted by her friend's approval, Brandee smiled. "Part of the new collection." In addition to running one of the most profitable ranches in Royal, Texas, Brandee still designed a few pieces of clothing and accessories for the fashion company she'd started twelve years earlier. "What do you think of the boots?"

"I'm sick with jealousy." Chelsea eyed the bright purple Tres Outlaws and grinned. "You are going to let me borrow them, I hope."

"Of course."

Brandee sat down, basking in feminine satisfaction. With all the hours she put in working her ranch, most saw her as a tomboy. Despite a closet full of frivolous, girlie clothes, getting dressed up for the sole purpose of coming into town for a leisurely lunch was a rare occurrence. But this was a celebration. Her first monthlong teenage outreach session was booked solid. This summer Hope Springs Camp was going to make a difference in those kids' lives.

"You made quite an impression on the terrible trio." Chelsea tipped her head to indicate the three newly minted members of the Texas Cattleman's Club. "They're staring at us and whispering."

"No doubt hating on what I'm wearing. I don't know why they think I care what they say about me."

It was a bit like being in high school, where the pretty, popular girls ganged up on anyone they viewed as easy prey. Not that Brandee was weak. In fact, her standing in the club and in the community was strong.

"It's pack mentality," Brandee continued. "On their own they feel powerless, but put them in a group and they'll tear you apart."

"I suppose it doesn't help that you're more successful than they are."

"Or that I've been blocking their attempts to run this club like their personal playground. All this politicking is such a distraction. I'd much rather spend my time holed up at Hope Springs, working the ranch."

"I'm sure they'd prefer that, as well. Especially when you show up looking like this." Chelsea gestured to Brandee's outfit. "You look like a million bucks. They must hate it."

"Except I'm wearing a very affordable line of clothing. I started the company with the idea that I wanted the price points to be within reach of teenagers and women who couldn't afford to pay the designer prices."

"I think it's more the way you wear your success. You are confident without ever having to build yourself up or tear someone else down."

"It comes from accepting my flaws."

"You have flaws?"

Brandee felt a rush of affection for her best friend. An ex-hacker and present CTO of the Hunt & Co. chain of steak houses, Chelsea was the complete package of brains and beauty. From the moment they'd met, Brandee had loved her friend's kick-ass attitude.

"Everyone has things about themselves they don't like," Brandee said. "My lips are too thin and my ears stick out. My dad used to say they were good for keeping my hat from going too low and covering my eyes."

As always, bringing up her father gave Brandee a bittersweet pang. Until she'd lost him to a freak accident when she was twelve, he'd been her world. From him she'd learned how to run a ranch, and the joys of hard work and a job well done. Without his voice in her head, she never would've had the courage to run from the bad situation with her mother at seventeen and to become a successful rancher.

"But you modeled your own designs for your online store," Chelsea exclaimed. "How did you do that if you were so uncomfortable about how you looked?"

"I think what makes us stand out is what makes us interesting. And memorable. Think of all those gorgeous beauty queens competing in pageants. The ones you remember are those who do something wrong and get called out or who overcome disabilities to compete."

"So the three over there are forgettable?" With a minute twitch of her head, Chelsea indicated the trio of mean girls.

"As far as I'm concerned." Brandee smiled. "And I think they know it. Which is why they work so hard to be noticed."

She'd barely finished speaking when a stir in the air raised her hackles. A second later a tall, athletically built man appeared beside their table, blocking their view of the three women. Shane Delgado. Brandee had detected his ruggedly masculine aftershave a second before she saw him.

"Hey, Shane." Chelsea's earlier tension melted away beneath the mega wattage of Shane's charismatic white grin. Brandee resisted the urge to roll her eyes. Shane would love seeing proof that he'd gotten to her.

"Good to see you, Chelsea." His smooth Texas drawl had a trace of New England in it. "Hello, Brandee."

She greeted him without looking in his direction. "Delgado." She kept her tone neutral and disinterested, masking the way her body went on full alert in his presence.

"You're looking particularly gorgeous today."

Across from her, Chelsea glanced with eyebrows raised from Shane to Brandee and back.

"You're not so bad yourself." She didn't need to check out his long legs in immaculate denim jeans or the crisp tan shirt that emphasized his broad shoulders to know the man looked like a million bucks. "Something I can do for you, Delgado?" She hated that she was playing into his hands by asking, but he wouldn't move on until he'd had his say.

"Do?" He caressed the word with his silver tongue and almost made Brandee shiver.

She recognized her mistake, but the damage was done. Her tone grew impatient as she clarified, "Did you just stop by to say hello or is there something else on your mind?"

"You know what's on my mind." With another man this might have been a horrible pickup line, but Shane had elevated flirting to an art form.

Brandee glanced up and rammed her gaze into his. "My ranch?" For years he'd been pestering her to sell her land so he could ruin the gorgeous vistas with a bunch of luxury homes.

To his credit, the look in his hazel eyes remained friendly and compelling despite her antagonism. "Among other things."

"You're wasting your time," she told him yet again. "I'm not selling."

"I never consider the time I spend with you as wasted." Honey dripped from every vowel as he flashed his perfect white teeth in a sexy grin.

Brandee's nerve endings sizzled in response. Several times in the last few years she'd considered hooking up with the cocky charmer. He possessed a body to die for and offered the perfect balance of risk and fun. Sex with him would be explosive and memorable. Too memorable. No doubt she'd spend the rest of her days wanting more. Except as far as she could tell, Shane wasn't the type to stick around for long. Not that she was looking for any-thing long-term, but a girl could get addicted to things that weren't necessarily good for her.

"In fact," he continued, sex appeal rolling off him in waves, "I enjoy our little chats."

"Our chats end up with me turning you down." She gave him her best smirk. "Are you saying you enjoy that?"

"Honey, you know I never back down from a challenge."

At long last he broke eye contact and let his gaze roam over her mouth and breasts. His open appreciation elec-trified Brandee, leaving her tongue-tied and breathless.

"Good seeing you both." With a nod at Chelsea, Shane ambled away.

"Damn," Chelsea muttered, her tone reverent.

"What?" The question came out a little sharper than Brandee intended. She noticed her hands were clenched and relaxed her fingers. It did no good. Her blood con-tinued to boil, but whether with lust or outrage Brandee couldn't determine.

"You two have some serious chemistry going on. How did I not know this?"

"It's not chemistry," Brandee corrected. "It's antago-nism."

"Po-tay-to. Po-tah-to. It's hot." Either Chelsea missed Brandee's warning scowl or she chose to ignore it as she continued, "How come you've never taken him for a test drive?"

"Are you crazy? Did you miss the part where he's been trying to buy Hope Springs Ranch for the last three years?"

"Maybe it's because it gives him an excuse to stop by

and see you? Remember how he came by the day after the tornado and stayed to help?" Two and a half years earlier an F4 tornado had swept through Royal. The biggest to hit in almost eighty years, it had taken out a chunk of the west side of town including the town hall and a wing of Royal Memorial Hospital before raging on to cause various degrees of damage to several surrounding ranches.

"He wasn't being altruistic. He was sniffing around, checking to see if because of the hit the ranch took whether I was in a position where I had to sell."

"That's not why he spent the next few days cleaning up the storm damage."

Brandee shook her head. Chelsea didn't understand how well Shane hid his true motives for being nice to her. He lived by the motto "You catch more flies with honey than vinegar." The smooth-talking son of a bitch wanted Hope Springs Ranch. If Brandee agreed to sell, she'd never hear from Shane again.

"Where Shane Delgado is concerned, let's agree to disagree," Brandee suggested, not wanting to spoil her lunch with further talk of Shane.

"Okay." Chelsea clasped her hands together on the table and leaned forward. "So, tell me your good news. What's going on?"

"I found out this morning that Hope Springs' first summer session is completely booked."

"Brandee, that's fantastic."

Since purchasing the land that had become Hope Springs Ranch, Brandee had been working to create programs for at-risk teens that helped address destructive behaviors and promote self-esteem. Inspired by her own difficult teen years after losing her dad, Brandee wanted to provide a structured, supportive environment for young adults to learn goal-setting, communication and productive life skills.

"I can't believe how well everything is coming together. And how much work I have to do before the bunkhouses and camp facilities are going to be ready."

"You'll get it all done. You're one of the most driven, organized people I know."

"Thanks for the vote of confidence."

It had taken years of hard work and relentless optimism, but she'd done her dad proud with the success she'd made of Hope Springs Ranch. And now she stood on the threshold of realizing her dream of the camp. Her life was perfect and Brandee couldn't imagine anything better than how she felt at this moment.

Shane strode away from his latest encounter with Brandee feeling like he'd been zapped with a cattle prod. Over the years, he'd engaged in many sizzling exchanges with the spitfire rancher. After each one, he'd conned himself into believing he'd emerged unscathed, while in reality he rarely escaped without several holes poked in his ego.

She was never happy to see him. It didn't seem fair when everything about her brightened his day. Usually he stopped by her ranch and caught her laboring beside her ranch hands, moving cattle, tending to the horses or helping to build the structures for her camp. Clad in worn jeans, faded plaid work shirts and dusty boots, her gray-blue eyes blazing in a face streaked with sweat and dirt, she smelled like horses, hay and hard work. All tomboy. All woman. And he lusted after every lean inch of her.

She, however, was completely immune to him. Given her impenetrable defenses, he should have moved on. There were too many receptive women who appreciated that he was easy and fun, while in Brandee's cool gaze, he glimpsed an ocean of distrust.

But it was the challenge of bringing her around. Of knowing that once he drew her beneath his spell, he would satisfy himself with her complete surrender and emerge triumphant. This didn't mean he was a bad guy. He just wasn't built to be tied down. And from what he'd noticed of Brandee's social life, she wasn't much into long-term relationships, either.

And so he kept going back for more despite knowing each time they tangled she would introduce him to some fresh hell. Today it had been the scent of her perfume. A light floral scent that made him long to gather handfuls of her hair and bury his face in the lustrous gold waves.

"Shane."

His mental meanderings came to a screeching halt. He nodded in acknowledgment toward a trio of women, unsure which one had hailed him. These three were trouble. Cecelia, Simone and Naomi. A blonde, brunette and a redhead. All three women were gorgeous, entitled and dangerous if crossed.

They'd recently been admitted to the Texas Cattleman's Club and were making waves with their demands that the clubhouse needed a feminine face-lift. They wanted to get rid of the old boys' club style and weren't being subtle about manipulating votes in their favor.

Brandee had been one of their most obstinate adversaries, working tirelessly to gather the votes needed to defeat them. She'd infiltrated the ranks of the oldest and most established members in order to preach against every suggestion these three women made. The whole thing was amusing to watch.

Shane responded to Naomi's wave by strolling to their table. "Ladies."

"Join us," Cecelia insisted. She was a striking platinum blonde with an ice queen's sharp eyes. As president of To The Moon, a company specializing in high-end children's furniture, Cecelia was obviously accustomed to being obeyed.

Putting on his best easy grin, Shane shook his head. "Now, you know I'd love nothing more, but I'm sorry to say I'm already running late." He glanced to where his best friend, Gabriel Walsh, sat talking on his cell phone, a half-empty tumbler of scotch on the table before him. "Is there something I can do for you ladies?"

"We noticed you were talking with Brandee Lawless," Simone said, leaning forward in a way that offered a sensational glimpse of her ample cleavage. With lush curves, arresting blue eyes and long black hair, she, too, was a striking blend of beauty and brains. "And we wanted to give you some friendly advice about her."

Had the women picked up on his attraction to Brandee? If so, Shane was losing his touch. He set his hands on the back of the empty fourth chair and leaned in with a conspiratorial wink.

"I'm always happy to listen to advice from beautiful women."

Cecelia nodded as if approving his wisdom. "She's only acting interested in you because she wants you to vote against the clubhouse redesign."

Shane blinked. Brandee was acting interested in him? What had these three women seen that he'd missed?

"Once the vote is done," Simone continued, "she will dismiss you like that." She snapped her fingers and settled her full lips into a determined pout.

"Brandee has been acting as if she's interested in me?" Shane put on a show of surprise and hoped this would entice the women to expound on their theories. "I thought she was just being nice."

The women exchanged glances and silently selected Naomi to speak next. "She's not nice. She's manipulating you. Haven't you noticed the way she flirts with you? She knows how well liked you are and plans to use your popularity to manipulate the vote."

Shane considered this. Was Brandee flirting with him? For a second he let himself bask in the pleasure of that idea. Did she fight the same intoxicating attraction that gripped him every time they met? Then he rejected the notion. No. The way she communicated with him was more like a series of verbal jousts all determined to knock him off his white charger and land him ass-first in the dirt.

"Thank you for the warning, ladies." Unnecessary as it had been. "I'll make sure I keep my wits about me where Brandee is concerned."

"Anytime," Naomi murmured. Her brown eyes, framed by long, lush lashes, had a sharp look of satisfaction.

"We will always have your back," Cecelia added, and glanced at the other two, garnering agreeing head bobs.

"I'll remember that." With a friendly smile and a nod, Shane left the trio and headed to where Gabe waited.

The former Texas Ranger watched him approach, a smirk kicking up one corner of his lips. "What the hell was that about? Were you feeding them canaries?"

"Canaries?" Shane dropped into his seat and gestured to a nearby waiter. He needed a stiff drink after negotiating the gauntlet of strong-willed women.

"That was a trio of very satisfied pussycats."

Shane resisted the urge to rub at the spot between his shoulder blades that burned from several sets of female eyes boring into him. "I gave them what they wanted."

"Don't you always?"

"It's what I do."

Shane flashed a cocky grin, but he didn't feel any satisfaction.

"So what did they want?" Gabe asked.

"To warn me about Brandee Lawless."

Gabe's gaze flickered past Shane. Whatever he saw made his eyes narrow. "Do you need to be warned?"

"Oh hell no." The waiter set a scotch before him and Shane swallowed a healthy dose of the fiery liquid before continuing. "You know how she and I are. If we were kids she'd knock me down and sit on me."

"And you'd let her because then she'd be close enough to tickle."

"Tickle?" Shane stared at his best friend in mock outrage. "Do you not know me at all?"

"We're talking about you and Brandee as little kids. It was the least offensive thing I could think of that you'd do to her."

Shane snorted in amusement. "You could have said *spank*."

Gabe closed his eyes as if in pain. "Can we get back to Cecelia, Simone and Naomi?"

"They're just frustrated that Brandee has sided against them and has more influence at the club than they do. They want to rule the world. Or at least our little corner of it."

On the table, Gabe's phone chimed, signaling a text. "Damn," he murmured after reading the screen.

"Bad news?"

"My uncle's tumor isn't operable."

Several weeks ago Gabe's uncle Dusty had been diagnosed with stage-four brain cancer.

"Aw, Gabe, I'm sorry. That really sucks."

Dale "Dusty" Walsh was a dynamic bear of a man. Like

Gabe he was a few inches over six feet and built to intimidate. Founder of Royal's most private security firm, The Walsh Group, he'd brought Gabe into the fold after he'd left the Texas Rangers.

"Yeah, my dad's pretty shook up. That was him sending the text."

Gabe's close relationship with his father was something Shane had always envied. His dad had died when Shane was in his early twenties, but even before the heart attack took him, there hadn't been much good about their connection.

"Hopefully, the doctors have a good alternative program to get Dusty through this."

"Let's hope."

The two men shifted gears and talked about the progress on Shane's latest project, a luxury resort development in the vein of George Vanderbilt's iconic French Renaissance château in North Carolina, but brimming with cutting-edge technology. As he was expounding on the challenges of introducing the concept of small plates to a state whose motto was "everything's bigger in Texas," a hand settled on Shane's shoulder. The all-too-familiar zap of awareness told him who stood beside him before she spoke.

"Hello, Gabe. How are things at The Walsh Group?"

"Fine." Gabe's hazel eyes took on a devilish gleam as he noticed Shane's gritted teeth. "And how are you doing at Hope Springs?"

"Busy. We've got ninety-two calves on the ground and another hundred and ninety-seven to go before April." Brandee's hand didn't move from Shane's shoulder as she spoke. "Thanks for helping out with the background checks for the latest group of volunteers."

"Anytime."

Shane drank in the soft lilt in Brandee's voice as he

endured the warm press of her hand. He shouldn't be so aware of her, but the rustle of her tulle skirt and the shapely bare legs below the modest hem had his senses all revved up with nowhere to go.

"See you later, boys." Brandee gave Shane's shoulder a little squeeze before letting go.

"Bye, Brandee," Gabe replied, shifting his gaze to Shane as she headed off.

All too aware of Gabe's smirk, Shane summoned his willpower to not turn around and watch her go, but he couldn't resist a quick peek over his shoulder. He immediately wished he'd fought harder. Brandee floated past the tables like a delicate gray cloud. A cloud with badass boots the color of Texas bluebonnets on her feet. He felt the kick to his gut and almost groaned.

"You know she only did that to piss off those three," Gabe said when Shane had turned back around. "They think she's plotting against them, so she added fuel to the fire."

"I know." He couldn't help but admire her clever machinations even though it had come with a hit to his libido. "She's a woman after my own heart."

Gabe laughed. "Good thing you don't have one to give her."

Shane lifted his drink and saluted his friend. "You've got that right."

Two

Afternoon sunlight lanced through the mini blinds covering the broad west-facing window in Brandee's home office, striping the computer keyboard and her fingers as they flew across the keys. She'd been working on the budget for her summer camp, trying to determine where she could siphon off a few extra dollars to buy three more well-trained, kid-friendly horses.

She'd already invested far more in the buildings and infrastructure than she'd initially intended. And because she needed to get the first of three projected bunkhouses built in time for her summer session, she'd been forced to rely on outside labor to get the job done.

Brandee spun her chair and stared out the window that overlooked the large covered patio, with its outdoor kitchen and fieldstone fireplace. She loved spending time outside, even in the winter, and had created a cozy outdoor living room.

Buying this five-thousand-acre parcel outside Royal four years ago had been Brandee's chance to fulfill her father's dream. She hadn't minded having to build a ranch from the ground up after the tornado had nearly wiped her out. In fact, she'd appreciated the clean slate and relished the idea of putting her stamp on the land. She'd set the L-shaped one-story ranch house half a mile off the highway and a quarter mile from the buildings that housed her ranch hands and the outbuildings central to her cow-calving operation.

The original house, built by the previous owner, had been much bigger than this one and poorly designed. Beaux Cook had been a Hollywood actor with grand ideas of becoming a real cowboy. The man had preferred flash over substance, and never bothered to learn anything about the ranching. Within eighteen months, he'd failed so completely as a rancher that Brandee had bought the property for several million less than it was worth.

Brandee was the third owner of the land since it had been lifted from unclaimed status ten years earlier. Emmitt Shaw had been the one who'd secured the parcel adjacent to his ranch by filing a claim and paying the back taxes for the five thousand acres of abandoned land after a trust put into place a century earlier to pay the taxes had run out of money. Health issues had later compelled him to sell off the land to Beaux to pay his medical bills and keep his original ranch running.

However, in the days following the massive storm, while Brandee was preoccupied with her own devastated property, Shane Delgado had taken advantage of the old rancher's bad health and losses from the tornado to gobble up his ranch to develop luxury homes. If she'd known how bad Beaux's situation had become, she would've offered to buy his land for a fair price.

Instead, she was stuck sharing her property line with his housing development. Brandee liked the raw, untamed beauty of the Texas countryside, and resented Delgado's determination to civilize the landscape with his luxury homes and fancy resort development. Her father had been an old-school cowboy, fond of endless vistas of Texas landscape populated by cattle, rabbits, birds and the occasional mountain lion. He wouldn't be a fan of Shane Delgado's vision for his daughter's property.

Her smartphone chimed, indicating she'd received a text message. There was a phone number, but no name. She read the text and her heart received a potent shock.

Hope Springs Ranch rightfully belongs to Shane Delgado. —Maverick

Too outraged to consider the wisdom of engaging with the mysterious sender, she picked up the phone and texted back.

Who is this and what are you talking about?

Her computer immediately pinged, indicating she'd received an email. She clicked to open the message. It was from Maverick.

Give up your Texas Cattleman's Club membership and wire fifty thousand dollars to the account below or I'll be forced to share this proof of ownership with Delgado. You have two weeks to comply.

Ignoring the bank routing information, Brandee double-clicked on the attachment. It was a scan of a faded, handwritten document, a letter dated March 21, 1899, written by someone named Jasper Crowley. He offered a five-thousand-acre parcel as a dowry to the man who married his daughter, Amelia. From the description of the land, it was the five thousand acres Hope Springs Ranch occupied.

Brandee's outrage dissipated, but uneasiness remained.

This had to be a joke. Nothing about the documentation pointed to Shane. She was ready to dismiss the whole thing when the name Maverick tickled her awareness. Where had she heard it mentioned before? Cecelia Morgan had spoken the name before one of the contentious meetings at the TCC clubhouse. Was Cecelia behind this? Given the demands, it made sense.

Brandee had been doing her best to thwart every power play Cecelia, Simone and Naomi had attempted. There was no way she was going to let the terrible trio bully their way into leadership positions with the Texas Cattleman's Club. Was this their way of getting her to shut up?

She responded to the email.

This doesn't prove anything.

This isn't an empty threat, was the immediate response. Shaw didn't search for Crowley's descendants. I did.

That seemed to indicate that Maverick had proof that Crowley and Shane were related. Okay, so maybe she shouldn't ignore this. Brandee set her hands on the edge of the desk and shoved backward, muttering curses. The office wasn't big enough for her to escape the vile words glowing on the screen, so she got up and left the room to clear her head.

How dare they? She stalked down the hall to the living area, taking in the perfection of her home along the way.

Everything she had was tied up in Hope Springs Ranch. If she wasn't legally entitled to the land, she'd be ruined.

Selling the cattle wouldn't provide enough capital for her to start again. And what would become of her camp?

Sweat broke out on Brandee's forehead. Throwing open her front door, she lifted her face to the cool breeze and stepped onto the porch, which ran the full length of her home. Despite the chilly February weather, she settled in a rocker and drew her knees to her chest. Usually contemplating the vista brought her peace. Not today.

What if that document was real and it could be connected to Shane? She dropped her forehead to her knees and groaned. This was a nightmare. Or maybe it was just a cruel trick. The ranch could not belong to Shane Delgado. Whoever Maverick was, and she suspected it was the unholy trio of Cecelia, Simone and Naomi, there was no way this person could be right.

The land had been abandoned. The taxes had ceased being paid. Didn't that mean the acres reverted back to the government? There had to be a process that went into securing unclaimed land. Something that went beyond simply paying the back taxes. Surely Emmitt had followed every rule and procedure. But what if he hadn't? What was she going to do? She couldn't lose Hope Springs Ranch. And especially not to the likes of Shane Delgado.

It took a long time for Brandee's panic to recede. Half-frozen, she retreated inside and began to plan. First on the agenda was to determine if the document was legitimate. Second, she needed to trace Shane back to Jasper Crowley. Third, she needed to do some research on the process for purchasing land that had returned to the government because of unpaid back taxes.

The blackmailer had given her two weeks. It wasn't a lot of time, but she was motivated. And if she proved Shane was the owner of her land? She could comply with Maverick's demands. Fifty thousand wasn't peanuts, but she had way more than that sitting in her contingency fund. She'd pay three times that to keep Shane Delgado from getting his greedy hands on her land.

And if she absolutely had to, she could resign from the Texas Cattleman's Club. She'd earned her membership the same way club members of old had: by making Hope Springs a successful ranch and proving herself a true cattleman. It would eat at her to let Cecelia, Simone and Naomi bully her into giving up the club she deserved to be a part of, but she could yield the high ground if it meant her programs for at-risk teenagers would be able to continue.

Bile rose as she imagined herself facing the trio's triumphant smirks. How many times in school had she stood against the mean girls and kept her pride intact? They'd ridiculed her bohemian style and tormented anyone brave enough to be friends with her. In turn, she'd manipulated their boyfriends into dumping them and exposed their villainous backstabbing to the whole school.

It wasn't something Brandee was proud of, but to be fair, she'd been dealing with some pretty major ugliness at home and hadn't been in the best frame of mind to take the high road.

When it came to taking care of herself, Brandee had learned how to fight dirty from her father's ranch hands. They'd treated her like a little sister and given her tips on how to get the upper hand in any situation. Brandee had found their advice useful after she'd moved in with her mother and had to cope with whatever flavor of the month she'd shacked up with.

Not all her mother's boyfriends had been creeps, but enough of them had turned their greedy gaze Brandee's way to give her a crash course in manipulation as a method of self-preservation.

And now those skills were going to pay off in spades.

Because she intended to do whatever it took to save her ranch, and heaven help anyone who got in her way.

Standing in what would eventually become the grotto at Pure, the spa in his luxury resort project, The Bellamy, Shane was in an unhappy frame of mind. He surveyed the half-finished stacked stone pillars and the coffered ceiling above the narrow hot tub. In several months, Pure would be the most amazing spa Royal had ever seen, offering a modern take on a traditional Roman bath with a series of soothing, luxurious chambers in which guests could relax and revive.

Right now, the place was a disaster.

"I'm offering people the experience of recharging in an expensive, perfectly designed space," Shane reminded his project manager. "What about this particular stone says expensive or perfect?" He held up a sample of the stacked stone. "This is not what I ordered."

"Let me check on it."

"And then there's that." Shane pointed to the coffered ceiling above the hot tub. "That is not the design I approved."

"Let me check on that, as well."

Shane's phone buzzed, reminding him of his next appointment.

"We'll have to pick this up first thing tomorrow." Even though he was reluctant to stop when he had about fifty more details that needed to be discussed, Shane only had fifteen minutes until he was supposed to be at his mother's home for their weekly dinner, and it was a twenty-minute drive to her house.

Shane wound his way through The Bellamy's construction site, seeing something that needed his attention at every turn. He'd teamed with hotelier Deacon Chase to create the architectural masterpiece, and the scope of the project—and the investment—was enormous.

Sitting on fifty-plus acres of lavish gardens, the resort consisted of two hundred and fifty luxury suites, tricked out with cutting-edge technology. The complex also contained fine farm-to-table dining and other amenities. Every single detail had to be perfect.

He texted his mother before he started his truck, letting her know he was going to be delayed, and her snarky response made him smile. Born Elyse Flynn, Shane's mother had left her hometown of Boston at twenty-two with a degree in geoscience, contracted to do a field study of the area near Royal. There, she'd met Shane's father, Landon, and after a whirlwind six-month romance, married him and settled in at Bullseye, the Delgado family ranch.

After Landon died and Shane took over the ranch, Elyse had moved to a home in Pine Valley, the upscale gated community with a clubhouse, pool and eighteen-hole golf course. Although she seemed content in her six-thousand-square-foot house, when Shane began his housing development near Royal, she'd purchased one of the five-acre lots and begun the process of planning her dream home.

Each week when he visited, she had another architectural design for him to look over. In the last year she'd met with no fewer than a dozen designers. Her wish list grew with each new innovation she saw. There were days when Shane wondered if she'd ever settle on a plan. And part of him dreaded that day because he had a feeling she would then become his worst client ever.

When he entered the house, she was standing in the doorway leading to the library, a glass of red wine in her hand.

"There you are at last," she said, waving him over for

a kiss. "Come see how brilliant Thomas is. His latest plan is fantastic."

Thomas Kitt was the architect Elyse was currently leaning toward. She hadn't quite committed to his design, but she'd been speaking of him in glowing terms for the last month.

"He's bumped out the kitchen wall six inches and that gives me the extra room I need so I can go for the thirty-inch built-in wine storage. Now I just need to decide if I want to do the one with the drawers so I can store cheese and other snacks or go with the full storage unit."

She handed Shane the glass of wine she'd readied for him and gestured to the plate of appetizers that sat on samples of granite and quartz piled on the coffee table.

Shane crossed to where she'd pinned the latest drawings to a magnetic whiteboard. "I'd go with the full storage. That'll give you room for an extra sixty bottles."

"You're right." Elyse grinned at her son. "Sounds like a trip to Napa is in my future."

"Why don't you wait until we break ground?" At the rate his mother was changing her mind, he couldn't imagine the project getting started before fall.

"Your father was always the practical one in our family." Elyse's smile faded at the memory of her deceased husband. "But you've really taken over that role. He'd be very proud of you."

Landon Delgado had never been proud of his son.

You've got nothing going for you but a slick tongue and a cocky attitude, his father had always said.

Elyse didn't seem to notice the dip in her son's mood as she continued, "Is it crazy that I like the industrial feel to this unit?" She indicated the brochure on high-end appliances.

Shane appreciated how much fun his mother was having with the project. He wrapped his arm around her and dropped a kiss on her head. "Whatever you decide is going to be a showstopper."

"I hope so. Suzanne has been going on and on about the new house she's building in your development to the point where I want to throw her and that pretentious designer she hired right through a plate-glass window."

Growing up with four older brothers gave Elyse a competitive spirit in constant need of a creative outlet. Her husband hadn't shared her interests. Landon Delgado had liked ranching and believed in hard work over fancy innovation. He'd often spent long hours in the saddle moving cattle or checking fences. His days began before sunup and rarely ended until long after dinner. When he wasn't out and about on the ranch, he could be found in his office tending to the business side.

To Landon's dismay, Shane hadn't inherited his father's love of all things ranching. Maybe that was because as soon as Shane could sit up by himself, his father had put him on a horse, expecting Shane to embrace the ranching life. But he'd come to hate the way his every spare moment was taken up by ranch duties assigned to him by his father.

You aren't going to amount to anything if you can't handle a little hard work.

About the time he'd hit puberty, Shane's behavior around the ranch had bloomed into full-on rebellion, and when Shane turned fifteen, the real battles began. He started hanging out with older friends who had their own cars. Most days he didn't come home right after school and dodged all his chores. His buddies liked to party. He'd been forced to toil alongside his father since he was three years old. Didn't he deserve to have a little fun?

According to his father, the answer was no.

You're wrong if you think that grin of yours is all you need to make it in this world.

"So what have you cooked up for us tonight?" Shane asked as he escorted his mother to the enormous kitchen at the back of the house.

"Apricot-and-Dijon-glazed salmon." Although Elyse employed a full-time housekeeper, she enjoyed spending time whipping up gourmet masterpieces. "I got the recipe from the man who catered Janice Hunt's dinner party. I think I'm going to hire him to cater the Bullseye's centennial party," Elyse continued, arching an eyebrow at her son's blank expression.

Shane's thoughts were so consumed with The Bellamy project these days, he'd forgotten all about the event. "The centennial party. When is that again?"

"March twenty-first. I've arranged a tasting with Vincent on the twenty-fourth of this month so we can decide what we're going to have."

"We?" He barely restrained a groan. "Don't you have one of your friends who could help with this?"

"I do, but this is *your* ranch we're celebrating and *your* legacy."

"Sure. Of course." Shane had no interest in throwing a big party for the ranch, but gave his mother his best smile. "A hundred years is a huge milestone and we will celebrate big."

This seemed to satisfy his mother. Elyse was very social. She loved to plan parties and when Shane was growing up there had often been dinners with friends and barbecues out by the pool. Often Shane had wondered how a vibrant, beautiful urbanite like his mother had found happiness with an overly serious, rough-around-the-edges Texas rancher. But there was no question that in spite of their differences, his parents had adored each other, and the way Landon had doted on his wife was the one area where Shane had seen eye to eye with his father.

At that moment Brandee Lawless popped into his mind. There was a woman he wanted to sweep into his arms and never let go. He imagined sending her hat spinning away and tunneling his fingers through her long golden hair as he pulled her toward him for a hot, sexy kiss.

But he'd noticed her regarding him with the same skepticism he used to glimpse in his father's eyes. She always seemed to be peering beyond his charm and wit to see what he was made of. He'd never been able to fool her with the mask he showed to the world. It was unsettling. When she looked at him, she seemed to expect…more.

Someday people are going to figure out that you're all show and no substance.

So far he'd been lucky and that hadn't happened. But where Brandee was concerned, it sure seemed like his luck was running out.

Three

After snatching too few hours of sleep, Brandee rushed through her morning chores and headed to Royal's history museum. She hadn't taken time for breakfast and now the coffee she'd consumed on the drive into town was eating away at her stomach lining. Bile rose in her throat as she parked in the museum lot and contemplated her upside-down world.

It seemed impossible that her life could implode so easily. That the discovery of a single piece of paper meant she could lose everything. In the wee hours of the morning as she stared at the ceiling, she'd almost convinced herself to pay Maverick the money and resign from the TCC. Saving her ranch was more important than besting the terrible trio. But she'd never been a quitter and backing down when bullied had never been her style. Besides, as authentic as the document had looked, there was no reason to believe it was real or that it was in the museum where anyone could stumble on it.

Thirty minutes later, she sat at a table in the small reference room and had her worst fears realized. Before her, encased in clear plastic, was the document she'd been sent a photo of. She tore her gaze from the damning slip of paper and looked up at the very helpful curator. From Rueben Walker's surprise when she'd been waiting on the doorstep for the museum to open, Brandee gathered he wasn't used to having company first thing in the morning.

"You say this is part of a collection donated to the museum after Jasper Crowley's death?" Brandee wondered what other bombshells were to be found in the archives.

"Yes, Jasper Crowley was one of the founding members of the Texas Cattleman's Club. Unfortunately he didn't live to see the grand opening of the clubhouse in 1910."

"What other sorts of things are in the collection?"

"The usual. His marriage license to Sarah McKellan. The birth certificate for their daughter, Amelia. Sarah's death certificate. She predeceased Jasper by almost thirty years and he never remarried. Let's see, there were bills of sale for various things. Letters between Sarah and her sister, Lucy, who lived in Austin."

Brandee was most interested in Jasper's daughter. The land had been her dowry. Why hadn't she claimed it?

"Is there anything about what happened to Amelia? Did she ever get married?"

Walker regarded Brandee, his rheumy blue eyes going suddenly keen. "I don't recall there being anything about a wedding. You could go through the newspaper archives. With someone of Jasper's importance, his daughter's wedding would have been prominently featured."

Brandee had neither the time nor the patience for a random search through what could potentially be years' worth of newspapers. "I don't suppose you know of anyone who would be interested in helping me with the research? I'd be happy to compensate them."

"I have a part-time assistant that comes in a few times a week. He might be able to assist you as soon as he gets back from helping his sister move to Utah."

"When will that be?"

"Middle of next week, I think."

Unfortunately, Maverick had only given her two weeks to meet the demands, and if the claims were true, she needed to find out as soon as possible. Brandee ground her teeth and weighed her options.

"Are the newspaper archives here?"

The curator shook his head. "They're over at the library on microfiche."

"Thanks for your help." Brandee gave Reuben a quick nod before exiting the building and crossing the street.

The library was a couple blocks down and it didn't make sense for her to move her truck. She neared Royal Diner and her stomach growled, reminding her she hadn't eaten breakfast. As impatient as she was to get to the bottom of Maverick's claim, she would function better without hunger pangs.

Stepping into Royal Diner was like journeying back in time to the 1950s. Booths lined one wall, their red faux leather standing out against the black-and-white-checkerboard tile floor. On the opposite side of the long aisle stretched the counter with seats that matched the booths.

Not unexpectedly, the place was packed. Brandee spotted local rancher and town pariah, Adam Haskell, leaving the counter toward the back and headed that way, intending to grab his seat. As she drew closer, Brandee noticed a faint scent of stale alcohol surrounded Haskell. She offered him the briefest of nods, which he didn't see because his blue bug-eyes dropped to her chest as they passed each other in the narrow space.

Once clear of Haskell, Brandee saw that the spot she'd been aiming for was sandwiched between an unfamiliar fortysomething cowboy and Shane Delgado. Of all the bad luck. Brandee almost turned tail and ran, but knew she'd look silly doing so after coming all this way. Bracing herself, she slid onto the seat.

Shane glanced up from his smartphone and grinned as he spotted her. "Well, hello. Look who showed up to make my morning."

His deep voice made her nerve endings shiver, and when she bumped her shoulder against his while sliding her purse onto the conveniently placed hook beneath the counter, the hairs on her arms stood up. Hating how her body reacted to him, Brandee shot Shane a sharp glance.

"I'm not in the mood to argue with you." She spoke with a little more bluntness than usual and his eyes widened slightly. "Can we just have a casual conversation about the weather or the price of oil?"

"I heard it's going to be in the midfifties all week," he said, with one of his knockout grins that indicated he liked that he got under her skin. "With a thirty percent chance of rain."

"We could use some rain."

Heidi dropped off Shane's breakfast and took Brandee's order of scrambled eggs, country potatoes and bacon. A second later the waitress popped back with a cup of coffee.

"Everything tasting okay?" Heidi asked Shane, her eyes bright and flirty.

"Perfect as always."

"That's what I like to hear."

When she walked off, Brandee commented, "You haven't taken a single bite. How do you know it's perfect?"

"Because I eat breakfast here twice a week and it's always the same great food." Shane slid his fork into his sunny-side up eggs and the bright yellow yolk ran all over the hash on his plate.

Brandee sipped her coffee and shuddered.

"What's the matter?" Shane's even white teeth bit into a piece of toast. He hadn't looked at her, yet he seemed to know she was bothered.

"Nothing." Brandee tried to keep her voice neutral. "Why?"

"You are looking more disgusted with me than usual." His crooked smile made her pulse hiccup.

"It's the eggs. I can't stand them runny like that." The same flaw in human nature that made people gawk at car accidents was drawing Brandee's gaze back to Shane's plate. She shuddered again.

"Really?" He pushed the yolk around as if to torment her with the sight. "But this is the only way to eat them with corn-beef hash."

"Why corn-beef hash and not biscuits and gravy?"

"It's a nod to my Irish roots."

"You're Irish?"

"On my mother's side. She's from Boston."

"Oh." She drew out her reply as understanding dawned.

"Oh, what?"

"I always wondered about your accent."

"You thought about me?" He looked delighted.

Brandee hid her irritation. Give the man any toehold and he would storm her battlements in a single bound.

"I thought about your accent," she corrected him. "It has a trace of East Coast in it."

Shane nodded. "It's my mom's fault. Even after living in Texas for nearly forty years, she still drops her *r*'s most of the time."

"How'd your mom come to live in Texas?"

Even as Brandee asked the question, it occurred to her that this was the most normal conversation she and Shane had ever had. Usually they engaged in some sort of verbal sparring or just outright arguing and rarely traded any useful information.

"She came here after college to study oil reserves and met my dad. They were married within six months and she's been here ever since." Shane used his toast to clean up the last of the egg. "She went back to Boston after my dad died and stayed for almost a year, but found she missed Royal."

"I'm sure it was you that she missed."

Shane nodded. "I am the apple of her eye."

"Of course." Brandee thanked Heidi as the waitress set a plate down on the counter. With the arrival of her breakfast, Brandee had intended to let her side of the conversation lapse, but something prompted her to ask, "She didn't remarry?"

Never in a million years would Brandee admit it, but Shane's story about his mother was interesting. Shane's father had died over a decade earlier, but Elyse Delgado had accompanied her son to several events at the TCC clubhouse since Brandee had bought Hope Springs Ranch. Her contentious relationship with Shane caused Brandee to avoid him in social situations and she'd never actually spoken to his mother except to say hello in passing. Yet, Brandee knew Elyse Delgado by reputation and thought she would've enjoyed getting to know the woman better if not for her son.

"There've been a couple men she's dated, but nothing serious has come out of it. Although she was completely devoted to my father, I think she's enjoyed her independence."

"I get that," Brandee murmured. "I like the freedom to run my ranch the way I want and not having to worry about taking anyone's opinions into account."

"You make it sound as if you never plan to get married." Shane sounded surprised and looked a little dismayed. "That would certainly be a shame."

Brandee's hackles rose. He probably hadn't intended to strike a nerve, but in the male-dominated world of Texas cattle ranching, she'd faced down a lot of chauvinism.

"I don't need a man to help me or complete me."

At her hot tone, Shane threw up his hands. "That's not what I meant."

"No?" She snorted. "Tell me you don't look at me and wonder how I handle Hope Springs Ranch without a man around." She saw confirmation in his body language before he opened his mouth to argue. "Thanks to my dad, I know more about what it takes to run a successful ranch than half the men around here."

"I don't doubt that."

"But you still think I need someone."

"Yes." Shane's lips curved in a sexy grin. "If only to kiss you senseless and take the edge off that temper of yours."

The second Brandee's eyes cooled, Shane knew he should've kept his opinion to himself. They'd been having a perfectly nice conversation and he'd had to go and ruin it. But all her talk of not needing a man around had gotten under his skin. He wasn't sure why.

"I have neither a temper nor an edge." Brandee's conversational tone wasn't fooling Shane. "Ask anyone in town and they'll tell you I'm determined, but polite."

"Except when I'm around."

Her expression relaxed. "You do bring out the worst in me."

And for some reason she brought out the worst in him. "I'd like to change that." But first he had to learn to hold his tongue around her.

"Why?"

"Because you interest me."

"As someone who sees through your glib ways?"

"I'll admit you've presented a challenge." Too many things in his life came easily. He didn't have to exert himself chasing the unachievable. But in Brandee's case, he thought the prize might be worth the extra effort.

"I've begun to wonder if convincing me to sell Hope Springs had become a game to you."

"I can't deny that I'd like your land to expand my development, but that's not the only reason I'm interested in you."

"Is it because I won't sleep with you?"

He pretended to be surprised. "That never even occurred to me. I'm still in the early stages of wooing you."

"Wooing?" Her lips twitched as if she were fighting a smile. "You do have a way with words, Shane Delgado."

"Several times you've accused me of having a silver tongue. I might have a knack for smooth talking, but that doesn't mean I'm insincere."

Brandee pushed her unfinished breakfast away and gave him her full attention. "Let me get this straight. You want us to date?" She laughed before he could answer.

He'd thought about it many times, but never with serious intent. Their chemistry was a little too combustible, more like a flash bang than a slow burn, and he'd reached a point in his life where he liked to take his time with a woman.

"Whoa," he said, combating her skepticism with light-hearted banter. "Let's not get crazy. How about we try a one-week cease-fire and see how things go?"

Her features relaxed into a genuine smile and Shane

realized she was relieved. His ego took a hit. Had she been dismayed that he'd viewed her in a romantic light? Most women would be thrilled. Once again he reminded himself that she was unique and he couldn't approach her the same way he did every other female on the planet.

"Does that mean you're not going to try to buy Hope Springs for a week?" Despite her smile, her eyes were somber as she waited for his answer.

"Sure."

"Let's make it two weeks, then."

To his surprise, she held out her hand like it was some sort of legal agreement. Shane realized that for all their interaction, they'd never actually touched skin to skin. The contact didn't disappoint.

Pleasure zipped up his arm and lanced straight through his chest. If he hadn't been braced against the shock, he might have let slip a grunt of surprise. Her grip was strong. Her slender fingers bit into his hand without much effort on her part. He felt the work-roughened calluses on her palm and the silky-smooth skin on the back of her hand. It was a study in contrasts, like everything else about her.

Desire ignited even as she let go and snatched up her bill. With an agile shift of her slim body, she was sliding into the narrow space between his chair and hers. Her chest brushed his upper arm and he felt the curve of her breasts even through the layers of her sweater and his jacket.

"See you, Delgado."

Before he got his tongue working again, she'd scooped her coat and purse off the back of the chair and was headed for the front cash register. Helpless with fascination, he watched her go, enjoying the unconscious sashay of her firm, round butt encased in worn denim. The woman knew how to make an exit.

"Damn," he murmured, signaling to the waitress that

he wanted his coffee topped off. He had a meeting in half an hour, but needed to calm down before he headed out.

A cup of coffee later, he'd recovered enough to leave. As he looked for his bill, he realized it was missing. He'd distinctly recalled Heidi sliding it onto the counter, but now it was gone. He caught her eye and she came over with the coffeepot.

"More coffee, Shane?"

"No, I've got to get going, but I don't see my bill and wondered if it ended up on the floor over there." He indicated her side of the counter.

"All taken care of."

"I don't understand."

"Brandee got it."

Had that been the reason for her brush by? In the moment, he'd been so preoccupied by her proximity that he hadn't been aware of anything else. And he understood why she'd paid for his meal. She was announcing that she was independent and his equal. It also gave her a one-up on him.

"Thanks, Heidi." In a pointless assertion of his masculinity, he slid a ten-dollar tip under the sugar dispenser before heading out the door.

As he headed to his SUV, he considered his action. Would he have been compelled to leave a large tip if Gabe or Deacon had picked up his tab? Probably not. Obviously it bothered him to have a woman pay for his meal. Or maybe it wasn't just any woman, but a particular woman who slipped beneath his skin at every turn.

Why had he rejected the idea of dating her so fast? In all likelihood they'd drive each other crazy in bed. And when it was over, things between them would be no worse. Seemed he had nothing to lose and a couple months of great sex to gain.

As he headed to The Bellamy site to see how the project was going, Shane pondered how best to approach Brandee. She wasn't the sort to be wowed with the things he normally tried and she'd already declared herself disinterested in romantic entanglements. Or had she?

Shane found himself back at square one, and realized just how difficult the task before him was. Yet he didn't shy from the challenge. In fact, the more he thought about dating Brandee, the more determined he became to convince her to give them a shot.

But how did a man declare his intentions when the woman was skeptical of every overture?

The answer appeared like the sun breaking through the clouds. It involved the project nearest and dearest to her heart: Hope Springs Camp for at-risk and troubled teenagers. He would somehow figure out what she needed most and make sure she got it. By the time he was done, she would be eating out of his hands.

Brandee left the Royal Diner after paying for Shane's breakfast, amusing herself by pondering how much it would annoy him when he found out what she'd done. She nodded a greeting to several people as she headed to the library. Once there, however, all her good humor fled as she focused on finding out whether there was any truth to Maverick's assertion that Shane was a direct descendant of Amelia Crowley.

It took her almost five hours and she came close to giving up three separate times, but at long last she traced his family back to Jasper Crowley. Starting with newspapers from the day Jasper had penned the dowry document, she'd scrolled through a mile of microfiche until she'd found a brief mention of Amelia, stating that she'd run off with a man named Tobias Stone.

Using the Stone family name, Brandee then tracked down a birth certificate for their daughter Beverly. The Stones hadn't settled near Royal but had ended up two counties over. But the state of Texas had a good database of births and deaths, and the town where they'd ended up had all their newspapers' back issues online.

Jumping forward seventeen years, she began reading newspapers again for some notice of Beverly Stone's marriage. She'd been debating giving up on the newspapers and driving to the courthouse when her gaze fell on the marriage announcement. Beverly had married Charles Delgado and after that Brandee's search became a whole lot easier.

At last she was done. Spread across the table, in unforgiving black and white, was the undeniable proof that Shane Delgado was legally entitled to the land where Hope Springs Ranch stood. A lesser woman would have thrown herself a fine pity party. Brandee sat dry-eyed and stared at Shane's birth certificate. It was the last piece of the puzzle.

In a far more solemn mood than when she'd arrived, Brandee exited the library. The setting sun cast a golden glow over the street. Her research had eaten up the entire day, and she felt more exhausted than if she'd rounded up and tagged a hundred cattle all on her own. She needed a hot bath to ease the tension in her shoulders and a large glass of wine to numb her emotions.

But most of all she wanted to stop thinking about Shane Delgado and his claim to her land for a short time. Unfortunately, once she'd settled into her bath, and as the wine started a warm buzz through her veins, that proved impossible. Dwelling on the man while lying naked in a tub full of bubbles was counterproductive. So was mulling over their breakfast conversation at the Royal Diner, but she couldn't seem to shake the look in his eye as he'd talked about kissing her senseless.

She snorted. As if her current problems could be forgotten beneath the man's chiseled lips and strong hands. She closed her eyes and relived the handshake. The contact had left her palm tingling for nearly a minute. As delightful as the sensation had been, what had disturbed her was how much she'd liked touching him. How she wouldn't mind letting her hands wander all over his broad shoulders and tight abs.

With a groan Brandee opened her eyes and shook off her sensual daydreams. Even if Shane wasn't at the center of her biggest nightmare, she couldn't imagine either one of them letting go and connecting in any meaningful way.

But maybe she didn't need meaningful. Maybe what she needed was to get swept up in desire and revel in being female. She'd deny it until she was hoarse, but it might be nice to let someone be in charge for a little while. And if that someone was Shane Delgado? At least she'd be in for an exhilarating ride.

The bathwater had cooled considerably while Brandee's mind had wandered all over Shane's impressive body. She came out of her musings to discover she'd lost an hour and emerged from her soaking tub with pruney fingers and toes.

While she was toweling off, her office phone began to ring. It was unusual to have anyone calling the ranch in the evening, but not unheard-of. After she'd dressed in an eyelet-trimmed camisole and shorts sleepwear set she'd designed, Brandee padded down the hall to her office, curled up in her desk chair and dialed into voice mail.

"I heard you're looking for a couple horses for your summer camp." The voice coming from the phone's speaker belonged to Shane Delgado. "I found one that might work for you. Liam Wade has a champion reining horse that he had to retire from showing because of his bad hocks. He wants the horse to go to a good home and is interested in donating him to your cause."

Brandee had a tight budget to complete all her projects and was doing a pretty good job sticking to it. When she'd first decided to start a camp, she'd done a few mini-events to see how things went. That was how she'd funded the meeting hall where she served meals and held classes during the day and where the kids could socialize in the evenings. Thanks to her successes, she'd forged ahead with her summer-camp idea. But that required building a bunkhouse that could sleep twelve.

With several minor issues leading to overages she'd hadn't planned for, getting a high-quality, well-trained horse for free from Liam Wade would be awesome. She already had three other horses slated for the camp and hoped to have six altogether to start.

Brandee picked up the phone and dialed Shane back. Knees drawn up to her chest, she waited for him to answer and wondered what he'd expect in return for this favor.

After three rings Shane picked up. "I take it you're interested in the horse."

"Very." Her toes curled over the edge of the leather cushion of her desk chair as his deep, rich voice filled her ear. "Thank you for putting this together."

"My pleasure."

"It was really nice of you." Remembering that he had the power to destroy all she'd built didn't stop her from feeling grateful. "I guess I owe you…" She grasped at the least problematic way she could pay him back.

"You don't owe me a thing."

Immediately Brandee went on alert. He hadn't demanded dinner or sexual favors in exchange for his help.

What was this new game he was playing? Her thoughts turned to the blackmailer Maverick. Once again she wondered whether Shane was involved, but quickly rejected the idea. If he had any clue she was squatting on land that belonged to his family, he would be up front about his intentions.

"Well, then," she muttered awkwardly. "Thank you."

"Happy to help."

After hanging up, she spent a good ten minutes staring at the phone. Happy to help? That rang as false as his "you don't owe me a thing." What was he up to? With no answers appearing on the horizon, Brandee returned to her bedroom and settled in to watch some TV, but nothing held her attention.

She headed into the kitchen for a cup of Sleepytime herbal tea, but after consuming it, she was more wide-awake than ever. So she started a load of laundry and killed another hour with some light housekeeping. As the sole occupant of the ranch house, Brandee only had her cook and cleaning woman, May, come in a couple times a week.

Standing in the middle of her living room, Brandee surveyed her home with a sense of near despair and cursed Maverick. If she found out who was behind the blackmail, she'd make sure they paid. In the meantime, she had to decide what to do. She sank down onto her couch and pulled a cotton throw around her shoulders.

Her choice was clear. She had to pay the fifty thousand dollars and resign from the Texas Cattleman's Club. As much as it galled her to give in, she couldn't risk losing her home. She pictured the smug satisfaction on the faces of the terrible trio and ground her teeth together.

And if Maverick wasn't one or all of them?

What if she'd read the situation wrong and someone else was behind the extortion? She had no guarantee that if she met the demands that Maverick wouldn't return to the well over and over. The idea of spending the rest of her life looking over her shoulder or paying one blackmail demand after another appalled Brandee. But what could she do?

Her thoughts turned to Shane once more. What if she could get him to give up his claim to the land? She considered what her father would think of the idea and shied away from the guilt that aroused. Buck Lawless had never cheated or scammed anyone and would be ashamed of his daughter for even considering it.

But then, Buck had never had to endure the sort of environment Brandee had been thrust into after his death. In her mother's house, Brandee had received a quick and unpleasant education in self-preservation. Her father's position as ranch foreman had meant that Brandee could live and work among the ranch hands and never worry that they'd harm her. That hadn't been the case with her mother's various boyfriends.

She wasn't proud that she'd learned how to manipulate others' emotions and desires, but she was happy to have survived that dark time and become the successful rancher her father had always hoped she'd be. As for what she was going to do about Shane? What he didn't know about his claim on Hope Springs Ranch wouldn't hurt him. She just needed to make sure he stayed in the dark until she could figure out a way to keep her land free and clear.

Four

At Bullseye Ranch's main house, Shane sat on the leather sofa in the den, boots propped on the reclaimed wood coffee table, an untouched tumbler of scotch dangling from the fingers of his left hand. Almost twenty-four hours had gone by since Brandee had called to thank him for finding her a horse and he'd been thinking about her almost nonstop. She'd sounded wary on the phone, as if expecting him to demand something in return for his help. It wasn't the response he'd been hoping for, but it was pure Brandee.

What the hell was wrong with the woman that she couldn't accept a kind gesture? Well, to be fair, he hadn't acted with pure altruism. He did want something from her, but it wasn't what she feared. His motive was personal not business. Would she ever believe that?

His doorbell rang. Shane set aside his drink and went to answer the door. He wasn't expecting visitors.

It was Brandee standing on his front porch. The petite blonde was wearing her customary denim and carrying a bottle wrapped in festive tissue. She smiled at his shocked look, obviously pleased to have seized the upper hand for the moment.

"Brought you a little thank-you gift," she explained, extending the bottle. "I know you like scotch and thought you might appreciate this."

"Thanks." He gestured her inside and was more than a little bewildered when she strolled past him.

"Nice place you have here." Brandee shoved her hands into the back pockets of her jeans as she made her way into the middle of the living room.

"I can't take the credit. My mom did all the remodeling and design."

"She should have been an interior designer."

"I've told her that several times." Shane peeled the paper off the bottle and whistled when he saw the label. "This is a great bottle of scotch."

"Glad you like it. I asked the bartender at the TCC clubhouse what he'd recommend and this is what he suggested."

"Great choice." The brand was far more expensive than anything Shane had in his house and he was dying to try it. "Will you join me in a drink?"

"Just a short one. I have to drive home."

Shane crossed to the cabinet where he kept his liquor and barware. He poured shots into two tulip-shaped glasses with short, stout bases and handed her one.

Brandee considered it with interest. "I thought you drank scotch from tumblers."

"Usually, but you brought me a special scotch," he said, lifting his glass to the light and assessing the color. "And it deserves a whiskey glass."

"What should we drink to?" she asked, snagging his gaze with hers.

Mesmerized by the shifting light in her blue-gray eyes, he said the first bit of nonsense that popped into his head. "World peace?"

"To world peace." With a nod she tapped her glass lightly against his.

Before Shane drank, he gave the scotch a good swirl to awaken the flavors. He then lifted the glass to his nose and sniffed. A quality scotch like this was worth taking the time to appreciate. He took a healthy sip and rolled it around his tongue. At last he swallowed it, breathed deeply and waited. At around the six-second mark, the richness of the scotch rose up and blessed him with all its amazing flavors—citrus, pears, apples and plums from the sherry barrels it was aged in, along with an undertone of chocolate and a hint of licorice at the very end.

"Fantastic," he breathed.

Brandee watched him with open curiosity, then held up her glass. "I've never been much of a scotch drinker, but watching you just now makes me think I've been missing out. Teach me to enjoy it."

She couldn't have said anything that pleased him more.

"I'd be happy to. First of all you want to swirl the scotch in the glass and then sniff it. Unlike wine, what you smell is what you'll taste."

She did as he instructed, taking her time about it. "Now what?"

"Now you're going to take a big mouthful." He paused while she did as instructed. "That's it. Get it onto the middle of your tongue. You'll begin to tease out the spice and the richness." He let her experience the scotch for a few more seconds and then said, "Take a big breath, swallow and open your mouth. Now wait for it."

She hadn't blinked, which was good. If she had, it would mean the scotch flavor was too strong. Her expression grew thoughtful and then her eyes flared with understanding.

"I get it. Tangerine and plum."

"The second sip is even better."

Together they took their second taste. The pleasure Shane received was doubled because he was able to share the experience with Brandee. She didn't roll her eyes or make faces like many women of his acquaintance would have. Instead, she let him lead her through an exploration of all the wonderful subtleties of the scotch.

Fifteen minutes later, they had reached a level of connection unprecedented in their prior four years of knowing each other. He was seeing a new side of Brandee. A delightful, sociable side that had him patting himself on the back for putting her in touch with Liam. Convincing her they should give dating a try was going to be way easier than he'd originally thought.

Brandee finished her last sip of scotch and set the glass aside. "I had another reason for dropping by tonight other than to say thank-you."

Shane waited in silence for her to continue, wondering if the other shoe was about to drop.

"I thought about what you said in the diner yesterday." She spoke slowly as if she'd put a lot of thought into what she was saying.

Shane decided to help her along. "About you needing to be kissed senseless?" He grinned when he saw the gap between her eyebrows narrow.

"About us calling a truce for two weeks," she countered, her tone repressive. "I know how you are and I realized that after those two weeks, you'd be back to pestering me to sell the ranch."

Right now, he didn't really give a damn about buying her ranch, but he sensed if he stopped pestering her about it she would forget all about him. "You have a solution for that?"

"I do. I was thinking about a wager."

Now she was speaking his language. "What sort of wager?"

"If I win you agree to give up all current and future attempts to claim Hope Springs Ranch and its land."

"And if I win?"

"I'll sell you my ranch."

A silence settled between them so loud Shane could no longer hear the television in the den. Unless she was convinced she had this wager all sewn up, this was a preposterous offer for her to make. What was she up to?

"Let me get this straight," he began, wanting to make sure he'd heard her clearly. "After years of refusing to sell me your land, you're suddenly ready to put it on the table and risk losing it?" He shook his head. "I don't believe it. You love that ranch too much to part with it so easily."

"First of all, what makes you think you're going to win? You haven't even heard the terms."

He arched one eyebrow. "And the second thing?"

"I said I'd sell the land. I didn't say how much I wanted for it."

He'd known all along that she was clever and relished the challenge of pitting his wits against hers. "Ten million. That's more than fair market value."

Her blue-gray eyes narrowed. She'd never get that much from anyone else and they both knew it.

"Fine. Ten million."

The speed with which she agreed made Shane wonder what he'd gotten himself into. "And the terms of our wager?"

"Simple." A sly smile bloomed. "For two weeks you move in and help me out at the ranch. Between calving time and the construction project going on at my camp, I'm stretched thin."

Shane almost laughed in relief. This was not at all what he'd thought she'd propose. Did she think he'd shy away from a couple weeks of manual labor? Granted, he rarely came home with dirt beneath his fingernails, but that didn't mean he was lazy or incompetent. He knew which end of the hammer to use.

"You need someone who knows his way around a power tool." He shot her a lecherous grin. "I'm your man."

"And I need you to help with the minicamp I have going next weekend."

Now he grasped her logic. She intended to appeal to his altruistic side. She probably figured if he got a close look at her troubled-teen program that he would give up trying to buy the land. This was a bet she was going to lose. He didn't give a damn about a camp for a bunch of screwed-up kids who probably didn't need anything more than parents who knew how to set boundaries.

"That's it?" He was missing something, but he wasn't sure what. "I move in and help you out?" Living with Brandee was like a dream come true. He could survive a few backbreaking days of hard work if it meant plenty of time to convince her they could be good together for a while.

"I can see where your mind has gone and yes…" She paused for effect. "You'll have ample opportunity to convince me to sleep with you."

A shock as potent as if he'd grabbed a live wire with both hands blasted through him. His nerve endings tingled in the aftermath. He struggled to keep his breathing even as he considered the enormity of what she'd just offered.

"You call that a wager?" He had no idea where he found the strength to joke. "I call it shooting ducks in a barrel."

"Don't you mean fish?" Her dry smile warned him winning wasn't going to be easy. "Getting me to sleep with you isn't the wager. You were right when you said I was lacking male companionship."

Well, smack my ass and call me a newborn. The phrase, often repeated by Shane's grandma Bee, popped into his head unbidden. He coughed to clear his throat.

"I said you needed to be kissed senseless."

She rolled her eyes at him. "Yes. Yes. It's been a while since I dated anyone. And I'll admit the thought of you and I has crossed my mind once or twice."

"Damn, woman. You sure do know how to stroke a man's ego."

"Oh please," she said. "You love playing games. I thought this would appeal to everything you stand for."

"And what is that exactly?"

"You get me to say I love you and I sell you the ranch for ten million."

He hadn't prepared himself properly for the devastation of that other shoe. It was a doozy. "And what needs to happen for you to win?"

"Simple." Her smile was pure evil. "I get you to say 'I love you' to me."

Brandee stood on her front porch, heart beating double-time, and watched Shane pull a duffel out of his SUV. In his other hand he held a laptop case. It was late afternoon the day after Brandee had pitched her ridiculous wager to Shane and he was moving in.

This was without a doubt the stupidest idea she'd ever had. Paying Maverick the blackmail money and quitting the TCC was looking better and better. But how would she explain her abrupt change of heart to Shane? No doubt he would consider her backpedaling proof that she was afraid of losing her heart to him.

At least she didn't have to worry about that happening. There was only room in her life for her ranch and her camp. Maybe in a couple years when things settled down she could start socializing. She'd discovered that as soon as she'd started thinking about seducing Shane, a floodgate to something uncomfortably close to loneliness had opened wide.

"Hey, roomie," he called, taking her porch steps in one easy bound.

Involuntarily she stepped back as he came within a foot of her. His wolfish grin was an acknowledgment of her flinch.

"Welcome to Hope Springs Ranch."

"Glad to be here."

"Let me show you to your room. Dinner's at seven. Breakfast is at six. I don't know what you're used to, but we get up early around here."

"Early to bed. Early to rise. I can get on board with the first part. The second may take some getting used to."

Brandee let out a quiet sigh. Shane's not-so-subtle sexual innuendo was going to get old really fast. It might be worth sleeping with him right away to get that to stop.

"I'm sure you'll manage." She led the way into the ranch house and played tour guide. "Kitchen. Dining room. Living room."

"Nice." Shane took his time gazing around the uncluttered open-plan space.

"Your room is this way." She led him into a hallway and indicated a door on the left. "Guest bedrooms one and two share that bathroom. I put you in the guest suite. It has its own bathroom and opens to the patio."

Shane entered the room she indicated and set his duffel on the king-size bed. "Nice."

The suite was decorated in the same neutral tones found

throughout the rest of the house. It was smaller than her master bedroom, but she'd lavished the same high-end materials on it.

"You'll be comfortable, then?" She imagined his master suite at Bullseye was pretty spectacular given what she'd seen of his living room.

"Very comfortable." He circled the bed and stared out the French doors. "So where do you sleep?"

He asked the question with no particular inflection, but her body reacted as if he'd swept her into his arms. She shoved her hands into her back pockets to conceal their trembling and put on her game face. She'd get nowhere with him if he noticed how easily he could provoke her.

"I'll show you."

Cringing at the thought of inviting him into her personal space, Brandee nevertheless led the way back down the hall and past the kitchen. When she'd worked with the architect, she insisted the master suite be isolated from the guest rooms. Passing her home office, Brandee gestured at it as she went by and then strode into her private sanctuary. It wasn't until Shane stood in the middle of her space, keen eyes taking in every detail, that she realized the magnitude of her mistake.

It wasn't that giving him a glimpse of her bedroom might clue him in to what made her tick. Or even that she'd imagined him making love to her here. It was far worse than that. She discovered that she liked having him in her space. She wanted to urge him into one of the chairs that faced her cozy fireplace and stretch out in its twin with her bare feet on his lap, letting him massage the aches from her soles with his strong fingers.

"Nice."

Apparently this was his go-to word for all things re-

lated to decorating. She chuckled, amusement helping to
ease her anxiety.

Shane shot her a questioning look. "Did I miss something?"

"You must drive your mother crazy."

"How so?"

"She loves to decorate. I imagine she's asked your opinion a time or two. Tonight, your reaction to every room
we've been in has been—" she summoned up her best
Shane imitation "—nice." Her laughter swelled. "I'm imagining you doing that to your mother. It's funny."

"Obviously." He stared at her as if he didn't recognize
her. But after a moment, his lips relaxed into a smile. "I'll
make an effort to be more specific from now on."

"I'm sure your mother will appreciate that."

Deciding they'd spent more than enough time in her
bedroom, Brandee headed toward the door. As she passed
Shane, he surprised her by catching her arm and using her
momentum to swing her up against his body.

"Hey!" she protested even as her traitorous spine softened beneath his palm and her hips relaxed into his.

"Hey, what?" He lowered his lips to her temple and
murmured, "I've been waiting too many years to kiss you.
Don't you think it's time you put me out of my misery?"

She should've expected he'd make his move as soon as
possible, and should've been prepared to deflect his attempt to seduce her. Instead, here she was, up on her toes,
flattening her breasts against the hard planes of his chest
and aching for that kiss he so obviously intended to take.

"I'm going to need a couple glasses of wine to get me
in the mood," she told him, stroking her fingers over his
beefy shoulders and into the soft brown waves that spilled
over his collar.

"You don't need wine. You have me." His fingers

skimmed the sensitive line where her back met her butt, sending lightning skittering along her nerve endings.

She trembled with the effort of keeping still. Seizing her lower lip between her teeth, she contained a groan, but the urge to rub herself all over him was gaining momentum. She needed to decide the smart move here, but couldn't think straight.

Summoning all her willpower, she set her hands on his chest and pushed herself away. "It's not going to happen, Delgado."

Shane raked both hands through his hair, but his grin was unabashed and cocky. "Tonight or ever?"

"Tonight." Lying to him served no purpose.

Given the seesaw of antagonism and attraction, she couldn't imagine them lasting two weeks without tearing each other's clothes off, but she refused to tumble into bed with him right off the bat.

"Fair enough."

Brandee led the way back into the main part of the house and toward the kitchen. When she'd made this wager, she hadn't thought through what sharing her home with Shane would entail. She hadn't lived with anyone since she'd run away from her mother's house twelve years earlier. Realizing she would have to interact with him in such close quarters threw her confidence a curve ball.

"I'm going to open a bottle of wine. Do you want to join me or can I get you something else?" She opened the refrigerator. "I have beer. Or there's whiskey."

"I'll have wine. It wasn't an I-could-use-a-beer sort of day."

Brandee popped the cork on her favorite Shiraz and poured out two glasses. "What sort of day is that?"

"One where I spend it in the saddle or out surveying the pastures." His usually expressive features lost all emotion.

And then he gave her a meaningless smile. "You know, ranch work."

"You don't sound as if you're all that keen on ranching."

Because he seemed so much more focused on his real-estate developments, she'd never considered him to be much of a rancher. He gave every appearance of avoiding hard work, so she assumed that he was lazy or entitled.

"Some aspects of it are more interesting than others."

With an hour and a half to kill before dinner, she decided to build a fire in the big stone fireplace out on her covered patio. The cooler weather gave her a great excuse to bundle up and enjoy the outdoor space. She carried the bottle of wine and her glass through the French doors off the dining room.

The days were getting longer, so she didn't have to turn on the overhead lights to find the lighter. The logs were already stacked and waiting for the touch of flame. In a short time a yellow glow spilled over the hearth and illuminated the seating area.

Choosing a seat opposite Shane, Brandee tucked her feet beneath her and sipped her wine. "You do mostly backgrounding at Bullseye, right?"

Backgrounding was the growing of heifers and steers from weanlings to a size where they could enter feedlots for finishing. With nearly fourteen thousand acres, Shane had the space to graze cattle and the skills to buy and sell at the opportune times. He had a far more flexible cattle business than Brandee's, which involved keeping a permanent stock of cows to produce calves that she later sold either to someone like Shane or to other ranches as breeding stock.

"I like the flexibility that approach offers me."

"I can see that."

She'd suffered massive losses after the tornado swept through her property and demolished her operations. She hadn't lost much of her herd, but the damage to her infra-structure had set her way back. And loss of time as she rebuilt wasn't the sort of thing covered by insurance.

Shane continued, "I don't want to give everything to the ranch like my father did and end up in an early grave." Once again, Shane's easy charm vanished beneath a stony expression. But in the instant before that happened, some-thing like resentment sparked in his eyes.

This glimpse behind Shane's mask gave Brandee a flash of insight. For the first time she realized there might be more to the arrogant Shane Delgado than he wanted the world to see. And that intrigued her more than she wanted it to.

She couldn't actually fall for Shane. Her ranch was at stake. But what if he fell in love with her? Until that sec-ond, Brandee hadn't actually considered the consequences if she won this desperate wager. And then she shook her head. The thought of Shane falling for her in two weeks was crazy and irrational. But wasn't that the way love made a person feel?

Brandee shook her head. She wasn't in danger of losing her heart to Shane Delgado, only her ranch.

Five

Tossing and turning, his thoughts filled with a woman, wasn't Shane's style, but taking Brandee in his arms for the first time had electrified him. After a nearly sleepless night, he rolled out of bed at five o'clock, heeding her warning that breakfast was at six. The smell of coffee and bacon drew him from the guest suite after a quick shower.

He'd dressed in worn jeans, a long-sleeved shirt and his favorite boots. He intended to show Brandee that while he preferred to run his ranch from his office, he was perfectly capable of putting in a hard day's work.

Shane emerged from the hallway and into the living room. Brandee was working in the kitchen, her blond hair haloed by overhead recessed lighting. With a spatula in one hand and a cup of coffee in the other, she danced and sang to the country song playing softly from her smartphone.

If seeing Brandee relaxed and having fun while she flipped pancakes wasn't enough to short-circuit his equilibrium, the fact that she was wearing a revealing white cotton nightgown beneath a short royal blue silk kimono hit him like a two-by-four to the gut.

Since she hadn't yet noticed him, he had plenty of freedom to gawk at her. Either she'd forgotten he was staying in her guest room or she'd assumed he wasn't going to get up in time for breakfast. Because there was no way she'd let loose like this if she thought he'd catch her.

The soft sway of her breasts beneath the thin cotton mesmerized him, as did the realization that she was a lot more fun than he gave her credit for being. Man, he was in big trouble. If this was a true glimpse of what she could be like off-hours, there was a damn good chance that he'd do exactly what he swore he wouldn't and fall hard. He had to reclaim the upper hand. But at the moment he had no idea how to go about doing that.

"You're into Florida Georgia Line," he said as he approached the large kitchen island and slid onto a barstool. "I would've pegged you as a Faith Hill or Miranda Lambert fan."

"Why, because I'm blond or because I'm a woman?"

He had no good answer. "I guess."

She cocked her head and regarded him with a pitying expression. "The way you think, I'm not surprised you have trouble keeping a woman."

He shrugged. "You got any coffee?"

"Sure." She reached into her cupboard and fetched a mug.

The action caused her nightgown to ride up. Presented with another three inches of smooth skin covering muscular thigh, Shane was having trouble keeping track of the conversation.

"What makes you think I want to keep a woman?"

"Don't you get tired of playing the field?"

"The right woman hasn't come along to make me want to stop."

Brandee bent forward and slid his mug across the concrete counter toward him, offering a scenic view of the sweet curves of her cleavage. In his day he'd seen bigger and better. So why was he dry-mouthed and tongue-tied watching Brandee fixing breakfast?

"What's your definition of the right woman?" She slid the plate of pancakes into the oven to keep them warm.

"She can cook." He really didn't care if she did or not; he just wanted to see Brandee's eyes flash with temper.

She fetched a carton of eggs out of the fridge and held them out to him. "I don't know how to make those disgusting things you eat. So either you eat your eggs scrambled or you make them yourself."

This felt like a challenge. His housekeeper didn't work seven days a week and he knew how to fix eggs. "And she's gotta be great in bed."

"Naturally."

He came around the island as she settled another pan on her six-burner stove and got a flame started under it.

"So as long as she satisfies what lies below your belt, you're happy?" She cracked two eggs into a bowl and beat them with a whisk.

"Pretty much." Too late Shane remembered that their wager involved her falling in love with him. "And she needs to have a big heart, want kids. She'll be beautiful in a wholesome way, passionate about what she does and, of course, she's gotta be a spitfire."

"That's a big list."

"I guess." And it described Brandee to a tee, except for the part about the kids. He had no idea whether or not she wanted to have children.

"You want kids?"

"Sure." He'd never really thought much about it. "I was an only child. It would've been nice to have a bunch of brothers to get into trouble with."

Her silk kimono dipped off her shoulder as she worked, baring her delicate skin. With her dressed like this and her fine, gold hair tucked behind her ears to reveal tiny silver earrings shaped like flowers, he was having a hard time keeping his mind on the eggs he was supposed to be cracking. His lips would fit perfectly into the hollow of her collarbone. Would she quiver as she'd done the evening before?

Silence reigned in the kitchen until Shane broke it.

"Do you do this every day?" He dropped a bit of butter into his skillet.

"I do this most mornings. Breakfast is the most important meal of the day and trust me, you'll burn this off way before lunch."

Based on the mischief glinting in her eyes, Shane didn't doubt that. What sort of plan had she devised to torment him today? It was probably a morning spent in the saddle cutting out heavies, the cows closest to their due date, and bringing them into the pasture closest to the calving building.

It turned out he was right. Brandee put him up on a stocky buckskin with lightning reflexes. He hadn't cut cows in years and worried that he wouldn't be up to the task, but old skills came back to him readily and he found himself grinning as he worked each calf-heavy cow toward the opening into the next pasture.

"You're not too bad," Brandee said, closing the gate behind the pregnant cow he'd just corralled.

She sat her lean chestnut as if she'd been born in the saddle. Her straw cowboy hat had seen better days. So had her brown chaps and boots. The day had warmed from the lower forties to the midsixties and Brandee had peeled off a flannel-lined denim jacket to reveal a pale blue button-down shirt.

"Thanks." He pulled off his hat and wiped sweat from his brow. "I forgot how much fun that can be."

"A good horse makes all the difference," she said. "Buzz there has been working cows for three years. He likes it. Not all the ones we start take to cutting as well as he has."

Shane patted the buckskin's neck and resettled his hat. "How many more do you have for today?" They'd worked their way through the herd of fifty cows and moved ten of them closer to the calving building.

"I think that's going to be it for now." Brandee guided her horse alongside Shane's.

"How many more are set to go soon?"

"About thirty head in the next week to ten days, I think. Probably another fifteen that are two weeks out."

"And it's not yet peak birthing season. What kind of numbers are you looking at in March?"

With her nearly five thousand acres, Shane guessed she was running around seven hundred cows. That translated to seven hundred births a year. A lot could go wrong.

"It's not as bad as it seems. We split the herd into spring and fall calving. So we're only dropping three to four hundred calves at any one time. This cuts down on the number of short-term ranch hands I need to hire during calving and keeps me from losing a year if a breeding doesn't take."

"It's still a lot of work."

Brandee shrugged. "We do like to keep a pretty close eye on them because if anything can go wrong, chances are it will."

"What are your survival rates?"

"Maybe a little better than average. In the last three years I've only lost four percent of our calves." She looked pretty pleased by that number. "And last fall we only had two that were born dead and only one lost through complications." Her eyes blazed with triumph.

"I imagine it can be hard to lose even one."

"We spend so much time taking care of them every day between feeding, doctoring and pulling calves. It breaks my heart every time something goes wrong. Especially when it's because we didn't get to a cow in time. Or if it's a heifer who doesn't realize she's given birth and doesn't clean up the calf or, worse, wanders off while her wet baby goes hypothermic."

Over the years he'd become so acclimated to Brandee's coolness that he barely recognized the vibrant, intense woman beside him. He was sucker punched by her emotional attachment to the hundreds of babies that got born on her ranch every year.

This really was her passion. And every time he approached her about selling, he'd threatened not just her livelihood but her joy.

"My dad used to go ballistic if that happened," she continued. "I pitied the hand that nodded off during watch and let something go wrong."

"Where's your dad now?"

Her hat dipped, hiding her expression. "He died when I was twelve."

Finding that they had this in common was a surprise. "We both lost our dads too early." Although Shane suspected from Brandee's somber tone that her loss was far keener than his had been. "So, your dad was a rancher, too?"

She shook her head. "A foreman at the Lazy J. But it was his dream to own his own ranch." Her gaze fixed on the horizon. "And for us to run it together."

Shane heard the conviction in her voice and wondered

if he should just give up and concede the wager right now. She wasn't going to sell her ranch to him or anyone else. Then he remembered that even if he was faced with a fight he could never win, there was still a good chance she'd sleep with him before the two weeks were up. And wasn't that why he'd accepted the wager in the first place?

At around two o'clock in the afternoon, Brandee knocked off work so she could grab a nap. It made the long hours to come a little easier if she wasn't dead tired before she got on the horse. Normally during the ninety-day calving season Brandee took one overnight watch per week. She saw no reason to change this routine with Shane staying at her house.

Brandee let herself in the back door and kicked off her boots in the mudroom. Barefoot, she headed into the kitchen for a cheese stick and an apple. Munching contentedly, she savored the house's tranquillity. Sharing her space with Shane was less troublesome than she'd expected, but she'd lived alone a long time and relished the quiet. Shane had a knack for making the air around him crackle with energy.

It didn't help that he smelled like sin and had an adorable yawn, something she'd seen a great deal of him doing these last three days because she'd worked him so hard. In the evenings he had a hard time focusing on his laptop as he answered emails and followed up with issues on The Bellamy job site.

Today, she'd given him the day off to head to the construction site so he could handle whatever problems required him to be there in person. She didn't expect him back until after dinner and decided to indulge in a hot bath before hitting her mattress for a couple hours of shuteye. It always felt decadent to nap in the afternoon, but she functioned better when rested and reminded herself that she'd hired experienced hands so she didn't have to do everything herself.

Since receiving Maverick's blackmail notice, she hadn't slept well, and though her body was tired, her mind buzzed with frenetic energy. Disrupting her routine further was the amount of time she was spending with Shane. Despite questioning the wisdom of their wager, she realized that having him in her house was a nice change.

Four hours later, Brandee was fixing a quiet dinner for herself of baked chicken and Caesar salad. Shane had a late business meeting and was planning on having dinner in town. He'd only been helping her for three days, but already she could see the impact he was having on her building project at the camp.

He'd gone down to the site and assessed the situation. Last night he'd studied her plans and budget, promising to get her back on track. As much as she hated to admit it, it was good to have someone to partner with. Even if that someone was Shane Delgado and he was only doing it to make her fall in love with him.

There'd been no repeat of him making a play for her despite the way she fixed breakfast every morning in her nightgown. Standing beside him in the kitchen and suffering the bite of sexual attraction, she'd expected something to happen. When nothing had, she'd felt wrung out and cranky. Not that she let him see that. It wouldn't do to let him know that she'd crossed the bridge from it's never going to happen to if it didn't happen soon she'd go mad.

Shane returned to the ranch house as Brandee was getting ready to leave. Her shift wouldn't begin for an hour, but she wanted to get a report on what had happened during the afternoon. As he came in the back door and met up with her in the mudroom, he looked surprised to see her dressed in her work clothes and a warm jacket.

His movements lacked their usual energy as he set his briefcase on the bench. "Are you just getting in?"

"Nope, heading out." She snagged her hat from one of the hooks and set it on her head. "It's my night to watch the cows that are close to calving."

"You're going out by yourself?"

She started to bristle at his question, then decided he wasn't being patronizing, just voicing concern. "I've been doing it for three years by myself. I'll be fine."

"Give me a second to change and I'll come with you."

His offer stunned her. "You must be exhausted." The words slipped out before she considered them.

He turned in the doorway that led to the kitchen and glared at her. "So?"

"I just mean it's a long shift. I spend between four to six hours in the saddle depending on how things go."

"You don't think I'm capable of doing that?"

"I didn't say that." Dealing with his ego was like getting into a ring with a peevish bull. "But you have worked all day and I didn't figure you'd be up for pulling an all-nighter."

"You think I'm soft."

"Not at all." She knew he could handle the work, but was a little surprised he wanted to.

"Then what is it?"

"I just reasoned that you don't…that maybe you aren't as used to the actual work that goes into ranching."

"That's the same thing."

Brandee regretted stirring the pot. She should have just invited him along and laughed when he fell off his horse at 2:00 a.m. because he couldn't keep his eyes open any longer.

"I don't want to make a big deal about this," she said. "I just thought you might want to get a good night's sleep and start fresh in the morning."

"While you spend the night checking on your herd."

"I took a three-hour nap." His outrage was starting to amuse her. "Okay. You can come with me. I won't say another word."

He growled at her in frustration before striding off. Brandee grabbed a second thermos from her cabinet. Coffee would help keep them warm and awake. To her surprise, Brandee caught herself smiling at the thought of Shane's company tonight. Working together had proven more enjoyable than she'd imagined. She didn't have to keep things professional with Shane the way she did when working with her ranch hands. She'd enjoyed talking strategy and ranch economics with him.

As if he feared she'd head out without him, Shane returned in record time. She handed him a scarf and watched in silence as he stepped into his work boots.

"Ready?" she prompted as he stood.

"Yes."

"Do you want to take separate vehicles? That way if you get…" She trailed off as his scowl returned. "Fine."

Irritation radiated from him the whole drive down to the ranch buildings. In the barn, she chatted with her foreman, Jimmy, to see how the afternoon had gone. H545 had dropped her calf without any problems.

"A steer," he said, sipping at the coffee Brandee had just made.

"That makes it fifty-five steers and fifty-two heifers." While the ratio of boys to girls was usually fifty-fifty, it was always nice when more steers were born because they grew faster and weighed more than the girls. "Anyone we need to keep an eye on tonight?"

"H729 was moving around like her labor was starting. She's a week late and if you remember she had some problems last year, so you might want to make sure things are going smoothly with her."

"Will do. Thanks, Jimmy."

The moon was up, casting silvery light across the grass when Shane and Brandee rode into the pasture. The pregnant cows stood or lay in clusters. A couple moved about in a lazy manner. H729 was easy to spot. She was huge and had isolated herself. Brandee pointed her out.

"She's doing some tail wringing, which means she's feeling contractions. I don't think she'll go tonight, but you can never tell."

"How often do they surprise you?"

"More often than I'd like to admit. And that drives me crazy because there's nothing wrong with nearly eighty percent of the calves we lose at birth. Most of the time they suffocate because they're breeched or because it's a first-calf heifer and she gets too tired to finish pushing out the calf."

"How often do you have to assist?"

"On nights like this it's pretty rare." The temperature was hovering in the low forties; compared to a couple weeks earlier, it almost felt balmy. "It's when we get storms and freezing rain that we have our hands full with the newborns."

Shane yawned and rubbed his eyes. Brandee glanced his way to assess his fatigue and lingered to admire his great bone structure and sexy mouth. It was an interesting face, one she never grew tired of staring at. Not a perfect face—she wasn't into that, too boring—but one with character.

"What?" he snapped, never taking his focus off the cows. Despite the shadow cast by the brim of his hat, Brandee could see that Shane's jaw was set.

"I was just thinking it was nice to have your company tonight."

For the briefest of moments his lips relaxed. "I'm glad to be here."

She knew that showing she felt sorry for him would only heighten his annoyance. Big strong men like Shane did not admit to weakness of any kind. And she rather liked him the better for gritting his teeth and sticking with it.

"That being said, you can take my truck and head back if you want. I don't think much of anything is going to happen tonight."

"I don't like the idea of you being alone out here."

"I've been doing this since I was ten years old."

"Not alone."

"No. With my dad. On the weekends, he used to let me ride the late-night watch with him."

"What did your mom say about that?"

"Nothing. She didn't live with us."

Shane took a second to digest that. "They divorced?"

"Never married."

"How come you lived with your dad and not your mom?"

Insulated by her father's unconditional love, Brandee had never noticed her mother's absence. "She didn't want me."

It wasn't a plea for sympathy, but a statement of fact. Most people would have said her mother was a bad parent or uttered some banality about how they were sure that wasn't true.

Shane shrugged. "You are kind of a pain."

He would never know how much she appreciated this tactic. Shane might come off as a glib charmer, but the way he watched her now showed he had a keen instinct for people.

"Yes," Brandee drawled. "She mentioned that often after my dad died and I had to go live with her."

Judging from his narrowed eyes, he wasn't buying her casual posture and nonchalant manner. "Obviously she wasn't interested in being a parent," he said.

Brandee loosed a huge sigh and an even bigger confession. "I was the biggest mistake she ever made."

Six

Shane's exhaustion dwindled as Brandee spoke of her mother. Although he'd grown up with both parents, his father's endless disappointment made Shane sympathetic of Brandee for the resentment her mother had displayed.

"Why do you say that?"

"She gave birth to me and handed me over to my dad, then walked out of the hospital and never looked back. After my dad died and the social worker contacted my mom, I was really surprised when she took me in. I think she wanted to get her hands on the money that my dad left me. He'd saved about fifty thousand toward the down payment on his own ranch. She went through it in six months."

"And you got nothing?"

"Not a penny."

"So your father died when you were twelve and your mother spent your inheritance."

"That about sums it up." Brandee spoke matter-of-factly,

but Shane couldn't imagine her taking it all in stride. No child grew up thinking it was okay when a parent abandoned them. This must have been what led to Brandee erecting her impenetrable walls. And now Shane was faced with an impossible task. The terms of her wager made much more sense. There was no way he was going to get her to fall for him.

After a slow circle of the pasture, Brandee declared it was quiet enough that they could return to the barn. Leaving the horses saddled and tied up, they grabbed some coffee and settled in the ranch office. While Brandee looked over her herd data, updated her birth statistics and considered her spring-breeding program, Shane used the time to research her.

"You started a fashion line?" He turned his phone so the screen faced her.

She regarded the image of herself modeling a crocheted halter, lace-edged scarf and headband. "A girl's got to pay the bills."

"When you were eighteen?"

"Actually, I was seventeen. I fudged my age. You have to be eighteen to open a business account at the bank and sell online."

"From these news articles, it looks like you did extremely well."

"Who knew there was such a huge hole in the market for bohemian-style fashion and accessories." Her wry smile hid a wealth of pride in her accomplishment.

"You built up the business and sold it for a huge profit."

"So that I could buy Hope Springs Ranch."

He regarded her with interest. "Obviously the fashion line was a moneymaker. Why not do both?"

"Because my dream was this ranch. And the company was more than a full-time job. I couldn't possibly keep up with both." She picked up her hat and stood. "We should do another sweep."

Back in the saddle, facing an icy wind blowing across the flat pasture, Shane considered the woman riding beside him. The photos of her modeling her clothing line had shown someone much more carefree and happy than she'd ever appeared to him. Why, if there'd been such good money to be made running a fashion company, had she chosen the backbreaking work of running a ranch?

Was it because she'd been trying to continue her father's legacy, molded by him to wake up early, put in a long day and take satisfaction in each calf that survived? From the way she talked about her dad, Shane bet there'd been laughter at the end of each day and a love as wide as the Texas sky.

He envied her.

"Is that the cow you were watching earlier?" He pointed out an animal in the distance that had just lain down.

"Maybe. Let's double-check."

When they arrived, they left their horses and approached the cow on foot. Judging from the way her sides were straining, she was deep in labor.

It struck Shane that despite spending his entire life on a ranch, he'd only witnessed a few births, and those had been horses not cows. He took his cue from Brandee. She stood with her weight evenly placed, her gloved hands bracketing her hips. Although her eyes were intent, her manner displayed no concern.

"Look," she said as they circled around to the cow's rear end. "You can see the water sack."

Sure enough, with the moon high in the sky there was enough light for Shane to pick out the opaque sack that contained the calf. He hadn't come out tonight expecting excitement of this sort.

"What did you expect?" It was as if she'd read his mind.

"Frankly I was thinking we'd be riding around out here while you kept me at arm's length with tales of your brokenhearted ex-lovers."

With her arms crossed over her chest, she pivoted around to face him, laboring cow forgotten.

"My brokenhearted what?"

"I don't know," he replied somewhat shortly. "I'm tired and just saying whatever pops into my mind."

"Why would you be thinking about my brokenhearted ex-lovers?"

"Are you sure she's doing okay?" He indicated the straining cow, hoping to distract Brandee with something important.

Unfortunately it seemed as if both females were happy letting nature take its course. Brandee continued to regard him like a detective interviewing a prime suspect she knew was lying.

"What makes you think that any of my lovers are brokenhearted?"

"I don't. Not really." In truth he hadn't given much thought to her dating anyone.

Well, that wasn't exactly true. To the best of his knowledge she hadn't dated anyone since moving to Royal. And despite the womanly curves that filled out her snug denim, she always struck him as a tomboy. Somehow he'd gotten it into his head that he was the only one who might've been attracted to her.

"So which is it?"

"Is that a hoof?"

His attempt to distract her lasted as long as it took for her to glance over at the cow and notice that a pair of hooves had emerged.

"Yes." And just like that she was back staring at him

again. "Do I strike you as the sort of woman who uses men and casts them aside?"

"No."

"So why would you think I would end my relationships in such a way that I would hurt someone?"

Shane recognized that he'd tapped into something complicated with his offhand remark and sought to defuse her irritation with a charming smile. "You should be flattered that I thought you would be so desirable that no one would ever want to break up with you."

"So you think I'm susceptible to flattery?"

He was in so deep he would need a hundred feet of rope to climb out of the hole he'd dug. What had happened to the silver-tongued glibness she liked to accuse him of having?

"Is she supposed to stand up like that?"

"Sometimes they need to walk around a bit." This time Brandee didn't spare the cow even a fraction of her attention. "She may be up and down several times."

"I think our arguing is upsetting her," he said, hoping concern for the cow would convince Brandee to give up the conversation.

"We're not arguing," she corrected him, her voice light and unconcerned. "We're discussing your opinion of me. And you're explaining why you assume I'd be the one to end a relationship. Instead of the other way around."

At first he grappled with why he'd said what he had. But beneath her steady gaze, he found his answer. "I think you have a hard time finding anyone who can match up to your father."

She obviously hadn't expected him to deliver such a blunt, to-the-point answer. Her eyes fell away and she stared at the ground. In the silence that followed, Shane worried that he'd struck too close to home.

Brandee turned so she was once again facing the cow.

The brim of her hat cast a shadow over her features, making her expression unreadable. Despite her silence, Shane didn't sense she was angry. Her mood was more contemplative than irritated.

"I never set out to hurt anyone," she said, her voice so soft he almost missed the words. "I'm just not good girlfriend material."

Was that her way of warning him off? If so, she'd have to work a lot harder. "That's something else we have in common. I've been told I'm not good boyfriend material, either."

Now both of them were staring at the cow. She took several steps before coming to a halt as another spasm swept over her. It seemed as if this would expel the calf, but no more of the baby appeared.

"Is this normal?" Shane asked. "It seems like she can't get it out."

"We should see good progress in the next thirty minutes or so. If we don't see the nose and face by then, there might be something wrong."

Shane was surprised at the way his stomach knotted with anxiety. Only by glancing at Brandee's calm posture did he keep from voicing his concern again.

"How do you do this?"

"I have around seven hundred cows being bred over two seasons. While I never take anything for granted, watching that many births gives you a pretty good feel for how things are going."

"Your business is a lot more complicated than mine." And offered a lot more potential for heartbreak.

He certainly wasn't standing in his field at three o'clock in the morning waiting for new calves to be brought into the world. He bought eight-month-old, newly weaned steers and heifers and sent them out into his pastures to grow up. Unless he was judging the market for the best time to sell, he rarely thought about his livestock.

"Not necessarily more complicated," Brandee said. "You have to consider the market when you buy and sell and the best way to manage your pastures to optimize grazing. There are so many variables that depend on how much rain we get and the price of feed if the pastures aren't flourishing."

"But you have all that to worry about and you have to manage when you're breeding and optimize your crosses to get the strongest calves possible. And then there's the problem of losing livestock to accidents and predators."

While he'd been speaking, the cow had once again lain down. The calf's nose appeared, followed by a face. Shane stared as she began to push in earnest.

"She's really straining," he said. "This is all still normal?"

"She needs to push out the shoulders and this is really hard. But she's doing fine."

Shane had the urge to lean his body into Brandee's and absorb some of her tranquillity. Something about the quiet night and the miracle playing out before them made him want to connect with her. But he kept his distance, not wanting to disturb the fragile camaraderie between them.

Just when Shane thought the whole thing was over, the cow got to her feet again and he groaned. Brandee shot him an amused grin.

"It's okay. Sometimes they like finishing the birthing process standing up."

He watched as the cow got to her feet, her baby dangling halfway out of her. This time Shane didn't resist the urge for contact. He reached out and grabbed Brandee's hand. He'd left his gloves behind on this second sweep and wished Brandee had done the same. But despite the worn leather barrier between them, he reveled in the way her fingers curved against his.

After a few deep, fortifying breaths, the cow gave one last mighty push and the calf fell to the grass with a thud. Shane winced and Brandee laughed.

"See, I told you it was going to be okay," Brandee said as the cow turned around and began nudging the calf while making soft, encouraging grunts.

A moment later she swept her long tongue over her sodden baby, clearing fluid from the calf's coat. The calf began to breathe and the cow kept up her zealous cleaning. Brandee leaned a little of her weight against Shane's arm.

That was when Shane realized they were still holding hands. "Damn," he muttered, unsure which had a bigger impact, the calf being born or the simple pleasure of Brandee's hand in his.

He hadn't answered the question before she lifted up on tiptoes and kissed him.

Being bathed in moonlight and surrounded by the sleepy cows seemed like an ideal moment to surrender to the emotions running deep and untamed through Brandee's body. At first Shane's lips were stiff with surprise and Brandee cursed. What had she been thinking? There was no romance to be found in a cold, windswept pasture. But as she began her retreat, Shane threw an arm around her waist and yanked her hard against his body. His lips softened and coaxed a sigh of relief from her lungs.

She wrapped her arms around his neck and let him sweep her into a rushing stream of longing. The mouth that devoured her with such abandon lacked the persuasive touch she'd expected a charmer like Shane to wield. It almost seemed as if he was as surprised as she.

Of course, there was no way that could be the case.

His reasons for being at her ranch were as self-serving as hers had been for inviting him. Each of them wanted to win their wager. She'd intended to do whatever it took to get Shane to fall in love with her. Her dire situation made that a necessity. But he'd been pestering her for years to sell and she was sure he'd pull out every weapon in his arsenal to get her to fall for him.

This last thought dumped cold water on her libido. She broke off the kiss and through the blood roaring in her ears heard the measured impact of approaching hooves all around them. It wasn't unusual for the most dominant cows in the herd to visit the newborn. Half a dozen cows had approached.

"He's looking around," she said, indicating the new calf. "Soon he'll be trying to get up."

Usually a calf was on its feet and nursing within the first hour of being born. Brandee would have to make sure her ranch hands kept an eye on him for the next twelve hours to make sure he got a good suckle. And they would need to get him ear-tagged and weighed first thing. The calves were docile and trusting the first day. After that they grew much more difficult to catch.

Brandee stepped away from Shane and immediately missed their combined body heat. "I think it's okay to head back."

"I'm glad I came out tonight," Shane said as they rode back toward the horse barn. A quick sweep of the pasture had shown nothing else of interest.

"You're welcome to participate in night duty anytime."

"How often do you pull a shift?"

"Once a week."

"You don't have to."

"No." But how did she explain that sitting on a horse in the middle of the night, surrounded by her pregnant cows, she felt as if everything was perfect in her world? "But when I'm out here I think about my dad smiling down and I know he'd be happy with me."

She didn't talk about her dad all that much to anyone. But because of Shane's awestruck reaction to tonight's calving, she was feeling sentimental.

"Happy because you're doing what he wanted?"

"Yes."

"How about what you want?"

"It's the same thing." Brandee's buoyant mood suddenly drooped like a thirsty flower. "Being a rancher is all I ever wanted to do."

"And yet you started a fashion business instead of coming back to find work as a ranch hand. You couldn't know that what you were doing with your clothing line would make you rich."

"No." She'd never really thought about why she'd chosen waitressing and creating clothing and accessories after running away from her mother's house over getting work on a ranch. "I guess I wasn't sure anyone would take me serious as a ranch hand." And it was a job dominated by men.

"You might be right."

When they arrived at the barn, this time Brandee insisted Shane take her truck back to the ranch house. She wasn't going to finish up work until much later. He seemed reluctant, but in the end he agreed.

The instant the truck's taillights disappeared down the driveway, Brandee was struck by a ridiculous feeling of loneliness. She turned on the computer and recorded the ranch's newest addition. Then, hiding a yawn behind her hand, she made her way to the barn where they housed cows and calves that needed more attention.

Cayenne was a week old. A couple days ago a ranch hand had noticed her hanging out on her own by the hay, abandoned by her mother. At this age it didn't take long for a calf to slide downhill, so it paid to be vigilant. Jimmy had brought her in and the guys had tended to a cut on her hind left hoof.

They'd given her a bottle with some electrolytes and a painkiller and the calf had turned around in two days. She was a feisty thing and it made Brandee glad to see the way she charged toward the half wall as if she intended to smash through it. At the very last second she wheeled away, bucking and kicking her way around the edge of the enclosure.

Brandee leaned her arms on the wood and spent a few minutes watching the calf, wondering if the mother would take back her daughter when they were reunited. Sometimes a cow just wasn't much of a mother and when that happened they'd load her up and take her to the sales barn. No reason to feed an unproductive cow.

Talking about being abandoned by her own mother wasn't something Brandee normally did, but it had proven easy to tell Shane. So easy that she'd also divulged the theft of her inheritance, something she'd only ever told to one other person, her best friend, Chelsea.

In the aftermath of the conversation, she'd felt exposed and edgy. It was partially why she'd picked a fight with him about his "brokenhearted ex-lovers" comment. She'd wanted to bring antagonism back into their interaction. Fighting with him put her back on solid ground, kept her from worrying that he'd see her as weak and her past hurts as exploitable.

At the same time his offhand comment had unknowingly touched a nerve. She'd asked if he saw her as the sort of woman who'd use a man and cast him aside. Yet she'd done it before and had barely hesitated before deciding to do so with Shane. She was going to make him fall for her and trick him into giving up his legal claim to Hope Springs Ranch. What sort of a terrible person did that make her?

Reminding herself that he intended to take the ranch didn't make her feel better about what she was doing. He had no clue about the enormity of their wager. Keeping him in the dark wasn't fair or right. Yet, if he discovered the truth, she stood to lose everything.

As during her teen years living with her mother, she was in pure survival mode. It was the only thing that kept her conscience from hamstringing her. She didn't enjoy what she was doing. It was necessary to protect what belonged to her and keep herself safe. Like a cat cornered by a big dog, she would play as dirty as it took to win free and clear.

Several hours later, after one final sweep of the pasture, she turned the watch over to her ranch hands and had one of them drop her off at home. She probably could've walked the quarter-mile-long driveway to her house, but the emotional night had taken a toll on her body as well as her spirit.

The smell of bacon hit her as she entered the back door and her stomach groaned in delight. With loud country music spilling from the recessed speakers above her kitchen and living room, she was able to drop her boots in the mudroom and hang up her coat and hat, then sneak through the doorway to catch a glimpse of Shane without him being aware.

Her heart did a strange sort of hiccup in her chest at the sight of him clad in baggy pajama bottoms, a pale blue T-shirt riding his chest and abs like a second skin. She gulped at the thought of running her hands beneath the cotton and finding the silky, warm texture beneath. While the man might be a piece of work, his body was a work of art.

"Hey." She spoke the word softly, but he heard.

His gaze shifted toward her and the slow smile that curved his lips gave her nerve endings a delicious jolt. She had to hold on to the door frame while her knees returned to a solid state capable of supporting her. He was definitely working the sexy-roommate angle for all it was worth. She'd better up her game.

"I'm making breakfast just the way you like it." He held up the skillet and showed her the eggs he'd scrambled. "And there's French toast, bacon and coffee."

Damn. And he could cook, too. Conscious of her disheveled hair and the distinctive fragrance of horse and barn that clung to her clothes, Brandee debated slinking off to grab a quick shower or just owning these badges of hard work.

"It all sounds great." Her stomach growled loudly enough to be heard and Shane's eyebrows went up.

"Let me make you a plate," he said, laughter dancing at the edges of his voice. "Here's a cup of coffee. Go sit down before you fall over."

That he'd misinterpreted why she was leaning against the doorway was just fine with Brandee. She accepted the coffee and made her way toward the bar stools that lined her kitchen island. Unconcerned about whether the caffeine zap would keep her awake, she gladly sipped the dark, rich brew.

"It's decaf," he remarked, sliding a plate toward her and then turning back to the stove to fill one for himself. "I figured you'd grab a couple hours before heading out again."

"Thanks," she mumbled around a mouthful of French toast. "And thanks for breakfast. You didn't have to."

His broad shoulders lifted in a lazy shrug. "I slept a few hours and thought you'd be hungry. How's the new calf?"

"On my last circuit he was enjoying his first meal."

"Great to hear." Shane slid into the seat beside her and

set his plate down. His bare feet found the rungs of her
chair, casually invading her space. "Thanks for letting
me tag along last night." He peered at her for a long moment before picking up his fork and turning his attention
to breakfast.

"Sure."

As they ate in companionable silence, Brandee found
her concern growing by the minute. The night's shared experience and his thoughtfulness in having breakfast ready
for her were causing a shift in her impression of him. For
years she'd thought of Shane as an egomaniac focused
solely on making money. Tonight she'd seen his softer
side, and the hint of vulnerability made him attractive to
her in a different way.

A more dangerous way.

She had to stay focused on her objective and not give
in to the emotions tugging at her. Letting him capture her
heart was a mistake. One that meant she would lose everything. Her home. Her livelihood. And worst of all, her
self-respect. Because falling for a man who wouldn't return her love was really stupid and she'd been many things,
but never that.

Seven

It was almost six o'clock in the evening when Shane returned from checking on the building site at Brandee's teen camp. As he entered the house through the back door, the most delicious scents stopped him dead in his tracks. He breathed in the rich scent of beef and red wine as he stripped off his coat and muddy boots. In stockinged feet, he entered the kitchen, where Brandee's housekeeper stood at the stove, stirring something in a saucepan.

"What smells so amazing?"

"Dinner," May responded with a cheeky grin and a twinkle in her bright blue eyes.

The fiftysomething woman had rosy cheeks even when she wasn't standing over the stove. She fussed over Brandee like a fond aunt rather than a housekeeper and treated Shane as if he was the best thing that had ever happened to her employer.

"What are we having?"

"Beef Wellington with red potatoes and asparagus."

Shane's mouth began to water. "What's the occasion?"

"Valentine's Day." May pointed toward the dining table, where china and silverware had been laid. There were white tapers in crystal holders and faceted goblets awaiting wine. "You forgot?"

Eyeing the romantic scene, Shane's heart thumped erratically. What special hell was he in for tonight?

"I've been a little preoccupied," he muttered.

Between helping out at Hope Springs, keeping an eye on the construction at The Bellamy and popping in at Bullseye to make sure all was running smoothly, he hadn't had five minutes to spare. Now he was kicking himself for missing this opportunity to capitalize on the most romantic day of the year to sweep Brandee off her feet.

Obviously she hadn't made the same mistake.

May shook her head as if Shane had just proven what was wrong with the entire male sex. "Well, it's too late to do anything about it now. Dinner's in half an hour." She arched her eyebrows at his mud-splattered jeans.

Catching her meaning, Shane headed for his shower. Fifteen minutes later, he'd washed off the day's exertions and dressed in clean clothes. He emerged from his bedroom, tugging up the sleeves of his gray sweater. Black jeans and a pair of flip-flops completed his casual look.

Brandee was peering into her wine fridge as he approached. She turned at his greeting and smiled in genuine pleasure. "How was your day?"

"Good. Productive." It was a casual exchange, lacking the push and pull of sexual attraction that typified their usual interaction. Time to step up his game. "Did May head home?"

"Yes. She and Tim were going out for a romantic dinner."

"Because it's Valentine's Day. I forgot all about it."

"So did I." Brandee selected a bottle and set it on the counter. With her long golden hair cascading over the shoulders of her filmy top, she looked like a cross between a sexy angel and the girl next door. White cotton shorts edged in peekaboo lace rode low on her hips and bared her sensational, well-toned thighs. "Can you open this while I fetch the glasses? The corkscrew is in the drawer to your right."

"I guess neither one of us buys into all the romantic mumbo jumbo," he muttered.

He should've been relieved that the fancy dinner and beautifully set dining table hadn't been Brandee's idea. It meant that she hadn't set out to prey on his libido. But that didn't mean the danger had passed.

"Or we're just cynical about love." She gazed at him from beneath her long eyelashes.

Shane finished opening the bottle and set it aside to breathe. He worked the cork off the corkscrew, letting the task absorb his full attention. "Do you ever wonder if you're built for a long-term relationship?" He recognized it was a strange question to ask a woman, but he suspected Brandee wouldn't be insulted.

"All the time." She moved past him as the timer on the stove sounded. Apparently this was her signal to remove the beef Wellington from the oven. "I don't make my personal life a priority. Chelsea's on me all the time about it."

"My mom gives me the same sort of lectures. I think she wants grandchildren." And he was getting to an age where he needed to decide kids or no kids. At thirty-five he wasn't over the hill by any means, but he didn't want to be in his forties and starting a family.

"I imagine she's feeling pretty hopeless about the possibility."

"Because I haven't met anyone that makes me want to settle down?"

Brandee shook her head. "I can't imagine any woman being more important to you than your freedom."

And she was right. His bachelor status suited him. Having fun. Keeping things casual. Bolting at the first sign of commitment. He liked keeping his options open. And what was wrong with that?

"And what about you, Miss Independent? Are you trying to tell me you're any more eager to share your life with someone? You use your commitment to this ranch and your teen camp to keep everyone at bay. What are you afraid of?"

"Who says I'm afraid?"

Bold words, but he'd seen the shadows that lingered in her eyes when she talked about her mother's abandonment. She might deny it, but there was no question in Shane's mind that Brandee's psyche had taken a hit.

"It's none of my business. Forget I said anything." Shane sensed that if he pursued the issue he would only end up annoying her and that was not how he wanted the evening to go.

"Why don't you pour the wine while I get food on the plates." From her tone, she was obviously content to drop the topic.

Ten minutes later they sat down to the meal May had prepared. Shane kept the conversation fixed on the progress she was making at her teen camp. It was a subject near and dear to her heart, and helping her with the project was sure to endear him to her. Was it manipulative? Sure. But he wanted to buy her property. That's why he'd accepted the bet and moved in.

Shane ignored a tug at his conscience and reminded himself that Brandee was working just as hard as he was to make him fall for her. He grinned. She just didn't realize that she'd lost before she even started.

"This weekend I'm hosting a teen experience with some of the high school kids," Brandee said. "Megan Maguire from Royal Safe Haven is bringing several of her rescue dogs to the ranch for the teens to work with. Chelsea is coming to help out. I could use a couple more adult volunteers." She regarded him pointedly.

The last thing he wanted to do was spend a day chaperoning a bunch of hormonally charged kids, but he had a wager to win and since he'd dropped the ball for Valentine's Day, he could probably pick up some bonus points by helping her out with this.

"Sure, why not." It wasn't the most enthusiastic response, but he hoped she'd be pleased he'd agreed so readily.

"And maybe you could see if Gabe is interested, as well?"

If it made Brandee go all lovey-dovey for him, Shane would do as much arm-twisting as it took to get his best friend on board. "I'll check with him. I'm sure it won't be a problem."

After putting away the leftovers and settling the dirty dishes in the dishwasher, Brandee suggested they move out to the patio to enjoy an after-dinner scotch. This time, instead of taking the sofa opposite him, she settled onto the cushion right beside him and tucked her feet beneath her.

While the fire crackled and flickered, Shane sipped his drink and, warmed by alcohol, flame and desire, listened while Brandee told him about the struggling calf they'd saved and reunited with her mother today. He told himself that when Brandee leaned into him as she shared her tale she was only acting. Still, it was all Shane could do to keep from pulling her onto his lap and stealing a kiss or two.

"You know, it is Valentine's Day," she murmured, tilting her head to an adorable angle and regarding him from beneath her long lashes.

With her gaze fixed on his lips, Shane quelled the impulses turning his insides into raw need. She was playing him. He knew it and she knew he knew it. For the moment he was willing to concede she had the upper hand. What man presented with an enticing package of sweet and spicy femininity would be capable of resisting?

"Yes, it is," he replied, not daring to sip from the tumbler of scotch lest she see the slight tremble in his hand.

"A day devoted to lovers."

Shane decided to follow her lead and see where it took him. "And romance."

"I think both of us know what's inevitable."

"That you and I get together?" To his credit he didn't sound as hopeful as he felt.

"Exactly." She leaned forward to kiss him. Her lips, whether by design or intent, grazed his cheek instead. Her breath smelled of chocolate and scotch, sending blood scorching through his veins. "I've been thinking about you a lot."

Her husky murmur made his nerve endings shiver. He gripped the glass tumbler hard enough to shatter it. "Me, too. I lay in bed at night and imagine you're with me. Your long hair splayed on my pillow." Thighs parted in welcome. Skin flushed with desire. "You're smiling up at me. Excited by all the incredible things I'm doing to you."

From deep in her throat came a sexy hum. "Funny." Her fingertips traced circles on the back of his neck before soothing their way into his hair. "I always picture myself on top. Your hands on my breasts as I ride you."

Shane winced as his erection suddenly pressed hard against his zipper. "You drive me crazy," he murmured. "You know that, right?"

He set down his drink with a deliberate movement before cupping her head. She didn't resist as he pulled her close enough to kiss. Her lashes fluttered downward, lips arching into a dreamy smile.

Their breath mingled. Shane drew out the moment. Her soft breasts settled against his chest and he half closed his eyes to better savor the sensation. This wouldn't be their first kiss, but that didn't make it any less momentous. Tonight they weren't in the middle of a pasture surrounded by cows. This time, the only thing standing in the way of seeing this kiss through to the end was if she actually felt something for him.

Was that what made him hesitate? Worry over her emotional state? Or was he more concerned about his own?

"Let's go inside," she suggested, shifting her legs off the couch and taking his hand. Her expression was unreadable as she got to her feet and tugged at him. "I have a wonderful idea about how we can spend the rest of the evening."

The instant they stepped away from the raging fire, Brandee shivered as the cool February air struck her bare skin. She'd dressed to show off a ridiculous amount of flesh in an effort to throw Shane off his game. Naturally her ploy had worked, but as they crossed the brick patio, she wished she hadn't left the throw behind. Despite how readily Shane had taken her up on her offer, she was feeling incredibly uncertain and exposed.

In slow stages during their romantic dinner, her plan to methodically seduce him had gone awry. She blamed it on the man's irresistible charm and the way he'd listened to her talk about the calf and her camp. He hadn't waited in polite silence for her to conclude her explanation about the program she and Megan Maguire had devised to teach the teenagers about patience and responsibility. No, he'd asked great questions and seemed genuinely impressed by the scope of her project.

But the pivotal moment had come when she saw a flash of sympathy in his eyes. She'd been talking about one particular boy whose dad had bullied him into joining the football team when all the kid wanted to do was play guitar and write music. Something about the story had struck home with Shane and for several seconds he'd withdrawn like a hermit crab confronted by something unpleasant. She realized they were alike in so many ways, each burying past hurts beneath a veneer of confidence, keeping the world at bay to keep their sadness hidden.

As they neared the house, a brief skirmish ensued. Shane seemed to expect that Brandee would want their first encounter to be in her bedroom. That was not going to happen. She'd invited him into the space once and it had been a huge mistake. Her bedroom was her sanctuary, the place she could be herself and drop her guard. She didn't want to be vulnerable in front of Shane. Seeing her true self would give him an edge that she couldn't afford.

"Let's try out the shower in your suite," she suggested, taking his hand in both of hers and drawing him toward the sliding glass door that led to his bedroom. "I had such fun designing the space and haven't ever tried it out."

"The rain shower system is pretty fantastic."

The four recessed showerheads in the ceiling and integrated chromotherapy with mood-enhancing colored lighting sequences were ridiculous indulgences, but Brandee had thought her grandmother would get a kick out of it and had been right.

Shane guided her through the bedroom. His hand on the

small of her back was hot through the semisheer material of her blouse and Brandee burned. How was it possible that the man who stood poised to take everything from her could be the one who whipped her passions into such a frenzy? They hadn't even kissed and her loins ached for his possession. She shuddered at the image of what was to come, a little frightened by how badly she wanted it.

While Shane used the keypad to start the shower, Brandee gulped in a huge breath and fought panic. How was she supposed to pretend like this was just a simple sexual encounter when each heartbeat made her chest hurt? Every inch of her body hummed with longing. She was so wound up that she was ready to go off the instant he put his hands on her.

Shane picked that second to turn around. Whatever he saw in her expression caused his nostrils to flare and his eyes to narrow. Her nerve collapsed. Brandee backed up a step, moving fully clothed into the shower spray. She blinked in surprise as the warm water raced down her face. Shane didn't hesitate before joining her.

As he circled her waist, drawing her against his hard planes, Brandee slammed the door on her emotions and surrendered to the pleasure of Shane's touch. She quested her fingers beneath his sweater, stripping the sodden cotton over his head. The skin she revealed stretched over taut muscle and sculpted bone, making her groan in appreciation.

Almost tentatively she reached out to run her palm across one broad shoulder. His biceps flexed as he slid his hands over her rib cage, thumbs whisking along the outer curves of her breasts. She shuddered at the glancing contact and trembled as he licked water from her throat. Hunger built inside her while her breath came in ragged pants.

The water rendered her clothes nearly transparent, but

Shane's gaze remained locked on her face. He appeared more interested in discovering her by touch. His fingertips skimmed her arms, shoulders and back with tantalizing curiosity. If she could catch her breath, she might have protested that she needed his hands on her bare skin. An insistent pressure bloomed between her thighs. She felt Shane's own arousal pressing hard against her belly. Why was he making her wait?

In the end she took matters into her own hands and stripped off her blouse. It clung to her skin, resisting all effort to bare herself to his touch. Above the sound of the rain shower, she heard a seam give, but she didn't care. She flung the garment aside. It landed in the corner with a plop. At last she stood before him, clad only in her white lace shorts and bra. And waited.

Shane's breath was as unsteady as hers as he slipped his fingers beneath her narrow bra straps and eased them off her shoulders. Holding her gaze with his, he trailed the tips of his fingers along the lace edge where it met her skin. Brandee's trembling grew worse. She reached behind her and unfastened the hooks. The bra slid to the floor and she seized Shane's hands, moving his palms over her breasts.

Together they shifted until Brandee felt smooth tile against her back. Trapped between the wall and Shane's strong body, hunger exploded in her loins. She wrapped one leg around Shane's hip and draped her arms over his shoulders. At long last he took the kiss she so desperately wanted to give and his tongue plunged into her mouth in feverish demand.

Brandee thrilled to his passion and gave back in equal measures. The kiss seemed to go on forever while water poured over his shoulders and ran between their bodies. Shane's hands were everywhere, cupping her breasts, roaming over her butt, slipping over her abdomen to the waistband of her shorts.

Unlike his jeans with their button and zipper, her lacy cotton shorts were held in place by a satin ribbon. He had the bow loosened and the material riding down her legs in seconds. A murmur of pleasure slipped from his lips when he discovered her satin thong, but it was soon following her shorts to the shower floor.

Naked before him, Brandee quaked. In the early years of her fashion line, she'd modeled all the clothes up for sale at her online store, even the lingerie. She'd lost all modesty about her body. Or so she'd thought.

Shane stepped back and took his time staring at her. She pressed her palms against the tile wall to keep from covering herself, but it wasn't her lack of clothing that left her feeling exposed. Rather, it was the need for him to find her desirable.

"You are so damned beautiful," he said, sweeping water from his face and hair. His lips moved into a predatory smile. "And all mine."

She hadn't expected such a provocative claim and hid her delight behind flirtation. Setting her hands on her hips, she shot him a saucy grin. "Why don't you slip out of those wet jeans and come get me?"

Without releasing her from the grip of his intense gaze, he popped the button on his jeans and unzipped the zipper. He peeled off black denim and underwear. Brandee's breath lodged in her throat at what was revealed.

The man was more gorgeous than she'd imagined. Broad shoulders tapered into washboard abs. His thighs were corded with muscle. The jut of his erection made her glad she still had the wall at her back because her muscles weakened at the sight of so much raw masculinity.

"Come here." She had no idea how her voice could

sound so sexy and calm when her entire being was crazy out of control.

He returned to her without hesitation and captured both her hands, pinning them against the wall on either side of her head. His erection pressing against her belly, he lowered his head and kissed her, deep and demanding. Brandee yielded her mouth and surrendered all control.

This was what she needed. A chance to let go and trust. He was in charge, and in this moment, she was okay with that.

When he freed her hands, she put her arms around his neck, needing the support as he stepped between her feet, widening her stance. His teeth grazed her throat while his hand slid between their bodies and found her more than ready for his possession.

She moaned feverishly as he slid a finger inside her, the heel of his palm grazing the over-stimulated knot of nerves. Gasping, she writhed against his hand while hunger built. She needed him inside her, pumping hard, driving her relentlessly into a massive orgasm.

It was hard to concentrate as he masterfully drove her forward into her climax, but Brandee retained enough of her faculties to offer him a small taste of the torment he was inflicting upon her. She cupped her palm over the head of his erection and felt him shudder.

"Jeez" was all he could manage between clenched teeth.

"We need a condom." She rode his length up and down with her hand, learning the texture and shape of him. "Now."

"Yes."

"Where?"

"Jeans."

"You're prepared." A bubble of amusement gave her enough breathing room to stave off the encroaching orgasm.

"Since I arrived."

She bit her lip as his hand fell away from her body, but kept the dissatisfied groan from escaping while he took a few seconds to reach into his jeans pocket and pull out a foil-wrapped pack.

"Let me." She plucked it from his fingers and deftly ripped it open.

He winced as she rolled the condom down his length. Another time, she might have made more of a production of it to torment him, but her body needed to join with his, so she skipped the foreplay.

Almost as soon as she was done, he was lifting her off the floor and settling her back against the wall once more. Brandee stared out the shower door at the mirror that hung over the double vanity. She could just make out the back of Shane's head and her fingers laced in his hair. Every muscle in her body was tensed. Waiting.

"Look at me."

She resisted his demand. She needed him inside her, but she couldn't let him see what it would do to her. This wasn't just sex. Something was happening to her. In the same way she'd liked having him in her bedroom and found comfort riding beside him out in the pasture, she craved intimacy that went beyond the merely physical.

"Look at me." His rough voice shredded her willpower. "You're going to watch what you do to me."

That did it. She could no longer resist him. Her eyes locked with his. A second later he began to slide inside her, and Brandee began to shatter.

Eight

Shane wasn't sure what he'd said to make Brandee meet his gaze, but from the way her big blue-gray eyes locked on him, he was certain he'd regret it later. The ache she'd aroused needed release, but he took his time sliding into Brandee this first time. He wanted to remember every second, memorize every ragged inhalation of her breath and quiver of her body.

The first flutters of her internal muscles began before he'd settled his hips fully against hers. Her eyes widened to a nearly impossible size and she clutched his shoulders, her fingernails biting into him. As the first shudder wracked her, it was all he could do to keep from driving into her hard and fast and taking his own pleasure. Instead, he withdrew smoothly and pressed forward again. He watched in utter fascination as a massive orgasm swept over her, nearly taking him with it.

"Damn, woman." He thought he'd known lust and desire before, but something about what had just happened with Brandee told him he was diving straight off a cliff with nothing at the bottom to keep him from crashing and burning. "That was fast."

She gave him a dreamy smile as her head dropped back against the wall. Her lashes appeared too heavy to lift. "It's been a while," she said weakly. At long last her gaze found his and a mischievous glint lurked in the depths of her eyes. "And you're pretty good at this."

"You haven't seen anything."

She slid her fingers up his shoulders and into his hair, pressing the back of his head to urge his mouth toward hers. "Then let's get this party started."

"I thought we already had."

Before she could come up with another sassy retort, he claimed her mouth. Apparently the orgasm hadn't dampened her fire because Brandee kissed him back with ardent intensity.

Shane began to move inside her once more, determined to take his time and make her climax again. Had he ever been with a woman as wildly sensitive and willing to give herself wholeheartedly to pleasure as Brandee? Her whispered words of encouragement accompanied his every thrust and drove his willpower beyond its limits. But he held on until he felt the tension build in her body again. At last he let himself go in a rush of pleasure as her body bucked and she began to climax again. Sparks exploded behind Shane's eyes as they went over together.

In the aftermath, there was only the hiss of water pouring from the showerheads and ragged gasps as they strained to recover. But these were distant noises, barely discernible over the stunned, jubilant voice in Shane's head. He'd known making love to Brandee would be a singularly amazing experience, but he'd underestimated the power claiming her would have on his psyche.

"You should put me down," she said, her low, neutral tone giving nothing away. "Before something happens."

Something had already happened. Something immense and unforgettable. Powerful and scary. He was both eager and terrified to repeat the experience. But not yet. First he needed a few seconds to recover. And not just physically.

As soon as she was standing on her own, he reached to turn off the water, and the instant he took his eyes off her, she scooted out of the shower. He started to follow, but was slowed when a towel shot toward his face. The emotions that had been gathering in him, unsettling yet undeniable, retreated as he snatched the thick terry from the air.

Brandee had used his momentary distraction to slip a robe off the back of the door and wrap it around herself. Water dripped from the ends of her blond hair as she whirled to confront him, chuckling as she caught up another towel and knotted it around her head. Cocooned in plush white cotton, she watched him wrap the towel around his waist.

"Wow," she said with a bright laugh. "I knew that was going to be fantastic, but you exceeded my expectations."

Her delight found no matching gladness inside him. From her nonchalant cheerfulness, the experience hadn't been as transformative for her as it had been for him.

"That's me," he said, straining for a light tone. "Satisfaction guaranteed."

"I'll make sure I rate you five stars online." She yawned. "Well, it's been quite a day. And I still need to get a little work done. See you tomorrow, Delgado."

Shane had assumed there'd be a round two and now watched in stunned silence as Brandee blew him a kiss and disappeared out the bathroom door. Shane retreated to his room, shadowed by an uneasiness he couldn't shake. Chasing after her would only give her the upper hand in this wager.

Few knew his inner landscape didn't match the witty, life-of-the-party exterior people gravitated to. If he went after Brandee right now, he honestly didn't think he could pull off the cocky, charming version of himself that was his trademark.

She'd blown his mind and then walked away, leaving him hungry for more. But it wasn't so much his body that was in turmoil, but his emotions. And not because he was worried she might not be as into him as he'd thought.

He'd intended to make love to her again and then spend the night snuggling with her.

Snuggling.

With a groan, Shane flipped open his laptop and stared at the screen, unable to comprehend anything on it. Brandee had definitely won this round. Now it was up to him to make sure that didn't happen again.

The following day, Shane agreed to meet Gabe for a drink at the TCC clubhouse bar before dinner. While he waited on his friend, he followed up on a text he'd received a few minutes earlier. The call wasn't going well.

"I thought I told you last week that I needed that changed," Shane snarled into his cell phone. "Get it done."

"Sheesh," Gabe commented as he slid into the empty seat beside Shane. "Did you wake up on the wrong side of the bed, or what?"

The question hit a little too close to home. In fact, he hadn't woken up at all. He'd never fallen asleep. After Brandee's abrupt departure the night before, he'd busied himself until two o'clock and then laid awake thinking about her and replaying what had happened between them in the shower. And afterward.

Never before had a woman bolted so soon after making love. If anyone put on their clothes and got out, it was him.

"Sorry," Shane muttered. "Things are way behind at The Bellamy and we're due to open in a couple months."

"Things are always running behind. You usually don't take it out on your contractors."

Shane wasn't about to get into why he was so cranky. Not even with his best friend. So he shrugged his shoulders, releasing a little of the tension, and sipped his scotch.

"I'm feeling stretched a bit thin at the moment," he said. "I told you that I'm helping Brandee with her ranch. It's made me lose sight of some of the details at The Bellamy and I'm annoyed at myself."

"Oh."

Just that. Nothing more.

"Oh, what?" Shane demanded, not sure he wanted to hear what his friend had to say.

"It's just this wager of yours…" Gabe looked deep into the tumbler before him as if he could find the answer to life's mysteries at the bottom.

"Yes?" Shane knew he should just let it drop, but whatever was or wasn't happening between him and Brandee was like an itch he couldn't quite reach. And if Gabe had some insight, Shane wanted to hear it.

"It's just that I know you, Shane. I've seen you around a lot of women. You like this one. I mean really like her."

His first impulse was to deny it, but instead, he said, "Your point?"

"Let's say you somehow win the bet and she falls madly in love with you. Then what?"

"I guess we keep dating."

"You guess?" Gabe shook his head. "Do you really think she's gonna want to have anything to do with the guy who made her fall in love with him so he could take away the ranch she loves?"

"I don't have to buy the ranch." In fact, after spending time on it, he didn't really want the ranch to become home to hundreds of luxury estates. "I could just tell her I changed my mind."

"Have you?"

"Maybe."

"Does anyone ever get a straight answer out of you?"

"It depends."

"And what happens if Brandee wins?"

"That's not going to happen. I might really like this woman, but that's as far as it goes. She and I are too much alike. Neither one of us is interested in a relationship. We talked about it and we agree. Sex is great. Romance is…"

He'd been about to say *tiresome*, but he had to admit that over the course of several dinners and long talks by the fireplace on the patio, he was enjoying himself a great deal.

"Romance is…?" Gabe prodded.

"Too complicated, and you know I like things casual and easy."

With a nod, Gabe finished the last of his drink. "As long as you realize what you're doing can have repercussions and you're okay with whatever happens, my job as your conscience is done."

"I absolve you of all responsibility for any missteps I make with Brandee."

Gabe didn't look relieved as he nodded.

"One last thing before we get off the topic of Brandee," Shane said, remembering his promise to her the night before. "She asked me if you'd be willing to help tomorrow with her teen group. Apparently Megan Maguire from Safe Haven is bringing by some of her rescue dogs for the kids to work with."

"Sure. Let me know what time I need to be there."

Brandee surveyed the camp meeting hall for any details left undone. It was nearly ten o'clock in the morning and she was expecting a busload of teenagers to arrive at any moment. Megan had brought fifteen dogs, one for each teenager. Currently the rescues were running around in the paddock, burning off energy.

"Thank you for helping me out today," Brandee said to Gabe.

"My pleasure."

He and Chelsea had moved tables and organized the kitchen, while Brandee had helped Megan with the dogs and set up the obstacle course they would use later in the afternoon.

The plan for the day was for Megan to talk about the benefits of dog training for both the owner and pet and demonstrate her preferred method of clicker training. Then they would turn the kids loose in the paddock with the dogs so everyone could get to know each other.

After lunch, the teenagers would be issued clickers and dog treats. Megan was in charge of pairing up child with dog. Some of the kids had been through this before, so they would be given less experienced dogs. And the dogs that were familiar with clicker training would be matched with newcomers.

"Have you heard from Shane?" Gabe asked. "I thought he was going to be here today."

"He promised he would be, but he had something to check on at his hotel project."

"Well, hopefully that won't take him all day."

Brandee heard something in Gabe's tone, but before she could ask him about it, the camp bus appeared around a curve in the driveway. She pushed all thought of Shane's absence to the back of her mind. They'd completed the preliminary work without him, and there wouldn't be much to do while Megan spoke. Hopefully, Shane would arrive in time to help with lunch.

"Here we go." Megan Maguire came to stand beside Brandee. The redhead's green eyes reflected optimism. With her kind heart and patient manner, Megan was one of the most likable people Brandee had ever met. "I hope this group is as good as the last one."

"Me, too. We had such a great time."

"Of the ten dogs I brought that day, three of them were adopted almost immediately. The little bit of training they get here really helps."

"I know most of the kids enjoy it. Some act as if they are just too good for this. But it's funny, a couple of those girls that gave us such a hard time last month are back to do it again."

Brandee wasn't sure if it was because their parents were forcing them or if deep down inside they'd actually had fun. And what wasn't fun about hanging out with dogs all day?

The bus came to a halt and the door opened. The first teenager who emerged was Nikki Strait. She was one of the girls who'd been so bored and put out the prior month. She looked no better today. Neither did her best friend, Samantha, who followed her down the bus steps. Brandee sighed. Perhaps she'd been a little too optimistic about those two.

"Welcome to Hope Springs Camp," she said as soon as all the teenagers were off the bus and gathered in an ungainly clump. "On behalf of Megan Maguire of Royal Safe Haven and myself, we appreciate you giving up your Saturday to help with the dogs."

There were a couple smiles. A lot of looking around. Some jostling between the boys. All normal teenage behavior.

"We'll start our day in the camp meeting hall, where Megan will demonstrate what you'll be doing today. If you'll follow me, we can get started."

The teenagers settled into the folding chairs Chelsea had set up and more or less gave Megan their attention as she began speaking about Royal Safe Haven and the number of dogs that people abandoned each year in Royal.

"Dogs are pack animals," Megan explained. "They need a pack leader. Today it will be your job to assert yourself and take on that role. This doesn't mean you will mistreat the dogs or get angry with them. Most dogs perform better with positive reinforcement. That's why we use this clicker and these treats to get them to perform basic tasks such as recognizing their name, and commands such as *sit* and *down*. We'll also work with them on recalls and a simple but potentially life-saving maneuver I like to call 'what's this.'"

Megan set about demonstrating with her dog how effective the method was. She then switched to a nine-month-old Lab mix that had come to the shelter only the day before and was full-on crazy rambunctious.

Brandee surveyed the teens, noting which ones seemed engaged in the process and which couldn't be bothered. To her surprise Nikki was one of the former. The same could be said for Samantha.

Next, Megan brought the kids to the paddock so they could meet the dogs. Brandee turned her attention to lunch preparations. May had helped with the food. She'd fixed her famous lasagna and they would be serving it with salad, warm garlic bread and brownies for dessert. Last month they'd done chili and corn bread. As for next month…who knew if she'd even be around. With Maverick causing trouble, and Shane acting distant one minute and amorous the next, there were too many variables to predict.

A much more animated group of teenagers returned to the meeting hall. Playing with a group of dogs would do that.

Shane still hadn't arrived by the time the tables were cleared and the teenagers got down to the serious business of clicker training. Brandee shooed Gabe and Chelsea out of the kitchen with plates filled with lasagna and began the tedious job of cleaning up. She wrapped up what was left of the main meal and put the pans into the sink to soak while she nibbled at some leftover salad and scarfed down two pieces of May's delicious garlic bread.

It was almost one o'clock when Shane strolled into the meeting hall. Brandee had finished washing the plates and the silverware. All that was left was to scrub the pans.

"How's it going?" he asked, snagging a brownie. Leaning his hip against the counter, he peered at her over the dessert before taking a bite. "This is delicious."

"It's going fine," Brandee said, more than a little perturbed that after promising to help, he hadn't. "I didn't realize your business was going to take you all morning. You missed lunch."

"That's okay, I grabbed something in town."

"I thought you had a meeting at The Bellamy."

"I did, then David and I needed to chat, so we headed over to Royal Diner." He was gazing out the pass-through toward the gathered teenagers. "I'm here now. What can I do?"

She was tempted to tell him everything was done, but then she remembered the lasagna pans and grinned. "You can finish the dishes." She flung a drying towel over his shoulder and pointed at the sink. "I always leave the worst for last and now they're all yours."

As she went to join the others, her last glimpse of Shane was of him rolling up his sleeves and approaching the sink as if it contained a live cobra. She doubted the man had ever done a dish in his life and reminded herself to double-check the pans later to make sure they were clean to her standards.

Banishing Shane from her thoughts, Brandee circled the room to check on everyone's progress. To her surprise, Megan had paired Nikki with the hyper Lab mix. Nikki had seemed so disinterested the previous month, but with the puppy, she was completely focused and engaged. Already the teenager had the puppy sitting and lying down on command.

Brandee sidled up to Megan. "After how she was last month, what made you think to put Nikki and the Lab mix together?"

Megan grinned. "She and her mom have come by the shelter a couple times to help with the dogs and she has a real knack with them. I think last month she was bored with Mellie. This puppy is smart, but challenging. You can see how well it's going."

Next, Brandee turned her attention toward Justin Barnes. He'd isolated himself in a corner and was spending more time petting the dog than training her. It had been like this last month, too. The high school sophomore was disengaged from what was going on around him. She glanced in Gabe's direction, thinking he might be able to engage Justin, but Gabe was helping Jenny Prichard work with an adorable but very confused shih tzu/poodle mix.

Shane's voice came from right behind her. "Who's the kid over there?"

"Justin. He's the one I told you about whose dad wants him to play football rather than the guitar."

"Sounds like he and I might have a few things in common."

Brandee wasn't sure what Shane could say that might help Justin, but she'd asked for Shane to come today. It seemed wrong not to give him a chance to pitch in. "Maybe you could talk to him about it?"

"It's been a long time since I was a teenager, but I can give it a try."

"Thanks." Any animosity Brandee might have felt for his tardiness vanished. "I'll finish up the pans."

"No need. They're done."

"Already?"

"Just needed a little elbow grease." He arched an eyebrow at her. "It's not good for my ego that you look so surprised."

"I'm sure your ego is just fine." It was familiar banter between them, yet for one disconcerting moment, Brandee craved a more substantive connection. She dismissed the feeling immediately. What was she thinking? That she was interested in a *relationship* with Shane Delgado? Her stomach twisted at the thought, but the sensation wasn't unpleasant. Just troubling.

"You're right." He smirked at her. "It's great being me."

She watched him walk away and laughed at her foolishness. Even if she'd never made the bet with Shane, falling in love with him would be a disaster. They were too much alike in all the bad ways and complete opposites in the good ones. Nope, better to just keep things casual and breezy between them. Fabulous, flirty, sexy fun. That was all either of them wanted and all she could handle.

As he ambled toward Justin, Shane passed Gabe and raised his hand in greeting. Gabe acknowledged him with a broad grin and Shane wondered if he saw a touch of relief in his friend's eyes. No doubt Gabe appreciated that he was no longer the only guy.

Snagging a spare chair, Shane carried it to Justin's corner and set it down beside the kid, facing the dog.

"Hey," he said as he dropped a hand on the dog's caramel-colored head. "How's it going?"

"Fine." Justin mumbled the word and punched down on the clicker. The dog's ears lifted and he focused his full attention on the treat in Justin's hand.

"What's his name?" Shane indicated the dog.

"*Her* name is Ruby."

"Hey, Ruby." He fussed over the dog for a bit and then slouched back in his chair. "I'm Shane."

"Justin."

With niceties exchanged, the two guys settled down to stare at the dog, who looked from one to the other as if wondering where her next treat was coming from.

After a bit, Shane ventured into the silence. "What are you supposed to be doing?"

"Clicker training."

"How does that work?"

"Ruby."

The dog met Justin's glance. He clicked and gave her a treat.

"That's great."

Justin nodded.

So, obviously this whole connecting-with-kids thing wasn't easy. Shane's respect for Brandee's dedication grew. He shifted forward in the chair, propped his forearms on his thighs and mashed his palms together.

"She made me do dishes," he murmured. "Can you believe that?"

"Who did?"

"Brandee. She's always making me do stuff I don't want to."

"That sucks." Justin cast a sidelong glance his way. "Why do you do it?"

"Because she's pretty and I really like her. I'm not sure

she likes me, though. Sometimes I feel like no matter what I do, it's not good enough, ya know?"

"Yeah." More silence, and then, "It's like that with my dad. He makes me play football, but I hate it."

"My dad was the same way." After all these years, Shane couldn't believe he still resented his father, but the emotion churned in him. And really, it was all about not being good enough in Landon Delgado's eyes. "He expected me to follow in his footsteps and take over the family ranch, but I hated it." And in a community dominated by ranching, it felt like treason to criticize your bread and butter.

"What did you want to do instead?" Justin was showing more interest than he had a few seconds ago.

"I dunno. Anything but ranching." Shane thought back to when he'd been Justin's age. There wasn't much he'd been interested in besides hooking up with the prettiest girls in school and hanging out with his friends. He could see where his dad might've found that frustrating.

"So what do you do now?"

"Still have the ranch. And I develop properties. Heritage Estates is mine. And right now I'm working on a luxury hotel outside town called The Bellamy."

Justin's eyes had dimmed when Shane admitted he still had the ranch. "So you did what your father wanted you to do after all."

"The ranch has been in my family for almost a hundred years," Shane explained, deciding he better make his point awfully fast or he'd lose Justin altogether. "It wasn't as if I could walk away or sell it after my dad died. But I found a way to make it work so that I can do what I want and also respect my father's wishes."

"It isn't that easy for me."

"What do you want to do instead of playing football?" Shane asked, even though he already knew the answer."

"Play guitar and write music."

"Sounds pretty cool. How long have you been into that?"

"My dad gave me the guitar for my birthday a couple years ago."

"If your dad didn't want you to play the guitar, why did he buy you one?"

"He'd rather I play football," Justin said, his tone defensive and stubborn.

"Do you know why?"

"Because he did in high school and he got a scholarship to go to college." Justin gave a big sigh. "But I'm not that good. No college is going to want to put me on their team."

"Maybe your dad is worried about paying for your college?"

"I guess." Justin shrugged. "But I'm not really sure I want to go to college. I want to write songs and have a music career."

"You're way ahead of where I was at your age in terms of knowing what you want. That's pretty great." Shane had used money he'd inherited from his grandmother to start his real-estate development company shortly after graduating from college. When his dad found out what he'd done, he hadn't talked to him for a month. "I didn't know what I was going to do when I graduated high school, so I got a degree in business."

"College is expensive and I don't know if it would help me get what I want."

Shane wanted to argue that Justin would have something to fall back on if the music didn't work out, but he could see from the determined set of the boy's features that he would have a career in music or nothing else. Shane hoped the kid had some talent to back up his ambition.

"I'm sure this thing with your dad and football is because he's worried about your future. Maybe you could agree to try football in exchange for him agreeing to helping you with your music."

"Is that what you did with your dad?"

Not even close. "Absolutely. We came to an understanding and I figured out a way to keep ranching and at the same time pursue my interest in real estate."

"Was he proud of you?"

The question tore into Shane's gut like a chain saw. "My dad died before my business really got going, but I think he saw the potential in what I was doing and was impressed."

Shane didn't feel one bit bad about lying to the boy. Just because Shane hadn't been able to communicate with his father didn't mean Justin would have the same problem. And maybe if someone had offered him the advice he'd just given to the teenager, things with his dad might've gone better.

"I'll give it a try," Justin said.

"And if you want to talk or if you want me to have a heart-to-heart with your dad, here's my card. Call me anytime."

"Thanks." Justin slid the business card into his back pocket and seemed a little less glum. Or at least he showed more interest in the dog training.

Shane stuck around to watch him for a little while longer and then excused himself to go help a girl who seemed to be struggling with a brown-and-white mop of a dog.

Over the next thirty minutes, he worked his way around the room chatting with each kid in turn. By the time Megan called for everyone to take the dogs outside to the obstacle course, Shane had gotten everyone's story.

"How do you do that?" Brandee joined him near the back of the crowd. "Everyone you talk to was smiling by the time you walked away. Even Justin."

"How do you not realize what a great guy I am?" He grinned broadly and bumped his shoulder into hers. "I would think after living with me this past week you'd have caught the fever."

"The fever?" she repeated in a dubious tone.

"The Shane fever." He snared her gaze and gave her his best smoldering look. "Guaranteed to make your heart race, give you sweaty palms and a craving for hot, passionate kisses."

Her lips twitched. "I'm pretty sure I'm immune." But she didn't sound as confident as she once had.

"That sounds like a challenge."

"It's a statement of fact."

"It's your opinion. And if I'm good at anything, I'm good at getting people to see my point of view. And from my point of view, you're already symptomatic."

"How do you figure?"

With everyone's attention fixed on Megan, Shane was able to lean down and graze his lips across Brandee's ear. He'd noticed she was particularly sensitive there. At the same time, he'd cupped his hand over her hip and pulled her up against his side. The two-pronged attack wrenched a soft exclamation from her lips.

A second later he let her go and greeted her glare with a smirk. "Tell me your heart isn't racing."

"You aren't as charming as you think you are," she said, turning her attention to what was going on among the poles, small jumps and traffic cones set up near the meeting hall.

He let her get the last word in because he'd already annoyed her once that day and that wasn't the way to this woman's heart.

"Do you think there's something going on between Gabe and Chelsea?" Brandee asked after a couple more kids had taken their dogs through the obstacle course.

Shane followed the direction of her gaze and noticed the couple standing together on the outskirts of the crowd. "Going on how?"

"Like maybe they could be interested in each other?"

"Maybe." Shane paid better attention to the body language between the two and decided there might be an attraction, but he was pretty sure neither one had noticed it yet.

For a second Shane envied the easy camaraderie between Gabe and Chelsea. With the bet hanging over their heads, he and Brandee couldn't afford to let down their guards. And maybe that was okay. Sparring with Brandee was exciting. So was making love to her. He liked the way she challenged him, and figuring out how to best her kept him on his toes.

Besides, he wasn't in this for the long haul. This was his chance to have some fun and try to win a bet. Eventually he would move out of Brandee's house and life would return to normal. But what if it didn't? What if he wanted to keep seeing Brandee? He snuck a peek at her profile. Would she be open to continuing to see where things went? Or was this just about the wager for her?

Shane didn't like where his thoughts had taken him. He liked even less the ache in his chest. Gabe's words from several days earlier came back to haunt him.

As long as you realize what you're doing can have repercussions and you're okay with whatever happens...

It was looking more and more like he had no idea what he was doing and the repercussions were going to be a lot more complicated than he'd counted on.

Nine

To thank Chelsea, Gabe and Shane for their help at Hope Springs Camp's mini-event, Brandee treated them to dinner at the Texas Cattleman's Club. Their efforts were the reason the day had gone so smoothly and Brandee was able to relax at the end of the successful event.

As soon as they finished dinner and returned to the ranch house, she and Shane headed out to the patio to sit by the fire.

Brandee tucked her bare feet beneath her and sipped at her mug of hot, honey-laced herbal tea. "Despite your very late start," she said to Shane, keeping her tone light, "you were a huge help today. I think it was good to have both you and Gabe there. Usually we have trouble keeping the boys on task."

"A couple of them were a little rowdy while they were waiting for their turn at the obstacle course, but once they got working with the dogs it was better."

"The clicker training keeps both handler and dog engaged. Megan was very satisfied how the day went."

"She said she might even get some adoptions out of it."

"I wish Seth Houser could be one of them. He's been working with Sunny for almost three months. And making great strides." The Wheaton terrier was a great dog, but way too hyper. He'd been adopted twice and returned both times. A talented escape artist with abandonment issues, he needed to go to someone as active as he was.

"I was really amazed by how well Seth handled him." Shane puffed out a laugh. "I think Tinkerbell and Jenny were my favorite pair."

The adorable shih tzu/poodle mix with the bad underbite had been recently turned in by a woman who had to go into a nursing home. Jenny was a goth girl of fifteen who'd shuffled through the day with stooped shoulders and downcast eyes. But she'd bonded with her short-legged black-and-white dog and together they'd won the obstacle course.

"Megan has a knack for matching the right dog to the perfect handler."

They lapsed into silence for a time while the fire popped and crackled. The longer they went without speaking, the more Brandee could feel the tension building between them. The last time they'd sat together out here, she'd ended up dragging Shane into the shower.

The day after, she'd been busy with her cattle herd and hadn't gotten home until late every night. Part of her wondered if she'd been avoiding Shane. The way she'd felt as he'd slid inside her for the first time had shocked her. She'd expected to enjoy making love with Shane, but couldn't have predicted to what extent. It was like all the best sex she'd ever had rolled into one perfect act of passion.

And ever since, all she wanted to do was climb into the

memory and relive it over and over. But not the aftermath when she'd bolted for the safety of her room before Shane could notice that her defenses were down. Standing naked in the bathroom, she'd been terrified that, with his appetite satisfied, he wouldn't want her to stick around. So, she'd fled.

Now, however, after a couple days to regain her confidence, she was ready to try again. Anticipation formed a ball of need below her belly button. The slow burn made her smile. She was opening her mouth to suggest they retire to his bedroom when he spoke.

"I see why you find it so rewarding."

Brandee sat in confused silence for several seconds. "What exactly?"

"Working with teenagers."

With a resigned sigh, Brandee turned down the volume on her libido. "I wish I could say it was all success and no failure, but these kids don't have nearly the sorts of issues of some I've worked with."

"You do a good job relating to them."

He hadn't done so bad himself. Watching him with Justin, Brandee had been impressed with the way he'd gotten the kid to stop looking so morose.

"I remember all too well what it was like to have troubles at home," she said.

"Your mom?" Shane asked gently.

For a second Brandee was tempted to give a short answer and turn the topic aside, but part of her wanted to share what her childhood had been like after losing her dad. "It wasn't easy living with someone who only wants you around so she can steal your money."

"I can't imagine." Shane shifted his upper body in her direction until his shoulder came into companionable contact with hers.

Brandee welcomed the connection that made her feel

both safe and supported. "It didn't make me the ideal daughter."

"You fought?"

"Not exactly." Brandee let her head fall back. Her eyes closed and images of the cramped, cluttered house filled her mind. A trace of anxiety welled as memories of those five suffocating years rushed at her. "She yelled at me, while I said nothing because I'd tried arguing with her and she'd just freak out. So I learned to keep quiet and let her have her say. And then I'd rebel."

"By doing what?"

"The usual. Partying with my friends. Drinking. Drugs. For a while my grades slipped, then I realized she didn't give a damn about any of it and I was only hurting myself."

"So, what happened?"

"I cleaned up my act. Not that she noticed anything going on with me." Or cared. "But I continued to avoid the house as much as possible."

"That sounds a lot like how I spent my teen years. I made sure I was gone as much as possible. That way I wasn't around when it came time to help out on the ranch. It drove my dad crazy." Shane fixed his gaze on the hypnotic dance of the flames, but didn't seem to be seeing the fire. "He was a firm believer in hard work, a lot like your dad. He was fond of telling me I wasn't going to make anything of myself if I wasn't willing to work for it. I didn't believe him. I was pretty happy with what I had going. I had a lot of friends and decent grades. I was having a good time. And all he cared about was that I wasn't in love with ranching like he was."

Brandee didn't know how to react to the bitter edge in Shane's voice. She loved her ranch and couldn't imagine giving it up. That ranching was something Shane only did out of obligation was a disconnect between them that

reinforced why she shouldn't let herself get too emotionally attached.

"What was it about the ranching you didn't like?" she
asked, shifting to face him and putting a little distance
between them.

"I don't honestly know. One thing for sure, I didn't see
the point in working as hard as my dad did when there were
more efficient ways to do things. But he wouldn't listen to
anything I had to say. He expected me to follow exactly in
his footsteps. I wasn't going to do that."

"What did you want to do?"

"Justin asked me that today, too. I guess I just wanted
to have fun." He grinned, but the smile lacked his typical
cocky self-assurance. "Still do."

She let that go without comment even as she was mentally shaking her head at him. "So, how'd you get into real-
estate developing?"

"A buddy of mine in college got me into flipping houses.
I liked the challenge." Satisfaction reverberated in Shane's
voice. He obviously took great pride in his past accom-
plishments. And present ones, too. From everything she'd
heard, The Bellamy was going to be quite a resort.

"I got my first job when I turned sixteen," Brandee said.
"Stocking shelves at a grocery store after school and on
weekends. It gave me enough money to buy a used junker
with no AC and busted shocks. I didn't care. It was freedom. I used to park it around the corner from the house
because I didn't want my mom knowing about it."

"What would've happened if she'd known about it?"

"She would've given it to Turtlehead or Squash Brain."
Those days were blurry in her memory. "Mom always had
some loser boyfriend hanging around."

"She lived with them?"

Brandee heard the concern in his voice and appreciated

it more than she should. "They lived with her. She rented a crummy two-bedroom house right on the edge of a decent neighborhood because she thought it was great to be so close to people with money. I don't know what she was like when my dad met her, but by the time I went to live with her, she wasn't what anyone would call a class act."

"What did she do?"

"She actually had a halfway-decent job. She cut hair at one of those chain salons. I think if she had better taste in boyfriends she might have been more successful. But all she attracted were harmless jerks." She thought back to one in particular. "And then Nazi boy showed up."

"Nazi boy?"

"A skinhead with the Nazi tattoos on his arms and all over his chest. For a while I just hung in there figuring he'd soon be gone like all the rest."

"But he wasn't?"

"No. This one had money. Not because he worked. I think he and his white-supremacist buddies jacked cars or ran drugs or something. He always had money for blow and booze." She grimaced. "My mom took a bad path with that one."

"How old were you?"

"I'd just turned seventeen."

"Did he bother you?"

"Not at first. He was more into my mom than a dopey-looking kid with bad hair and ill-fitting clothes. But his friends were something else. I think initially they started to bug me out of sheer boredom. I was used to having my ass grabbed or being shoved around by some of the other guys my mom hooked up with. Nazi boy's friends were different, though."

As she described her encounters, Shane's muscles tensed. "Did they hurt you?"

She knew what he was asking. "If you're trying to be delicate and ask if I got raped, the answer is no."

Shane relaxed a little. "So what happened?"

"For a while it was okay. I was hiding behind bad hygiene and a dim-witted personality. Then one day I was taking a shower and thought I was alone in the house."

"You weren't?"

"Nazi boy had taken off with his buddies to go do something and I wasn't expecting them back. I never showered when he was home. Most days I either took clothes to school and cleaned up there or did the same thing at a friend's house."

"That's pretty extreme."

The unfinished mug of tea had gone cold in Brandee's hands, so she set it on the coffee table. "I'd seen how he could be around my mom and it made me feel way too vulnerable to be naked in the house."

"So he came home unexpectedly and caught you in the shower?"

Those days with her mom weren't something she liked talking about and part of her couldn't believe she was sharing this story with Shane. The only other person she'd told was Chelsea.

"I was coming out of the bathroom wearing nothing but a towel. The second I saw him, I jumped back into the bathroom and locked the door. He banged on the door, badgering me to open it for twenty minutes until my mom came home."

"Did you tell her what happened?"

"No. Why bother? She'd just accuse me of enticing him. Either she was scared of him or she liked the partying too much. This one wasn't going away anytime soon."

"Did he come after you again?"

"For a while I tried to stay away as much as possible,

but sometimes I had to go home. When I did, I was careful to do so when my mom was home. He left me alone while she was around."

"I don't suppose you had a teacher or adult that could help you out."

"That might have been smart. But I felt like all the adults I'd reached out to had failed me. Instead, I found the biggest, meanest football player in our school and made him the most devoted boyfriend ever." She batted her eyelashes and simpered. "Oh, Cal, you're just so big and strong." Her voice dripped with honey. "Do you think you could get that terrible man who lives with my mother to stop trying to put his hands all over me?"

"Did that work?"

"Like a charm. Nazi boy was all talk and glass jaw. He knew it and I knew it. At five-ten and 170, he might have scared me, but he was no match for a six-five, 280-pound linebacker."

Shane regarded her with admiration and respect. "So your linebacker kept you safe until you finished high school?"

Brandee shifted her gaze out toward the darkness beyond the patio and debated lying to him. "I didn't actually finish high school."

"How come?"

"Because two months before graduation my mom finally figured out that her boyfriend was coming on to me and rather than kicking him to the curb, she blamed me. That's when I ran away for good."

Shane's first instinct was to curse out her mother, but the way Brandee was braced for his reaction, he knew he had to take a gentler approach or risk her fleeing back behind her defenses.

"Wow, that sucks."

This part of her story was different than the last. As she'd spoken of her difficulties with Nazi boy, she'd sounded strong and resilient. Now, however, she was once again that abandoned child, learning that she was the biggest mistake her mother had ever made. Her loneliness was palpable and Shane simply couldn't stand to be physically separated from her. He reached for her hand and laced their fingers together, offering her this little comfort.

"What did you do?" he asked.

"I should've gone to live with my grandmother in Montana."

"Why didn't you?"

Her fingers flexed against his as she tightened her grip on him. A second later she relaxed. "Because I was angry with her for not taking me in after my dad died."

"So what did you do instead?"

"I stayed with my best friend for a couple days until I found a room and a waitressing job that paid better."

"When did you start your business?"

"I'd learned how to crochet and knit from one of my friends' moms and had been making headbands and adding lace embellishments to stuff I found at the thrift store. I bought a used sewing machine and started doing even more stuff. It was amazing how well things sold online. All I did was waitress, sew and market my stuff."

"The rest is history?"

"Not quite. Nazi boy and his friends tracked me down. Fortunately I wasn't home. But the homeowner was. They shoved her around and scared her pretty good. After that they went into my room and took everything, including the five hundred dollars I'd saved."

"What happened then?"

"The homeowner pressed charges and they all got

picked up by the cops. But she kicked me out. Once again I had nowhere to go and nothing to show for all my hard work."

"Did you stay in Houston?"

"Nope. I moved to Waco and lived out of my car for two weeks."

"At seventeen?"

"Haven't you figured out I'm tougher than I look?" She gave a rueful laugh. "And I'd turned eighteen by then. In fact, I'd been out celebrating my birthday with friends when Nazi boy robbed me."

"What happened after that?"

"That's when things get boring. I found another waitressing job and another place to live. Took a second job at a tailoring shop. The owner let me use the machines after hours so I could create my designs. In four months I was making enough by selling my clothes and accessories online to quit my waitressing job. In a year I moved into a studio apartment and was bringing in nearly ten thousand a month."

Shane had a hard time believing her numbers could be real. "That's a lot for a solo operation."

"I didn't sleep, was barely eating and the only time I left my apartment was to get supplies or ship product."

"How long before it got too big for you to handle?"

"By the time I turned twenty, I had four seamstresses working for me and I was in over my head. I was paying everyone in cash and eventually that was going to catch up to me. So I talked to a woman at the bank I really liked and Pamela hooked me up with a website designer, lawyer and an accountant. But between the designing and running things, there was still too much for me to do, so I hired Pamela to manage the business side. And then things really took off."

"And now here you are running a ranch." He smiled ruefully. "It's not an ordinary sort of career move."

"Probably not, but it's a lot better for me. While I loved designing and promoting my fashion lines, I'm not cut out to sit in an office all day looking at reports and handling the myriad of practical decisions a multimillion-dollar business requires."

"You'd rather ride around in a pasture all night, keeping an eye on your pregnant cows."

She nodded. "Exactly."

"So, you sold the business."

"A woman in California bought it and has plans to take it global." Brandee shook her head. "It's still a little surreal how much the company has grown from those first few crocheted headbands."

"I can't help but think it was a lot to give up."

"It wasn't my dream. Hope Springs Ranch is. And I still design a few pieces each year. So, I get to be creative. It's enough. And now I expect to be busier than ever with Hope Springs Camp starting to ramp up."

His gaze fastened on her softly parted lips and a moment later, he'd slid his hand beneath the weight of her long hair and pulled her toward him. After the first glancing slide of his mouth over hers, they came together in a hungry crush.

Tongues danced and breath mingled. Shane lifted her onto his lap, the better to feel her soft breasts press against him through her cotton shirt. With her fingers raking through his hair, Shane groaned her name against the silky skin of her long neck. Despite the longing clawing at him these past few days, he'd underestimated his need for her.

"I can't wait to be inside you again," he muttered, sliding his tongue into the hollow of her throat while his fingers worked her shirt buttons free. "You are like no woman I've known."

Brandee stripped off her shirt and cast it aside. "You're pretty awesome yourself, Delgado." Her fingers framed his face, holding him still while she captured his gaze. "You've made me feel things I've never known before."

Her mouth found his in a sweet, sexy kiss that stole his breath. He fanned his fingers over her back, reveling in her satiny warmth, the delicate bumps of her spine and the sexy dimples just above her perfect ass. This time around, Shane was determined to take his time learning everything about what turned her on.

He shifted so that her back was against his chest and his erection nestled between her firm butt cheeks. This gave him full access to her breasts, stomach and thighs, while she could rock her hips and drive him to new levels of arousal. As trade-offs went, it wasn't a bad one.

Shane unfastened her bra and set it aside. As the cool night air hit her nipples, they hardened. He teased his fingertips across their sensitive surface and Brandee jerked in reaction. Her head fell back against his shoulder as a soft *yes* hissed past her teeth.

"Do that again," she murmured, her eyelids half-lowered, a lazy smile on her lips. "I love the feel of your hands on me."

"My pleasure."

He cupped her breasts and kneaded gently, discovering exactly what she liked. Each breathy moan urged his passion higher. His fingers trembled as they trailed over her soft, fragrant skin. Her flat stomach bucked beneath his palm as he slipped his fingers beneath the waistband of her leggings and grazed the edge of her panties.

"Let's get these off." His voice was whisky-rough and unsteady.

"Sure."

She helped him shimmy the clingy black cotton material over her hips and down her legs. He enjoyed sliding his hands back up over her calves and knees, thumbs trailing along the sensitive inner thigh. Catching sight of her lacy white bikini panties, Shane forgot his early determination to make her wait.

He dipped his fingertips beneath the elastic and over her sex. She spread her legs wider. Her breath was coming in jagged gasps and her body was frozen with anticipation as he delved into her welcoming warmth.

They sighed together as he circled her clit twice before gliding lower. He found a rhythm she liked, taking his cues from the way her hips rocked and the trembling increased in her thighs. She gave herself over to him. She was half-naked on his lap, thighs splayed, her head resting on his shoulder, eyes half-closed. She sighed in approval as he slid first one, then two fingers inside her.

The tension in her muscles increased as he slowly thrust in and out of her. He noted how her eyebrows came together in increased concentration, saw the slow build of heat flush her skin until all too soon, her lips parted on a wordless cry. And then her back arched. She clamped her hand over his and aided his movements as her climax washed over her in a slow, unrelenting wave. He cupped her, keeping up a firm, steady pressure, and watched the last of her release die away.

"We need to take this indoors," he murmured against her cheek, shuddering as she shifted on his lap, increasing the pressure of her backside against his erection. The sensation made him groan.

"Give me a second," she replied. "I'm pretty sure I can't walk at the moment."

Wait? Like hell.

"Let me help you with that." He lifted her into his arms and stood.

"Your room," she exclaimed before he'd taken more than two steps. "Please. I've been imagining you all alone in that big bed and thinking about all the things I'd like to do to you in it."

He liked the way her mind worked. "I've been picturing you there, as well." He slipped through the French doors and approached his bed. "We'll take turns telling each other all about it and then acting every scenario out."

"Sounds like we're going to have a busy night."

"I'm counting on it."

Tonight, he'd make sure she didn't have the strength to leave until he was good and ready to let her go.

Ten

The Royal Diner was packed at nine o'clock on Sunday morning, but Brandee had gotten there at eight and grabbed a table up front. As Chelsea slid into the red vinyl booth across from her, Brandee set aside the newspaper she'd been reading.

"Thanks for meeting me," Brandee said. "I needed to get out of the house. This thing with Shane is not going as I'd hoped."

"I told you it was a bad idea."

Brandee winced. "Let's put it down to me being in a desperate situation and not thinking straight."

"So, have you finally given in to that wild animal magnetism of his?"

"I haven't *given in* to anything," Brandee retorted. "However, we have been having fun." A lot of fun.

"You are such a fake." Chelsea laughed. "You act all cool chick about him, but I watched you yesterday. When he was talking to the kids, you were all moony. You've got it bad."

Brandee wasn't ready to admit this in the relative safety of her mind much less out loud to her best friend in a public restaurant. "It's just sex. I've been out of circulation for a long time and he's very capable."

Chelsea shook her head in disgust and picked up her menu. "Is that why you look so tired out this morning?"

"No. I actually got a good night's sleep."

That was true. After they'd worn each other out, Brandee had fallen into the deepest slumber she'd had since Maverick had sent that vile demand. Snuggling in Shane's arms, his breath soft and warm against her brow as she'd drifted off, she'd gained a new perspective on the amount of time she spent alone. Where she'd thought she was being smart to direct her energy and focus toward the ranch, what she'd actually done was maintain a frantic pace in order to avoid acknowledging how lonely she was.

"Thanks again for your help yesterday," Brandee said once they'd put in their breakfast orders and the waitress had walked away. "I couldn't have managed without you and Gabe and, once he showed up, Shane. I hope this wasn't my last mini-event."

"Anything new from Maverick?"

"No, but my resignation from the TCC and the money are due in two days. And I don't know if Shane's going to sign away his claim to Hope Springs Ranch before the deadline."

"You don't think Shane is falling in love with you?"

Brandee's heart compressed almost painfully at Chelsea's question. "I don't know. Do you think he is? Even a little?" She sounded very insecure as she asked the question.

"It's hard to tell with Shane. He hides how he feels nearly as well as you do." Chelsea eyed her friend over the rim of her coffee cup. "But given the way he looked at you during dinner last night, I'd say that he's more than a little interested."

Brandee still felt an uncomfortable pang of uncertainty. "That's something, I guess."

"Which makes the whole wager thing a bummer because it's going to get in the way of you guys being real with each other."

Thinking over the prior evening's conversation and the lovemaking that followed, Brandee wasn't completely sure she agreed. She'd felt a connection with Shane unlike anything she'd ever known before. Maybe sharing their struggles with their parents had opened a gap in both their defenses.

"I'd like to call off my wager with Shane," Brandee admitted. "What started out as a good idea has gotten really complicated."

"So do it."

"How am I supposed to explain my change of heart to Shane?"

"You could tell him that you really like him and want to start with a clean slate."

Brandee threw up her hands, her entire body lighting up with alarm. "No. I can't do that. He'll think he's won and I'll have to sell him Hope Springs."

Besides, leaving herself open to be taken advantage of—or worse, rejected—went against all the instincts that had helped her to survive since she was twelve years old. She didn't want to be that girl anymore, but she was terrified to take a leap of faith.

Chelsea blew out her breath in frustration. "This is what I'm talking about. You have to stop working the angles and just trust that he feels the same way."

"But what if he doesn't?" Already Brandee had talked

herself out of canceling the wager. "What if it's just that he's done a better job of playing the game than me?"

"And what if he's really fallen for you and is afraid to show it because that means you'll win the wager? Shane loves a challenge. You two have squared off against each other almost from the day you met. Frankly, I'm a little glad this Maverick thing came along to bring you two together."

Chelsea's frustrated outburst left Brandee regarding her friend in stunned silence. She'd never considered that being blackmailed could have an upside. Yet she couldn't deny that her life was a little bit better for having gotten to spend time with Shane.

The sound of angry voices came from a table twenty feet away.

Chelsea, whose back was to the drama, leaned forward. "Who is it?"

"Looks like Adam Haskell and Dusty Walsh are at it again." The two men hated each other and tempers often raged when they occupied the same space. "I can't quite tell what it's about."

"You're nothing but an ignorant drunk." Walsh's raised voice had the effect of silencing all conversation around him. "You have no idea what you're talking about."

"Well, he's not wrong," Chelsea muttered, not bothering to glance over her shoulder.

Brandee's gaze flickered back to her best friend. "He needs to learn to mind his own damn business." She remembered how when she first bought Hope Springs Ranch, Adam had stopped by to inform her that ranching wasn't women's work.

"You're gonna get what's coming to you." Haskell's threat rang in the awkward silence that had fallen.

"You two take it outside." Amanda Battle stepped from

behind the counter and waded into the confrontation. "I'll not have either of you making a ruckus in my diner."

Most people probably wouldn't have tangled with either Haskell or Walsh on a normal day, much less when they were going at each other, but Amanda was married to Sheriff Nathan Battle and no one was crazy enough to mess with her.

"He started it," Walsh grumbled, sounding more like a petulant five-year-old than a man in his sixties. It was hard to believe that someone like Dusty could be related to Gabe. "And I'm not done with my breakfast."

"Looks like you're done, Adam." Amanda glanced pointedly at the check in his hand. "Why don't you head on over to the register and let Karen get your bill settled."

And just like that it was over. Brandee and Chelsea's waitress appeared with plates of eggs, biscuits and gravy, and a waffle for them to share. She returned a second later to top off their coffee and the two women dug in.

After a while Brandee returned to their earlier conversation. "I've been thinking more and more about what Maverick brought to light."

"That it's not really fair to keep Shane from knowing that his family is the rightful owners of the land Hope Springs sits on?"

"Yes. I can't exactly afford to walk away from ten million dollars, but I can make sure that after I'm gone the land will revert back to his family."

Chelsea was silent for a long time. "This really sucks."

"Yes, it does." Brandee was starting to think that no matter what she did, her time with Shane was drawing to a close. "Whoever Maverick is, the person has a twisted, cruel personality."

"Still think it's one or all of the terrible trio?"

"I can't imagine who else." Brandee hadn't given up on her suspicions about Cecelia, Simone and Naomi. "Although it seems a little extreme even for them."

"But you've really been a burr in their blankets and I could see them siding with Shane."

"And considering what Maverick wants..."

"Money?"

"Fifty grand isn't all that much. I think Maverick asked for money more to disguise the real purpose of the blackmail, which was getting me out of the Texas Cattleman's Club." Something she could see the terrible trio plotting to do. "Regardless of what I do or don't know, the fact is that I can't afford for Shane to find out the truth."

"But if you don't win the wager, what are you going to do?"

"As much as I hate the idea, I think I'm going to do as Maverick demands."

"So, what does that mean for you and Shane?"

"I think from the beginning we were both pretty sure this thing was going to end up in a stalemate."

"So neither of you is going to admit that you've fallen for the other."

"Nope."

"And yet I'm pretty sure you've fallen for him."

"I can't let myself go there, Chels." Brandee rubbed her burning eyes and let her pent-up breath go in a ragged exhale. "There's too much at stake."

"And if the fate of your ranch didn't hinge on you admitting that you had it bad for him?"

"The problem is that it does." As much as Brandee wished she was brave enough to risk her heart, she could point to too many times when trusting in things beyond her control hadn't worked in her favor. "So, I guess that's something we'll never know."

* * *

The rain began shortly after three o'clock that afternoon. Brandee fell asleep listening to it tap on the French doors in the guest suite, a rapid counterpoint to the steady beat of Shane's heart beneath her ear. It was still coming down when she woke several hours later.

They hadn't moved during their nap and his strong arms around her roused a contentment she couldn't ignore. For as long as she could remember, she'd bubbled with energy, always in motion, often doing several things at once and adding dozens of tasks to the bottom of her to-do list as she knocked off the ones at the top.

Around Shane she stepped back from the frenetic need for activity. He had a way of keeping her in the moment. Whether it was a deep, drugging kiss or the glide of his hands over her skin, when she was with him the rest of the world and all its problems slipped away.

"Ten more minutes," he murmured, his arms around her tensing.

"I'm not going anywhere."

His breath puffed against her skin as his lips moved across her cheek and down her neck. "I can feel you starting to think about everything that needs to get done in the next twelve hours."

"I'm only thinking about the next twelve minutes." She arched her back as his tongue circled her nipple. A long sigh escaped her as he settled his mouth over her breast and sucked.

In the end it was twenty minutes before she escaped his clever hands and imaginative mouth and made her way on shaking legs to her shower. As tempted as she'd been by his invitation to stay and let him wash her back, they'd already lingered too long.

They grabbed a quick dinner of May's chili to fortify

them for the long, cold night, before heading out. With the number of cows showing signs of delivering over the next twenty-four hours, it was all hands on deck.

Icy rain pelted Shane and Brandee as they maneuvered the cows. By three o'clock in the morning, Hope Springs Ranch had seen the addition of two heifers and three steers. On a normal night, emotions would be running high at all the successful births, but a sharp wind blew rain into every gap in their rain gear, leaving the group soaked, freezing and exhausted.

Brandee cast a glance around. Although most of the newborns were up on their feet and doing well, a couple still were being tended to by their moms. That left only one cow left to go. The one Brandee was most worried about: a first-time heifer who looked like she was going to be trouble.

"We might want to take this one back to the shed," Brandee shouted above the rain, moving her horse forward to turn the heifer they'd been keeping tabs on in the direction of the ranch buildings.

Her water had broken at the start of the evening and now she'd advanced to the stage where she was contracting. They'd been watching her for the last twenty minutes and things didn't seem to be progressing.

Shane shifted his horse so that the cow was between them and they could keep her heading where they wanted. It seemed to take forever and Brandee's nerves stretched tighter with each minute that passed. As many times as she'd seen calves drop, each birth held a place of importance in her heart.

They got the heifer into the barn and directed her into a chute. At the far end was a head gate that opened to the side and then closed after the cow stuck her head through. Once the heifer was secure, Brandee put on a long glove and moved to her back end.

"I've got to see what's going on up there," she explained to Shane, who watched her with interest.

"What can I do?"

"There's an obstetric chain, hooks and a calf puller over there." She indicated a spot on the wall where the equipment was kept. "Can you also grab the wood box propped up against the wall, as well?" Two feet square and four inches high, the box was used to brace against the heifer when she started pulling the calf out.

"Got it."

Now that they had the cow inside where it was dry and light, Brandee needed to examine the birth canal to determine the size and position of the calf. She was dreading that the calf was breeched. Most calves were born head-first, but sometimes they were turned around, and if the legs were tucked up, it would mean she'd have to go rooting around an arm's-length distance to see if she could find a hoof and wrap the chain around it.

Brandee knew she was in trouble almost immediately. Chilled to the bone, exhausted and anticipating a hundred things that could possibly go wrong with this birth, she cursed.

"Problem?" Shane stood beside her with the equipment.

"Calf's breeched." She took the chain from Shane and indicated the puller. "You can put that aside. We're not going to need it yet."

She hoped not at all. If she could get the calf straightened out, the cow's contractions might be able to help her. Brandee just hoped the heifer wasn't worn-out from pushing the breeched baby.

"What do you do with that?" Shane indicated the chain. It was several feet in length with circles on each end, reminiscent of a dog's choke collar.

"I need to get this around the calf's legs so I can get

them straightened out. Right now its hind end is toward the birth canal and its legs are beneath it."

"Isn't this something a vet should handle?"

"Only if things get complicated." And she hoped that wouldn't happen. "I've done this before. It's just tricky and time-consuming, but doable."

"What can I do to help?"

Her heart gave a silly little flutter at his earnest question. Usually she had one of the guys helping her with this, but they were all out, tending to little miracles of their own. She could handle this.

She eyed Shane's beefy shoulders with a weary but heartfelt grin. "I'm going to let you show off your manly side."

"Meaning?" He cocked an eyebrow at her.

"You get to do all the pulling."

Her last glimpse of Shane before she focused all her attention on the cow was of his sure nod. He had his game face on. This aspect of ranching was one he'd never known, but he'd stepped up and she respected him for that.

Brandee made a loop with one end of the chain and reached in until she located the calf's legs. The snug fit and the way he was positioned meant that getting the chain over the hoof required dexterity and patience. To block out all distractions, Brandee closed her eyes and "saw" with her fingers. Before she could get the loop over the hoof, she lost the opening and the chain straightened out.

Frustration surged. The miserable night had worn her down. Feeling raw and unfocused, she pulled her arm out and re-created the loop before trying once more. It took her three attempts and ten agonizing minutes before she'd captured both hooves. She was breathing hard past the tightness in her throat as she turned to Shane.

"Okay, now it's your turn." Her voice was thick with

weariness and she struggled not to let her anxiety show. "We'll do this slow. I need you to pull one side and then the other to get his hooves pointed outward. I'll let you know which to pull and when."

Working together in slow stages, they got the calf's back legs straightened so that both were heading down the birth canal. Both Brandee and Shane were sweating in the cool barn air by the time stage one was complete.

"What now?" Shane asked, stepping back to give Brandee room to move around the heifer.

"We need to get her down on her right side. It's the natural position for birthing. I want as little stress on her as possible."

Brandee slipped a rope around the cow right in front of her hip bones and tightened it while rocking her gently to get her to lie down. Once the heifer was on her side, Brandee made sure the chains were still properly positioned around the calf's cannon bones.

"Good," she said, noting that the cow was starting to contract once more. "Let's get this done."

She sat down on the ground and grabbed the first hook. When the cow contracted, Brandee pulled. Nothing happened. She set her foot against the cow for leverage and switched to the second hook. With the next contraction, she pulled again without success. This breeched baby was good and stuck.

"Let me help." Shane nudged her over and sat beside her.

After alternating back and forth between the two chains a few times, Brandee dropped her head onto her arms as frustration swallowed her whole.

"Damn it, I don't want to use the calf puller." But it was very much appearing like she'd have to.

An uncharacteristic urge to cry rose in her. She wanted

to throw herself against Shane's chest and sob. Brandee gritted her teeth. She never got emotional like this.

"Come on," Shane said, bumping her shoulder with his in encouragement. "We can do this."

His focus was complete as he timed his exertions with the cow's contractions. Following his example, Brandee put her energy into willing the damned calf to move. The heifer groaned, Shane grunted and Brandee's muscles strained.

After four more contractions, they were able to get more of the legs out and Brandee felt some of the tension ease from her chest. There was still no guarantee that the calf would be alive when they were done, but at least they were making progress.

"Here," she said, shifting the wood platform and sliding it against the cow's backside between the calf's legs and the floor. Now she and Shane had a better brace for their feet. "He's starting to loosen. A few more contractions and we'll have him."

Then like a cork coming loose from a champagne bottle, the rear half of the calf was suddenly out. They scooted back to make way and then scrambled to their feet. With one final contraction and two mighty pulls from Brandee and Shane, the calf slipped free in a disgusting expulsion of amniotic fluid and blood.

Shane gave a soft whoop as he and a very relieved Brandee dragged the limp calf ten feet away from the cow.

"Is it alive?" Shane bent down and peered at the unmoving calf while Brandee peeled the sack from its face and cleared fluid from its nostrils.

"It sure is." She exuberantly roughed up its coat in a simulation of its mother's rough licking and watched it begin to draw breath into its lungs.

Shane peeled off the rubber gloves he'd donned and

turned them inside out to avoid transferring the gore to his skin. "What a rush."

"It can be." Brandee released the head gate and walked out of the birthing area. "Let's get out of here so she can get up and smell her baby."

The calf still hadn't moved, but now the cow got to her feet and managed a lumbering turn. She seemed a little disengaged from what had just happened.

"She doesn't seem too interested in her baby," Shane commented, his voice low and mellow.

"Give her a minute."

And sure enough the cow ambled over to the baby and gave him a good long sniff. This seemed to stimulate the calf and he gave a little jerk, which startled the cow for a second. Then Mama gave her baby another couple sniffs and began licking.

"What do you know." Shane gently bumped against Brandee. "Looks like we did okay."

She leaned her head on his shoulder. "We sure did."

Within an hour the calf was on its feet and Brandee wanted very badly to get off hers. Several hands had swung by to check in and thumped Shane on the back when they found out he'd participated in his first calf pulling.

"I think we can leave these two for now," Brandee said, pushing away from the railing. "I really want a shower and some breakfast."

"Both sound great."

Twenty minutes later, clean and dressed in leggings and an oversize sweater, Brandee pulled her damp hair into a topknot and padded into the kitchen, where Shane had already put on a pot of coffee and was staring into the refrigerator. He hadn't noticed her arrival and she had an unguarded few seconds to stare at him.

He'd been a huge help tonight. She wondered if he still

disliked ranching as much as he had when he'd first arrived. Seeing his face light up as they'd pulled the calf free had given her such joy. She was starting to get how being partners with someone could be pretty great. Too bad there was a sinkhole the size of Hope Springs Ranch standing between them.

He must have heard her sigh because he asked, "What are you hungry for?"

He turned to look at her and she realized he was the manifestation of every longing, hope and fantasy she'd ever had. She had closed the distance and was sinking her fingers into his hair before the refrigerator door closed.

"You."

Eleven

Shane's arms locked around her as their mouths fused in a hot, frantic kiss. She was everything sweet and delicious. And sexy. He loved the way her hips moved against him as if driven by some all-consuming hunger. He sank his fingers into them and backed her against the counter.

If he'd thought she made him burn before, the soft moans that slipped out when he palmed her breast awakened a wildness he could barely contain. The big island in the kitchen had enough room for them both, but before he could lift her onto it, she shook her head.

"My room."

For an instant he froze. Over the last week, she'd made it pretty clear that her bedroom was off-limits. What had changed? He framed her face with his hands and peered into her eyes. She met his gaze with openness and trust. His heart wrenched and something broke loose inside him.

"You're the most amazing woman I've ever known,"

he murmured, dipping his head to capture her lips in a reverent kiss.

She melted into his body and he savored the plush give of her soft curves. Before the kiss could turn sizzling once more, Shane scooped Brandee off her feet and headed to her bedroom.

She'd left the nightstand lamps burning and he had no trouble finding his way to her bed. Setting her on her feet, he ripped off his T-shirt and tossed it aside. She managed to unfasten the button on his jeans before he pushed her hands aside and finished the job himself. Once he stood naked before her, he wasted little time stripping off her clothes.

Together they tumbled onto the mattress and rolled. Breathless, Shane found himself flat on his back with a smiling Brandee straddling him. Gloriously confident in her power, she cupped her breasts in her hands and lifted them in offering to him.

Shane's erection bobbed against her backside as he skimmed his palms up her rib cage and lightly pinched her tight nipples. He wanted what happened between them tonight to be something neither one would ever forget and tangled one hand in her hair to draw her mouth down to his.

Again they kissed with more tenderness than passion. The heat that had driven them earlier had given way to a curious intimacy. Shane kissed his way down her throat and sucked gently at the spot where her shoulder and neck came together. Her fingers bit into his shoulder as she shivered.

"You like that," he said, teasing the spot with his tongue and smiling at her shaky laugh.

"I like a lot of things that you do to me."

"Like this?" He brushed his hand over her abdomen.

Her thighs parted in anticipation of his touch, but he went no lower.

"Not like that," she murmured, pushing his fingers lower. "Like this." Her back arched as he slid a finger along the folds that concealed her intimate warmth. "Almost, but not quite…there."

Her shudder drove his willpower to the brink. Sensing she'd rush him if he let her, Shane eased down her body, gliding his mouth over the swell of one breast, and then the other. Brandee's fingers sifted through his hair as she sighed in pleasure.

But when his tongue drew damp patterns on her belly, she tensed, guessing his destination. His mouth found her without the preliminaries he usually observed. This time he wasn't here to seduce, only to push her over the edge hard.

Her body bowed as he lapped at her. A moan of intense pleasure ripped from her throat. The sound pierced him and drove his own passion higher. In the last week he'd learned what she liked and leveraged every bit of knowledge to wring his name from her lips over and over.

With her body still shaking in the aftermath of her climax, she directed him to her nightstand and an unopened box of condoms. The sight of it made him smile. She'd been planning to invite him to her room. This meant that her walls were crumbling, if only a little. Was he close to winning their bet?

The thought chilled him. If she fell in love with him and he took away the ranch that meant so much to her, would she ever be able to forgive him?

He slid on the condom and kissed his way up her body. She clung to him as he settled between her thighs and brought his lips to hers for a deep, hot kiss. Her foot skimmed up the back of his leg as she met his gaze. Then she opened herself for his possession. He thrust into her, his heart expanding at the vulnerability in her expression.

She pumped her hips, taking him all the way in, and he hissed through his teeth as her muscles contracted around him. For a long second he held still, breathing raggedly. Then he began to move, sliding out of her slowly, savoring every bit of friction.

"Let's go, Delgado," she urged, her nails digging into his back. She wrapped her leg around his hip, making his penetration a little deeper, and rocked to urge him on.

"You feel amazing." At the end of another slow thrust, he lightly bit her shoulder and she moaned. "I could go like this all night." He was lying.

Already he could feel pleasure tightening in his groin. He was climbing too fast toward orgasm. He surged into her, his strokes steady and deep, then quickening as he felt her body tighten around him. She was gasping for air, hands clamped down hard on his biceps as they began to climax nearly at the same moment. He'd discovered timing his orgasm to hers required very little attention on his part. It was as if some instinct allowed their bodies to sync.

But tonight Shane grit his teeth and held off so he could watch Brandee come. It was a perfect moment, and in a lightning flash of clarity, he realized that he'd gone and done it. He'd fallen for her. Hard. Caught off guard by the shock of it, Shane's orgasm overcame him, and as his whole body clenched with it, pleasure bursting inside him, a shift occurred in his perception.

This was no longer a woman climaxing beneath him, but his woman. He couldn't imagine his life without her in it. He wanted her in his bed. Riding beside him on a horse. Laughing, teasing, working. Yes, even working. He wanted to be with her all the time.

Stunned by what he'd just admitted to himself, Shane

lay on his back and stared at the ceiling while Brandee settled against his side, her arm draped over his chest, her breath puffing against his neck. Contentment saturated bone, muscle and sinew, rendering him incapable of movement, but his brain continued to whirl.

Brandee was already asleep, her deep, regular breathing dragging him toward slumber. Yet, despite his exhaustion, something nagged at him. As perfect as their lovemaking had been, there was a final piece of unfinished business that lay between them.

Leaving Brandee slumbering, Shane eased out of bed. He needed to do this while his thoughts were clear. He suspected doubts would muddy his motivation all too soon.

The first night he'd arrived, she'd shown him the two contracts. He'd taken both copies to his lawyer to make sure there was nothing tricky buried in the language. Turned out, it had been straightforward. If he signed the paperwork, he agreed to give up all claim to the land. If she signed, she agreed to sell him the land for ten million.

Several times in the last two weeks, she'd reminded him that his contract awaited his signature in her office. He headed there now. Turning on the desk light, he found a pen and set his signature to the document with a flourish.

As he added the date, it occurred to him he was declaring that he'd fallen for her. Opening himself up to rejection like this wasn't something he did. Usually he was the one making a break for it as soon as the woman he was dating started getting ideas.

Except Brandee wasn't like the women he usually went for. She was more like him. Fiercely independent. Relentlessly self-protective. And stubborn as all get-out.

Shane reached across the desk and turned off the lamp. A second after Brandee's office plunged back into darkness, her cell phone lit up. The text message caught his eye.

Pay up tomorrow or Delgado gets your land back.

Shane stared at the message in confusion. "Your land back"? Those three words made no sense. And what was this about "pay up tomorrow"? As far as Shane knew, Brandee owned the land outright. Could there be a lien on the property he didn't know about? Shane was still puzzling about the text as he sat down in Brandee's chair, once again turned on the lamp and pulled open her file drawer.

Her organizational skills betrayed her. A hanging file bearing his name hung in alphabetical order among files for property taxes, credit card and bank statements, as well as sketches for her upcoming clothing line. Shane pulled out his file and spread the pages across the desk.

His heart stopped when he saw the birth certificates going back several generations. He reviewed the copy of Jasper Crowley's legal document that made the Hope Springs Ranch land his daughter's dowry. After reading through the newspaper clippings and retracing his ancestry, Shane understood. Brandee intended to cheat him out of the land that should belong to his family.

Leaving everything behind, he returned to the bedroom to wake Brandee and demand answers. But when he got to the room, he stopped dead and stared at her sleeping form. He loved her. That was why he'd signed the document.

Not one thing his father had ever said to him had hurt as much as finding out he'd fallen in love with a woman who was using him.

Torn between confronting her and getting the hell away before he did something else he'd regret, Shane snatched his clothes off the floor and headed for the back door. He slid his feet into his boots, grabbed his coat with his truck keys and went out into the night.

* * *

Brandee woke to a sense of well-being and the pleasant ache of worn muscles. She lay on her side, tucked into a warm cocoon of sheets and quilts. Her bedroom was still dark. The time on her alarm clock was 5:43 a.m.

The room's emptiness struck her. There was no warm, rugged male snoring softly beside her. She didn't need to reach out her hand to know Shane's side of the bed was cool and unoccupied. After the night they'd shared, she didn't blame him for bolting before sunrise. The sex had been amazing. They'd dropped their guards after the difficult calf birthing, permitting a deeper connection than they'd yet experienced.

Part of her wanted to jump out of bed and run to find him. She longed to see the same soul-stirring emotion she'd glimpsed in his eyes last night. But would it be there? In her gut, she knew he felt something for her. No doubt he was as uncomfortable at being momentarily exposed as she'd been.

As much as she'd grown accustomed to having him around and had put aside her fierce independence to let him help, she was terrified to admit, even to herself, that she craved his companionship as much as his passionate lovemaking. But was it worth losing her ranch?

Brandee threw off the covers and went to shower. Fifteen minutes later, dressed in jeans and a loose-fitting sweater, she headed for the kitchen, hoping the lure of freshly made coffee would entice Shane.

And she'd decided to come clean about Maverick, Hope Springs Ranch and the blackmail.

Over a hearty breakfast, she would explain her fear of losing the ranch and see if he would agree to letting her keep it for now as long as she agreed to leave it to him in her will.

While she waited for the coffee to brew, Brandee headed to her office to get the document Maverick had sent to her as well as the ones she'd found during her research. Dawn was breaking and Brandee could see her desk well enough to spy the papers strewn across it. She approached and her heart jerked painfully as she realized what she was staring at.

With her stomach twisted into knots, Brandee raced from the room and headed straight for her guest suite. The room was empty. Next she dashed to the back door. Shane's coat and boots were gone. So was his truck. Her knees were shaking so badly she had to sit down on the bench in the mudroom to catch her breath.

No wonder he'd left so abruptly during the night. He knew. Everything. She'd failed to save her ranch. She'd hurt the man she loved.

It took almost ten minutes for Brandee to recover sufficiently to return to her office and confront the damning documents. How had he known to go into her filing cabinet and look for the file she'd made on him? Had he suspected something was wrong? Or had Maverick tipped him off early?

The answer was on her phone. A text message from Maverick warning her time was almost up. But how had Shane seen it? She gathered the research materials together and returned them to the file. It was then that she noticed Shane's signature on the document revoking his claim to her land.

She'd won.

It didn't matter if Shane knew. Legally he couldn't take her ranch away from her.

But morally, he had every right to it.

Brandee picked up the document. While the disclosure she'd been about to make was no longer necessary, the solution she'd intended to propose was still a valid one.

Brandee grabbed the document and her coat and headed for her truck. As she drove to Bullseye, the clawing anxiety of her upcoming confrontation warred with her determination to fix the situation. It might be more difficult now that he'd discovered she'd been lying to him all along before she had a chance to confess, but Shane was a businessman. He'd understand the value of her compromise and weigh it against an expensive court battle.

Yet, as she stood in the chilly morning air on his front steps, her optimism took a nosedive. Shane left her waiting so long before answering his doorbell that she wondered if he was going to refuse to see her. When he opened the door, he was showered and dressed in a tailored business suit, a stony expression on his face.

She held up the document he'd signed and ignored the anxious twisting of her stomach. "We need to talk about this."

"There's nothing to talk about. You won. I signed. You get to keep the ranch."

Brandee floundered. On the way over, she hadn't dwelled on how Shane might be hurt by her actions. She'd been thinking about how to convince him of her plan so they both got what they wanted.

"I didn't win. And there's plenty more to talk about. I know what you must think of me—"

He interrupted, "I highly doubt that."

"You think I tricked you. You'd be right. But if I lose the ranch, I lose everything." Immediately she saw this tack wasn't going to be effective. So, maybe she could give him some idea of what she was up against. "Look, I was being blackmailed, okay? Somebody named Maverick sent me the Jasper Crowley document."

"That's your story?" Shane obviously didn't believe her. "You're being blackmailed?"

"Maverick wanted fifty thousand dollars and for me to resign from the Texas Cattleman's Club." To Brandee's ears the whole thing sounded ridiculous. She couldn't imagine what would convince Shane she was telling the truth. "I should've done as I was asked, but I really thought it was…"

Telling him that she suspected Cecelia, Simone and Naomi wasn't going to make her story sound any more sympathetic. Shane liked those women. Brandee would only come off as petty and insecure if she accused them of blackmail without a shred of proof.

"Look," she continued, "I should've come clean in the beginning. Maybe we could've worked something out." She took a step closer, willing him to understand how afraid she'd been. "But when I proposed the wager, I didn't know anything about you except that for years you've been after me to sell. I didn't think I could trust you."

"Were you ever going to tell me the truth?"

The fear of opening herself up to rejection and ridicule once again clamped its ruthless fingers around her throat. "Last night…" She needed to say more, but the words wouldn't come.

"What about last night?"

"It was great," she said in a small voice, barely able to gather enough breath to make herself heard.

"You say that after I signed away my rights to *my family's* land."

Why had he? He could have torn up the agreement after finding out he owned the land, but he hadn't. He'd left it for her to find. Why would he do that?

"Not because of that," she said, reaching deep for the strength to say what was in her heart. "I say it because I think I might have fallen in love with you."

His face remained impassive, except at the corner of his

eyes where the muscles twitched. "Is this the part where I say I'm not going to pursue legal action against you?"

She floundered, wondering if that was what he intended. "No, this is me talking to you without this between us." She tore the document he'd signed down the middle, lined the pieces back up and tore them again.

"Is that supposed to impress me? Do you think that document would've stood up in court?"

Brandee hung her head. "It was never supposed to get that far."

"I imagine you were pretty confident you could get away with cheating me," Shane said, the icy bite of his voice making her flinch.

"I wasn't confident at all. And I wasn't happy about it. But the ranch is everything to me. Not just financially, but also it's my father's legacy. And the camp could have done so much good." Brandee ached with all she'd lost. "But I am truly sorry about the way I handled things. I didn't do it to hurt you."

He stared at her in silence for several heartbeats before stepping back.

"You didn't."

And then the door swung shut in her face.

Twelve

Five days and four long, empty, aching nights after Shane slammed the door in Brandee's face, he slid onto the open bar stool beside Gabe at the Texas Cattleman's Club and ordered a cup of coffee.

Ignoring the bartender's surprise, he growled at his friend, "Okay, you got me here. What's so damned important?"

Gabe nodded toward a table in the corner. A familiar blonde sat by herself, hunched over an empty glass. Brandee's long hair fell loosely about her face, hiding her expression, but there was no misreading her body language. She was as blue as a girl could be.

"Yeah, so?" Shane wasn't feeling particularly charitable at the moment and didn't have time to be dragged away from The Bellamy. He had his own problems to contend with.

"You don't think there's something wrong with that picture?" Gabe nodded his head in Brandee's direction.

There was a lot of something wrong, but it wasn't Shane's problem.

"Tell me that's not why you dragged me here. Because if it is, you've just wasted an hour of my time."

Gabe's eyes widened at Shane's tone. "I think you should talk to her."

"As I explained yesterday and the day before and the day before that, I'm done talking about what happened. She screwed me over."

"In order to keep her ranch," Gabe replied, his quiet, calm voice in marked contrast to Shane's sharp tone. "She stood to lose everything. How would you have behaved if the situation was reversed and you were about to lose Bullseye?"

It wasn't a fair comparison.

"I'd say good riddance." Shane sipped his coffee and stared at the bottles arranged behind the bar. "I would've sold it years ago if I thought it wouldn't upset my mom."

"You don't mean that."

"I do."

Or he mostly did. Ranching had been in his father's blood and Shane associated Bullseye with being bullied and criticized. Every memory of his father came with an accompanying ache. He'd never be the rancher his father wanted. In some ways it had been a relief when Landon had died. There, he'd admitted it. But by admitting it, he'd lived up to his father's poor opinion of him. He was a bad son. Guilt sharpened the pain until it felt like spikes were being driven into his head.

"I've never seen you like this." Gabe leaned back in his seat as if he needed to take a better look at his friend. "You're really upset."

"You're damned right," Shane said. "She intended to cheat me out of what belongs to my family."

"But you said the land was unclaimed…"

"And what really gets me—" Shane was a boulder rolling down a steep grade "—is the way she went about it."

She'd made him fall in love with her. There. He'd admitted that, too. He was in love with Brandee Lawless, the liar and cheat.

Shane signaled the bartender. Maybe something strong was in order. "Give me a shot of Patrón Silver."

She'd ruined scotch for him. He couldn't even smell the stuff without remembering the way she'd tasted of it the first night they'd made love. Or her delight when he'd introduced her to the proper way to drink it. And his surprise when she'd poured a shot of it over him and lapped up every drop.

Shane downed the tequila shot and signaled for another.

"Are you planning on going head down on the table, too?" Gabe's tone had a mild bite.

"Maybe." But instead of drinking the second shot, Shane stared at it. "You gonna sit around and watch me do it, or are you going to make sure she gets home safe?"

"I've already taken care of Brandee." Gabe nodded his head toward the entrance, where Chelsea had appeared. "If you feel like drowning your sorrows, I'll stick around to drive you home."

Shane rotated the glass and contemplated it. He'd spent the last four nights soaking his hurt feelings in alcohol and after waking up that morning with a whopping hangover had decided he was done moping. He pushed the shot away.

"No need. I'm getting out of here."

But before he could leave, Chelsea had gotten Brandee to her feet and the two women were heading toward the door. Despite how Brandee had looked staring morosely into the bottom of her glass, she wasn't at all unsteady on her feet.

Not wanting to risk bumping into her, Shane stayed where he was and turned his back to the departing women. He couldn't risk her or anyone else noticing the way his hungry gaze followed her. She'd ditched her jeans and was wearing another of those gauzy, romantic numbers that blew his mind. This one was pale pink and made her look as if a strong wind could carry her all the way to Austin. Gut-kicked and frustrated that she still got to him, he reminded himself that she was strong, independent and could take care of herself.

"Look at you three sitting here all smug and self-important." Brandee's voice rang out and conversations hushed. "Well, congratulations, you got your way."

Gabe caught Shane's eye and gave him a quizzical look. "Any idea why she's going after Cecilia, Simone and Naomi?"

With an abrupt shake of his head, Shane returned to staring at his untouched drink, but he was far less interested in it than he was the scene playing out behind him.

"I'm not going to be around to oppose you any longer. I've resigned from the Texas Cattleman's Club. It's all yours." Brandee didn't sound intoxicated exactly. More hysterical and overwrought than anything.

"We don't know what you're—" Cecelia Morgan began, only to be interrupted.

"Where do you three get off ruining other people's lives?"

The entire room was quiet and Brandee's voice bounced off the walls. None of the women answered and Brandee rambled on.

"You must have thought it would be great fun, but blackmail is an ugly business. And it will come back to bite you in the ass."

At the mention of blackmail, Shane turned around in

time to see Brandee push herself back from the table where she'd been looming over the three women. They were all staring at Brandee in openmouthed shock and fear.

Brandee punched the air with her finger. "Mark my words."

As Chelsea tugged Brandee toward the exit, the trio of women erupted in nervous laughter.

"I don't know what that was about," Simone said, her voice pitched to carry around the room. "Obviously she's finally snapped."

"It was only a matter of time," Naomi agreed, tossing her head before sipping her fruity drink.

Only Cecelia refrained from commenting. She stared after Brandee and Chelsea, her eyes narrowed and a pensive expression on her beautiful face. Moments later, however, she joined her friends in a loud replay of the clash. Around them, side conversations buzzed. News of Brandee's behavior and her wild accusations would spread through the TCC community before morning.

"She thinks those three blackmailed her?" Gabe glanced at Shane. "Did you know she was planning to resign from the TCC?"

"I don't know why she needed to. I signed her damned document giving up my right to the ranch." Yet, when Brandee had come to his house to apologize, he had refused her attempt to make amends.

"You said she tore it up."

"Well, yeah." Guilt flared. But Shane refused to accept blame for Brandee's overwrought state. "None of that had anything to do with me."

"That—" Gabe gestured at the departing women "—has everything to do with you." His features settled into grim lines. "Of all the times you should have come through and helped someone."

"What's that supposed to mean?"

Gabe looked unfazed by Shane's belligerent tone. "Everybody thinks you're a great guy. You make sure of that. You've always been the life of the party. But when it comes to helping out…" The former Texas Ranger shook his head.

Shane heard the echoes of his father's criticism in Gabe's words and bristled. "Why don't you come right out and say it? No one can count on me when it comes to things that need doing."

"Mostly you're good at getting other people to do stuff."

Shane recalled the expression on Megan Maguire's face when she'd spotted him helping out with Brandee's teen day. She'd been surprised.

And if he was honest with himself, Brandee's tactics to hold on to her land weren't all that different from his own way of doing things. He'd held back important information a time or two. And what Gabe had said about his getting other people to volunteer when there was work to be done…

Growing up, his father had accused him of being lazy and Shane had resented it, despite knowing there was a bit of truth to it. So, what was he supposed to do? Change who he was? He was thirty-five years old and far too accustomed to doing things his way.

"How is it I'm the bad guy all of a sudden?" Shane demanded. "And where do you get off making judgments about me?"

"I just want to point out that while Brandee may have manipulated you, it's not like you haven't done the same to others. She's not perfect. You're not perfect. But from watching you both, you might be perfect together."

And with that, Gabe pushed away from the bar and headed out, abandoning Shane to a head filled with recriminations and a hollow feeling in his gut.

* * *

It took until Brandee was seated in Chelsea's car before the full import of what she'd just done hit her. By the time Chelsea slid behind the wheel, Brandee had planted her face in her hands and was muttering incoherent curses.

As she felt the car begin to move forward, Brandee lifted her head and glared at her best friend. "Why didn't you stop me?"

"Are you kidding?" Chelsea smirked. "You said what half the membership has been dying to. Did you see the look on their faces?"

The brisk walk across the chilly parking lot had done much to clear Brandee's head, but she was still pretty foggy. When was the last time she'd had this much to drink? She didn't even know how many she'd had.

"All I saw was red." Brandee groaned and set her head against the cool window. "Take me to the airport. I'm going to get on a plane and fly to someplace no one has ever heard of."

Chelsea chuckled. "Are you kidding? You're going to be a hero."

"No, I'm not. No one deserves to be talked to like that. I run..." She gulped. Hope Springs Camp was an impossibility now that Shane knew he owned her ranch. "I had hoped to run a camp that gave teenagers the skills to cope with their problems in a sensible, positive way. And what do I do? I stand in the middle of the Texas Cattleman's Club and shriek at those three like a drunken fishwife." The sounds coming from the seat beside her did not improve Brandee's mood. "Stop laughing."

"I'm sorry, but they deserved it. Especially if any one or all three is Maverick."

"Do you really think it's possible they're behind the blackmail?"

"I think someone needs to look into it."

"Well, it isn't going to be me. I'm going to be sitting on a beach, sipping something fruity and strong."

"You'll get a new guy? He'll have it going on?"

Despite her calamitous exit from the TCC clubhouse, Brandee gave a snort of amusement as Chelsea twisted the Dierks Bentley song lyrics from "Somewhere on a Beach" to suit the conversation. Then, despite her dire circumstances and the fact that she'd just humiliated herself, Brandee picked up the next line and in moments the two girls were singing at the top of their lungs.

They kept it up all the way to Chelsea's house, where Brandee had agreed to spend the night. She couldn't bear to be alone in her beautiful custom-tailored ranch home that she would soon have to pack up and move out of.

Tucked into a corner of Chelsea's couch, wrapped in a blanket with a mug of hot chocolate cradled in her hands, Brandee stared at the melting mini marshmallows and turned the corner on her situation. It wasn't as if it was the first time she'd lost everything. And in the scheme of things, she was a lot better off than she'd been at eighteen, broke and living out of her car.

"I guess I get to re-create myself again," she said, noticing the first hint of determination she'd felt in days.

"I think you should fight for your ranch. Take Shane to court and make him prove the land belongs to him."

Brandee didn't think she had the strength to take Shane on in a legal battle. She was still too raw from the way he'd slammed the door in her face.

"I'll think about it."

Chelsea regarded her in concern. "It isn't like you to give up like this."

"I know, but I'm not sure."

"Brandee, you can't just walk away from a ten-million-dollar property."

"It sounds crazy when you say it, but that's what I intend to do. Legally I might be able to get a court to determine the land is mine, but I think morally it belongs to Shane's family."

"What are you going to do?"

"Sell everything and start over?" The thought pained her more than she wanted to admit, but in the last five days she'd come to terms with her loss. "I wasn't kidding about finding a beach somewhere and getting lost."

"You can't seriously be thinking of leaving Royal?"

The pang in Chelsea's voice made Brandee wince. "I don't know that I want to stay here after everything that's happened." Just the thought of running into Shane and seeing his coldness toward her made her blood freeze. "Look, it's not like I have to do anything today. It's going to take me a while to sell my herd and settle things on the ranch. With The Bellamy still under construction and taking up all his energy, Shane isn't going to have time to start developing the ranch right away."

"And maybe you and Shane can work out an arrangement that will benefit you both."

"Did you see the way he acted as if I didn't exist?" Brandee shook her head, fighting back the misery that was her constant companion these days. "No, he hates me for what I tried to do to him and there's no going back from that."

"Now, aren't you glad we warned you off of Brandee Lawless?"

"Did you see how she spoke to us?"

"I think she had too much to drink. And happy hour's barely started."

"I've said from the beginning that she has no class."

"She must've had a reason for going after you," Shane said.

He recalled what had happened to Wesley Jackson, and thought there'd been some buzz around the clubhouse that Cecelia had been behind it. An anonymous hacker had exposed Wes as a deadbeat dad on social media and it had blown a major business deal for him. What had happened to Brandee was in the same vein.

"She's been out to get us from the moment we joined the Texas Cattleman's Club."

"That's not true," Shane said, a hint of warning in his tone. "She just hasn't bought into what you want to do with the place. A lot of people haven't."

"But she's been actively working to drum up resistance," Naomi said.

"That doesn't make her your enemy." Shane shook his head. "Not everyone wants the clubhouse to undergo any more changes, especially not the kind you're interested in making."

"Well, it doesn't matter anymore. She resigned her membership."

"And with her gone, the others will come around," Cecelia said. "You'll see."

"Sounds like everything is going your way." Shane set his hands on their table the way Brandee had and leaned forward to eye each woman in turn. "If I find out any of you three were behind what happened to Brandee, you'll have to answer to me."

He loomed menacingly for several heartbeats, taking in each startled expression in turn. Instinctively, they'd leaned back in their chairs as if gaining even a small amount of distance would keep them safe. At long last, satisfied they'd received his message, he pushed upright, jostling the table just enough to set their cutlery tingling and their drinks sloshing.

"Ladies." With a nod, he headed for the exit.

Icy gusts blew across the parking lot as Shane emerged from the clubhouse. He faced the north wind and lifted his hat, not realizing how angry he'd been until he dashed sweat from his brow. Damn Brandee for making him rush to defend her. He should've left well enough alone.

The cold reduced his body temperature to normal as he headed toward his truck. A row back and a few spaces over, he caught sight of her vehicle.

"Great."

Now he'd have to make sure she wasn't driving in her condition. But the truck was empty. Brandee was long gone. Shane headed to his own truck.

As he drove the familiar roads on his way to The Bellamy, he tried to put Brandee out of his thoughts, but couldn't shake the image of her going after Cecelia, Simone and Naomi. The outburst had shocked more than a few people.

Brandee's public face was vastly different from the one she showed in private. Not once in all the years that he'd pursued her to sell the ranch had she ever cracked and lost her temper with him. Because of her cool, composed manner, he'd worked extra hard to get beneath her skin. From getting to know her these last two weeks, he recognized that she put a lot of energy into maintaining a professional image. It was why she was so well respected at the male-dominated Texas Cattleman's Club.

Today, she'd blown that. Her words came back to him. Why had she quit the TCC? Did she really think he had any intention of taking her ranch? Then he thought about how she'd torn up the document he'd signed, relinquishing his claim. The damned woman was so stubborn she probably figured she'd turn the place over to him regardless of what he wanted.

And if she did? What would she do? Where would she go? The ranch was everything to her. With her capital tied up in her land and her cows, she probably figured she'd have to downsize her herd in order to start over.

After checking to make sure everything was on track at The Bellamy, he headed home and was surprised to see his mother's car as well as a catering van in the driveway. Shane parked his truck, drawing a blank. He was pretty sure he'd remember if there was a party scheduled.

When it hit him, he cursed, belatedly remembering he'd promised his mother to help her make catering decisions this afternoon for the party being held in four weeks to celebrate Bullseye's hundred-year anniversary. He'd neglected to add the appointment to his calendar any of the four times she'd reminded him of the event.

He rushed into the house and found everything set up in the dining room. "Hello, Mother." He circled the table to kiss the cheek she offered him.

"You're late," she scolded, more annoyed than she sounded.

The way she looked, he was going to need a drink. "I'm sorry."

"Well, at least you're here now, so we can begin."

Until that second, Shane had been hoping that his mother had already sampled everything and made her decisions. Now he regarded the food spread over every available inch of table and groaned. The appetizers ran the gamut from individual ribs glazed in sweet-smelling barbecue sauce to ornate pastries begging to be tasted. Three champagne flutes sat before Elyse. She gestured toward the dining chair nearest her with a fourth glass.

"Vincent, please pour my son some champagne so he can give his opinion on the two I'm deciding between."

"I'm sure whatever you decide is fine," Shane said, edging backward. He was in no mood to sit through an elaborate tasting.

"You will sit down and you will help me decide what we are going to serve at your party."

If her tone hadn't been so severe, he might have protested that the party hadn't been his idea and he couldn't care less what they served. But since he'd already alienated Gabe today and ruined any hope of future happiness with the woman he loved several days earlier, Shane decided he needed at least one person in his corner.

It took a half an hour to taste everything and another fifteen minutes for them to narrow it down to ten items. Elyse generously included several selections Shane preferred that she'd described as too basic. He wondered if she gave him his way in appreciation of his help tonight or if it was a ploy to make him more pliable the next time she asked for his assistance.

And then he wondered why he was questioning his mother's motives. Was this what playing games had turned him into? Had he become suspicious of his own mother?

And what about Brandee? Was she solely to blame for the way she'd tried to trick him? If he'd been more like Gabe, honest and aboveboard, might she have come to him and negotiated a settlement that would have benefited both of them? Instead, because he liked to play games, she'd played one on him.

"I'm sorry I forgot about today," he told his mother as Vincent packed up his edibles and returned the kitchen to its usual pristine state.

She sipped champagne and sighed. "I should be used to it by now."

Shane winced. With Gabe's lecture foremost in his thoughts, he asked, "Am I really that bad when it comes to getting out of doing things?"

"You're my son. And I love you." She reached out and patted his hand. "But when it comes to doing something you'd rather avoid, you're not very reliable."

It hurt more than he imagined it would to hear his mother say those words. Realizing he wasn't his mother's golden child humbled Shane. "Dad yelled at me about that all the time, but you never said a word."

"Your father was very hard on you and it certainly decreased your willingness to help around the ranch. You didn't need to feel ganged up on."

From where he was sitting, he could see the informal family portrait taken when he'd been seventeen. His father stood with his arm around his beaming wife and looked happy, while Shane's expression was slightly resentful. He'd always hated it because he was supposed to be on a hunting trip with friends the weekend the photo shoot had been scheduled. The photo seemed to sum up how he'd felt since he was ten.

Mother and son chatted for over an hour after the caterer departed about Elyse's upcoming trip to Boston for her brother Gavin's surprise sixty-fifth birthday party. She and Gavin's wife, Jennifer, were planning a tropical-themed bash because Gavin was also retiring at the end of the month and he and Jennifer were going to Belize to look at vacation properties.

"I need to get going," Elyse said, glancing at her watch. "I promised Jennifer I would call her to firm up the last few details for Gavin's party." She got to her feet and deposited a kiss on Shane's cheek. "Thank you for helping me today."

"It was my pleasure." And in fact, once he got over

his initial reluctance, he'd enjoyed spending time with his mom, doing something she took great pride in. "Your party-planning skills are second to none and the centennial is going to be fantastic. Let me know what else I can do to help you."

His mother didn't try to hide her surprise. "You mean that?"

"I do. Send me a list. I'll get it done."

"Thank you," she said, kissing him on the cheek.

After his mom left, Shane remembered something else he'd been putting off. His keys jingled as he trotted down the steps to the driveway. He needed to pick up his stuff from Brandee's. He'd been in such a hurry to leave that he hadn't taken anything with him.

He didn't expect to see her truck in the driveway and it wasn't. It was nearly seven o'clock. The sun was below the horizon and a soft glow from the living room lights filled the front windows. Shane got out of his truck and headed for the front door, remembering the first time he'd stepped onto her porch two weeks ago. So much had happened. So much had gone wrong.

First he tried the doorbell, but when that went unanswered, he tried knocking. Was she avoiding him? Or had she come home, consumed more alcohol and passed out? Shane decided he needed to see for himself that she was okay and used the key she'd given him to unlock the door.

As he stepped across her threshold, he half expected her to come tearing toward him, shrieking at him to get out. Of course, that wasn't her style. Or he hadn't thought it was until he'd witnessed her going after Cecelia, Simone and Naomi today.

He needn't have worried. The house had an unoccupied feel to it.

A quick look around confirmed Brandee hadn't come

home. Shane headed to the guest suite and was surprised to find none of his things had been touched. Moving quickly, he packed up his toiletries and clothes. He kept his gaze away from the luxurious shower and the big, comfortable bed. Already a lump had formed in his throat that had no business being there. He swallowed hard and cursed.

What the hell had he expected? That they would live happily-ever-after? Even before he found out she'd been keeping the truth from him about the ranch, that ending hadn't been in the cards. All along Brandee had said she didn't need anyone's help. She'd never wanted a partner or a long-term lover. They might have enjoyed each other's company for a while, but in the end both of them were too independent and afraid of intimacy for it to have worked.

Eager to be gone, Shane strode toward the front door, but as he reached it, a familiar ringtone began playing from the direction of the kitchen. He stopped walking and, with a resigned sigh, turned toward the sound. Brandee had left her smartphone on the large concrete island.

Though he knew he should just leave well enough alone, Shane headed to check out who might be calling. Brandee always made a point of being available to her ranch hands and with her not being home, they would have no way of knowing how to get in contact with her.

Shane leaned over and peered at the screen. Sure enough, it was her ranch foreman. Now Shane had two choices. He could get ahold of Chelsea and see if Brandee was staying there, or he could find out what was up and then call Chelsea.

"Hey, Jimmy," Shane said, deciding to answer the call. "Brandee isn't around at the moment. She left her phone behind. Is there something you need?"

"Is she planning on coming back soon?"

Shane recalled how she'd looked earlier. "I doubt it. She

went into town and I think she might be staying the night at Chelsea's. Is there something wrong?"

"Not wrong, but we've got a half-dozen cows showing signs of calving and she said if we needed her to help out tonight to call. But it's okay, we'll make do."

As Jimmy was speaking, Shane's gaze fell on something he hadn't noticed before. A large poster was tacked on the wall near the door to the mudroom. It held pictures of all the teenagers and their dogs surrounding a big, glittery thank-you in the middle. It was a gaudy, glorious mess and Shane knew that Brandee loved it.

He closed his eyes to block out the sight. Brandee didn't have to give her time or energy to a bunch of troubled kids, but she did it because even small events like the one with the rescue dogs had the power to change lives. He'd seen firsthand how her program had impacted each of the teens in some way, and with her camp she was poised to do so much more.

"Why don't I stop down and give you a hand." The last thing he wanted was to spend an endless, freezing night outside, but he knew it was the right thing to do.

"That would be a big help." Jimmy sounded relieved. "But are you sure? Between the cold and the number of cows ready to go, it's going to be a long, miserable night."

"I'm sure. See you in ten."

The way Shane was feeling at the moment, he was going to be miserable regardless. And to his surprise, as he headed back to the guest suite to change into work clothes, his mood felt significantly lighter. Maybe there was something to this helping-others thing after all.

Thirteen

Brandee came awake with a jolt and groped for her cell phone. Jimmy was supposed to check in with her last night and let her know if he needed her help with the calving. Had she slept through his call? That had never happened before.

Yet here she was, six short days after her reckoning with Shane, and already she was disengaging from her ranch. Had she really given up on her dream so easily? She couldn't imagine her father being very proud of her for doing so. And yet what choice did she have? All her capital was tied up in the land and her livestock. With the land returned to Shane, she didn't have a place for her cows and calves. It only made sense to sell them.

When she didn't find her phone on the nightstand, she realized why. This wasn't her room. She'd spent the night at Chelsea's after making a scene at the Texas Cattleman's Club. Brandee buried her face in the pillow and groaned.

She hadn't been anywhere near drunk, but her blood had been up and she'd consumed one drink too many.

Thank goodness she'd never have to set foot in the clubhouse again. Of course, that didn't mean she wouldn't be running into members elsewhere. Maybe she could hide out for a month or so while she settled her business with the ranch stock and figured out what to do next.

Should she move away from Royal? The thought triggered gut-wrenching loneliness and crippling anxiety. She couldn't leave behind so many wonderful friends. Two weeks ago, she might have considered herself self-sufficient, but after living with Shane she realized she was way needier than she'd let herself believe.

After sliding out of bed and feeling around the floor, Brandee broke down and turned on the bedside light. Her cell phone wasn't beneath the bed or lost among the sheets. Feeling a stir of panic, she considered all the places she might've left it.

A quick glance at the clock told her it was six o'clock in the morning. Too early for Chelsea to be awake, and Brandee would not borrow her friend's computer to check on her phone's location without permission. She could, however, use Chelsea's landline to call her foreman.

He answered after the third ring. "Hey, boss."

"I can't find my phone. I'm sorry I didn't check in sooner. Is everything okay?"

"It was a pretty crazy night, but me and the boys handled it."

"That's great to hear. I'm sorry I wasn't there to help you out."

"It's okay. Shane said you were staying the night at Chelsea's."

A jolt of adrenaline shot through her at Jimmy's words.

"How is it you spoke with Shane?" Annoyance flared. Was he already taking over her ranch?

"He answered your phone when I called."

"Did he say how he'd gotten my phone?" Had she left it in the parking lot of the Texas Cattleman's Club?

"He said you left it at your house." Jimmy's voice held concern. "You okay?"

For a long moment Brandee was so incensed she couldn't speak. What the hell was Shane doing in her house? "I'm fine. I need to get my truck and then I'll be by. Maybe an hour and a half, two hours tops." Cooling her heels for an hour until it was reasonable to wake Chelsea was not going to improve her temper.

"No rush. As I said, we have everything under control."

To keep herself busy, Brandee made coffee and foraged in Chelsea's pantry for breakfast. She wasn't accustomed to sitting still, and this brought home just how hard it was going to be to give up her ranch.

As seven o'clock rolled around, she brought a cup of coffee to Chelsea's bedside and gently woke her friend.

"What time is it?"

"Seven." Brandee winced at Chelsea's groan. "I made coffee," she said in her most beguiling voice.

"How long have you been up?"

"An hour." She bounced a little on the springy mattress.

"And how much coffee have you had?"

She extended the coffee so the aroma could rouse Chelsea. "This is the last cup."

"You drank an entire pot of coffee?"

"I didn't have anything else to do. I left my phone at home and didn't want to use your computer. I think the boys had a rough night and need me back at the ranch."

Chelsea lifted herself into a sitting position and reached

for the coffee. "Give me ten minutes to wake up and I'll take you to your truck."

"Thank you." She didn't explain about how Jimmy had spoken with Shane or the anxiety that overwhelmed her at the thought of him giving orders to her hands.

An hour later, Brandee had picked up her truck, driven home, changed clothes and was on the way to the ranch buildings. A familiar vehicle was parked beside the barn where they kept the cows and calves who needed special attention. Brandee pulled up alongside and shut off her engine. It ticked, cooling as she stared toward the barn.

What was Shane doing here?

Brandee slid from the truck and entered the barn. She found Shane standing in front of the large enclosure that housed the breeched calf they'd brought into the world. He stood with his arms on the top rail of the pen, his chin resting on his hands.

"Hey," she said softly, stepping up beside him and matching his posture. "What are you doing here?"

"Jimmy said these two are ready to head to the pasture today."

"So you came to say goodbye?" The question didn't come out light and unconcerned the way she'd intended. Anxiety and melancholy weighed down her voice.

"Something like that."

Since Brandee didn't know what to make of his mood, she held her tongue and waited him out. She had nothing new to say and reprising her apology wouldn't win her any points. The silence stretched. She could ask him again why he'd come out to the ranch or she could demand to know why he'd entered her house without asking.

He probably figured he was entitled to come and go anytime he wanted since the land beneath the house belonged to him. Frustration built up a head of steam and she took a deep breath, preparing to unleash it. But before she could utter a word, Shane pushed away from the fence.

"I'd better go." He looked into her eyes, tugged at the brim of his hat in a mock salute and turned away.

Deflated, Brandee watched him go. She couldn't shake the feeling that she'd missed an opportunity to say or do something that would span the gap between them. Which was ridiculous. Shane hated her. She'd tricked him into giving up all claim to his family's land and he would never forgive her.

Her throat closed around a lump and suddenly she couldn't catch her breath. Tears collected and she wiped at the corners of her eyes before the moisture could spill down her cheeks. All at once she was twelve again and hearing the news that her dad was dead. Faced with an equally uncertain future, she'd gotten on her horse and rode off.

She'd ridden all day, tracing the familiar paths that she'd traveled beside her dad. At first she'd been scared. Where would she go? Who would take her in? Her mother's abandonment had hit her for the first time and she'd cried out all her loneliness and loss until she could barely breathe through the hysterical, hiccuping sobs. Once those had passed, she'd been an empty vessel, scrubbed clean and ready to be filled with determination and stubbornness.

She felt a little like that now. Empty. Ready to be filled with something.

Leaving the cow and calf, Brandee headed for the horse barn and greeted her ranch hands. They looked weary, but smiled when they saw her. Apparently the cows had kept them busy, but the night had passed without serious incident. Next she headed to the ranch office to look for Jimmy. Her foreman was staring blankly at the computer, a full mug of coffee untouched beside the keyboard.

"You should head off," she told him, sitting in the only other chair. "I can handle entering the information."

"Thanks. I'm more beat than I thought."

"I'm sorry I wasn't here," she said again, pricked by guilt.

"It's okay. We had Shane's help and everything worked out fine."

"Shane was here all night?" Brandee's heart jumped.

"He came right after answering your phone. About seven or so."

Shane had been helping out at her ranch for over twelve hours? Why hadn't he said anything just now? Maybe he'd been waiting for her to thank him. If she'd known, she would have. Damn. No wonder he'd left so abruptly. She'd screwed up with him again.

But this she could fix. She just needed to come up with a great way to show her appreciation.

Shane wasn't exactly regretting that he'd promised his mother he'd help with Bullseye's centennial party, but he was starting to dread her texts. This last one had summoned him back to the ranch on some vague request for his opinion.

He parked his truck next to her Lexus and took the porch steps in one bound. Entering the house, he spied her in the living room and began, "Mother, couldn't this have waited…" The rest of what he'd been about to say vanished from his mind as he noticed his mother wasn't alone.

"Oh good." Elyse Delgado got to her feet. "You're home."

Shane's gaze locked on Brandee and his heart stopped as if jabbed by an icicle. "What is she doing here?"

"Shane, that's rude. I raised you better than that." Elyse set her hands on her hips and glared at her son. "She came to see me about this disturbing business about her ranch belonging to our family."

"Let me get this straight," Shane began, leveling his gaze on Brandee. "You called my mother to intervene on your behalf?"

"She did no such thing."

"It was Gabe's idea," Brandee said, a touch defensive. "He said you'd listen to her."

It was all too much. First Gabe, now his mother. Shane crossed to the bar and poured himself a shot of scotch. As soon as he lifted it to his lips, he recognized his mistake and set it back down.

"I don't know what you want," he said, dropping two ice cubes into a fresh glass and adding a splash of vodka.

"I brought this as a thank-you for helping out at the ranch the other night." While he'd had his back turned, she'd approached and set a bottle on the bar beside him.

"I don't want your thanks." Mouth watering, he eyed the rare vintage. "Besides, you've ruined scotch for me." He lifted his glass of vodka and took a sip. It took all his willpower not to wince at the taste.

Her lips curved enticingly. "It's a thirty-five-year-old Glengoyne. Only five hundred were released for sale."

"You can't bribe me to like you."

At his aggressive tone, all the light went out of her eyes. Once again she became the pale version of herself, the disheartened woman hunched over an empty glass in the TCC clubhouse.

"Shane Robert Delgado, you come with me this instant." Elyse didn't bother glancing over her shoulder to see if her son followed her toward the French doors leading out to the pool deck. She barely waited until the door had shut behind him before speaking. "How dare you speak to Brandee like that. She's in love with you."

"She tried to cheat us out of our family's land." He tried for righteous anger but couldn't summon the energy. The accusation had lost its impact.

"I don't care. We have more than enough wealth and Bullseye is one of the largest ranches around Royal. Besides, that land was unclaimed for over a hundred years and she paid for it fair and square. If anyone cheated us, it was the person who claimed the land without doing due diligence on the property's heirs."

"So, what do you want me to do? Be friends with her again?"

"I'd like for you to give up feeling sorry for yourself and tell that girl how much she means to you."

"What makes you think she means anything to me?"

"From what I hear, you've been an ornery, unlikable jerk this last week and I think it's because you love that girl and she hurt you."

Shane stood with his hands on his hips, glaring at his mother, while in his chest a storm raged. He did love Brandee, but the emotion he felt wasn't wondrous and happy. It was raw and painful and terrifying.

"Now," his mother continued, her tone calm and practical. "I'm going to go home and you are going to tell that girl that you love her. After which the two of you are going to sit down and figure out a way to get past this whole 'her ranch, our land' thing. Because if you can't, she told me she's going to sell everything and leave Royal. You'll never see her again and I don't think that's what you want."

Shane stared out at the vista behind the ranch house long after the French door closed behind his mother.

When he reentered the house, Brandee was still standing by the bar where he'd left her. "You're still here."

"I came with your mother and she refused to give me a ride back to her house, where my truck is parked." She took a step in his direction and stopped. After surveying his expression for several seconds, her gaze fell to his feet. "Look, I'm sorry about what I did. Whatever you want me to do about the land, I will."

"I don't give a damn about the land and I'm certainly not going to kick you off and take away everything you worked so hard to build." He sucked in a shaky breath.

This was his chance to push aside bitterness and be happy. He'd lost his father before making peace with him and was haunted by that. Losing Brandee would make his life hell.

"What I want more than anything is…" He dug the heels of both hands into his eyes. Deep inside he recognized that everything would be better if he just spoke what was in his heart. Shane let his hands fall to his sides and regarded her with naked longing. "You."

Her head came up. Tears shone in her eyes as she scanned his expression. "Are you sure?" she whispered, covering her mouth and staring at him with a look of heart-breaking hope.

"I am." Shane crossed the distance between them and put his arms around her. For the first time in a week, everything was perfect in his world. "I love you and I can't bear to spend another second apart."

His lips claimed hers, drinking in her half sob and turning it into a happy sigh.

When he finally let her come up for air, she framed his face with her fingers and gazed into his eyes. "Then you're not mad at me anymore?"

"For what? Trying to save your ranch and your dreams?" He shook his head. "I don't think I was ever really angry with you for that. I fell in love with you and when I found the documents I thought you'd been playing me the whole time."

"I should have told you about the blackmail after we made love that first time. I knew then that I was falling for you, but I didn't know how to trust my feelings and then there was that stupid bet." She shook her head.

"You weren't the only one struggling. I lost interest in your land after the tornado tore through Royal. I only agreed to the wager to spend time with you. All along I'd planned to lose."

She stared at him, an incredulous expression spreading across her features. "Then why did you work so hard to win?"

"Are you kidding?" He chuckled. "The bet was for you to fall for me. That was the real prize."

"I love you." Brandee set her cheek against his chest and hugged him tight. "I can't believe I'm saying this, but I'm really glad Maverick blackmailed me. If it hadn't happened, I never would've invited you to move in."

Shane growled. "I'll buy Maverick a drink and then knock his lights out."

"We don't know who he or she is."

"I asked Gabe to investigate. He'll figure out who Maverick is." Shane scooped Brandee off her feet and headed for the master suite. "In the meantime, I'd like to see how you look in my bed."

Brandee laughed and wrapped her arms around his neck. "I'm sure not much different than I looked in mine."

There she was wrong. As he stripped off her lacy top and snug jeans, the shadows he'd often glimpsed in her eyes were gone. All he could see was the clear light of love shining for him. There was no more need for either of them to hide. This was the first step toward a new partnership. In love and in life.

With her glorious blond hair fanned across his pillow and her blue-gray eyes devouring his body while he peeled off his clothes, Shane decided she was the most incredible woman he'd ever known.

He set his knee on the bed and leaned forward to frame her cheek with his fingers. His thumb drifted over her full lower lip. "You're looking particularly gorgeous today."

She placed her hand over his and turned to drop a kiss in his palm. With her free hand, she reached up to draw him down to her. "You're not looking so bad yourself, Delgado."

And when their lips met, both were smiling.

* * * * *

REUNITED WITH THE RANCHER

SARA ORWIG

With many thanks to
Stacy Boyd and Charles Griemsman
for working with me on this.
Thank you to Tahra Seplowin.
Also, thank you to Maureen Walters.

With love to my family—you are so special to me.

One

Tom Knox hurried down the hall of the Texas Cattleman's Club, his footsteps muffled by the thick carpet. The dark wood-paneled walls held oil paintings and two tall mirrors in wide ornate frames. There were potted palms and chairs covered in antique satin. Tom was so accustomed to his surroundings he paid no attention until a woman rounded the corner at the end of the long hall.

Tom's insides clutched and heat filled him as he looked at his estranged wife, Emily Archer Knox. Physical attraction, definitely lust, hit him as his gaze swept over her.

Wavy honey-brown hair framed her face. Her hair was always soft to touch. There was no way to shut off the memories, no matter how much they hurt or stirred him. A red linen suit with a matching linen blouse and red high heels added to her attractiveness. The red skirt ended above her knees, leaving her shapely legs bare to her ankles. His imagination filled in how she would look without the red linen. While desire ran rampant, at the same time, a shroud of guilt enveloped him. He had failed her in the worst way possible.

Each time he saw Emily, guilt gnawed at him for failing to save the life of their four-year-old son, Ryan, after a tour bus accident on a family ski vacation in Colorado. It had been five long, guilt-ridden years since then, and a chilly bitterness had settled in between them. His life had improved only slightly last year when he'd moved out of the house to the guesthouse on their ranch. They could go for weeks without crossing paths.

In many ways it was better to be apart, because then he could let go of the burden of guilt. That's why he had joined the Army Rangers for three years after the accident. After the death of his close friend, Jeremy, he wanted out of the Rangers. He couldn't be with Emily without thinking about how he had failed her and how unhappy she had been with him.

At the moment when they approached each other, Emily looked up and her green eyes widened. They avoided each other most of the time but couldn't today. He kept walking, his heart drumming while desire and guilt continued to war within him. Would he ever be able to face her without an internal emotional upheaval? Her smile was polite, the kind of smile usually reserved for strangers. When she came closer, her smile vanished before she greeted him with a quiet, "Hi, Tom."

"Good morning. You look great," he couldn't keep from saying.

Her gaze shifted to the briefcase in his hand. "Are you at the club for a meeting?"

"Yes. The finance committee. How about you?"

"I'm having lunch with a friend," she answered. How polite they were, yet a storm was going on within him. Guilt, hurt, too much loss plagued him each time he saw Emily or talked to her.

"Have a good time," he said as he passed her.

Her perfume stirred memories of holding her in his arms while he kissed her. Longing tore at him along with anger at himself. Why couldn't he let go completely? He and Emily didn't have anything together any longer. Only he knew that wasn't true. There was one thing they still had that hadn't vanished—a physical attraction that he felt each time she came into his sight. It was something he couldn't understand and didn't want to think about.

On a physical level, he knew she felt that chemistry as much as he did. She couldn't hide her reactions completely, and neither could he. But each time he encountered her, he was reminded that they both needed a chance for a fresh start, and that maybe the best thing he could do would be to give her a divorce and get out of her life completely.

After lunch at the Texas Cattleman's Club and an afternoon at her photography studio in downtown Royal, Emily drove home to Knox Acres, the cattle ranch she shared with Tom. She still couldn't stop replaying their brief encounter at the Texas Cattleman's Club. Since she first met him, she'd had a strong physical reaction to Tom. She still got tingles from just seeing him. Through good times, through the worst of times, Tom had dazzled her since they had fallen in love at sixteen. She had no comparison, but she didn't think that mattered. Tom was the best-looking, most appealing guy she had ever known.

Even so, other aspects of their marriage outweighed sheer lust. And they had lost what was essential in a marriage—that union of hearts, that joy in each other.

Their happiness had shattered the night their tour bus had skidded on an icy Colorado highway, going into a frozen pond. Tom had almost died pulling Ryan from the frigid water. Tom had ended up with pneumonia, a deep cut on his knee and a broken collarbone, broken ribs and a ruptured spleen. But in the end, he hadn't been able to save their son's life. After three days Tom could travel and they flew Tom, Emily and Ryan to a big hospital in Denver. They couldn't help Ryan, either. In eight more days, Ryan succumbed to his injuries. Somehow, amid all the grief, she and Tom composed themselves long enough to donate Ryan's organs to spare other parents the agony of losing a child.

The vacation had been Tom's family reunion, and twenty-three members of his family were on the bus. Besides Ryan, Tom's aunt died from drowning. Three other people, including two children, died in the accident, but they weren't in the Knox party.

Weeks turned into months and months into years, and her memories became more precious. In an effort to strengthen their marriage, they had tried to conceive again, but a new baby—a new start—never happened for them. Emily felt she had failed Tom in this; it was another blow to their marriage. They'd lost their son, and eventually their love, and their relationship became more strained until Tom moved out and they hardly saw each other any longer. It was general knowledge with most people they knew that they were estranged. Sometimes that still shocked her as much as everything else that had happened to them. She had been so in love with Tom when they married, she never would have believed the day would come when they barely spoke and hardly saw each other.

Hoping to put Tom out of her thoughts, she talked to her big white cat that had been a kitten given to Ryan when he was four. After feeding Snowball, she turned on her computer to read her email, and in seconds, a message caught her attention.

It was harsh, simple: Guess you weren't woman enough to hold his interest. Here's his real family, his secret family—until now. Frowning and puzzled, Emily scanned the subject: Today—for your eyes only. Tomorrow—for all of Royal to see.

She froze when she read the sender's name: Maverick. She had no idea who Maverick was. No one in Royal knew the identity of the hateful troll who'd been threatening and blackmailing people in town for the past few months. There were rumors Maverick might be the work of the three snooty stepsisters—that's how she pictured the clique of women, Cecelia Morgan, Simone Parker and Naomi Price, who seemed to think they owned the Texas Cattleman's Club and everything else in Royal these days. They always made Emily feel that she wasn't good enough to be included in their company.

Another chill slithered down Emily's spine when she opened the email attachment. It was a photograph. She stared at Tom in the picture, and shock hit her. As a professional photographer, Emily knew at a glance this picture was real. A smiling, earthy redhead with her hair fastened up in a ponytail posed with Tom, who stood close and had his arm draped around her shoulders. In front of them were two adorable children. The boy she guessed to be around four—the same age their Ryan had been when they had lost him. The little red-haired girl was pretty. In the background was a gingerbread dream house and beside the boy was a show-worthy golden retriever. They looked like the perfect family.

So this was Tom's preferred family. That made her the world's biggest fool. She and her husband had been growing apart for the past five years, and now she could see an additional reason why. Fury made her hot. There was a whole different side to Tom she had never seen— a deceitful side. She had trusted him completely. She stared at the picture, which was absolute evidence that their marriage was built on lies. Tom had another family. He was leading a double life. The realization was almost a physical blow.

If she wanted proof that their marriage was irrevocably broken, she had it now. Fresh out of excuses to delay the inevitable, heartsick and furious with Tom for his deception, she could see no other option: she planned to file for divorce. She would give him his official freedom to stop being secretive about the family he loved.

Shaking with anger, she leaned in closer to the computer screen to study the photo intently. The woman looked familiar, but Emily didn't know who she was. Were she and her kids in Royal?

And was the message on target—was Emily not woman enough to hold Tom? She shivered as she admitted to herself that the message was accurate, dead-on accurate. She couldn't give Tom the family he wanted.

It had been Tom's idea to move out to the guesthouse. He'd said separating would give them a chance to think clearly about their futures. He was the one who'd said they needed to get the physical attraction out of the way so they could straighten out their emotions and feelings for each other.

Knowing the real reason Tom wanted to move out of the house, away from her, hurt Emily badly.

She looked again at the sender's email signature. She had no idea who Maverick was. Could the rumors be right, that Cecelia Morgan, Simone Parker and Naomi Price were behind the nasty emails and the blackmail? Those three were successful businesswomen, so it didn't seem likely in a lot of ways. They might be snooty, but that didn't mean they were this evil.

Someone intended to make Tom's secret public to people in Royal. When that happened, Emily knew she would be viewed with pity and there would be laughter behind her back. That was insignificant next to the pain that consumed her over Tom's deception. How could he have been so duplicitous? It seemed totally unlike the man she knew and loved.

Would Maverick write Tom and threaten to go public? Had he—or she—already tried to extort money from Tom for silence? Emily could easily imagine Tom telling Maverick to go to hell first.

Emily couldn't stop her tears as her growing fury overwhelmed her. All this time, Tom had had a wife to love, to love him in return, precious children and a home. No wonder she couldn't get back together with him.

She intended to confront Tom with the truth. Their marriage was over. Completely finished. She needed a divorce to go on with her life. She had lost their son, and evidently, she'd lost Tom long ago, too. He was a lying, two-faced man she hadn't ever really known. She had never suspected that side of Tom. She had never even had a hint of it before now. Tom had seemed totally honest, kind—how he had fooled her! She wanted to scream at him and tell him how deceitful and hurtful he was. She wanted him out of her life, and this would ensure that happened.

She spent a sleepless night and drove into Royal the next day. Angry and hurt, she filed for divorce. Tom was now home from the military after his tour of duty with the Rangers, and he had taken over running the ranch. She had her photography studio and had just inherited her uncle Woody's old home in Royal. She and Tom could go their separate ways.

After work later that day, she went by the three-story house she had inherited from her uncle, the man who had raised her. The house was all she had left of family, so she intended to hang on to it and restore it so she could live there. She would be close to her photography studio and off the ranch, away from Tom. She didn't want to live in the palatial house on the ranch that they had built before Ryan was born anymore.

Tom drove back to the guesthouse after working outside all day on first one job and then another. Hard physical labor was the best way to drive the hurtful memories away, at least temporarily. It was early March, and the days were growing longer and warmer. It was spring—a time that used to be exciting and filled with promise. Now one day was like another and he spent time thinking over how he should plan his future.

At the present moment he wanted a shower and a beer and wished he had someone, a friend, to spend the evening with. Nights were long and lonely, and weekends were the worst.

As he pulled up, he saw a car parked in front of his house. It surprised him even more when he realized it was Emily's.

Why was she here? She never came to see him. Worried something might have happened to a friend, he frowned. Emily really had no family—only older cousins she didn't see. He parked and stepped out, slamming the pickup door behind him. He watched her open her car door to get out. She wore stiletto heels with black straps on her shapely feet. Her jeans fit her tiny waist snugly and were tight enough to emphasize her long, long legs. She wore a pale blue short-sleeved sweater that hugged her lush curves. In jeans, high heels and the sweater, she looked stunning. Her hair fell loosely around her face—the way he liked it best.

When his gaze raked over her, his pulse jumped. In spite of all their troubles, he was as physically drawn to her as ever. She was a good-looking woman—he'd always thought so and he still did. At the sight of her, memories tormented him, moments when he'd held and kissed her and wanted her with all his being. They'd had steamy nights of sexy loving, exciting days filled with happiness—a time that seemed incredibly far away and impossible to find ever again. He had failed her in the biggest possible way and now their love had ended. They had been through too much upheaval and loss to ever regain what they'd had.

Even so, desire for Emily was intense. He remembered that silky curtain of honey-brown hair spilling over his bare shoulders. Thoughts of kissing her haunted him. Memories of her softness, her voluptuous curves and her hands fluttering over him made him hot. She stood only a short distance away, pure temptation, and he wanted to reach for her…until he thought about all the problems between them. And it had to be a problem of some kind that brought her to see him. One glance in her big green eyes and he knew she was angry.

"Hi," he said. "What brings you here?"

Glaring at him, Emily waved papers in his face and then shoved them into his hand while she snapped, "You're welcome."

Startled out of his fantasy, Tom focused on her. "What am I welcome for? What are these papers?" he asked, looking down and turning over the official-looking forms in his hands before he looked up at her again. Puzzled, he met her fiery green eyes that flashed with fury.

"You can thank me now, because I've given you what you want—your freedom. You're free to marry the mother of your children."

"What the hell are you talking about?" She was rarely in a rage, but he could see she was boiling.

"Your secret is out, Tom," she said, her voice quivering with wrath. "You hid your family well. Have you paid Maverick to keep your secret? Or has it already spread all over Royal?"

Mystified, he saw that while she was shaking with rage, she was also fighting to hold back tears. "What the hell are you talking about, and what are these papers? And why are you talking about Maverick? What do you know about Maverick?"

"I think you know the answers to some of those questions," she said in a tight voice. "You have your divorce papers. You'll be free to be with your other wife."

"Other wife?" Stunned, Tom repeated the words as he frowned. "Emily, what are you talking about? There is no other wife—"

"Oh, please. I have proof. I've seen the picture of you and your family." She started to turn away.

Tom reached out to take her arm. As she yanked free of his grasp, the pain of her rejection made him hurt from head to toe. In three long strides, he caught up with her and held her arm more tightly this time.

"Emily, I don't understand what you're talking about.

Mother of my children? You're not leaving until you tell me what's going on."

"You can drop the lies and false front now that I know the truth," she snapped, twisting away to head back to her car.

Shocked, he went after her again with long strides that closed the distance between them. He grasped her shoulder to turn her to face him. "I have no idea what you're talking about or what brought this divorce on so suddenly without us talking about it."

"We're through and you know it. Your other family is what brought it on. I got an email from Maverick about them." She yanked free from him again and turned to open her car door.

He closed her door and stepped between her and the car. In minutes she would be gone and he wouldn't have any answers. He placed his hand on her shoulder. "You can't pop in and tell me we're getting divorced and then leave. Tell me what the hell all this is. And tell me about this email from Maverick. That troll who's blackmailing people in town? When did you get that?"

She twisted free again. "Get out of my way."

"Like hell I will. You're not going until you tell me. There is no secret family. That's nonsense."

"Oh, no? Tom, how could you be so deceitful?" she asked, sneering at him as she fumbled in a pocket to pull out a wrinkled piece of paper and wave it in front of him. "Here's proof, Tom. Here's your picture with your family. You have your arm around your secret wife. How could you lie to me like this?" Tears filled Emily's eyes, her cheeks were red and her voice was tight with anger. "How could you do this?" she repeated. "You've hurt me again, but this will be the last time."

"Give me that," he said, taking the paper from her to smooth it out and look at it. As he did, she wiggled away and opened her car door.

Determined to get answers from her, Tom reached out to push the car door closed again, stepping close with his hip against the door so she couldn't get inside while he smoothed the paper more to look at it. "Don't go anywhere, Emily, until we get this straightened out."

"Don't you dare tell me what to do," she said in a low voice that was filled with rage.

He paid no attention to her as he focused on the computer printout. Startled, Tom realized it was a copy of a very familiar snapshot.

Two

"Emily," he said, his anger changing to curiosity, "you got this in an email? This is Natalie Valentine and her kids. She's Jeremy Valentine's widow, who owns the Cimarron Rose Bed-and-Breakfast. Why have you filed for divorce over Natalie Valentine?"

Wide-eyed, Emily looked up at Tom and then glanced at the picture. "Jeremy Valentine?" she repeated, sounding dazed. "That's his wife? You told me about his death."

"That's right. I told you how he died on a mission and my promise to him to take care of his family if he didn't make it back."

"I remember that," Emily said, sounding stunned and confused. "She looked vaguely familiar, but I was in so much shock, I just didn't put anything together." She sagged against the car.

"Jeremy was shot," Tom reminded her. "We were on a mission in Iraq to rescue three hostages and Jeremy was shot twice. I promised him if he didn't make it, I'd take care of his family," Tom said, momentarily lost in remembering the battle, the blood, the noise of guns and men yelling. Tom looked at Emily, who had grown pale. Her eyes no longer held anger but uncertainty; he was sure she remembered him telling her about Jeremy's death.

"He was so worried about his family because he didn't expect to make it. I told him I'd be there for them if he couldn't." Tom held out the picture. "This is Natalie, and she's doing a great job being brave and upbeat and pouring herself into taking care of their two kids."

"Heavens, Tom," Emily whispered, shaking her head. "Those kids are Jeremy Valentine's? I've made a terrible mistake."

"Jeremy was their dad. They're really sweet kids. Colby is four—just like our Ryan when we lost him. Colby has autism. He's gotten accustomed to me and he's pretty relaxed around me. Lexie is two and thinks she's seventeen. She's pretty and cute. I just try to help out, because there's always something that needs fixing at the B and B. I try to be a man in the kids' lives and do things around the place or with the kids that Jeremy would do. Jeremy was one of the best."

Emily focused on him with a piercing look. "Tom, have you slept with Natalie?"

"Never," he answered with a clear conscience. "That isn't what this is about. I'm helping Natalie out, for Jeremy. That's all there is to it. He was a buddy and he died for his country." Tom gazed into Emily's green eyes and wondered whether she believed him or not. "It would be a good idea if you two met. Natalie has a sweet family."

"Oh, Tom," Emily said. She looked as if she'd been punched in the gut. Her shoulders sagged and she frowned. She ran her hand across her brow. "I've made a big mistake then," she repeated.

"I think you did," he said quietly. "But not one that can't be fixed."

Emily nodded. "I owe you an apology, because I believed this, even though it was so unlike you. The picture really shocked me."

"Forget that. We've got this ironed out between us now as far as I'm concerned, and I'll arrange for you and Natalie to meet."

"You never told me about seeing them. If it was just to be a help and do this for Jeremy, why didn't you tell me? I could have done some things for them, too."

He felt a ripple of impatience. "You haven't been interested in anything I've done for a long time. We don't keep up with each other any longer. I don't know any more about what you're doing than you know about what I'm doing. We're out of each other's lives now." He looked down at the papers in his hand. "This divorce was inevitable."

Clamping her lips shut, she nodded. "That's true. I can see why you didn't tell me." She frowned. "So this troll just sent the message to upset and hurt me," Emily said quietly, as if more to herself than to Tom, but he heard her.

"You got this from Maverick?"

"Yes."

"Damnation," Tom said, his temper rising as he thought about someone hiding behind a fictitious name, sending hateful messages to try to hurt Emily, who had already suffered the worst possible losses. He had failed Emily in the worst possible way before, but he wasn't going to fail her this time. "There's too much damn hate in this world and we don't need this going on in Royal. Maverick." He said the name with distaste. "Someone has hurt you once, but I damn well can see that he doesn't hurt you again. First of all, unless you've already called him, I'm calling Nathan Battle and letting him know about this," Tom said, pulling his phone out of his pocket.

"Sheriff Battle?"

"Yes. This week it's a hateful message to you. Who knows what this might escalate into next or how much this troll might hurt someone else? For some reason, he or she or they want to hurt you or you wouldn't have received that email. But I can't imagine you have an enemy in this world."

"Frankly, Tom, I didn't think about calling the sheriff. I was thinking more about us."

"I'm glad to hear you say that. If you get another message from Maverick, call me the minute you do."

"You saw the message—it was on target," she said quietly, and his anger increased at hearing the pain in her voice.

"It was a lie meant to hurt you. I'll call Nathan right now."

Tom's anger boiled and he was frustrated not to be able to take more direct action. When Nathan answered, Tom quickly told him about the email. After a minute or two, he turned to Emily. "Nathan wants to come pick up your CPU. He knows it most likely won't do any good, but he doesn't want to overlook anything."

"I don't mind if he checks the CPU and the email," she answered. "Goodness, I have nothing to hide. I'm going back into town, so I can drop it off at his office."

Tom smiled, then went back to talking to the sheriff for a minute before ending the call. "We'll go by his office. I'll help you get your CPU."

"That's fine. How do you suppose someone got that picture? Do you remember who took it?"

"There was some guy, about seventy years old, staying at the bed-and-breakfast. He was taking pictures. I'm sure he didn't know any of us."

"Well, then, how did Maverick get the picture?"

"The guy was using a camera. Maybe he got the prints made at a store. Those can be handled by several people. It wouldn't be hard to get a copy." He tilted his head to look at her. "Do you have plans tonight?"

"Not at all," she answered.

"Good. Because I'm moving back in," Tom announced in an authoritative voice that she assumed he'd developed in the Rangers. "I want to stay close, because no one knows Maverick's ultimate intentions."

Startled, Emily stared at him. "I appreciate your offer but it's not necessary. I'm not staying on the ranch any longer. I'm going to restore Uncle Woody's house and move in there. I've put a cot in a bedroom and I'm already living in Royal."

"You've moved off the ranch?" Tom said, frowning. "Look, Maverick isn't getting the reaction from us that he, she or they expected, which will increase the hatred and anger toward you. Move back to the ranch until this Maverick gets caught. You'll be safer here."

She might have been tempted to do what he asked, except he was asking for the wrong reason. She wasn't moving back because of an email message. And now that she knew the truth and Tom still was the same Tom she had always known, she had lost her anger toward him. But they still had all the problems they'd had for the past five years. She was going to move into town and Tom wasn't going to stop her.

As she calmed down, the feelings and responses she had always had began to return, including noticing his thick black hair that was a tangle over his forehead but always looked appealing to her. She could remember running her fingers through his hair. Her gaze slid down and she thought about his strong arms holding her against his rock-hard chest.

She sighed, because the memories were a torment and she couldn't keep them from happening. The breeze caught locks of his hair and blew them slightly. Everything about him made her want to walk into his arms and hold him close. She had always thought he was good-looking, and as the years went by, he seemed more handsome than ever. Or did she feel that way just because he was more off-limits than ever? She wasn't staying on the ranch no matter what he said, because they had been too unhappy together there. There were too many bad memories in the big house on the ranch.

"I'll be fine in town," she said, knowing that was the best place for her to be. "I'm working at my studio four days a week now, and the other days, I can work on the house."

"Okay, I'll get a sleeping bag and stay with you in Royal. You don't know if you're in any danger from this troll. Just because nothing's happened in the past doesn't mean it won't in the future."

Startled, she stared at him. "You can't live in Royal—you have a ranch to run," she blurted, feeling a sudden panic that they would be in close quarters. No matter what problems they had, when they were together, the physical attraction was impossible to resist. She had been trying to get over him and build a new life. If they lived together, she wouldn't be able to resist him.

"You don't need to spend all that time driving back and forth every day from Royal to the ranch," she said. She was pleased that he was concerned and had made the offer, and overwhelmingly relieved to discover that the troll's message hadn't been true and Tom was still the same trustworthy person she had always thought he was, but her panic about spending nights under the same roof again began to revive. She gazed into his thickly lashed hazel eyes, which made her get a tightness low inside and think about his kisses that could melt her.

"If you're in danger and something happened to you in Royal while I'm out here on the ranch," he said, "I couldn't live with it. You'd do the same if the situation were reversed."

She had to smile at the thought of being a bodyguard for Tom. "That's such a stretch of the imagination, I can't picture it. Don't even think about moving to Royal, but thank you for the offer, which is nice of you," she said, running her fingers along his forearm, feeling the solid muscles. She had meant it as a friendly gesture of gratitude, but the minute her fingers touched his arm, a sizzling current spiraled in her and she thought again of having his strong arms around her.

As she drew a deep breath, she saw his eyes narrow. Either he felt something, too, or he knew that she had—or both.

She dropped her hand instantly and stepped back. "Thanks anyway," she said, dismissing his offer.

"Give some thought to this. For all we know, you might be in danger. The safest possible place would be in the guesthouse. I can protect you the easiest there."

"I don't think that's necessary at all. According to the rumors I've heard, Maverick hasn't done anything except send terrible messages, trying to blackmail Royal citizens and stir up trouble. I need to work in town and I don't want to drive back and forth. I'm staying at my uncle's. Thank you for your concern, but you don't need to stay with me," she said firmly.

"I've already lost one of the most important people in my life," he said in a tight voice. "I don't intend to let anything happen to you." His hazel eyes looked darker, as they did when he was emotional or making love. "I'm going to ask Nathan to have someone drive by Natalie's and check on her to make sure she and her family are protected and okay." Tom removed his phone from his

pocket again. Emily wondered who he was calling now
until she heard him say hello to their foreman.

"Hey, Gus. I need to be away from the ranch for a
while."

Even as she stepped in front of him and shook her
head, trying to discourage him, she knew the futility of
her efforts. Tom had made up his mind that she should
have protection and she wouldn't be able to stop him.
She threw up her hands and walked away as he gave
instructions to Gus. How was she going to be able to
resist Tom if they were under the same roof? Maybe
he would stay downstairs and she could stay upstairs,
or vice versa.

"There, now," he said when he finished talking to
the foreman. "I'll bring my sleeping bag and stay in the
old house with you. I won't be in your way, and I can
help you with the restoration."

Exasperated, she stared at him. While she was annoyed, she knew this alpha male attitude was part of
why she had been drawn to him in the first place. He
was decisive and got things done. In high school it had
been part of his appeal. Now she was glad he could
make a decision and solve problems, but this time she
really didn't want him interfering in her life by taking
charge. Each time she thought about being back under
the same roof with him all night, her heart pounded. If he
was going to help with the restoration of the old house,
they would be working together. And she couldn't trust
her physical response to Tom. He would stir up all those
latent longings again. Tom had a virile, sexy body. He
was superbly fit from the Rangers and from ranch work.

Tom turned to her. He had his hands on his hips and he stood close. He had the shadow of stubble on his face and his tangled hair added to his disheveled attraction. He looked more appealing than ever in a rugged, sexy way. She realized where her thoughts were drifting and tried to pay attention to what he was saying.

"Nathan told me that Case Baxter, president of the TCC, plans to have an emergency meeting this coming week. Case agrees with Nathan that Maverick has to be stopped. To do so, they need to learn Maverick's true identity. I'm going to that meeting, and I'd like you to come with me."

"Sure, I'll go. But I don't think I can help in any way."

"It won't hurt, and the more of us who are informed and keep in touch with Nathan, the more likely he'll be able to catch Maverick. If you go, remember, Maverick may be sitting in the audience."

She shivered. "That's creepy."

"Hopefully, his emails and threats on social media won't escalate into violence, but no one knows right now. What he's doing now is bad enough. He hasn't really hurt us, but he could have, and he can hurt others badly."

After a pause, Emily steered the conversation to an equally unpleasant topic. "Tom, when we've waited a bit, we need to sit down and talk about the divorce and how we'll divide things. I was so angry when I filed. The picture was so convincing."

He nodded. "I don't think we'll have a problem dividing up the ranch, the house, the cars or the plane."

"You can definitely have the plane," she remarked, and he gave her a fleeting smile that made her smile in turn.

"I'll sign the divorce papers. We're there anyway, and you can have a life."

She turned away before he saw tears in her eyes. He was right. They were as good as divorced now, and she couldn't give him children. Their marriage had such devastating memories. Even so, it still hurt when divorce became reality; she had filed and the papers were in his possession. It was one more big loss in her life and this one she took responsibility for because she'd been unable to get pregnant again. If she had been, it would have held them together. She'd wanted so badly to give Tom another child like Ryan. There was adoption—Tom had been willing—but it wasn't the same and she was against it. She wanted to have another child like Ryan.

Now she and Tom were estranged, and if they got divorced, they could each go ahead with life. But it was difficult to imagine ever loving another man.

And it didn't help that Tom had proved Maverick wrong and was trying to help her. It was easy to file for divorce when she was so angry with Tom because she thought he had deceived her. To know that he was still the same guy she had always admired and trusted made the divorce hurt.

"Emily?"

She blinked in surprise, turning to face him again. His eyes narrowed, and he studied her intently. "I'm sorry, Tom. My thoughts drifted back to Maverick," she said, her cheeks burning with embarrassment. She suspected he could guess exactly why she hadn't heard him.

"You said you're going back to Royal from here. Let me grab a sleeping bag and a few things. I'll take you."

She opened her mouth to protest, but before she said a word, he waved his hand. "I'm taking you to Royal. Tomorrow we'll come back and get your car. I'd just as soon let everyone see us together—it'll give me pleasure. Hopefully, the damned troll will see us and realize that email did no harm. Far from it. How's that for a plan?"

She shrugged. "I have a feeling if I didn't like it at all, I would still end up doing it. I think you're right about letting Maverick see us together. That gives me a sense of getting even with the troll."

"We can flaunt that we're getting along. It doesn't take long for word to get around Royal."

"I agree. While it's good to be seen together, you don't need to stay with me," she argued again. "I'll be in town, where I can call for help at any hour and someone will be right there."

"I'm staying, Emily. This is someone with a grudge and you're on the list. That was a damn hateful message you received. Look at the results. You filed for divorce. If rumors started, they could have hurt Natalie, which in turn would have hurt her kids. Frankly, I'm not ready to divorce you when it's because of a bunch of lies from a vengeful creep."

"You have a point, Tom," she said, wishing he had said he didn't want the divorce for other reasons, yet knowing he was right. "And while we've been talking, I've been thinking—Maverick has to be somebody who lives in Royal, or has lived in Royal until recently, to know this about you and Natalie and to know to send the picture to me."

"That's right." He looked down at his dusty boots, his mud-splattered jeans. "Can you have a seat inside and let me take a quick shower? I can be speedy."

"You were never speedy when I showered with you," she teased and then blushed. "I don't know where that came from," she said. "Forget it."

"Hell, no, I won't forget it," he said, his voice getting soft. "You were teasing like you used to, and that's allowed, Emily. We can have some fun sometimes—let it happen. We've got too much of the sad stuff. At this point in our lives, it really isn't going to change anything to have a laugh or two," he said.

She nodded. "I suppose you're right," she said quietly, thinking he was the way he used to be before the bad times set in. Relaxed, kind, understanding, practical, sexy. He had been fun, so much fun, so sexy. She waved her hand at him. "Go on, Tom. Shower. I can go get the CPU while you're in there."

"Nope. I want to be with you. This Maverick bothers me, I'll admit. I can't imagine why you're on anyone's hit list. That's worrisome. You're softhearted, generous—"

"Oh, my! We've turned into a mutual-admiration society, thanks to a troll."

"It's not thanks to the damned troll. It's time we have something between us again that isn't sad, even if it's just for five minutes."

"Tom, I agree with everything you just said. For just a few minutes, it was sort of the way it used to be, at least a tiny bit," she said, suddenly serious, thinking it was a lot better than not speaking and avoiding each other. "I know we can't turn back the clock, but we can at least be civil to each other."

"Damn right. Don't disappear while I go shower," he said, starting inside and holding the screen door. He paused, looking over his shoulder at her. "Unless you want to come inside and join me."

She shook her head. "No, thank you."

He grinned. "After your remark, I had to try." He let the door slam shut behind him and disappeared.

"Don't make me fall in love with you all over again," she whispered, and wound her fingers together, trying to think of seeing Nathan Battle, of her appointments tomorrow, of anything except Tom in the shower.

In less than ten minutes Tom reappeared, his hair slightly damp. He wore a clean navy T-shirt, fresh jeans, black boots and a black hat. He carried a rolled-up sleeping bag and a satchel. "I'll put up my truck and get the car and we'll go get the CPU."

"Sure," she said, walking out with him and waiting on the porch until he pulled up in a black sports car. He was out and around the car by the time she got to it. He held the door for her, and as she passed him, she glanced up and received another scalding look. She was close, her shoulder brushing his arm as he held the car door open. Their gazes met and she couldn't catch her breath. For just a moment, she forgot everything except Tom, pausing to look into his thickly lashed hazel eyes that immobilized her. The differences between them fell away, and all-consuming lust enveloped her.

It took an effort to tear her gaze from his. In that brief moment, she had wanted his arms around her and his mouth on hers.

"Thanks," she said, hating that it came out breathlessly. She slipped into the passenger seat and gazed ahead as he closed the door. He strode around the car. Handsome, purposeful, filled with vitality, he would be married again after their divorce, she was certain. Tom was too appealing to live alone, and he liked women. The idea of Tom marrying hurt even though they had no future together and no longer had the joy and happiness of their first years together.

She rode in silence as they drove the short distance from the guesthouse to the mansion they had shared. Now it stood silent and empty. They had been happy in the sprawling, palatial two-story house until they lost their son. She didn't want to live in it alone. It was too big, too empty without Tom. He'd seemed to fill it with his presence when he would come home. When they had Ryan, his childish voice and laughter had also seemed to fill the big house. At present, she found it empty, isolated and sad. She didn't like living alone in it and she didn't intend to ever again. This wasn't the place for her any longer.

The house had a somber effect on her and Tom seemed to react the same way. They both were quiet as they walked to the door. Tom still had a key and opened the door to hold it for her. She walked through into the spacious entryway, switching on lights as she went, although it wasn't dark outside yet.

She suddenly thought about Ryan running around in front of the house when he was so small. Tears came and she wiped them away quickly. Pausing, she glanced over her shoulder at Tom, and he looked stricken. She guessed that he, too, was thinking of Ryan and hurting because he hadn't been in the house in almost a year. He rubbed his eyes—the tough, decorated Ranger who had been in combat, been wounded, been a prisoner until he escaped. She couldn't bear his grief, which compounded her pain. When she turned away, crying silently while she tried to get control of her emotions, Tom put his arm around her.

"Come here," he whispered. Sobbing, she turned to him and they held each other. His strong arms around her felt wonderful and she tightened her hold on him as if she could squeeze out some of his strength, transferring it from him to her. He was a comfort and she hoped she was for him. She stroked his back, relishing holding him. It had been so long since she had been in his arms.

"I'm sorry, Tom. Sometimes I just lose it and I guess you do, too. Having you here helps," she said, wiping her eyes with a tissue.

He looked down at her, easing his hold on her slightly. "I'm glad I'm here for you. It helps me. Grieving is part of it that we can't escape." She nodded as he released her. She missed his strong arms around her.

"I'm okay now. Thanks."

They went through the house to the large room that

was her office. "I'll get the CPU out for you, Emily," he said and strode past her. "I'm sure this is futile, but it would be ridiculous for Nathan not to check it out."

"While you do that, Tom, I'll pick up a few things to take to Royal."

"Where's that white cat of yours?"

"Your cook has Snowball until I get settled in Royal. You don't care, do you?"

"No, I don't care where your cat is."

It seemed natural to be in the house with Tom again. She watched him hunker down to disconnect the CPU, the fabric of his jeans pulling tightly over his long legs. Desire swept through her, and she turned to leave the room abruptly to get away from him.

In less than half an hour they were on their way to Royal. They rode together in silence. She knew he was bound in his own thoughts as much as she was in hers, and they had little to say to each other. While they didn't talk, she was acutely conscious of him. She hadn't been around him this much in a long time. And their time together was just starting. How could she live under the same roof with him again without being in his arms and in his bed and back on an emotional roller coaster?

She glanced at his hand on the steering wheel. He had a scar across the back of it that had healed long ago. He had scars all over his body from his time in the military.

His hands were well shaped, nails clipped very short, veins showing slightly. Too easily she could remember his hands drifting over her when they had made love—strong hands that could send her to paradise.

She realized her thoughts were carrying her into a place she didn't want to go. "I think you're right about the divorce. We'll get it—that's inevitable—but I don't like getting a divorce because of Maverick, either."

"Let's table the divorce for now. I'll try to find out how much effort Nathan is devoting to catching this troll. The meeting Monday at the club may shed more light. If we don't divorce and we both stay at the house in Royal—"

"Maverick will know you've become my body-guard," she said, shaking her head.

"Not necessarily. If I help you restore the old house, it'll look as if we're back together. For all anyone knows, we're fixing it up for you to sell. For a few weeks, maybe we should keep quiet that I'm worried about your protection and that we're not really together anymore."

"That's fine with me. Anything to defeat Maverick. Frankly, I'm still amazed I'm a victim. I'm not the sweetest person, but I usually get along with people I know and work with, neighbors, church friends."

"I'll ask you the question that Nathan is going to ask—do you have any enemies? Anyone who doesn't like you or you've angered?"

She laughed softly. "Tom, I may have people who don't like me, but if so, I don't know anything about it. I don't have enemies. I can't think of anyone."

"The whole world loves you," he remarked. "That's what you'll hear from Nathan, I'll bet."

"The one person I've made the most unhappy is you," she answered quietly, and he glanced quickly at her and back at the road. When she looked again, she saw his knuckles had tightened on the wheel.

"Hell, Emily, I loved you with all my being, but we've just had so much happen between us there is no way we can go back to that life we had. When I ask if you have angered anyone, I'm talking real enemies."

"I know you are," she said, hurting inside because she'd answered with the truth. There was no one who had been as hurt by her or more at odds with her or more disappointed by her than Tom. "We're not real enemies and you're a good guy."

"Thanks for that much, Em. Think about it. Think if there is anyone you've crossed who might hold a grudge."

She gave a small laugh. "Darla from our class in high school. Oh, did she have a crush on you. Now if this had happened when we were sixteen instead of now when we're thirty-two, I'd give out her name in a flash, but the last I heard she's married and has three kids."

"I hate to say this, but I don't even remember the person you're talking about."

"One of your groupies."

"I didn't have groupies."

"Every cute football captain has groupies."

"May have seemed so to you, but I didn't. And I haven't been called cute since I was five."

"You were cute. That was the general consensus with all the girls. Ooh, long eyelashes, broad shoulders, cute butt, sexy, to-die-for—"

"Stop it." He laughed. "If I had only known then— you didn't tell me all that when we were in school."

"Of course not. It would have just gone to your head—or elsewhere."

"Oh, damn, we should have had this conversation long ago," he said, grinning at her. And once again, for just an instant, she was reminded of old times with him.

"Kidding aside, Emily, keep thinking. It's important. Could it have to do with your business?"

"I take pictures of kids and families—there's nothing in my work that should anger anyone. I've never had an irate customer."

"I'm sure you haven't—you're a damn good photographer."

"The result wasn't what Maverick intended, so let's not worry too much about it right now," she said, placing her hand on Tom's knee in a gesture that at one time would have been casual. It wasn't now. He turned to stare at her, and she saw his chest expand as he took a deep breath.

She removed her hand and looked out the window, turning from him and trying to make light of the moment. She was thankful he couldn't hear or feel her racing heart.

"I'll try to think, but I'm blank. I know I'm overlooking something or I wouldn't have received that email."

"That's right, so work on it," he said, and they lapsed into silence as they drove toward Royal.

She thought over what Tom had said. What enemies did she have? "Tom, maybe Maverick was getting at you through me."

"That occurred to me, and I've been trying to think

of anyone in these parts I could have really annoyed. Frankly, Emily, I can think of some. I've fired cowboys who didn't want to work. I was in the military—there are people in the area who don't like that or what I did. Politically, they don't agree with me. There are guys I competed with in college and high school sports. There are guys I've competed with in rodeos. I'll talk to Nathan about it. He's got to catch this troll. It has to be someone really low-down mean to hurt you after what you've been through."

"I haven't been through any more than you have," she said, and he was silent. His jaw was set and she suspected he was frustrated and angry.

"You have been through more than I have," he said quietly. "You lost Ryan, you lost your uncle, your dad split when you were two, your mom died when you were nine, the man who raised you and the last close member of your family died this past year and you haven't had another child. You don't need more anguish, much less to get hassled by a rotten coward."

It hurt to hear Tom say that she couldn't have more children, but everything he said was the truth. As their conversation trailed off, she was acutely aware of him so nearby. She had been doing fairly well when she didn't see him or talk to him on a regular basis, but now to be with him, to joke around with him, even just this tiny bit, drew her to him. And the memories were tormenting her. They had been so wildly in love when they were dating and first married. Her world had crashed and would never again be the same. She had been slowly adjusting to life without Tom, and now he was coming right back into it. Would she be able to cope with living in the same house again? Could she resist the intense, scalding attraction she always felt for him? What would happen if he tried to seduce her?

The questions came at her constantly, and there were no answers.

Three

When they got to town, Tom parked in front of the sheriff's office and carried the CPU inside. Nathan greeted them and shook Tom's hand. "We don't have much in the way of good leads and I don't expect to get anything from your computer, but I need to check it out. I hope both of you will go to the meeting Monday."

"We plan to," Tom said. "I'll help in any way I can. Just let me know."

"Thanks," Nathan said. The sheriff was tall and had friendly brown eyes. "I'd like to talk to each of you, one at a time. Emily, want to go first?"

"Sure," she answered, smiling at him. He was slightly older than Tom and she, but she knew him and his wife, Amanda, who owned the Royal Diner, which was a town fixture.

Emily went into his office and tried to answer his questions. She was with him only a short time and then he talked to Tom. Their session was also brief.

Soon both men came out of Nathan's office. "If either one of you think of anything to tell me, just call, no matter what the hour is. I want this Maverick caught."

"I think most of the people in Royal probably want him caught quickly," Emily said.

"Sorry we weren't more help, Nathan," Tom said. "I'll keep thinking about any possibilities."

"Sure. Both of you try to make the meeting Monday. I'm shocked that Emily was a target. And it could have been to get at you, but why you? You don't have any real enemies around these parts."

"You never know—you can aggravate someone without even knowing it. Since there are several people now who've received these Maverick messages, I'd say this is a sour character who has a lot of grudges."

"You're right. I want to catch him—or her. I'm sure Emily's computer will be the same as the others—we can't trace where the messages originated. Maverick may be mean, but he's not stupid."

Nathan followed them outside, and the three of them stood for a moment in the late-afternoon sun. "Emily, since you've moved into your uncle's house here in town, if you need us at any time, just call. I'm glad Tom is there now, because that takes away some worries."

"We'll keep in touch," Tom promised as he took Emily's arm lightly. He was saying goodbye to the sheriff, paying little attention to her, but with each of Tom's touches, the contact was startling. How could he still do this to her when they were no longer in love and headed for divorce? They had no future together, she was annoyed he had taken charge of her life and was staying with her, yet the slightest contact was electrifying. She hoped her reaction didn't show.

They told Nathan goodbye and walked to the car. As they drove away, Tom glanced at her. "Let's stop at the diner and get a burger."

"Sure," she answered, knowing Tom was probably hungry, but suspecting he wanted people in Royal to see them together.

Everything they did reminded her of old times with him, which made her sad, but at the same time, she couldn't keep from enjoying his company.

They drove the short distance down Main and stopped at the Royal Diner for burgers. Too many things she did with Tom reminded her of their life when everything was exciting and they were in love. The reminders hurt and made her realize how her expectations had been destroyed and there wasn't any putting their marriage back together. They might fool Maverick, but it was going to cost her peace of mind to have Tom hovering around.

They sat down in a booth upholstered in red faux leather. "How many times have we eaten burgers or had a malt here?" she couldn't resist asking Tom.

He smiled at her. "Too many to keep track, but my mind was never on the burgers or the malts."

"I doubt mine was, either," she said, remembering

how exciting he was to her. "This is the first place you asked me to go with you—to get a malt."

"I remember," he said, focusing on her with a direct gaze that made her warm. "After you ran into my car."

"That was one of the first times I ever took the car. I just didn't see you when I pulled out of the school parking lot. It's a good thing you had quick reflexes, because it would have been a worse wreck if you hadn't put on your brakes."

"That seems so long ago. Your uncle Woody was understanding about the whole thing. His insurance paid for my car and he had faith in you. He knew you'd learn to drive, and I guess he figured you'd be more careful after hitting my car."

"I was definitely more careful."

"It was worth it to get you to pick me up every morning and take me to school while my car was being fixed," Tom said, smiling at her.

"I thought so, too," she said, loving to see him smile. The sad times they'd experienced had taken away smiles and laughter, but before that she had always had more fun with Tom than anyone else. "I liked picking you up, except it was embarrassing, too, because everyone in school knew what I'd done."

He leaned across the table, and his voice dropped as he spoke softly. "Remember our first kiss? I do."

She looked into his bedroom eyes and drew a deep breath. But it felt as if all the air in the diner suddenly vanished. She couldn't keep from glancing at Tom's mouth, thinking about his kisses, remembering them in exacting detail and wanting to kiss him again.

"Of course I do, but I'm surprised you do."

"I do. Why do you think I asked you out again?" he said, those hazel eyes twinkling.

"It was all exciting, Tom," she said, full of regret.

"Then don't cry about it now. Happy memories. Take the ones that were special and exciting and concentrate on them."

"Thank you, Doctor," she said lightly, smiling at him.

Their burgers came. She ate half of hers, reflecting on how she didn't want Tom staying with her but finding no way to avoid it, especially after Nathan said it was a good arrangement.

They left and she felt certain they would never eat burgers together in the Royal Diner again. She glanced up at Tom as she walked beside him. He was still exciting to her, which was something she didn't want to feel, because they had no future and all too soon they would officially be divorced. Why did that hurt so badly when it was what they both wanted? Now with him moving in to stay in the same house with her, was she going through another emotional upheaval that would be more difficult and painful to get over than the last time?

"Want to make a quick stop and see my studio?" she asked impulsively. "It isn't something you have to do."

"No, I'd like to see it."

"Turn at the next corner." She gave him directions and they drove just two more blocks and parked in front. She was sandwiched in between a law office and a popular bakery that had delicious bread. He paused to look at the pictures of babies and dogs and families on display in her front window.

"Very nice, Em. You've turned your hobby into a good business. You're very good."

"Thank you," she said, feeling he was being polite.

"I think I may just stand out here and smell the bread," Tom remarked.

"It's fantastic. We can pick up a loaf to take with us. They have specialties. Come in. This is tiny, but big enough for me."

He walked around the waiting room, looking at more pictures on the walls. Some of the people he recognized, a lot he didn't, especially the children. Then he came upon a large framed picture of their son when he was two years old.

"Em, this is a wonderful picture of Ryan. I want a copy."

"I'll get you one. I'm glad you like it. It makes me happy to see his picture when I come to work."

Tom continued looking at the framed photographs. There was one from when the tornado hit Royal, of the damaged town hall with three floors destroyed and the clock tower left standing. "You're very good at this," he said, moving to another picture of a black horse in a pasture, the wind blowing its tail, sunlight spilling over its satiny black coat. Tom glanced at her.

"This looks like my horse Grand."

"It is. He's photogenic and cooperative."

"Wow. I'd like a copy of that picture, too." He leaned closer. "I don't see a price on these."

"You're special. You can have that picture compliments of the house."

"You don't need to do that."

"I want to," she said, smiling at him.

"Thanks. It's a great picture of him."

"Come see where I take pictures and my desk."

He walked around and bent down to look through a camera set on a tripod. Across from him was a backdrop of a field of green grass.

"Tom, let me take your picture."

He grinned at her. "You're kidding. You know what I look like."

She took his arm. "Come stand and let me have a picture of you. I might want it on cold winter nights when you're not with me."

His smile faded. "You're serious. All right, I will if you'll let me take one of you on my phone."

She laughed. "Sure I will."

"And promise you won't stick me out there in the window."

"I wouldn't think of it," she said. "Your picture will go home to my bedroom," she said, expecting a laugh or sexy reply, but he stood quietly looking at her and she wondered what he was thinking. "You stand right here," she said, motioning to him.

Behind the camera, she adjusted the settings and took a picture. "Now turn slightly and look over your shoulder a little at me and smile."

"Em, I feel silly."

"Smile and cooperate. I'll buy you a loaf of bread when we leave."

"You're really good at this bribery business." He turned and smiled and she snapped some more.

"Now, want to see your pictures? I can get proofs for you while we go get that loaf of bread."

"I don't really care about seeing my picture, but I definitely care about that bread. You don't have to buy it. I'll go get it and you get your proofs or whatever you do. What kind do you want me to get?"

"I love the sourdough."

"Sourdough, coming up. I'll be back." He left and she worked quickly on the proof. She was examining them when she heard the bell in front. She scooped up the proofs, turned off lights and hurried to meet him.

"I have two loaves of bread and they smell almost too good to wait to eat. Ready to go?"

"Yes, look. You take a very appealing picture."

She held a couple of proofs out for him to see. He barely glanced at them but smiled at her. "I'm a very appealing subject," he said and she smiled.

The sun was low in the west when they left her shop. As soon as they were in the car, she turned to him slightly. "When we leave here, get ready for a shock. The house is in terrible condition. At the last, Uncle Woody was so ill—"

"Emily, I've meant to tell you that I'm sorry I missed being at his funeral."

"There wasn't any reason for you to fly back from your business trip in Wyoming. I never asked you if you bought the ranch," she said, realizing how far apart they had grown. In times past he would have been at her side for her uncle's last hours and through the service. She would have known whether Tom bought another ranch in Wyoming and he would have discussed his decision with her before he did anything. They were moving farther apart and the divorce was inevitable, but right now, she didn't want to give any satisfaction to Maverick and neither did Tom, so they'd stay together.

"No, I didn't buy it. If I buy another ranch, it'll be in this part of the country," he said. "I'm beginning to rethink getting someone else to run it. I have to be hands-on with a ranch."

She was quiet when they turned on the street where she had lived from the time she was nine years old until she had married Tom. Big sycamores and oaks lined the road. Tiny green leaves covered some branches, but many had bare limbs. The aging sidewalk was pushed up by tree roots. Tom slowed in front of the three-story house and turned onto a driveway where grass filled the cracks of aged concrete that had disappeared beneath a cover of weeds.

Tom parked beside the back corner of the aged house. "I want the car out here where it can be seen. If anyone has been watching you, whoever it is will know this isn't your car. I want Maverick to know I'm here with you, that the email didn't work and didn't hurt either one of us."

"It gives me the shivers to think someone might be watching me," she said. "I never even thought of that."

Tom gave her a look and smiled. "You're trusting."

He cut the engine while he gazed at the house, and she studied it with him. Long ago it had been painted white, but now the paint was peeling. There were gables on the front and west sides with a shingled roof that needed replacement. The large round tower on the east side had broken windows and all the ground floor windows were broken. The house had a wraparound porch with wooden gingerbread decoration that had shattered through the years and ornate spindles that were broken.

She sat a moment looking at the dilapidated condition: peeling paint, shutters hanging awry or gone, broken windows, concrete steps crumbling. She remembered one night when Tom had brought her home and parked on the drive. They had gotten out of his car and he had kissed her beneath the mulberry tree. A kiss became kisses and then he asked her to marry him. They both had a year of college left and they'd talked about waiting, but that night was the night he proposed. Before she went in, they agreed they wouldn't do anything official until they finished their senior year.

"What are you thinking about?" he asked.

Startled, she turned to him and wondered if he had guessed that being with him at the house had triggered memories. "I have a lot of windows to repair," she said.

"Yeah," he said in a gruff voice, and she wondered if he remembered the same moments she had. "So this is where you want to live instead of the house on the ranch. This is going to be a job and a half," Tom said, looking at it in the dusk as the last sunlight slipped away into darkness. "It's also the least secure place you could pick to stay."

"I'm in Royal, which is a peaceful town."

"A peaceful town that has a hateful troll spreading grief."

"I know I have a lot of work to do here, but I work in town now and the house is my only tie to my past and my family. The ones I was really close to are all gone. I hardly know my cousins, and they live in Oregon and Vermont. I never see them. This house is my tie to Mom and Uncle Woody."

"It's a fine old home, but your uncle couldn't keep up with it and it'll be an expense for you."

"He didn't want me to hire anyone to work on it, so I did what he wanted."

"Honoring his wishes was probably more important. Well, we can fix it up and hire people to do some of the work."

"It's not a *we* thing, Tom. This isn't where you'll live. It's not your house and it's not your problem," she said. "You don't need to be concerned with it, and I still think you could go back to the ranch."

He frowned, his jaw clamped shut. The happy moments they'd had disappeared with her request for him to leave. Jolted by regret, she reminded herself it was for the best. She didn't need Tom staying with her, and it would complicate both their lives—he had a ranch to run and she didn't need him hovering.

"People will have seen us together and your car here and they'll talk about it. You don't need to stay longer," she added when he didn't say anything.

"You may not want me, but I'm staying," he said in a gruff tone. "Think of me as a bodyguard and maybe you can tolerate my presence. You might need me."

"Suit yourself," she said, still wondering how she would get through the night with him in the house.

She reached for the door handle and he placed his hand on hers.

Startled, she looked up at him.

"I don't feel right about you walking into this big empty house. Anybody could be in there, because there is not one lick of security here. They could step in through any one of downstairs windows. Do you even lock the doors?"

"Actually, no. What's the point with windows broken out?"

"You just wait here in the car while I check the place. Keep the car keys and give me your house key."

"Tom—"

"I know I'm being cautious, but it only takes minutes and we have time. I'll feel better. Now you stay locked in this car, and if you see anyone call me instantly. And if anyone tries to get in the car—"

"I'll just run over them," she couldn't resist saying, because she thought he was being ridiculous.

He didn't laugh. "Emily, I've seen a guy walk into a house and get his throat slashed. I know we're in Royal, but I don't see one damn reason to take a chance."

"Ah, Tom. Sorry," she said. "I know you're trying to help, but this isn't a war zone, it's Royal, and so far, Maverick has only sent emails." She waved her hand. "I'll do as you say. You check out the house." She knew his warrior background had kicked in and there was no use arguing.

Nodding at her, he stepped out of the car and closed the door quietly.

She couldn't imagine any danger, but then she had

never expected to receive such a hateful message from Maverick, either. And so now she was under the same roof with Tom again—that seemed the biggest threat, but it was a threat to her heart when she was just pulling herself together and beginning to establish a life without Tom in it.

He vanished into the house. It was still dusk. She could still see outside, but inside the old house, darkness would prevail. She could imagine Tom checking out each room. He would be thorough and silent.

Her nerves were on edge by the time the lights were switched on in the house and she could see him coming through the kitchen. As she took in his broad shoulders and purposeful stride, she knew she would feel totally safe with Tom in the house. In the past she had always felt completely safe when he was around, but then, in the past, she hadn't worried about any kind of threat.

He passed by the windows and a light went off in what Uncle Woody called his front parlor. Next the hall light went off and she realized Tom was going to turn off all the lights and leave the downstairs in darkness.

She didn't even see him coming when he tapped on the car window.

He opened the door for her, pushing a button to keep the car light off. "Thanks for humoring me. I feel better about the house now." She stepped out and closed the door. He reached to help her, taking her arm. It was casual, something he obviously wasn't thinking about, but like any physical contact with him, she was intensely aware of his touch.

"Emily, you have no security here. You don't have

one damn window covering except in a bathroom downstairs, and anyone watching can see where you are in the house at any time. We've got some work ahead of us. Do you have curtains or sheets here?"

"I have sheets."

"Okay, come on. Let's get moving. We need some windows covered, and you need to move upstairs."

"I don't suppose there is any point in arguing with you about moving upstairs."

"No, there isn't," he said. "That's what you're going to do."

"When did you get so take-charge?"

"When someone threatened you. You're on that troll's hit list, and until he or she is caught, don't forget that for a moment. You've crossed someone in some way and they want to get even. It could be me they're after, but if it is, that's a damn roundabout way to get at me. Just remember someone wants to hurt you."

"I don't think you're going to let me forget it."

They walked around to the back door and entered the dark house. Night had fallen and there was no moon. She realized he hadn't left any lights on in the back hall entrance.

Tom took her arm and, again, the minute his fingers touched her, she had the usual tingles from head to toe. How would she live with him in the same house, work with him to restore it? How would she get through this one night? She was always attracted to him, but she needed to resist him now. She couldn't bear to go through all the emotional upheaval she had in the past. There were no solutions to their problems, and their divorce would be finalized as soon as this threat from Maverick ended.

"Tom—"

In little more than a whisper, his breath warm on her ear, he said, "Wait until we're upstairs."

Four

They moved silently in the dark through the back hall into the breakfast room and then the main hall. When they stopped for a second, Emily collided with him.

Tom slipped his arm around her waist. The minute he did, everything changed. He became aware of her softness, the faint trace of perfume, her hair spilling across his hand. He held her lightly. Her soft blue sweater fit snugly and he could feel her warmth, her lush curves, her soft breasts pressing against his arm. Desire was sudden and intense.

Off balance, she grabbed his arm, but he held her and she wasn't going to fall. It took an effort to hold her lightly, to keep from wrapping his arms around her and kissing her until she responded. She was soft, alluring, warm.

Time disappeared and took along with it memories of the bad times and the loss. At the moment memories of holding her and kissing her consumed him, making his heart race. He tightened his arms to pull her close, feeling her slender arm slide around his neck.

"Some things between us haven't changed," he said quietly. He shifted, fitting her against him, still holding her close. The pounding beat of his heart was loud and he fought to keep control. Even though he knew the trouble it would cause, he wanted to hold her, to kiss her, to make love to her all night long.

"We can't do this, Tom," she whispered.

He couldn't answer. He was hot, hard and he wanted her. It was physical, a hungry need because he had been alone so long. He had to let her go and get upstairs, but he didn't want to release her. It had been so damned long since he had held her, kissed her or even just touched her.

He released her slightly, still holding her arm. "Are you okay?"

"Yes, I'm fine. I just stumbled," she answered. She sounded breathless and tense, and that just added to his desire. He tried to focus on the situation and stop thinking about kissing her.

"I don't want to turn on a light. You have all these damn windows. With your sunroom, you have thirty-two windows downstairs that are not covered, and anyone looking in can see what you're doing. Let's take this gear upstairs."

"I know this house even in the dark," she said. They talked in quieter tones, but he wasn't sure he was making sense, because all he could think about was kissing her. He was already tied in knots over her. Even while they talked, he continued to hold her arm and she had hers on his shoulder.

"I'm glad you know this house. We won't have to turn on lights until we're upstairs. Can you get up the steps in the dark?" he asked.

She leaned closer to his ear, her breath warm on his neck. "How many times do you think I turned out all the lights downstairs and tiptoed upstairs in total darkness after you brought me home from a date later than I was supposed to stay out? I can't recall you worrying then whether I could get up the steps in the dark."

Her words eased some of his tension and he chuckled softly. "Okay, you go ahead and I'll follow."

Reluctantly, he released her. Today, there had been moments when tension fell away. It was the way things used to be. This was a bubble in their lives—when they could live together again while Nathan and others tried to discover Maverick's identity.

Tom stayed right behind her as she silently went up the steps in the dark, leading him to a large bedroom at the back of the house. "We're in my room, Tom. I'm going to turn a light on now."

"Go ahead. I've checked out the house and we're the only ones in it. I've been in the attic and basement. No wonder these old houses are in scary movies. Plunk one of these in a scene and you already have atmosphere before you even start."

"I love this old house and there isn't anything scary about it, including the basement."

"I'm glad to hear you say that. Let's start hanging sheets and get you some privacy. Tomorrow you buy whatever you want—shutters, shades, curtains. Get something that will be easier to deal with than sheets on the windows for these upstairs rooms. Downstairs we can hang sheets and leave them."

Lost in thoughts about Emily, Tom worked fast. He was tall enough to hang sheets in front of a lot of windows without getting on a ladder, but he needed a stepladder for others.

"This place doesn't have an alarm system. You should go ahead and get one tomorrow and make arrangements to have it installed as soon as possible. I can recommend a good one. The guy who has the franchise is an ex-Ranger and a friend. He'll do a rush job."

"You're getting really bossy," she said. Her voice was light and he knew she was teasing.

Tom got hot working, so he yanked off his shirt. When he turned around to reach for another sheet, he glanced at Emily. She stood transfixed as her gaze danced over his chest. Her cheeks were pink, her breathing fast, and desire filled her expression as she stared at him. She looked up and met his gaze, making his pulse speed up.

Without breaking eye contact, he crossed the room to her. The temperature in the room climbed and memories tugged at him—of holding her, of kissing her, of making love. Desire intensified as he looked down into her green eyes. He slipped his hand behind her head, feeling her soft hair, looking at her mouth. Memories tore at him of kissing her and how soft her mouth was.

She looked up at him with a dazed expression as she shook her head.

"No," she whispered. "Tom, I was just getting adjusted to being on my own—I don't want to do this."

He could barely hear her over his pounding heart. "The hell you don't." His voice was low and gruff. "Emily, it's been so long. A kiss won't change anything. We can kiss and walk away." He was fighting to control desire because he wanted her more than he had dreamed possible. He hadn't made love to her in so long and there had been no other women. He was hard, ready, with visions taunting him of Emily naked in his arms. Memories poured over him of how she responded, of her scalding kisses and her hungry zest for making love.

He pulled her to him and kissed her passionately, wanting to take her now, hard and fast, yet knowing when she agreed to sex, he should take his time. And he felt she would agree. One look into her big green eyes and he could tell she was as ready as he was. Maybe not tonight, but soon, so soon. Heat filled him at the thought.

He bent over her and continued the kiss, dimly aware that her arms were wrapped around him and she held him tightly, rubbing against him, moaning with pleasure.

She was soft, warm, luscious in his arms. He slipped his hand over her breast and felt he would burst with hungry need to just take her now. Fighting for control, he caressed her. Her softness sent his temperature soaring. She wriggled out of his embrace and stepped back, gulping air.

"I can't do this. I just can't. It's emotional turmoil and I get too worked up and torn up. We're not good for each other. We're getting divorced."

He turned away, trying to control his desire and emotions. She wanted him out of her life. "I'll be downstairs," he said, yanking on his shirt and leaving the room, knowing he had to get that divorce and move on, let go of Emily because he made her unhappy.

He went down the steps, moving quietly, his gaze adjusting to the darkness as he reached the first floor. He looked over his shoulder and saw the light in the hall that spilled from her upstairs bedroom. She had been right—how were they going to stay in the same house, live together and not constantly hurt each other?

He wanted her, but the damned attraction between them that had been so exciting, sexy and fantastic in the early years was now an albatross for both of them.

Yet he had to stay with her. He couldn't walk out of here and leave her alone in this big rambling house that came straight out of a horror movie. She had zero security. She might not want him here any more than she had in the big house on the ranch, but he had to stay until she repaired the windows and installed alarms. Maverick scared him. What could either of them have possibly done to make someone so angry?

Tom stepped outside, letting his eyes adjust to the dark. Was anyone watching Emily? Was she in any danger?

He looked up at the house. The second story in front was as dark as the downstairs. Tom walked back to the porch and sat in the dark, trying to cool down, to stop thinking about her kiss or how soft she was. To stop thinking about divorcing Emily. It still seemed impossible.

He remembered that night on the bus in Colorado. They'd spent the day on the ski slopes near a new lodge with an indoor water park. By the time they started back to the hotel where they were staying, the weather had changed and the driver said they would skip the planned stop for dinner. In a short time, it had turned into a blizzard.

On a curve on the side of a mountain, the bus hit ice and slid off the road. Going down the mountainside, the bus crashed into trees and then rolled. Seat belts gave way and people and belongings were tossed into the aisle. The sounds of screams, yelling and crying rose above the howling wind. Emily had screamed to him to get Ryan. He wanted to protect both of them, but she was right that he had to focus on trying to help their son. Tom had tried to hold Ryan in his seat and protect him as the bus crashed down the mountain. Ryan kept crying, "Daddy! Daddy!" until his screams went silent.

Something had struck Tom, causing pain to shoot across his shoulder and arm as the bus slid on one side. Another blow brought oblivion. Seconds—or minutes—later, he'd come to and fought to stay conscious. The headlights were still on and Tom had seen a sheet of gray ice illuminated in the bus's headlights and fading into darkness—and he'd realized the momentum was carrying the bus to a frozen pond.

To Tom's horror, Ryan and the seat he had been buckled into were gone. "Ryan!" Tom's shout had been lost in all the chaos and noise. His cousin appeared and Tom yelled to Jack to look for Emily. People screamed and children cried. Most chilling of all, he couldn't hear his son's voice, and in the darkness he hadn't been able to see.

The front of the bus had lurched as it slid onto the frozen pond. At the same time, he'd heard the loud crack of ice breaking. The bus tilted and in seconds the bus slid partially underwater. Water gushed into the bus through gashes ripped in the sides and windows broken during the slide down the mountain. He'd had only minutes to find Ryan and get them both to the surface before the bus slipped deeper into the water.

It probably only took a minute for him to find his son, but it had seemed like forever. Holding Ryan's unconscious body against his chest and with his own lungs about to burst, Tom fought to get out of the wreck and to the surface. When he finally broke through, he swam the short distance to shore, where someone hauled him up onto the ground.

Red-and-blue lights flashed, sirens sounded, people were crying and yelling and screaming. To his relief there were already ambulances, and Tom had fought to get Ryan on one and climbed in with him when Jack appeared with Emily. Tom hauled her into the ambulance. An attendant started to say something to him, looked at Tom and merely nodded. The paramedics hovered over Ryan after a cursory look at Tom and Emily.

She had a head wound with blood streaming over her face and into her hair. Tom collapsed in the ambulance. He had broken bones, sprains, a ruptured spleen, deep cuts and pneumonia. He and Ryan each ended up in surgery. Tom was moved off the critical list after a day, but Ryan lived eleven days on life support.

Tom would never forget the day they'd returned to the ranch and walked into the empty house. Emily had started sobbing. He had embraced her, holding her while she cried quietly, and he'd felt as if his heart was shattering. He couldn't console her. All he could do was tell her he was sorry.

"You couldn't save him. I couldn't save him. We've lost our baby," she cried.

Tom couldn't keep back tears and his throat was raw. He held her close and stroked her head and knew there were no words to console her.

It was a crushing loss they would have to live with all their lives. Her words—"You couldn't save him"— would also be with him the rest of his life.

As he reflected on the difficult times, Tom wiped his eyes, then ran his hand over the scar on his knee. He would always have scars on his body and his heart from that night. Tom put his head in his hands. He should have been able to save Ryan. It was his fault and he had failed Emily.

He was beginning to get some peace in his life from working on the ranch, beginning to be reconciled to their separation, when Maverick sent the message to Emily.

Now Tom was back with her, and there was no way he could stop their attraction. She was irresistible, yet when they were together, it conjured up all the old hurts.

Tonight was the first time he had kissed Emily since

he moved out of the house last year. It had stirred his desire and probably ruined his chances of sleep for the night. How long would they be together? Was she in danger, or was Maverick just a coward who would go away after a while?

Until Tom knew, he wasn't going to leave her alone. He should have saved Ryan. He damn well wasn't going to let Emily get hurt.

He just hoped Nathan caught Maverick soon so life would settle down and he could try to pick up the pieces of his torn-up life again and move on.

He sat for an hour on the porch, gazing into the night, listening for any strange noises. He heard the sound of a frog croaking somewhere nearby. There was a slight breeze. There were no cars on the residential street. He dozed and woke and finally decided he should be closer to Emily, so he went inside. Emily had kept some odd pieces of her uncle's furniture, like the kitchen table and a rocker, but she'd gotten rid of the beds and sofas, leaving nowhere to sleep except the floor or his sleeping bag. Or with Emily.

"Damn," he whispered, thinking he had to get her out of his thoughts or he would not have another peaceful night until they caught Maverick. Then he went upstairs quietly and crossed the room adjoining hers with a door between them left open. He stretched out on his sleeping bag. He was asleep instantly. Twice in the night he stirred and went back to sleep, only to wake before sunrise.

He showered and dressed and went to the kitchen, where he cooked oatmeal.

As he poured orange juice, he heard footsteps and then Emily appeared. He was unable to resist letting his gaze drift to her toes and back up again. His breath caught in his chest.

"There goes peace and quiet for today," he said. "What are you trying to do to me, Emily?"

"What? I'm not doing anything except getting ready to fix breakfast and go to work on this house. What are you talking about?" she asked.

He walked closer and put his hands on his hips to look at her. She wore a blue cotton shirt tucked into cutoffs, ankle socks and tennis shoes. His gaze roamed over the V-neck of her blouse, down over her tiny waist and her long, long shapely legs. When his gaze slowly drifted up again, she shook her head.

"That's ridiculous. You've seen me like this hundreds of times."

"I'm used to being on the ranch with a bunch of cowhands."

"I think you better work. This place needs a lot done, and you insisted on being here."

"I'll try to concentrate on painting. Right now, I have a pot of oatmeal waiting. There are blueberries, strawberries, orange juice. Let's partake and then I'll work at the opposite end of the house."

She laughed. "You're being ridiculous," she said.

He couldn't smile. By nightfall, she would have him tied in knots. "I hope I can get my hands on this Maverick for just a few minutes," he said quietly. She heard him and smiled, shaking her head because she probably thought he was joking.

As they ate, Tom sipped coffee and looked around. "I sent a text to my friend and he'll be out this morning to look at the house and give you an estimate on the cost of the alarm. I told him it's a rush."

"That's fast, Tom."

"I'm a very good customer. I send a lot of business their way by telling friends and other ranchers about them."

"You're taking charge again."

"I'm just helping you get organized and telling you what I can do to help. I can do other things," he said, unable to resist flirting with her. When she walked into the room, she brought cheer and sunshine that drove away his demons from the night. "We're eating together and we'll work together."

"We'll work together. With you here, I don't know why I need an alarm. Now if you're planning on leaving—" she said cheerfully before he interrupted.

"I'm not leaving you. I'll take you with me if I need to. I'm here until they get Maverick. This place is going to take a whole lot to fix," he said, looking around.

"It's all I have," she answered quietly, looking at the high ceiling in the kitchen. "It's a tie to Mom and Uncle Woody and, really, a tie to when we first got married and after Ryan was born. Uncle Woody was always so happy to see Ryan."

"I remember staying here with you after we married when your uncle went to Chicago to his Shriner convention."

"I remember, too, and all we did was stay in bed. But we're not going to reminisce about that."

"Might be more fun than painting the house," Tom said, and she smiled as she shook her head.

She stood and leaned forward over the table. "You're so good at giving orders. Well, so am I. You clean the kitchen while I get out the paint and brushes."

"Where did Uncle Woody keep his paintbrushes?"

"In the workshop at the back of the garage."

"I think I'll go with you to get them and then I'll clean the kitchen."

"Tom—"

"We've been over this. You don't know how angry Maverick is. Besides, you'll enjoy my company."

"Too bad you don't have more confidence."

He walked around the table as they both carried their dishes to the sink.

"You win," she said with a sigh. "Let's both clean the kitchen and then we'll both go get the paint and brushes."

He worked fast, glancing at her. He had been teasing, but what he'd said to her was the truth. He had been dealing with guys who worked for him, cattle, horses, dusty fields and new calves. To work with her dressed in shorts and a cotton shirt was dazzling, and it was going to be difficult to keep his mind on anything else. Emily was good-looking, and it seemed to him she had gotten more so in the past year. He turned to watch her.

He thought about their kiss yesterday and just as quickly knew that was the way to disaster. He needed to think about getting the house safe. He needed to think about anything except kissing or making love to her. He turned again to look at her, taking his time because her back was still to him. She couldn't reach a shelf to put a bowl away. He crossed the room, took the bowl from her and placed it on the shelf, turning to her.

"Thank you," she said. Her words came out breathless and he knew he should walk away quickly.

He stopped at the door. "Ready to go get paint?"

"Sure. I think we better get to work," she said, heading for the kitchen door. He crossed the room to follow her out. They were kidding and flirting—something that hadn't happened in an incredibly long time, since before he moved out.

Did she want to make love? The thought made the temperature in the room rev up several notches. Did he want the emotional storm again? Looking at her legs and thinking about yesterday's kiss, he realized he did. If he had a chance, he'd take it even if it meant hurting later when they said goodbye. And he knew they would say goodbye no matter what they did during this time while Maverick was on the loose. Their problems were unsolvable and permanent. They had lost their son, and Emily could not get pregnant again and would not adopt because she had wanted a child exactly like Ryan, with their blood in his or her veins. And she blamed him for Ryan's death. Tom knew he had failed her, failed Ryan, and there was never a day that passed that he didn't think about it.

None of that could stop this lusty desire to seduce her, though.

Tom held the door for her and they walked to the garage, which was dark and stuffy. Tom took one look at the ladder and shook his head. "No way."

"Here we go again. Are you going to tell me I can't use that ladder?"

"I sure as hell am." He stepped on the bottom rung and put all his weight on it. It snapped in two and he dropped to the ground.

"Want to fall today? I'll be glad to catch you. Go ahead and try."

She shook her head. "Okay. You made your point—a new ladder."

He looked around. "Em, you need new paint, new brushes and a new ladder. When was the last time you or your uncle used this stuff?"

"Probably when I was seventeen. I don't remember." She laughed again. "You win that one. Let's go."

He placed his hand on her waist and she stopped instantly, looking up at him. "This reminds me of when we dated. I remember being out here once with you."

She blushed again. "I think we better go."

"Want to know how to make work a little bit fun? Do you remember being here with me?"

"Yes, I remember every single second. You know full well what you can do to me," she answered and this time she was breathless. They might both have regrets, but right now he thought she wanted to kiss as much as he did. Sliding his arm around her waist, he leaned down to kiss her.

The minute his mouth touched hers, he lost the casual, playful attitude he'd had. His tongue went deep as she stood on tiptoe, wound her arms around his neck and pressed against him. She kissed him in return, setting him on fire with longing. He might be sorry tomorrow, but right now, he wanted to kiss her for the rest of the day and the night.

He wound his fingers in her thick, soft hair and ran his other hand down over her enticing bottom. He could easily get his fingers inside her tiny shorts. She gasped and moaned with pleasure, thrusting her hips against him. He wanted her and he was hot, on fire, melting from her kisses and from touching her intimately.

She finally stepped out of his arms and gasped for breath. "We're going to have regrets," she said and turned, walking away swiftly. "You close up," she said over her shoulder and kept going.

He wanted to seduce her. Even knowing that it would cause a world of pain later and complicate his life, that he would have regrets because nothing was going to change between them, he wanted to make love to her all night long.

He'd known when he told her he was going to stay with her until they caught Maverick that he was walking straight into more heartache. He kicked one of the paint cans and it rolled across the floor and hit a wall. Why did she have to be so damned sexy? She'd always appealed to him, and that had never changed no matter what kind of heartaches they had between them.

And she wanted to make love. She was at war with herself and trying to maintain control, but he could tell what she wanted. When he touched and kissed her, her response was instant and intense.

He looked at the ladder; it was a piece of junk. He

gathered it up along with the paint cans and took them out to the big trash barrel. He went back to close the garage door and fasten the lock. As he walked back to the house, he wondered if he could seduce her. He had a sleeping bag and she had a cot. He didn't care if he had to stand on top of the car, he wanted her. "Stay away from her," he said aloud. "Leave her alone. She's trouble. Pure trouble," he added.

He didn't find her downstairs, but before he could go up to the second floor to look for her, she appeared at the top of the stairs. She wore a long-sleeved T-shirt and jeans and had her hair in a pigtail.

She came down fast and paused on the bottom step. "Now I should look much more ordinary and unappealing. Less...something."

"Go ahead and say it—less sexy. You'll never look unappealing to me and there will never be a time you are not tempting. But I know we have things to do, so I'll try to avoid looking below your chin or at your cute butt when you walk away. I'll warn you, no matter how you dress, my thoughts are wicked and sinful."

"I believe that one," she said, smiling, and he smiled in return.

"I'm glad we can still get along, Emily."

"Time helps," she said, and she sounded earnest. All the playfulness left her voice. He felt as if there was a very thin veneer of joy and fun and sex appeal, of what they used to have together, and in this rarefied atmosphere, they could enjoy each other's company again. But beyond that, nothing had changed—their close, loving relationship had ended long ago.

Tom's friend came from the alarm company and Tom joined her while they settled on the alarm system with the stipulation that it would be installed Monday...

At noon, they decided to take a break from their errands and went to the Royal Diner again for another burger.

"Yesterday when we left here, I didn't think I would ever be here again to eat a burger with you. Here I am less than twenty-four hours later. I didn't think that would be possible," Emily said.

"Just goes to show, expect more and maybe you'll get more."

"Right."

After a few minutes, he smiled at her. "I'm glad your photography is going well."

"I like it and I'm getting customers from other towns. I may just move to Dallas if business continues to grow. I'll keep Uncle Woody's house—"

"Em, it's your house now. You can stop calling it Uncle Woody's," Tom said, but his thoughts were on her moving to Dallas. When she said that, he felt another stab of loss. Instantly, he knew that was ridiculous because when their divorce went through, he and Emily would go their separate ways. He tried to avoid thinking about the future and pay attention to what she was saying to him.

"It's difficult to remember that this is my house now. Frankly, it's still Uncle Woody's to me even though I own it." She sipped her malt and after a few minutes asked, "Do you miss the military?"

Tom shook his head. "No. I've served and I'm glad

to be on the ranch now. Life hasn't turned out the way I expected it to, but I love the ranch. Frankly, Em, losing Jeremy took it out of me. That one hurt more than the others. Maybe it's because of losing Ryan and because I'm older now, but I've had enough of death and my buddies getting hurt."

"You were patriotic serving your country," she said, placing her hand on his. Instantly, he inhaled. She blinked and started to jerk her hand away, but he covered it and held it between his.

"That's nice. Don't pull away," he said softly.

"We're both doing things that will make it worse. We'll be hurt all over again because our future hasn't changed and isn't going to."

He felt a pinch to his heart and released her hand. "You're right," he said. "If I pass the sheriff's office and Nathan is there, I'll see what I can find out. I'm sure nothing eventful has happened or we would have heard something."

"We'll have the meeting at the TCC Monday morning."

"I hope this balmy spring weather holds, because we can keep the house aired out as we paint." He nodded and they lapsed into silence as they finished their burgers and then left to get her painting supplies.

When they returned to the house, she propped the front door open. "Tom, the paint fumes will be awful. There's an attic fan that will draw fresh air through and take out the fumes. I want to open the windows that are left and turn it on."

"That's fine with me. Another thing—I'll do the ceilings. Let me do the high stuff and you stay off the ladder."

"There's no end to your orders. You're no longer in the military, remember?"

"And you never were in it and you don't take orders worth a damn," he said, smiling and shaking his head.

"That definitely isn't so. Here you are, staying with me. I didn't think that one up. I'm not getting on the ladder. I didn't make that decision. I'm getting an alarm because of you. I've moved upstairs because of you."

"You won't let me kiss you. I have to catch you by surprise and then you run me off," he said, moving closer and looking into her big green eyes.

"Not so," she said, smiling. "You kiss me every time you decide you want to and you know it," she said, poking his hard stomach with her forefinger as if to emphasize what she was saying. "Mmm, that's impressive," she said, poking him again.

"Let's see if you'll let me kiss you just any old time," he said, wrapping his arms around her and leaning over her. His mouth covered and opened hers, his tongue going deep as he leaned farther until she clung to him and kissed him in return and he forgot their silly conversation. Holding her tightly, he straightened up and his arm tightened around her waist while he slowly ran his hand down her back and over her bottom. Then his hand drifted up and he unbuttoned her blouse as he kissed her. He caressed her breast, pushing away her bra.

She finally caught his hand and held it. "Tom, wait. Don't complicate our lives. You know where we're headed—for more hurt," she whispered, looking up at him. He gazed at her intently. He was aroused, hard and ready. He wanted her and he didn't think she would argue. As he gazed at her, he thought about the rift between them and knew she really didn't want his loving.

"You're right. We've hurt each other enough," he said softly. "I'll get the windows open and start painting downstairs."

Five

Tom stood on the new ladder, painting the front parlor ceiling, while Emily painted upstairs in one of the big bedrooms. He'd been at it for hours. At a certain point, he had changed to cutoffs and a sleeveless T-shirt because the air-conditioning was off since the house was open.

As Tom worked he thought about her living in the big house all alone. She might be thinking the same thing about him on the ranch, but he never felt alone there. He worked with guys all day and he could go find someone whenever he wanted to. And when they divorced he would be able to get a date when he wanted. But at this point in his life, he couldn't imagine wanting to go out with someone. The thought of Emily doing so was another deep hurt.

His estrangement from Emily had left Tom numb and hurting, and his life would have to change a lot before he would ever want to get involved with someone again. He was surprised how well he was getting along with Emily, because it really hurt to be together and he knew it hurt her. Their divorce had merely been tabled until later but definitely loomed in the near future.

He thought about the big, expensive mansion they had built on the ranch. He didn't want to go back to it, yet it was a tie to Ryan—it was where they'd brought him home from the hospital. Where they'd rocked him to sleep and read to him, sung him songs.

What could Tom do with the house? He had no idea, and he didn't intend to worry about it now.

He wiped his sweaty forehead and tried to concentrate on his brushstrokes and keep working steadily. When he finished this side of the room, he was taking a break and going to find Emily.

After another hour of work, Tom ordered pizzas for dinner. When they were done with their break they returned to painting.

It was after 11:00 p.m. when he went to find her again in the front parlor. She was on her knees, painting the baseboard, and his gaze roamed over her trim, very sexy ass. He inhaled deeply and knocked on the open door.

Emily looked up and sat back on her haunches as Tom entered. "You're just in time. I'm getting tired of this and I think the paint fumes are getting to me even with the windows open and the fans blowing."

"Let's knock off for tonight, sit on the porch and have

a cold drink, and just relax. It's do-nothing time." He crossed the room to her and took her brush. "I'll clean the brushes."

"And I'll get the drinks," she said, standing and looking at the painting she had done. Tom put the lid on her paint can and then picked up the other brushes.

"Let's get out of here. We need fresh air and I want a cold beer."

"I want a drink, too. See you on the porch."

She got there first and sat in one of the big wooden rocking chairs. She had brought beer for Tom and iced tea for herself. It was cool on the porch, and in minutes her eyes adjusted to the darkness. Tom came out and picked up a small table with their drinks to place it slightly in front of their chairs and then moved his rocking chair closer to hers.

"Now the view is better here," he said when he sat down.

"Liar. You can't enjoy the view in all this darkness. You just wanted to sit closer together," she said, amused by him. "It's nice out here."

"Yes, it is, and it's nicer closer together."

"It's wonderful you've been helping the Valentines. You're a good guy and I still feel so foolish for believing that email. That was a huge mistake."

"Forget that, Em. We worked it out, and Natalie invited us to a picnic in the park next Saturday, if you want. I told her I'd call her after I talk to you."

"Saturday's fine."

"Can you skip painting long enough for a picnic?"

"Of course. I have your help with painting and I

hadn't planned on that. I'd like to meet them. Once again, I hope whoever Maverick is, word gets back that we're all having a good time together."

"The way word gets around Royal, I suspect it will. You'll like Natalie. After her loss, she understands ours in a way some people really don't. Jeremy was a great guy. We were close—he was almost like a brother to me. Sometimes the stuff you go through when your life is at stake creates a real bond."

"I should have known you wouldn't have a secret family."

"As you said, the picture was convincing."

They sat quietly in the dark while she sipped her raspberry tea and Tom drank his beer. She watched the shifting shadows on the lawn. "I still think you should go back to the ranch. I can get this done."

"Nope. I'm staying, and you should let me do the high stuff in every room."

"Oh, my. If you're volunteering to paint the ceilings in this old house, I will take you up on that with joy. I figured I would hire a painter to do the ceilings, but if you're sure, that fun task is yours. I'm thrilled because I can't do them."

"I'll start on the ceilings and see how far I can get. When and if they catch Maverick, I'm gone. You know that."

"Of course. I know you didn't move in permanently."

"Somehow I can't imagine you here permanently."

"I don't know why—I lived here when we met. We were together in this house lots of times."

"I was just noticing how dark it is out here. The

branches of these big oaks almost touch the ground, and they give a lot of privacy. When I move out, I think you should have yard lights and motion detectors installed."

"By the time you get through, I'll have a chain-link fence with razor wire at the top and spotlights. You were in the Rangers too long and in scary, violent situations too much. This is Royal, Tom. All the precautions aren't necessary. We're safe here. And no one cares what we're doing behind the branches of the oak tree."

"You think?" he asked, setting down his bottle of beer. "Well, if we have privacy and no one cares what we do, I think I'm wasting a really good night by sitting over here alone." He stood and she wondered what he was up to now.

He leaned over to pick her up and then sat down again with her on his lap. She gasped in surprise and started to protest, but she liked being in his arms again, so she closed her mouth and wrapped her arm around his neck instead. "It's as dark as a cave out here tonight. I can't see you," she said quietly. "What brought this on?"

"Why not? We've got privacy to do what we want— you just said so. Why not forget our problems for ten minutes and enjoy each other's company and a few kisses besides? Or more."

She smiled as she ran her fingers through his hair. "You really have a one-track mind."

"No, I've been alone for a long time," he replied. "And now I'm with you. That's the biggest part of it."

His voice was low, the way it got when he was lusty. She was aware of being in his arms, on his lap. Even more, she was aware of his arousal. He flirted and teased the way he used to, so it was fun to be with him.

"You're not only a good guy. You're a very sexy guy."

"Is that right? On a scale of one to ten, where do I rate?" he asked, nuzzling her neck.

"Somewhere around one hundred," she said, her words coming out breathlessly and as if she barely thought about what she said. "But I'm not going to let you complicate my life tonight. I've spent the past year picking up the pieces and I'm on a shaky foundation—"

"This will get you on something solid."

"You're naughty, Tom," she replied as he trailed kisses across her neck and ran his tongue around the curve of her ear.

"But, oh, so sexy. You just said so." He kissed away her answer. His mouth covered hers, his arm tightening around her as he leaned her against his shoulder. She clung to him, kissing him in return. His kisses sizzled, making her want more loving from him.

He raised his head and yanked off his shirt, tossing it aside while she said, "For just a minute more, Tom. That's all we—"

He leaned close to kiss her again and end her talk. And she didn't care. She clung to him, thinking he was the most exciting man on earth and trying to avoid thinking about all the painful things that had come between them.

He caressed her breast and then slipped his hand beneath her shirt. His hand was warm, his palm rough and callused. He unfastened her bra easily and pushed it away. She moaned with pleasure as her breast filled his hand. His thumb circled the taut peak and she shifted her hips closer against him—as close as possible while she arched her back and gave him more access to caress her further. For the moment she was lost to the sensations he stirred up. His hands on her, his mouth on her—it seemed natural and right and made her want more. But the memories of past heartache were still strong. Suddenly she thought back to the last time they'd made love—he'd moved out immediately after.

"Tom, wait." She paused to look at him as she placed her hand on his jaw and felt the short stubble beneath her fingers and palm. "You're going to bring back all that we're trying to get away from."

"Live a little, darlin'. We should just let go and enjoy each other and the night. You can't tell me you don't like this."

"You know I love everything you do," she said, "but we've tried every way possible to work things out and haven't even come close." She wiggled away and slipped off his lap. "It's time for me to go upstairs."

He didn't answer. She left her drink and turned to hurry inside. She wanted to be in his arms, ached to have him carry her to bed and make love to her all night long. But if he did, morning would come and with it painful choices. They would go back to the way they were and it would hurt more than ever. She couldn't stay on that seesaw of hot sex and then estrangement. He couldn't have it both ways. Besides, she knew the night he moved out to the guesthouse, he had meant it to be for good.

She rushed upstairs, fighting with herself silently

every second because she really wanted to go right back to him. But it would be futile and lead to more hurt. She grabbed clothes and went to her shower, hoping he didn't come upstairs until she was asleep.

Finally she was settled beneath the sheets on her cot. The house was still open, the windows flung wide, but Tom would take care of everything downstairs and lock up. She didn't have to worry about any of it. What she had to worry about was Tom causing her to fall in love with him again.

She rolled over on her back and stared at the open windows. Her thoughts were on tonight and Tom. She couldn't fall in love with him again. She wasn't going through what they had before. She couldn't get pregnant and give him another son. Or a daughter. It wasn't going to happen. It had hurt to tell him over and over that she was not pregnant.

It was more than an hour later when she heard a board creak and then all was quiet. She closed her eyes and lay still, wondering if he would come see if she was asleep. She couldn't deal with him again tonight. She was torn between wanting to pull him down on the cot with her and avoiding any physical contact. His love-making could take her out of the world, but then later, regret would consume her.

The next morning she showered and dressed, pulling on a sleeveless pale blue cotton dress to wear to church. She brushed her wavy hair that fell loosely around her face. Stepping into blue high heels, she picked up her envelope purse, took a deep breath and went downstairs to breakfast.

When she entered the kitchen, Tom came to his feet and her heart lurched as her gaze ran over his white shirt, red tie and navy suit. "You look handsome enough to have breakfast with," she said. "Oh, my."

"You look gorgeous, Em," he said in a husky voice. "I fixed cheese grits with shrimp. Your orange juice is poured."

"Thank you," she said. She had already left her purse on a folding chair in the front room. She crossed the room to pour coffee. "Let me guess—you're going to church with me because of Maverick."

"That and because you're the best-looking, sexiest woman in the county."

She laughed and turned toward him. He took the coffee from her hand and set it on the counter, and her pulse raced. His arm circled her waist and she placed her hand lightly against his chest. "You'll wrinkle me," she said, trying to ignore the heat building inside her.

He dropped his hand, leaned forward and placed his mouth on hers without touching her anywhere else. She was as lost in his kiss as she would have been if he had embraced her. Desire rocked her, and she wrapped her arms around him, stepping close to hold him tightly while she kissed him in return and forgot about wrinkles and her dress.

He made a sound deep in his throat and his arms wrapped around her tightly, holding her against him. His kiss was demanding, making her want to kiss him back and shower kisses on him the rest of the day.

Instead, she stepped away and gulped for breath. "Do you do that just to see if you still can? If that's why, I'll tell you that yes, you can turn me to mush and set me on fire at the same time." She stared at him a moment and then walked away quickly. "I'm going to church."

"Come eat your breakfast. You have time and I'll get out of here," he said and left the room.

She closed her eyes momentarily, trying to get composed. Her lips tingled and she wanted to make love. She ate a few bites of the cheese grits, drank some orange juice and coffee and left it all until later to clean. She hurried upstairs and brushed her teeth. When she came back downstairs and grabbed her purse, Tom was nowhere around. She had already decided it would be a good day for her to walk.

She opened the door to leave, and as she crossed the porch, he stepped up to walk beside her. "I'll drive you there."

"I was going to walk."

"Let's take the car. You'll be a few minutes early. When you walk, you may be as safe as money in the bank vault, but humor me. I don't like you getting a message from Maverick and I can't relax about it."

"I understand," she said, trying to be patient but thinking he was being overly protective.

"You win the prize for the correct answer."

"I'm trying, too, Tom. I know your background makes you think the way you do and I know this will end. Maverick will be caught or stop sending messages and disappear. Before long we'll go our separate ways," she said, feeling a tightness in her chest when she said those last words.

"We'll get the divorce as soon as this is over," he said, sounding tense. "I've been thinking about that. We can work it out ourselves, turn it over to our attorneys."

"I think we can work this out. I know you'll be not only fair but generous, because that's the way you are."

"Thanks," he said in a flat voice that indicated this was hard for him. He held open her car door, closing it after she was seated.

As he drove away from the house, he glanced at her. "I've thought about our divorce. We can get a dollar figure on what the ranch and livestock are worth and I can buy you out. We can add the vehicles and the plane to that estimate and I'll pay you for those. You keep your car. We won't count it."

His hands gripped the steering wheel tightly. She knew him well, and knew by his tone of voice that he was unhappy.

"We don't have to decide yet," she said.

"We might as well make the decisions and be ready. When the time comes, it'll be easier and quicker and then we can say goodbye." He drew a deep breath and she hurt inside.

When he parked at the church, he walked around the car to open the door for her.

"Thank you," she said as she emerged into sunshine.

"Smile. We don't know this troll's identity, but I want Maverick to see that his damned email didn't do anything except get us together." She smiled and he took her arm. She thought they probably looked like a happy

couple. She hoped the person hiding behind the name
Maverick thought they were happily together again.
Then she recalled how shocked she had been looking
at the picture of Tom and the Valentines. Next Saturday
she would meet them, and she was looking forward to
it. She glanced up at Tom, sorry she had doubted him.
He was a wonderful guy who had been a good dad and
husband. That's what hurt so badly.

After church he took her to eat at the Texas Cattleman's Club, and afterward they drove back to her house
to paint again. It was the first Sunday in March and it
was a perfect spring day. She pulled on cutoffs and another T-shirt.

She found him downstairs in the front parlor, prying
open a can of white paint. Plastic drop cloths covered
the hardwood floor. The ladder stood to one side and he
had papers spread with brushes and stir sticks laid out.

"Calm yourself, because you've seen me in shorts
and less plenty of times," she said when she joined him
to get the can of paint he had opened for her.

He straightened, turning to look at her.

"Although I think I'm the one who might not be able
to concentrate," she amended, fanning herself as her
gaze roamed over him. Tom was all muscle, in excellent
physical shape and incredibly strong. She tried to avoid
memories of making love and how exciting he could
be. As her gaze drifted over him again, she looked up
and met his hazel eyes.

"We could put off painting," he said in a husky voice.

She shook her head even though she didn't want
to. "Did you open a can of paint for me?" Her voice

was raspy and she couldn't stop looking at his broad shoulders.

He stepped over the paint cans and approached her. She threw up both hands. "I'm going to work. Give me the paint. I have to get this house painted, and you're here now and can help."

"What room? I'll carry it for you," he said.

"The front bedroom," she said, turning to go. He walked beside her. "We've already lost the morning and part of the afternoon. I want to get something done today." She felt as if she was babbling. In the bedroom she waved her hand. "Thanks. I'll start here and work my way around."

He put the can on the floor, turned to her, stepped close and caught her chin lightly in his fingers. "You want to kiss and so do I."

"I'm trying to be sensible and not complicate our lives more. Not to mention getting my house painted."

"See which you like best," he said and drew her close, leaning down to kiss her. She stood in his arms for about two seconds before she hugged him back, sliding her hand over his broad shoulders and down one arm over rock-hard biceps. Then she wrapped her arms around his narrow waist. It always amazed her how narrow his waist was and how flat his stomach. She finally stopped him and stepped back, trying to catch her breath, pulling her T-shirt down.

"We could make love and get that out of our systems."

She smiled at him. "Good try."

He grinned and shrugged. "It's definitely worth a

try. I might bring that up again after you've painted for seven or eight hours and the sun goes down."

"You can try me and see," she said in a sultry voice, unable to resist flirting with him.

Something flickered in the depths of his eyes, and a faint smile raised the corner of his mouth. "Ah, I think I'm on the right track. I will try again. That's a promise." He stepped close and touched the corner of her mouth. "It's good to see you smile and laugh. We used to have lots of smiles and laughs and it's nice to share them again."

"It's temporary, Tom. Nothing has changed," she stated, hurting because of all they had lost and still stood to lose.

His smile faded. "I know."

"Now, it's time for you to go to work, too, and make yourself useful. You insisted on this," she said, picking up a brush.

He leaned close and placed his hand on her shoulders. She looked into his eyes and was aware his mouth was only inches away. She drew a deep breath, wanting to kiss him and knowing she should not.

"I can make myself not only useful, but indispensable," he said as he ran his hands so lightly along her bare thighs, then sliding them to the insides of her legs.

She placed a paintbrush in his hand. "You go paint and stop with the seduction scene."

"I thought I was doing pretty good."

She leaned forward so her nose almost touched his. "You know you're doing damn good, so you have to go or this house will never get painted," she said.

"Suit yourself, darlin'. I'm ready, willing and able."

"Ready, willing and able to pick up a brush and paint? Great. Go do it and I will, too. Goodbye, Tom." She turned away and bent over to pick up the paint can and received a whistle of appreciation from him. She straightened up and spun around, but he was already going out the door. Smiling, she shook her head. It was all a lot of foolishness, but if she had taken him up on any of his offers they would be making love now, and that made her hot and tingly and wanting him back holding her close.

She dreaded going through the divorce. It would be another wrenching, painful loss, but it was inevitable. They had tried to stay married, but it didn't work and just hurt more as time passed.

She got busy painting, a routine chore that left her thoughts free. And Tom filled them. Before Maverick's email, she'd thought she was beginning to achieve some peace. She'd been adjusting to life without Tom, as well as the realization that he would be out of her life for good when they divorced. Life on the ranch, which she had loved in so many ways, would also be gone. But she was beginning to find a life for herself as a photographer. She had made the move from the ranch to Royal. Now she had been thrown a curveball when Tom came to stay with her. They were flirting, laughing together—something that didn't happen after they lost Ryan. A week ago she wouldn't have guessed that they could be this relaxed together again. Maybe it was because they had lost everything they'd once had between them. Now the worst had happened and she didn't feel as tense. Maybe she had worried too much about disappointing Tom, and the fear was a self-fulfilling prophecy. It was fun to tease and flirt again. She missed what she'd once had with Tom.

Whatever the reasons, working with him on the house now reminded her of old times together when they could flirt and kiss and laugh. It was also going to hurt a lot more to tell him goodbye after being here together.

It was almost midnight when they settled in the rocking chairs on the porch. Tom had his cold beer and she had her raspberry tea and they sat quietly rocking.

"I remember when Uncle Woody would come out here and mow the lawn. He'd wave to anyone who passed and talk to neighbors who walked by."

"Your uncle was a friendly man. I liked him. When you and I dated, sometimes he gave me a look and I wondered if he was going to tell me to get lost and leave you alone."

"No. Uncle Woody liked you and thought you were good for me."

"That's nice to hear."

"I'm glad he didn't know about our divorce. I think losing Ryan is what—" She paused, because she hadn't ever voiced aloud her theory about her uncle's death. Tears threatened and she was grateful for the dark.

"Was what?" Tom asked and his voice had changed, deepened and become serious.

"I think he just died of a broken heart. He wasn't well, but he wasn't that ill. He had a heart problem, but when Ryan died, part of Uncle Woody died and there was never a time I saw him after that when he didn't cry over Ryan. It broke his heart. So I lost them both."

Tom sat in silence and she wondered what was going through his mind. She wiped her eyes, gradually regaining her composure.

"I'm going for a walk around the place. I have my phone if you want me," he said tersely. Then he faded into the darkness.

Tom walked around the property, staying in shadows, moving without making noise and taking his time.

Emily's revelation about her uncle's death hurt. Tom had no doubt that Woody had blamed him for his failure to save Ryan. He felt equally certain Woody had blamed Tom for Emily's unhappiness. He was just one more person who was important to Tom that he had failed.

He finally decided to rejoin Emily on the porch or just sit there alone if she had gone inside. But when he got back to the front of the house, she was still there. He climbed the steps to sit by her.

"You're back. This is nice, Tom. I'll miss us out here together when you go," she said quietly.

"Maybe I'll come visit and we can sit and talk. I like this, too. This is peaceful, and I can always hope I might get a kiss or two or get you to sit on my lap."

"No," she said, a note of sadness in her voice. "After our divorce, you'll go out, fall in love and marry again. You'll have a family, because that is what you were meant for. You're wonderful with kids. You and I will go our separate ways and our marriage will just be memories that fade into oblivion." She stood. "I'm going inside."

He came to his feet swiftly and wrapped his arms around her to kiss her, a hard, possessive kiss that took only seconds before she responded.

When he slipped his hand beneath her shirt and caressed her, she moaned softly, holding him until she suddenly stepped away.

"I can't go there. We'll just hurt each other more. I've disappointed you in the past and I don't see any future. Making love just binds us together for more heartache. I'm going in." She swept past him and he let her go.

She didn't want him in her life. He had failed her, disappointed her, hurt her. He needed to let her go and keep his distance and hope they caught Maverick soon. He couldn't live under the same roof with her much longer without making love, and he had no doubt that he could get her to agree, but afterward, their relationship might be worse than ever because that wasn't what Emily wanted. She wanted him out of her life. She was moving to Royal, taking up photography, finding a new life for herself, and he should do the same. He should find happiness with someone he hadn't failed and hurt and disappointed.

He stepped off the porch to circle around the big yard, wishing he could catch the troll and end his worries about Emily once and for all.

Six

Monday morning they drove the short distance to the Texas Cattleman's Club for the emergency meeting about Maverick.

Tom parked and they walked together toward the front door. Emily looked at the dark stone-and-wood clubhouse. In recent years, the TCC had voted to include women. It still hurt to walk in the front door and see the children's center where she had taken Ryan occasionally.

She waited while Tom checked his black Stetson. He wore a tan sport coat, a white dress shirt open at the throat and dark jeans, and just looking at him, her heart beat faster.

He turned and his gaze swept over her, and for another moment, she forgot everyone around them and saw only Tom. She took a deep breath. She would soon be divorced from him. Their marriage was over. Life was changing, and it was difficult to worry about Maverick when she had lost Ryan and now was losing Tom. Their happy marriage had been gone a long time, though, even if the past few days with him had reminded her of how it used to be.

Looking back now, she realized she had made a big mistake with Tom in being so desperate to get pregnant. That had made her tense and nervous on top of the grief they both dealt with daily.

Now she realized she had driven Tom away. For the past few days, she hadn't had her old worries about her inability to get pregnant, and she was relaxed with him.

At the time she hadn't realized what a mistake she'd made with him, and now it was too late to undo it.

"You look pretty," he said when he walked up to her. He leaned close to speak in her ear. "When you get home, take your hair down."

She smiled at him as she reached up, unfastened the clip that held her hair and shook her head. Her wavy, honey-brown hair fell around her face and on her shoulders.

"I like that," he said softly. He took her arm. "Let's get a seat." He turned and she walked beside him. They went through the foyer lined with oil paintings of past members. The motto of the club from its early days—Loyalty, Justice and Peace—was emblazoned on the wall in big letters for all to see.

They went past a lounge, and Emily saw a boar's head hanging above a credenza that held a crystal decanter on a silver tray. Some members wanted the stuffed animal heads removed. But they'd had been fascinating to Ryan, and as far as Emily was concerned, they could stay because other little kids might find them just as interesting.

She and Tom greeted friends as they walked through the club. Taking in her surroundings, she couldn't believe the club was more than a hundred years old. It had been founded around 1910 by Henry "Tex" Langley and other local ranchers. Tex wouldn't recognize a lot of things about the club now, particularly that women had been accepted as members, which had resulted in a child-care center where the billiard room once was.

They finally arrived at the large meeting room and settled in near the back. She had an eerie feeling when she thought about how Tom had said Maverick might be present at the meeting. As the room began to fill, she wasn't surprised to see the mean girl trio, Cecelia, Simone and Naomi, arrive and take seats near the front. Could the three women be behind the emails and blackmail? That was the rumor. But Emily couldn't imagine them doing something that wicked and then coming to this meeting. They were members of the TCC and had had background checks, friends in the club and people to vouch for them. They might be snooty, but she didn't think any one of them would do something criminal. She'd heard that Maverick blackmailed Brandee Lawless. And why would they have come after her, sending her that photo of Tom with the Valentines? How would they have even gotten such a photo?

"There's Nathan," Tom said and she glanced around the room. Sheriff Battle stood to one side, leaning against the wall, looking as if he wasn't paying attention, but she knew he probably wasn't missing anything that was happening in the big room.

At the stroke of the hour, Case appeared. Whenever she saw him, he looked in a hurry. Often he talked fast. His brown suit matched his short dark brown hair, and he looked as if he hadn't shaved for a couple of days.

"Good morning and thanks for coming," he said, holding a mike and stepping out from behind a podium they had set up for him.

People in the audience answered with an enthusiastic, "Good morning."

"Everyone here knows why we're having this meeting. We have a problem in Royal. Someone going by the name of Maverick is harassing and blackmailing people using social media and email. We need to put a stop to it." Case paused to allow for applause.

"I'd like to form a TCC committee to investigate, coordinating with the sheriff to back up his department's work. We're not law enforcement—just a group of concerned club members, citizens of Royal, who will make a big effort to keep their eyes and ears open for anything that might aid Sheriff Battle. You can sign up at the door and you'll be notified when we'll have our first meeting.

"Also, Chelsea Hunt has asked if she may speak. She has some ideas of her own that should help. Chelsea, why don't you come up here?"

Wearing head-turning designer jeans with a tucked-in white silk shirt and a leather vest, Chelsea walked up to join Case, amid more applause. Her high-heeled ankle boots made Chelsea appear to be the same height as the club president.

"Here comes the tech genius. She'll get things moving," Tom said quietly as he applauded. Emily knew that Chelsea was considered the cyber expert in Royal, so she was a good one to have at the meeting.

"I'm glad all of you are here today. I'm fully committed to the TCC's grassroots investigation into these cyber attacks. I'll have a tablet here at the front, so when the meeting is over, if you have computer skills and want to help me with the technical aspects of the investigation, please sign up. There has to be a way to find Maverick. There will be a trail of some sort, and I think if we pool resources, we can trace these messages."

Everyone applauded again and Chelsea thanked Case and sat down.

Tom stood and Case turned to him. "Tom?"

"I think we need to get word out to citizens in Royal. If they get a message from Maverick, they need to let Sheriff Battle know, even if there's blackmail involved. We can't do anything if we don't know who Maverick is targeting."

"I think we can all work on getting that message out," Case said, nodding. "Thanks." Tom sat back down.

Emily wondered how many people already knew she had received an email. She knew Tom and Nathan would only tell people on a need-to-know basis, so she suspected that not many were aware of her situation.

"Simone," Case said, recognizing Simone Parker, one of the mean girls triumvirate. There was instant quiet. Simone's striking looks, her blue eyes and long black hair usually commanded everyone's attention.

"I think we should have another meeting here in a month so the committee can bring the rest of us up-to-date on what's been done. The more informed TCC members are, the better we can deal with what's happening."

"We can do that," Case said. "If there are things Sheriff Battle thinks should not be made public, then they won't be, but otherwise, we'll meet again next month. Unless Maverick is caught in the meantime."

As Emily listened to the other speakers' suggestions, she looked over the club members in attendance. Once again she couldn't help wondering if the troll was in the audience.

How would they ever catch Maverick? What had she done to make herself a target of this troll? She still couldn't imagine someone being so angry with her that they would send that nasty message with the picture.

Finally, the meeting was over and Tom left her side to sign up for the committee. When he was done, he found Emily and took her arm to lead her out. His touch was as electrifying as ever. Why did he have that effect on her after all they had been through?

"I hope that meeting helped," she said as they drove back to her house. "Tom, shouldn't you go back to the ranch and check on things?"

"I will later this week. I talk to Gus several times a day and I'm available. This isn't the first time I've been away from there, and it hasn't been long yet. We're just getting started on this. It may take a long time to catch this Maverick character, but I have high hopes in Chelsea. If I were the troll and had Chelsea after me, I would be worried. Nathan, too. Nathan is quiet and easygoing, but he's tough and he doesn't miss a thing."

"I hope they can discover something soon," she said, wondering if living with Tom much longer would make it even more difficult to part again.

"I hope so, too," he said, but he didn't sound too happy about it.

"Stop at the grocery and let's pick up what we need to make sandwiches for lunch. It's a pretty day and we can eat on the porch. I don't even have a table."

"Take some furniture from the house at the ranch. The guys will move it for you. Just tell me or Gus what you want."

"Thank you. There are a few things I'd like, but in general, I don't want to move much from the ranch. Your cook likes Snowball so much, I may leave him with her because he likes the ranch."

"That's fine with me."

They bought groceries and when they were back in the car, he turned to her. "Why don't you buy a bed while I'm with you—"

She started laughing. "You've always been a little more subtle in your approach than this. Getting tired of your sleeping bag, or do you think you're going to coax me into bed?"

He raised his eyebrows. "Now that's a thought. I might give that one a try. Seriously, I suggested a bed because I can help you get it moved where you want it. You can get one delivered and set up, but they aren't going to move it around while you make up your mind where you would like it. As I recall on the last bed, I moved it until I wanted to put wheels on it."

"It wasn't that bad," she said, knowing he was teasing her. "When I get a bed, I'll probably go to Dallas or Midland. Though Royal has a good furniture store, so I suppose we can look here."

"Good. Let's look on the way back to the house. You can wait a few more minutes for lunch, I'm sure."

"Okay. We'll get a bed, Tom, but I still think you have at least one other motive besides helping me move it around," she said, watching him drive and wishing they could be like this all the time.

He smiled. "I might. We'll see if you object."

"You usually get what you want," she said, wanting to reach over and touch him just to have a physical connection. At one time she wouldn't have hesitated, but again, those times were over.

"That's interesting. Why do you think I get my way?"

"It's your good looks, your charm, your incredibly sexy body and your seductive ways, of course," she said in a sultry voice, teasing him.

"I may wreck the car. Now I know you need to hurry up and buy that bed."

"Don't rush me."

"I wouldn't think of rushing you to bed. This is something that will take some testing and touching to see if it feels right," he drawled in an exaggeratedly husky voice.

"Stop it," she said, smiling. "I never, ever guessed you and I would go shopping for a bed again."

"Life's full of surprises, and this is a damn fine one."

"I agree," she said, turning toward him as much as her seat belt would allow. "This is like our lives used to be."

"I told you before and I'll tell you again—we can still enjoy each other even though there are some terrible times behind us and some rough times up ahead."

"I've made big mistakes, and I can't undo them. But I'm glad you forgave me for the mistake I made believing Maverick's message. I'm thankful for that."

"We've both made mistakes," he said, suddenly serious, and she wondered what he felt he had done wrong. "Here we are," he said, stopping to park in the shade in front of the furniture store. He stepped out of the car and the moment for discussing their past was gone.

They shopped for almost an hour before she finally pointed to a fruitwood four-poster with a high, intricately carved headboard.

"I like this four-poster. And I like that sleigh bed. What do you think?" she asked, too aware that his opinion didn't matter because she would not be sharing the bed with him.

"I think the four-poster is great. Sleigh beds—even king-size sleigh beds—are too short. There is a tiny off chance I might get into this bed sometime."

"Shall we take bets on how many hours after purchase?" she asked sweetly and he grinned. "A sleigh bed is never too short for me," she said, studying the two frames. "Okay, I guess I'll get the four-poster."

"That's an excellent choice. Let's find the mattresses."

"You're very anxious to get a bed in my house," she said.

"I want you to be comfortable. You never know when you'll really want a bed. I'm sure you're enjoying your cot as much as I'm enjoying my sleeping bag," he said and then frowned slightly. "What's wrong, Em?"

"I started to say I should get a bed for the guest room now, too, but I don't have family. Uncle Woody was the last except the cousins, and I never see them. My family is gone. You and I will get our divorce and you'll be gone. I don't need a guest bed."

He put his arm around her shoulders. "You'll have a family soon enough. I know you'll marry again. You can wait and get another bed for the guest room some other day, but you need one for yourself now."

She felt the tears threatening. "What happened to us, Tom?"

He pulled her around to hug her. There was no one in that corner of the store and he really didn't care if there was. "We had the most devastating loss, and we just made too many mistakes dealing with that. But maybe some of them can be fixed," he said, holding her close.

She pulled away and wiped her eyes. "We're in public. I'll pull myself together. It's just a little scary to know I'm alone."

"You're not alone. Look, you can call me anytime you want."

She smiled at him. "Sure, Tom. I'm sure your next wife will just be thrilled to hear that you told your ex to call you anytime."

"Don't marry me off so fast. Let's get the bed, a mattress and springs, and go home and eat. Then they'll deliver the bed and mattress and we can try it out," he said, licking his lips and looking at her.

She smiled, shaking her head.

As they drove to the house, he went through what they had already done to the house, what they had lined up to do and what else should be added to the list. "Now I know you need a new roof, and I know a really good roofer. I'll call and get you a couple of estimates."

"Tom, I don't want to pay for all this at once. I have lots of windows. I'm having a security system installed. I've bought a lot of paint. I'll have bills and more bills."

He kept his attention on his driving as he talked. "Em, put all of this on the ranch expenses. We're still married. We're still a couple and we'll pay it out of the ranch budget."

"That simply means you'll pay it all," she said, looking at him in surprise. "You're divorcing me. Why would you pay for all this?"

He reached over with his free hand to squeeze hers. "You're my wife right now, and this divorce is not out of anger. Don't fuss. I'll just add it to the ranch tab. You forget about it."

She was surprised he would do that, but was more lost in his remark about how their divorce was not out of anger. But what difference did that make? They had made mistakes and hurt each other and soon would part.

"You're worrying. Don't. It's taken care of. Uncle Woody's house, which is now Emily's house, is getting a makeover."

"Thank you, Tom."

He reached over to give her hand another squeeze. "Sure. I intend to do some things right."

"You do a lot of things right," she said. She was amazed that he would do this for her. She rode the last two blocks in silence wondering what Tom really felt and wanted.

When they got home, they had to deal with the first window company. They were so impressed, they decided to skip getting the other estimates and go with this firm.

It was two in the afternoon before they ate lunch and she washed her new sheets. Then they went back to painting. As she painted, her thoughts were on Tom.

He worked fast and efficiently. He'd already taken care of the alarm system. The downstairs windows would be installed in two weeks, which was a rush job for custom-made windows. Going ahead without discussing it, Tom had also hired a professional outfit to paint the outside of the house and they had started this morning. And now he was going to pay all her repair bills.

Tom got things done, and with his help, it was going to take her far less time to finish restoring the house. How long would he stay? Trying to catch Maverick, if it was even possible, could take a long time. So far, she didn't think anyone had come close to learning the true identity of this monster. Maybe she would be the last victim—but how long would Tom feel she might need protection?

In some ways they were getting along better than they had, or maybe she had just relaxed about being with him. She was looking forward to meeting the Valentines Saturday. Tom liked them and his voice softened when he talked about them.

Like shifting sands beneath her feet, she felt as if her world was changing again, slight changes that might make a big difference later. She thought about Tom holding her in the store and telling her she wasn't alone. She expected Tom to eventually get the divorce and they would no longer be in each other's lives. He probably expected to marry again and she was sure he would. He probably expected her to marry again and she was sure she would not. She still wanted the divorce and she was certain he did. As great as Tom was, they could not have happiness together. Tom needed a family, and she couldn't give him his own kids.

The following day after the store delivered the bed, she got out her new sheets and Tom helped. He wore cut-offs, boots and another T-shirt with the sleeves ripped away, and it kept her tingly and physically aware of him every second they were together.

They made the bed and she spread a comforter on top with some new pillows. She stood back to admire it. "I think it's beautiful."

"I agree," he said, picking her up. His voice had lowered. "Let's try it out. I've been waiting for this moment."

"Aw, Tom, don't get me all torn up when I'm getting over what we went through," she said, but at the same time, joy rocked her and she loved being in his arms.

She put her arm around his neck and he carried her to the bed, placing his knee on the mattress to lower her.

While she wanted to kiss him, she didn't want to get tied up in emotional knots again. "Tom, we can't do this."

"Sure, we can. Try me and see," he said, stretching beside her and holding her in his arms as his mouth covered hers. She felt as if she were in free fall, the world spinning around her as his tongue stroked hers and he ran his hand over her breast and down to slip beneath her T-shirt. She tightened her arms and thrust her hips against him and felt his hard erection. Pushing aside her bra, he caressed her, his hand warm against her skin.

For a moment, she thought, *just for a moment...* She ran her hands over him, beneath his shirt as he had done, feeling his smooth back, the solid muscles. But she knew she was getting into deep trouble and would get hurt all over again. She slipped out of his embrace and stepped off the bed, shaking her head.

"I can't go through all that pain."

He gazed at her solemnly. She wanted to go right back into his arms, but she knew the futility of that, because it would lead straight to more unhappiness with nothing solved between them.

She turned and went downstairs and outside, trying to find something she could work on far away from him, away from the new bed that had been one more big mistake. The thought of sleeping in a comfortable bed instead of a narrow cot night after night had seemed so marvelous, but a bed and Tom—the mere thought made her hot and tingly.

He still could melt her with a look. She was headed for more heartbreak if she wasn't careful and didn't keep up her guard. Tom was a wonderful, sexy man, but they had no future together. She needed to stay aware of that all the time with him. They had relaxed now and had fun a lot of the time. But with hot sex and fiery passion, she would soon want him back on a permanent basis and then the problem of her inability to have children would come crashing down on her again and Tom would say goodbye.

She returned to her painting, working fast, focusing on her task and trying to avoid thinking about Tom. Then around four o'clock he stepped into the room. She heard his boot heels as he approached the open door and stepped inside.

"How're you doing?"

"Painting away and getting a lot done. You're an inspiration," she said, trying to keep things light and impersonal again, where they seemed to get along the best.

"I'm glad to hear I inspire you. And I'm glad you're okay. Shall I get carryout or do you want to go to a restaurant, or what?"

"I think carryout will be perfect."

"You had your chance to go out to dinner." He turned and was gone and she went back to painting. It was a couple of hours later when he sent her a text that he was leaving and taking orders. Smiling she sent him a reply and kept painting.

Half an hour later, she heard a loud whistle. Startled, she smiled and put down her brush. She went into the hall to look over the banister. He stood below with his hands on his hips and his hair in its usual tangle.

"I'm here and dinner's here, so come on down."

"I have a brush full of paint. You should have given me a warning."

"Bring your brush and I'll take care of it." He turned away without waiting for an answer. Smiling, she picked up her paintbrush and went downstairs.

They ate salads, barbecued ribs and corn bread on the porch and then went back to painting. It wasn't until ten o'clock when they sat back down together on the porch. As usual, she had raspberry tea and he had his cold beer.

"I'm amazed how much you've gotten done. I don't recall you being that fast before."

"I'm getting better as I age."

"Maybe we both are," she said, smiling in the dark.

They sat and talked until midnight and then walked up the stairs together. "Now you sleep tight in your big, cushy new bed while I crawl into my sleeping bag on the floor."

At the top of the stairs as they started down the hall, he put his arm across her shoulders. She smiled. "I will remind you, you insisted on staying here. I told you there was nowhere for you to sleep."

"Not quite true now. If you get lonesome, just whisper. I'll hear you."

She laughed. "Good night, Tom. You can have my cot."

"No, thanks. I'll wait for your invitation." He switched off the lights and she could hear him rustling around and then all was quiet. She suspected it would be a long time before she would get to sleep.

What would it be like when he went back to the ranch

and she was in this big old house all by herself? She knew she was going to miss him badly.

In the night a clap of thunder rattled the windows and jolted her awake. She could hear the wind whistling around the house outside and felt the cool breeze coming through the open windows. She got out of bed and slipped on flip-flops to go turn off the attic fan.

Brilliant flashes of lightning illuminated the interior of the room, so she could see as went out into the hall. She bumped into Tom, who steadied her. "Did the thunder wake you?" she asked, aware of his hands still on her arm and waist.

As if to emphasize her words, thunder rumbled again and a flash of lightning cast a silvery brilliance in the hall and was gone, followed by the hiss of a sudden downpour.

"I hoped you'd be scared of thunder and jump into my arms. You can get in my sleeping bag and be cozy."

"Are you trying to wrangle an invitation to sleep in my new bed?"

He ran his finger lightly over her collarbone. "My darlin', if I get an invitation to get on your new bed, I will not sleep. I can think of wonderful ways to try out that new bed." Lightning flashed and she gazed up at him. "Damn, I want you, and it's been a hell of a long time and we're still married." He drew her to him and leaned close to kiss her on the threshold of her bedroom. "You know you want to kiss," he whispered. "Live a little, Em."

Seven

Emily's breath caught as her arms slipped around his neck. Common sense went with the wind. Tom was right. She wanted him, it had been a long time and they were married.

She relished being in his strong arms, held tightly against his virile body that for an hour or two could drive every problem into oblivion.

His hand roamed over her, caressing her breasts, sliding down over her bottom and drifting over her, setting her on fire with wanting him. "Why do we have this effect on each other?" she whispered, more to herself than to him.

"I can't answer your question," he said between kisses. His tongue followed the curve of her ear and then he tugged away the T-shirt she slept in, drawing it over her head and dropping it to the floor. He cupped her soft breasts in his callused hands while his thumbs caressed her, drawing circles so lightly, making her shake and gasp with pleasure.

"I can't resist you. I never could." She sighed.

He framed her face with his hands. "That's damn mutual. You would have been free of me a long time ago if we could walk away from each other, but we can't. You take my breath away, Em. I dream about you. I still want you even when I should let you go."

She didn't reason out what he said to her. Instead, she kissed him and stopped all conversation. His arms tightened around her and he peeled away her pajama bottoms, tossing them aside while holding her tightly.

It had been too long, aeons, since they had made love, and his body beneath her hands was fit and strong. She wanted that strength, his passion for life, hot kisses and lovemaking that could shut out the pain of loss.

He was an exciting man, and all the things she couldn't be—physically strong, a decorated warrior, tough, sexy. Her world had been caring for her aging uncle, raising her baby, taking pictures of families and children and pets.

For right now, Tom's kisses drove away the heartbreaking problems between them. At the moment nothing was as important as Tom. Making love tonight would not satisfy anything except carnal lust, but she wanted him and he was here with her. If they made love, maybe she could be more relaxed with him, less sexually responsive to even the slightest touch—although that had never happened in the past. Sex with him had always had just the opposite effect, as she knew it would tonight. If they made love, she would want to make love again soon. She would want more instead of less because making love with Tom was fantastic.

She ran her hands over him. Her fingers shook as she peeled away his briefs.

His dark hair was tangled, falling on his forehead. She ran her hands over his broad, muscled shoulders, letting her hand slide down over his flat stomach, his narrow waist.

He was hard, ready to love, and she caressed him, wanting him, wanting to take her time. They hadn't made love in a year and now that they'd started, she couldn't stop and she was certain Tom didn't want to stop. He picked her up and moved to her new bed. He lay down, holding her against him while he stroked and kissed her and moved over her.

He showered kisses on her, starting at her ankle, and then stretched beside her and drew her closer, his leg moving between hers, parting her legs as he caressed her intimately.

She held him tightly, kissing him, the pressure building while desire intensified. Her hips moved and she arched against his hand, straining for release.

His fingers drove her, and then his mouth was on her, his tongue sending her over the edge as she thrashed and burst with release and need for all of him.

She moved over him to kiss him, taking him in her mouth, using her tongue and hands while she rubbed her breasts against him.

With a growl deep in his throat, he rolled her over and moved between her legs to look down at her.

"You're beautiful. I'll be right back," he said, starting to leave.

"I don't need protection," she replied, the moment changing as reality invaded the passionate idyll they had created. "I can't get pregnant, Tom."

He kissed her again, another devastating kiss that made her want him inside her and drove her wild with need. Shifting away swiftly, she got on her knees.

"We're doing this, so let's take our time. I haven't been loved by you in so very long. Take the night and drive away our sorrows. Let's grab joy here and hold it tight. I'm going to make you want me like you never have before," she said, her tongue stroking his thick manhood. "Turn over."

She caressed the backs of his legs, her hands trailing lightly over sculpted, hard muscles. She slowly ran her tongue, hot and wet, up the backs of his thighs, her fingers moving between his legs, her hand playing over his hard butt. Then he rolled back over, pulling her on top of him to kiss her passionately.

As she looked down at him, she wondered why he dazzled her so much and always had. "I can't resist you," she said.

"That's my line," he replied solemnly. "You have it all mixed up—I'm the one who can't resist."

She swung her leg over him to kneel beside him, running her tongue over him again while her fingers stroked and toyed with him. He fondled her breasts, his hands warm, his fingers brushing her nipples. Then he shifted, turning to take her breast in his mouth and run his tongue over the taut peak.

She tried to caress and kiss every inch of him until Tom knelt between her legs, putting her legs on his shoulders, his hands driving her to more heights.

"Come here," she demanded, tugging his hip with one hand, holding his rod with her other. "I want you inside me."

He shifted, coming down to give her a deep kiss that made her heart pound as she clung to him. "Tom, love me. I want you more than you can imagine."

He entered her slowly, filling her and almost withdrawing, moving with slow strokes that drove her wild as she tugged at him. She locked her long legs around his waist, clinging to him, wanting to consume him and for both of them to reach ecstasy and release.

He kissed her as he took his time, driving her wild with need. And then he thrust deep and faster, pumping and taking her with him as tension built until she climaxed, bursting with release, rapture, crying out.

"I love you," she gasped without thought.

Tension gathered swiftly again, built, and she achieved another orgasm. Tom kept up his relentless thrusts, and in minutes, his shuddering release came as she gasped and cried out with another. They clung tightly to each other and gradually her breathing slowed to normal. Then they were finally still, locked in each other's arms.

He showered light kisses on her temple, her ear, her cheek while he finger-combed her long hair away from her face.

Shifting, he held her close and kept her with him as he rolled to his side and faced her, all the while continuing to brush light kisses on her body and lips.

She knew when she let him go and the idyll ended, their problems would emerge, as omnipresent as ever. The problems they had between them would last a lifetime. Nothing could take them away. The moments of lovemaking only briefly blocked everything else out.

Feeling sadness seep back, she held Tom. She couldn't give him more children and he didn't want to stay married.

"You have to be the sexiest man ever."

One corner of his mouth rose in a slight smile. "I don't think you have a lot of experience to compare, but I'm glad you think that," he said gently. "Em, there aren't words for how much I wanted to make love to you."

"We didn't solve anything tonight," she said, voicing aloud her thoughts. "I don't care. I wanted you to kiss me. I wanted to make love." He was damp with sweat, his hair a tangle. She wound her fingers in it, running them down over the stubble on his jaw. Then her fingers played over the red lightning bolt tattoo on his right shoulder. She stroked his back, sliding her hand over his butt, down to the back of his thigh.

His arm tightened around her waist, pulling her closer against him. "You're right. It didn't change anything, but I wanted to hold you and kiss you again. Let me stay here with you a bit. You have the rest of your life to get away from me," he said. And that hurt. Reality was coming back and she couldn't stop it.

"Sure, Tom," she said, holding him, staying in his arms as they remained quiet. She couldn't have regrets for their lovemaking.

She finally shifted slightly. "You can stay here in my bed tonight."

Turning, he drew her against his side. "This seems right in so many ways."

She kissed his shoulder lightly in agreement and felt a pang, wishing they could go back to where they could love each other freely. Where they could feel they were doing right by the other person and their marriage was good. For tonight it was an illusion and she could pretend, but tomorrow, she would have to live with the truth.

He held her close and she clung to him, her arm wrapped around his narrow waist. She wished she could go back a couple of years and have a second chance, because she could see how she had driven Tom away. She ran her finger along his jaw and tried to think about the present, tonight, about loving him and having him in her arms, and forget everything else for now. Tomorrow the problems would all be right there for her to live with and try to cope.

With morning he drew her into his arms to kiss her awake. It was two hours later before they showered together and more than another hour before they went their separate ways to dress.

After breakfast they mopped up where the rain came in last night.

"You have a working alarm system now, in the house and in the yard."

"You've put motion-detector lights all over the place. The door locks all work. If you need to go to the ranch even for just a few days, go ahead."

"If I have to go, I'll tell you. Otherwise, I'm here for a while longer." He turned to face her. "I'll work outside now, so if you want me, I'll be on the east side of the house."

"I'll paint inside," she said and left him.

As Emily painted, she thought about living with Tom.

How would she cope when he walked out of her life? Would they say goodbye and never see each other again? Maybe she would see him at the Texas Cattleman's Club. But if she didn't like living in the old house she had inherited, she would move to Dallas. She would move if she got enough clients and business from the area. If she lived there, she didn't think she would ever see Tom. There were questions about her future that she couldn't answer.

Now, looking around her at the house she had inherited, the smell of fresh paint still filling the air, she thought about her future, when she would have to deal with another parting with Tom. This time a permanent one.

Saturday morning sunshine spilled in through the open windows and Tom was eager to wake Emily. Today was their picnic with the Valentines and he was excited. She'd told him to act as her human alarm clock if she slept past six thirty. It was ten seconds past six thirty now.

He stood beside her bed for seconds, looking at her sleep, her hair spread on the pillow, the sheet down to her waist, her breasts pushing against her T-shirt. He slipped beneath the sheet and pulled her into his arms.

She stirred, wrapped an arm around his neck and rolled over. He couldn't resist. He kissed her. He started out in fun, expecting her to wake instantly, the way she usually did. But the minute he was in bed with her and had her in his arms, all playfulness left him and he wanted to make love to her. He knew he was weaving a web of trouble that would ensnare both of them when they moved on in their lives.

By eleven, after they'd made love, showered, dressed and had breakfast, they were ready to go. Tom was in jeans and a navy T-shirt while she wore capri pants and sandals with a red-white-and-blue-striped cotton blouse. Tom had spent the past half hour packing the truck with provisions for the picnic. Then they locked up the house, setting the new alarm, and left for Royal's big park by the Texas Cattleman's Club.

When they got to the park, Tom noticed Emily's expression as she gazed out the car window. "Look at all the new trees," she said. "They've replaced a lot of the ones that were destroyed by the tornado."

"This is a great park. We could have gone to the Cattleman's Club, but a lot of people there would have wanted to join us. Another time, that would be fun, but I want you to meet and get to know the Valentines when it's just us and them."

Emily had been chatting, but as he wound slowly alongside a silvery pond toward where he and Natalie had agreed to meet, she became silent, and he knew she was remembering the last time she had been in the park. "This is the way we used to come when we brought Ryan," she said softly.

Tom glanced at Emily and pain stabbed him. She had her head turned away from him. He changed course and drove to a deserted parking area. He stopped the car, unfastened his seat belt and placed his hand on her shoulder. He hurt, and his pain was greater because he knew she felt it, too. She put her head in her hands. "I'm sorry."

A knot in his throat kept him from answering and tears burned his eyes. He braced for her to tell him to leave her alone as he pulled her into his arms as much as he could in his pickup. She put her arms around his neck and clung to him, which made him feel better because he had expected her to shove him away.

"I'm sorry, Tom. I thought I could do this without tears. It's a happy occasion and I've looked forward to meeting Natalie and her family and I really mean that—" Emily couldn't finish. She cried while he held her tightly, stroking her head.

"This is the first time I've been back in the park since Ryan was alive," she said between pauses to cry. She spoke so softly he could barely hear her. "We all came here together, remember?"

"I know it, darlin', and I wondered if this would tear you up. I've been here with Natalie and the kids once. This is the main park in Royal and where the Valentines always go. The kids love it here just like Ryan did."

"Then it's a good place to come. I'll be all right in a minute."

"I knew you might have difficulty, and I'm not surprised." He buried his head against her, holding her tightly while she clung to him and they cried. "It hurts like hell, Em, but we don't have a choice. I figure there's a little angel in heaven who loves us as much as we love him."

"Why is life—" She couldn't finish through her tears.

"So damn hard?" he offered. "I don't know. There aren't answers for some questions. When I'm ninety— if I make it that far—I'll cry for my son. As long as I live, I'll miss him."

"I will, too. Why aren't we more of a comfort to each other?"

"I don't know. I guess because that loss is a mountain of sadness and blame and guilt between us. It hurts, so go ahead and cry," he said quietly.

She looked up at him while tears still ran down her cheeks. Tom pulled out a clean, folded handkerchief and dabbed at her cheeks as they gazed at each other.

"You're a comfort to me now. I wish I could be for you, but I can see in your eyes that I'm not."

"Shh, Em. There's a point where it's just too much pain. Over our baby I should have saved. Guys that should have made it home and didn't."

"You just seem to go somewhere where I can't reach you."

He pulled her close again and held her tightly.

She stopped sobbing and became quiet. Raising her head, she wiped her eyes. "I'm making us late."

"If there is anyone on earth who will understand

people stopping to grieve, it's Natalie. She and Jeremy were so in love. Take your time. The kids will play and Natalie will be fine. I'll call her. We're only a minute or two from where we're going. She'll understand, believe me." Tom continued to stroke Emily's head lightly, wishing he could do more but knowing he couldn't.

"I'm sorry Natalie is widowed, but I'm glad we'll be with someone who will understand if I lose it again. That doesn't usually happen when I'm out with people, but this is different."

"I know it is, and sometimes the memory of losing Ryan just comes at you out of the blue."

When she shifted to brush a light kiss on his cheek, he looked down at her. "You're a great guy, Tom. I've been lucky."

He frowned, studying her intently. "Thanks, Em. That makes me feel better. We've had some rough times and we'll have more. I want to help, not be part of the problem."

She looked straight ahead. "You are a help. We got through the rough times until now, so hopefully, we'll get through what's ahead," she said. Her voice held a sad note, and he wondered if she dreaded the divorce or wished they could go ahead sooner and get it now.

He put his hand behind her head and pulled her close to kiss her lightly, tenderly, hoping he conveyed the bond he knew they would always have. Even after they divorced and went their separate ways, memories of Ryan would always be there between them.

She moved away from him and he let her go. "I'm

ready. She'll know I've been crying, but you said she would understand."

"She definitely will, and I told her this might be tough for you. It was for me the first time I was in the park after the wreck."

"Let's go meet them. I'm pulled together. Thanks for being patient and understanding."

"I feel the same as you do, so it's damn easy to be understanding."

He pulled out and returned to the main drive, winding through the park beneath tall oaks until he got to another parking spot near the pond, where a picnic table was already spread.

"There they are—including their dog," Tom said. "Miss Molly is a well-trained golden retriever and as long as we're the only folks out here, she's okay running free, because she sticks close to the kids. She loves those kids. If other families come out, Natalie has a lead she can put Miss Molly on.

"I told you about Colby. He's standoffish, but he'll warm up. He knows me well now, so he's usually responsive around me. I try to not push him," Tom said as he parked. "They're really great kids."

Emily lightly placed her hand on his arm. "You sound happy. You like being with a family and kids. That's what you need, Tom, your own family, your own kids. The sooner we divorce, the sooner you'll have that life."

Frowning slightly, he parked and studied her. "If you marry again, would you be willing to adopt a child?"

"I've never thought about that. I suppose I would,

because the only reason I didn't want to with us was I wanted another Ryan for you," she replied. "The only way we could have a child who would be like you would be if you fathered the child. That's why I held out to not adopt. I kept expecting to get pregnant. If I marry someone else—that wouldn't matter, so yes, I'd adopt."

He had decided long ago they would each be better off if they divorced. Now he knew they would. Emily would have a family and the life she wanted.

He needed to call Nathan and see if they had found any more clues about Maverick. Because Tom felt more strongly than ever that he needed to get out of Emily's life.

Eight

Emily got out when Tom did and they both gathered all they picnic supplies they could handle. Tom carried a big cooler loaded with ice and bottled drinks. He slung a tote bag on his shoulder, with pinwheels and kites sticking out of it. Emily carried a big sack with two beach balls. Two little wooden flutes were in the bottom of the sack. Tom also had an electronic toy for Colby and a little box containing a tiara, a feather boa, bangles and a beaded purse for Lexie to play dress-up. Before he picked up the cooler, he waved and Natalie waved back.

Miss Molly saw them and came bounding over. She went to Tom, but was too well behaved to jump all over him. He put down everything he carried to pet her and scratch her ears. It was obvious the dog loved him and it was mutual. She looked at Emily, who held her hand out, and Tom stepped closer to her. "Here's Miss Molly. She's friendly and has been through obedience school, so she's well trained."

Miss Molly sniffed Emily's hand and looked up expectantly. Tom took a doggie treat from his pocket and handed it to Emily. "Give her this and she will love you forever."

"That's a bribe."

"And it works beautifully. Try," he said.

She held out the treat, which Miss Molly politely took and ate, wagging her tail. She moved closer and looked up at Emily expectantly.

"See, you have a friend now," Tom said, picking things up to carry to the picnic spot.

Emily smiled as she petted Miss Molly and retrieved what she had been carrying. Miss Molly ran to catch up with Tom and walk beside him, moving around to his left side.

Natalie was sitting at the picnic table with a little redheaded girl on her lap. "Lexie is a little doll," Tom said. "At two, Lexie is too young for outdoor games, so I brought some toys and musical instruments. And I have two beach balls and two kites, but we'll need more wind than this. I have some pinwheels, too."

"You're a walking toy store. No wonder they're excited to see you."

As they drew close, Natalie set Lexie on the ground. The minute her feet touched the grass, she ran with her arms out. Tom put down his things and scooped her up, laughing as he said hello. He looked around and walked over to pick up Colby with the other arm. "Hi, Colby," he said easily. "Isn't this fun? We're at the park and I brought some toys and some things to do." The children were both talking to him and he laughed, setting them on their feet.

"Wait a minute. I need to mind my manners. We have someone new with us. Emily, meet Lexie and Colby. This is my wife, Miss Emily to you two." He looked at Emily. "Lexie's still a toddler, so no telling what you'll be called."

"Whatever she settles on, it'll be fine."

Emily greeted them with a smile while they politely said hello. She barely heard Colby, who shyly looked away.

"We'll get to what I brought, but first, I want to talk to your mama," Tom told them.

As they approached the picnic table, which already had a red-and-white-checkered plastic tablecloth covering it, Emily saw Natalie Valentine turn and come forward to greet them, smiling.

"Emily, I'm Natalie. I'm glad to finally meet you."

"I'm glad to meet you," Emily answered politely, amazed Tom hadn't fallen in love with Natalie, who was pretty with huge green eyes.

Natalie held out her hands. "Let me carry something."

"Here's a cake you can carry," Emily said, handing a covered pan to the other woman.

"Lexie woke up an hour earlier than usual this morning because she was so excited about the picnic today. The kids love to see Tom. He's wonderful with them and he's good to share his time. Jeremy picked the right guy to be friends with, and I know why."

"He's good with kids," Emily said, watching him hunker down to let Lexie and Colby look in the sack he'd brought and pull something out. They each got a pinwheel and stepped away to swing them through the air and make them spin. It was obvious they had played with them before.

"Tom has been a lifesaver for us," Natalie continued. "Last month he installed two new motion-detector lights outside at the B and B. And then I had an appointment to take Colby to the dentist and Miss Molly had an appointment at the groomer at the same time—both hard to change—so Tom took Lexie with him to get Miss Molly to be groomed while I took Colby to the dentist. He even took Lexie to the pediatrician when she had to get a tetanus shot because she cut her foot on a rusty piece of metal. He held her hand while she got her shot, took her for ice cream and then to the bookstore."

Emily continued to listen to Natalie talk about how much Tom had helped her. She was so effusive in her praise for Tom, talking about all the things he had done for her and her family, that Emily realized she had pushed Tom away and hadn't let him take care of her when that was probably what he needed to do.

It was what he was doing now, but she had been fighting him on it every step of the way, while Natalie accepted his help and was grateful for it.

In the past Emily had robbed him of his need to be her protector, a need she decided after listening to Natalie that was as essential to his life force as breathing.

He had tried in the days after they lost Ryan, but she had wrapped herself in a shell and withdrawn from him. She hadn't relied on him then and she wouldn't have now, but he'd simply taken charge because of worrying about what Maverick might be intending to do.

She thought about Tom telling her that he had lost Ryan, but he wasn't going to lose her to a troll.

She watched him with the kids and wondered if part of the reason they were getting along so much better now was because he felt he was helping her and doing things for her. If so, she had made really big mistakes by shutting him out of parts of her life after Ryan's death.

"I know you and Tom have been estranged in the past," Natalie said quietly. "I don't want to intrude, but it looks as if you might be getting back together. I just want to say you have a wonderful husband who has been so good to us and a marvelous substitute for Jeremy with the kids."

"Tom loves kids. He's got six nieces and nephews, but this past year we haven't seen them often, because all three of his brothers have moved farther away."

"Jeremy picked well when he got Tom for a friend. But Tom's gone through a lot at home and abroad. Jeremy told me about some of what they did and it was rough. Tom's a tough guy, but losing his son has really been hard on him. Just as I know it's hard on you. That's something we all share. But enough about our lives."

As Emily started to unpack the things they'd carried from the car, her thoughts were on all Natalie had said.

The more Emily thought about it, the more she realized that pushing Tom away after Ryan's death, doing things herself and shutting him out had been disastrous. But now she was accepting his help, and they both seemed to be thriving. He was getting the house in shape far faster than she would have been able to do. And since Tom appeared, she hadn't had any more messages from Maverick.

At least this part was good. She was happy to meet Natalie and the kids, who'd made her realize that it would have helped Tom heal more after they lost Ryan if she hadn't shut him out. He needed her to rely on him, to need him—which was something he had found with the Valentines.

Emily wondered if it was too late for her. Was having Tom working on Uncle Woody's house and staying with her for protection enough to meet the need he had to be a provider in her life and in the marriage?

Natalie watched as the kids played with the beach balls. Tom patiently helped Lexie, who was too little to keep up with her brother or do much of anything with her beach ball except toss it around and let Tom bring it back and roll it to her.

As soon as Emily and Natalie were done unpacking everything, the kids started dancing around Tom, asking him to create bubbles for them to pop.

"They'll keep him busy," Natalie said, turning to look at Emily. "Tom told me about the hateful email you got. It's terrible, but I'm so glad you two got it straightened out between you." She gave a faint smile and shook her head. "Tom's secret family. He is so good to us. I would have been sick if I thought all he's done for us would cause you both pain. Tom is a wonderful person."

"Yes, he is, and he thought your husband was. He told me about Jeremy, but that was a while ago. When I saw that picture, I didn't put it together and think about your husband. I just accepted the email as truth."

"I hope they catch this person before someone else gets hurt."

"I hope so, too. I'm sorry, Natalie, about Jeremy. Tom thought so much of him."

"Thanks," Natalie said. "I'm sorry for your loss. Tom is good to always spend time with the kids. Both kids love him. He's so patient with them and good for Colby."

"He's good with kids because he really likes them," Emily said quietly, hurting as she watched Tom play with Lexie and Colby. "And he's patient," she said, thinking again if she could have gotten pregnant, they might not be getting the divorce. Tom had been wonderful with Ryan.

"We've both lost so much," Natalie said quietly. "I hope you and Tom can work things out, because he should have his own family, his own kids."

"I agree with you about that and I know we have a mutual bond in losing someone we love deeply." She looked around. "We better start getting food ready, or there will be other kinds of tears shed."

"Indeed, there will be," Natalie said, smiling. "Before you and Tom arrived, they were coming to me every five minutes to ask when you'd get here and how soon we'll eat. Let's get some of this set up and then we can go join them and play for a short time. If you don't want to, that's okay," Natalie said.

"It'll be fun. Look at Tom. He has to be having a good time."

They paused a moment and watched Tom open a bottle, dip a wand inside and then wave it, leaving a stream of big bubbles. Laughing, both kids began to chase and pop bubbles while Tom kept producing more.

Another pang struck Emily as she looked at Tom. Wind tangled his hair. He was agile and strong, playing with the kids and obviously enjoying it. This was a fun few hours, but their lives were not a constant picnic with kids included. Their marriage was over and that was one more thing she had to accept and learn to live with. Tom was handsome, so appealing—she turned from watching him, focusing on the kids and laughing at their antics.

"Your children are wonderful."

"Thank you," Natalie answered. "They have their moments, and Colby has special needs and special abilities. They're good kids and I love them with all my heart."

Looking at both kids, Emily hurt because she wanted her own. She wanted to run and join the fun and play with them, too, but she didn't want to leave Natalie and they didn't need three adults mixing with the bubbles. "Lexie is so cute."

Natalie laughed. "She thinks so. She would love to have my shoes and makeup. I can't imagine what I'm in for when she's a teen."

Emily smiled. Tom glanced their way and said something to Colby and Lexie. He turned to walk toward Emily and Natalie.

"Hey, when do we get to eat around here?"

"We can any time you want to fire up that grill and do burgers," Natalie said.

"I'll tell Colby and Lexie and go to work at the grill."

"I'll tell them," Natalie said. "You get the food. Emily and I can play with them while you cook. I think we have everything else out and ready."

"Good deal," he answered.

Emily spread a blanket and gave each child a new box of crayons and tablets of plain paper so they could draw.

Natalie joined her and after a few minutes, Emily left to help Tom with the cooking and getting last-minute things on the table.

When they all sat down to eat, she felt as if she were part of the family. Natalie was easy to get to know and Emily already loved the kids. Colby was quiet, sometimes a little withdrawn, but he liked all the toys and gadgets Tom had brought. She took pictures of them and of everybody.

They had homemade strawberry ice cream for dessert along with chocolate chip cookies Natalie had made. As they sat in the shade and ate ice cream and cookies, Miss Molly stretched out at Tom's feet. Tom ran the toe of his boot back and forth behind her ear and she looked serenely happy.

When they put things away after the picnic, Lexie ran up to grab Tom's hand and tug. Colby stood back, holding one of the beach balls. "Back to work," Tom said, getting up to join the kids again. "Don't carry anything to the cars. I can do that later."

"I'll go with you," Emily said, smiling at Natalie. "Take a break and sit in the shade. We'll play with Lexie and Colby. It'll be fun."

Natalie smiled. "Thanks. Stop whenever you've had enough."

Tom and Colby moved yards apart while Emily stood near Lexie, who was too little to play but wanted to participate. The adults tossed the beach ball first to one child and then the other. Lexie couldn't catch it, but she chased it to bat it and Emily helped.

By late afternoon, Lexie was sitting on a blanket alternately playing with a doll and drawing while Colby played with the electronic game that Tom had brought. The three adults sat in the shade and talked.

Emily enjoyed being with all of the Valentines. Lexie brought over her drawing and scrambled up onto her lap. Emily held her, admiring her drawing and talking to her about making another picture. The minute she climbed on her lap, Emily thought of Ryan. She looked down at Lexie's red hair, thinking she was an adorable child. She took the crayons to draw. As she drew, Lexie listened attentively while Emily made up first one story and then another to go with the pictures. When she finished, she asked Lexie to draw a story and watched and listened as the little girl spoke of a mouse and an elephant and drew unrecognizable creatures. But she was happy with her story and her drawings.

"Emily, you don't have to do that the rest of the evening," Natalie said, smiling. "I think you've served your time."

Shaking her head, Emily smiled. "I'm having a good

time, too. As long as she wants to. When I want to stop, I will."

Lexie tugged on her hand. "Let's do another one," she said.

"Do you want to tell another story?" Emily asked, looking at Lexie and thinking how wonderful it was to have a little child in her lap again.

Lexie's eyes sparkled as she nodded. "I have a story about a kitty and a butterfly."

Emily listened, smiling and smoothing Lexie's hair, thinking Natalie had a wonderful family. She glanced up to see Tom watching her. Their gazes met and she wondered what he was thinking.

The sun was below the treetops in the west when Natalie announced they needed to pack things up and get home. She called to Miss Molly, and the big dog loped to her side.

"We'll follow you home and I can help carry things inside," Tom said.

"You don't need to do that," she said, smiling at him. "Emily told me how you're helping her get her house painted. I know how big a job that can be. Besides, I have four couples at the bed-and-breakfast, just getting away from city life for a weekend. The guys carried the things out for me this morning and have already told me they would carry the stuff in when I get back. Their reward will be the strawberry ice cream," she said, smiling at them.

"Come see me," Lexie said, taking Emily's hand. Her tiny hand felt so small, and Emily's heart lurched when she thought about Ryan holding her hand.

"I'd love to see your room and Colby's, too," Emily said, and Lexie's smile broadened.

"We'll be happy to have you come visit," Natalie said.

They let Miss Molly jump into the back of the SUV and then the kids climbed in and buckled into their car seats, with Natalie checking on Lexie's. Natalie got into the front and Tom closed her door.

Tom draped his arm across Emily's shoulders as they walked to the pickup. She wondered if he even gave any thought to what he was doing, but she was aware of it. The minute he put his arm across her shoulders, she was reminded of old times with him. And then she became aware of how close they were. All day he had looked virile, filled with energy, strong and incredibly appealing to her. How much would it tear her up to go back to the house and sleep with him? The thought of making love tonight made her draw a deep breath; she just couldn't suppress her eagerness.

Tom held the pickup door open and she climbed inside. He got in and waited while Natalie backed out and turned to drive away. Then he followed.

"They look like the all-American family, Tom. Especially with the dog hanging out the window," Emily said.

"Except the all-American dad was shot dead on foreign soil, defending his country so we can go on picnics. He's not in that car with his wife and kids and dog."

Emily wanted to reach for Tom's hand, just to hold it. At one time in her life that's what she would have done, but not now. Now they were going their separate ways soon and reaching for him would be almost like reaching to hold a stranger's hand. "You knew that when you joined the service," she said.

"I know I did, but sometimes when I'm with Natalie and the kids, it gets to me, because Jeremy should be with them instead of me."

"You've really kept your promise to Jeremy. She's so grateful for all you've done for them."

"I'm trying," he said. "When I think of the sacrifice he made, there's never enough I can do."

"You're a good guy," Emily said, and meant it. Tears threatened because she had lost Tom and there were moments it hurt badly. After a few minutes, she pulled herself together. "Natalie appreciates everything you've done and it's obvious the kids love you. You should have your own kids," she said quietly. He shot her a quick, startled glance but said nothing.

She felt another wave of sadness that she couldn't give Tom another little boy. If only she had been able to get pregnant, they might have had a chance to save their marriage. But that wasn't what had happened.

"They are cute kids. Lexie knows she is," Tom said, smiling. "That little girl can steal the show when she wants to. I'm glad you and Natalie met. I should have done that long ago, but you and I have been out of each other's lives for a long time now."

"I'm glad to meet her. I understand her loss and she understands mine—actually, ours."

"Yes. She's done well, but she has moments. She keeps a good front for the kids' sakes, so that helps in a way."

Emily thought about how all three of them—she, Natalie and Tom—had been targets of Maverick in a way. But Maverick's hateful lies had backfired, bringing them closer together instead of driving them all apart.

When they got back to her house, she was astonished again by the difference only a week had made. The new coat of paint was beginning to transform the house into the home she remembered and loved and always thought was so beautiful. Tom had started working on the yard because the days were getting warmer. He'd made two beds ready for spring planting. Filled with energy, Tom got things done, but she always had been impressed by his strength and vigor.

"It's just been a week and you've made a giant difference. It doesn't look like the same house."

"I'm glad you noticed, and you sound happy with it."

"I am happy with it. It's done and it looks nice and thank you."

"Good. It's a hell of a lot safer and more secure, too," Tom said. He parked at the side of the house, leaving the pickup so it could be seen from the street.

"You're not getting out of the pickup," she said, looking at him sitting still, staring straight ahead.

"No, I'm looking at the garage."

"Oh, heavens, what now, Tom? There must be something I need to fix."

"There sure as hell is. Emily, that garage is as old as this house. That big mulberry tree with giant roots is pushing the garage over and the driveway up."

"You want me to get rid of the garage?"

"Yes. You need to get estimates—I'll do it—on a

new driveway and a new garage and come into this century. Or even come into the last half of the last century. That thing is simply going to collapse someday soon and you don't want to be in it when it does."

She looked at the old garage and the cracked slabs of concrete driveway that had been pushed several inches into the air.

"Do you remember when your uncle Woody stopped using it?" Tom asked.

"I was probably about twelve. Okay. You're right about the garage."

Tom smiled. "So I'm finally right about something concerning this house."

"You're right about everything concerning this house. Tom, it is definitely better. It would have taken me months to get done what you've done. I'm grateful for your help," she said.

"I'll get your estimates on a driveway and the cost for a new garage. This will be a garage today's car will fit into," he said, grinning and shaking his head. "That thing was built for a Model T."

Together they carried the picnic things into the house. "It's a pretty Saturday night," he remarked. "After we get through putting the stuff away, let's sit on the porch, have a drink and enjoy the evening."

"Sure," she said, knowing if they did that many more times, she would miss having him here when he returned to the ranch. "But I need a shower first—I've been outside all day, in the grass, petting the dog—"

"Right. I know one thing that would make taking a shower better—"

"It's not going to happen tonight."

He grinned. "I have to keep trying. I can really be fun to take a shower with, or maybe you remember. I remember you're lots of fun to shower with. It would make this a superspecial Saturday."

"Will you stop?" she said, laughing and shaking her head. "No, we don't shower together. What would you like to drink? Let me guess—a cold beer."

"Ah, you know me too well. All the mystery is gone."

"There's plenty of mystery about you—I'm surprised you haven't fallen in love with Natalie Valentine. She is so sweet and has a wonderful family. And you love that dog."

He came back to put his hands on her shoulders and she wondered what chord she had struck. Was he falling in love with Natalie? She gazed into his seductive hazel eyes.

"I'll tell you what, darlin'. I don't fall in love with someone because of their dog. Or their kids—and those are adorable kids. Natalie is beautiful, but she's Jeremy's widow and she still loves him. And he was my buddy."

"You're a good guy, Tom," she said, turning back to her task.

When they were done putting things away in the kitchen, she turned to him. "I'm going upstairs to shower—alone. I'll meet you on the porch. The first one done can get drinks. See you in thirty minutes."

"Fine. I'll go upstairs and shower, too." At the head of the stairs he turned to her. "The invitation is still open."

"I'll have to admit, I'm tempted—"

"Oh, darlin'," he said, holding his arms out. "Come

join me. We'll have a shower you'll never forget." She laughed and he laughed with her. "See, I told you I can be fun in the shower," he said. "We're not even there yet and I have you laughing."

"You are fun, you devil," she said, squeezing his jaw and looking into his mischievous eyes. "As fun as you are, I'm going to shower all by myself and then enjoy sitting with you on the porch," she said.

He placed his arms casually on her shoulders. "We can still enjoy each other's company. It's been a good day."

"It has. The Valentines are wonderful."

"Yes, they are, but the good time today wasn't just because of the Valentines. You and I can laugh and enjoy each other. We haven't totally lost it," he said with so much confidence she felt a thrill.

"I know we can as long as we stay away from real life and the serious stuff."

"I'll settle for what we can get. We can do a lot of things together," he said, his voice changing, becoming deeper while his hands slid down to rub her bare arms lightly.

"I know we can."

Her heartbeat raced as his gaze lowered to her mouth. Her lips parted.

"Tom," she whispered, his name an invitation. She might have huge regrets very soon, but at this moment she wanted to kiss him. What would one kiss hurt?

When his mouth covered hers, she opened to him and felt on fire. Their tongues mingled as he wrapped his arm around her and pulled her tightly against him.

She hugged him around his waist and ran one hand over his muscled back.

She had no idea how long they kissed, but when she felt his hand on her breast, she placed her hand over his. "Wait," she whispered, looking up at him. "I want to shower and sit on the porch and talk and maybe kiss again—okay?"

He inhaled deeply and nodded. "Okay." He caressed her nape and tugged lightly on her braid. "Take your hair down."

"I will. I'll see you on the porch." She walked away, hearing his boots as he went into the room where he kept his things. Now what would she agree to after her shower? She better think before she brought pain and regret crashing back down on them.

When she came down, he was already on the porch. She wore navy capri pants, flip-flops, a pale blue sleeveless cotton blouse and a clip in her hair to hold it behind her head. The minute he saw her, Tom stood up. His gaze drifted over her from her head to her toes, making her tingle. She took in tight jeans, his black boots and short-sleeved navy T-shirt. To her, he was still the most handsome man she knew. And definitely the sexiest. She strolled to the empty chair beside him and picked up the drink he'd prepared for her.

He stepped closer and smiled at her, making her heart race as she gazed into his eyes. "You look as good as a million dollars."

"Thank you. You look rather good yourself." She didn't want to admit how appealing he did look to her.

"Let's fix this," he said, reaching over to take the clip out of her hair and placing it on the table. She smiled at him as she shook her head, letting her hair fan out over her shoulders.

As they rocked and talked, she felt as if she was standing on the edge of a high cliff and a misstep could mean ruin. She thought about what she should do and what she wanted to do. She wanted to be in his arms, making love again. How much would that hurt later? It wouldn't change anything. It just might mean more heartache.

"Think you'll stay in Royal or move to Dallas after our divorce?" he asked after a long silence.

"Right now, after a fun day together, I don't want to think about the divorce." She gazed into the darkness and sipped her tea. "I'll probably stay in this area unless some opportunity with my photography comes up and causes me to move on. We'll cross paths, I'm sure."

With his feet propped on another chair, Tom was silent. While he sipped his beer, he idly rubbed one knee and she remembered how he ran and played with the kids. She also remembered how badly his knee was hurt in the bus wreck and the big scar he still carried.

"Does your knee hurt?"

He looked around. "Not really. I guess rubbing it sometimes has gotten to be a habit from when it did hurt."

"That's good. It used to bother you some after a long day like today," she said.

"I don't think about it much any longer. We'll both carry that night with us in our memories forever, but the pain isn't as constant as it was."

"I agree. I'm sorry that you got hurt so badly. I was scared I'd lose you both," she said, thinking about all they had been through.

"I'm sorry I made it and Ryan didn't," he said quietly.

"Tom, don't ever apologize because you survived," she said, turning to stare at him. "I didn't want to lose either one of you," she said. "I was terrified when they told me you were on the critical list along with Ryan. I called your brother and that's why you were on so many prayer lists, because he got the word out. Don't ever apologize for surviving."

"I figured you wished I had died instead of Ryan," Tom replied. Stunned, she stared at him in the darkness while she clutched his hand.

Nine

"If one of us could have lived and one couldn't, I would rather it had been Ryan, too," Tom continued.

Shocked, she shook her head. "Tom, I never felt that way," she said, staring at him in the dark. "That's dreadful. I never for one second wanted to lose you."

He didn't answer and she wondered if he doubted her. "It has never occurred to me you could have thought I wished it had been you. I loved you. I loved you so much." When he still didn't answer her, she hurt to think he had been carrying that idea around all this time. "I was so scared you wouldn't make it. I stayed awake all through that first night praying for you and Ryan."

Setting her glass of tea aside, she got up and stepped over to sit in his lap. She framed his face with her hands so she could look into his eyes even though it was dark on the porch. "I never wished you had died instead of Ryan. Not for one part of a second. Oh, how I loved you."

His arms tightened around her and he shifted, cradling her against his shoulder as he leaned over to kiss her, a possessive kiss that made her insides seize up. She kissed him back as if she could erase all the heartaches and differences with their kiss. She leaned away again and cupped his chin in her hand.

"Don't ever think or say that again. With my whole heart I wanted you and Ryan, both of you, to survive." Holding him tightly, she resumed their kiss.

Minutes later, she raised her head. "Tom, I never for one second wanted you to die," she said.

He gazed intently at her and started to say something, but she stood, taking his hand. She pulled lightly and he came to his feet to sweep her into his arms.

If she couldn't convince him with words, she wanted to show him with her loving, with kisses and caresses to give him all the sensual pleasure possible. As if he knew what she wanted, he carried her inside. Holding her close, he climbed the staircase and switched on the light in the upstairs hall.

In her bedroom beside the new bed, he stood her on her feet and kissed her. The instant his mouth covered hers, she trembled with desire. She stepped back to take off her blouse, moving slowly while he watched her. When she had her blouse off, she stepped forward to pull off his shirt and rake her hands over his chest and shower kisses there, running her tongue over the flat, hard nipples, tangling her fingers in his thick chest curls.

He caressed her breasts, cupping them and stroking her nipples lightly with his thumbs while she peeled away her capri pants. She unfastened and pulled off his belt as they kissed. Then she unfastened his jeans and pushed them down his legs.

Tom paused to kick off his boots and pull off the rest of his clothes and her lace panties. He placed his hands on her hips and stepped back to look at her. "You're beautiful. I've dreamed about you and spent hours re-membering." His fingers again drifted over her breast, a faint brush of his hand that was as electrifying as his hungry gaze.

His look was as sexy and stimulating as his touch, making her quiver. She twisted and turned, rubbing her warm, naked body against him, all the while caressing him, touching him, stroking his thick manhood.

"Ah, Em, this is good with you, so good." He leaned down to take her nipple in his mouth and circle the tip with his tongue. Intense sensation shot through her from each hot brush of his tongue and she gasped with pleasure.

"Tom, my love," she whispered. Her fingers trailed over his scars, some new, most old and familiar. She followed with her tongue.

Reaching for her, he watched her expression as he cupped her breasts again.

She clung to his shoulders, closing her eyes and drowning in sensation. "I want to take all night to give you pleasure, to show you how wrong you were."

He kissed her fiercely, holding her tightly as if it might be their last kiss, and she clung to him.

When he released her, he gazed into her eyes. "Tonight is for memories of the good times, for a day well spent, to celebrate being alive."

Emily tangled her fingers in his chest hair as she kissed him. He stood with his eyes closed as she knelt to lick and kiss and stroke him, until he picked her up and placed her on the bed. He propped himself up on an elbow beside her, watching her, and then leaned down to shower kisses and caresses over every inch of her.

He pushed her over onto her stomach, his tongue trailing down her spine, over her smooth, round bottom, lower between her legs and then over the backs of her legs while his hands were everywhere caressing her.

She moaned softly, her hands knotted in the sheets on the bed. She turned to face him, her gaze raking over his muscled body and thick manhood. He stretched out beside her to pull her into his arms and kiss her hard while his hand was warm between her legs, rubbing her, driving her to new heights. She arched against him and ran her hand over his legs, over his thick rod that was hot and hard and ready for her.

With a murmur deep in his throat, he stepped off the bed and picked her up. They looked into each other's eyes while he pulled her up onto her toes. He looked fierce, desire blazing in his expression.

As he kissed her, he braced himself. She locked her long legs around his waist and he lowered her onto his thick shaft.

Gasping with pleasure, she dug her nails into his muscled shoulders and then wrapped her arms around him, clinging tightly to him She wanted his lovemaking to drive her to oblivion, to make love until pain and hurt and loss were mere shadows that couldn't affect her.

And then all thought was gone as she rode him. He thrust hard and fast, driving her to a brink and then over. She cried out with ecstasy before kissing him again, a kiss of love, of longing and of rapture.

Time and hurt didn't exist. She was wrapped in his arms, one with him, and for this moment it felt as if she was enveloped in his love once again.

When she finally slid down to stand, she gazed into his eyes that looked filled with love. For this moment they had recaptured the past. Gently, he picked her up to place her on the bed and stretched out beside her. She lay in his arms, exhausted, pressed against his hard length. Tom held her close against him, slowly combing his fingers through her hair. "This is good, Em," he said in a raspy tone.

She placed her hand on his cheek. They lay quietly, holding each other, touching, stroking each other gently, and she wished the night would stretch into eternity.

"We're way ahead of the schedule for fixing the house, aren't we?" he asked, his deep voice soft in the silent night.

"Yes, thanks to you and your dynamo energy."

"How about going to the ranch for a few days to get a break? You've already blocked off time from your photography. Honestly, I can use a little time on the ranch. Would you do that? A little break won't hurt."

She gazed at him as she thought it over. "Just a few days?"

"Sure. Just a break. I think we've earned one. I've

hired a company to get these hardwood floors back in shape for you."

"Tom—you didn't tell me. Are they putting in new floors?"

"No. It's a cleanup and polish, that sort of thing. If you want something more, though, now is the time to say so."

"No, that will be wonderful. That's all I intended to do. Thank you."

"You're welcome. Let's go to the ranch tomorrow and I'll call and tell them to come do the floors. I know the guy that owns the company, and we can trust him with the house key."

She laughed. "Sure. What's to steal here?" she asked, looking around at an empty room. "Very well. Yes, I'll go to the ranch—what? A week, four days, two days?"

"How is four days?"

"Four days it is. Thanks. I'll make arrangements and we'll go after lunch.

"Where are we staying?"

He leaned close. "Let's try the main house together. Our house. I can stay in a separate bedroom if you want, but four days—let's try, Em."

"You can always get your way with me. You know all you have to do is look at me, touch me or even just stand close and I'm putty."

"Very sexy putty, I'd say."

"Don't try to butter me up now," she said, smiling at him.

"Ah, butter. That's something we haven't tried. Maybe I will butter you up one night."

She laughed and hugged him. "Why can't it stay this way?"

"I can't answer that one."

The next afternoon, they were packed, had the house locked up and were in the car by two o'clock. On the ride back to the ranch, they reminisced about their high school days and dating. Emily wondered if they could maintain their relaxed, friendly attitude on the ranch, where so many painful memories came up day after day.

She would soon know. They moved into the big house and she had a chill run down her spine because she had a feeling they were making a big mistake by coming back when they didn't have to. Standing in the entryway beneath the Waterford crystal chandelier, she looked around.

"Tom, I'll take the guest bedroom on the far west side."

"Good idea. I'll take the one next to it unless you'll just let me move in with you from the start."

She laughed. "Let's see how we're doing by nightfall. We don't have a good track record in this house."

He took her hand and stepped close in front of her. With his other hand he caressed her nape lightly. "We had the best track record possible until that bus wreck. That's when it all went to hell. But we've been doing pretty well together in town these past weeks."

She nodded but still had the feeling of foreboding.

"I need to go see Gus and check on some things. I'm sure you can entertain yourself, and if nothing else, just take a four-day vacation."

"That sounds awesome," she said, smiling at him. "You get going and my vacation will start. I may go swim."

"Better check the pool over first for critters. No one has been here except a skeleton garden and cleaning staff."

"Oh, yes. I look before I jump in."

"So you do." He smiled at her. "See, we're doing pretty well. Kiss me and we'll see if we are still speaking to each other."

She laughed, but she really didn't feel lighthearted. He stepped close to embrace and kiss her, startling her for one second, and then she held him and returned his kiss, wondering if he would still want to kiss her in four days.

In minutes, he picked her up and carried her to a downstairs bedroom, setting her down only to yank the covers off the bed.

"Tom—" she protested.

"We're alone. What I'm going to do can wait. This can't," he rasped. In seconds, their clothing was gone and he picked her up as he kissed her. She locked her legs around him and he spread his feet apart, letting her slide down on his thick rod while they kissed.

Emily held him tightly, moving on him, her cries of ecstasy smothered by his kisses. She moved fast with him as he thrust deeply and groaned when he reached a shuddering climax.

She finally sagged against him, placing her head on his shoulder as he placed her in bed and then stretched out beside her.

"You are fantastic and leave me frazzled and in paradise at the same time."

She smiled. "You're never frazzled. We'll shower soon, but for a minute I want you close to me. This is a good way to start our current life here."

They talked softly, stroking each other, and he seemed to enjoy the moment as much as she did until he finally rolled over.

"I hate to go, but I have several things to do. First I'm going to talk to Gus. Then I'm going to my office in the guesthouse, because I need to find some old records for our accountant to do the taxes. No one will be here today except me, so do whatever you want. We should have dinners in the freezer and a couple in the fridge. I won't be gone long."

"I hope not. I don't do well in this big house by myself."

Something flickered in his gaze. "We had a lot of good years here and really good memories. We both need to try to remember to hang on to those times."

She leaned close to kiss him tenderly. "You've been my world since I was sixteen. Then, when the crash happened—"

"A day at a time," he said solemnly. "I'm going to shower and see you later. You find something in that freezer to thaw for us."

"Sure will." She watched him get up and leave the room. He was naked, handsome, all muscle. He had scars, but she barely noticed them. Desire stirred and she wondered if there was any hope for them to have a future together. Was the sex between them blinding them to the problems they faced—or was it helping to work those problems out?

Sex for them had always been good, but they couldn't stay married on that alone, and they really hadn't solved any problems between them. Or had they? There was her discovery that Tom thought she wished he had died instead of Ryan. They'd been able to clear the air about that. And she realized how tense and uptight she had been about getting pregnant, and how that might have driven him away from her. So maybe they were making progress.

After she showered and dressed, she walked through the house, closing off some rooms because she wanted to avoid seeing them.

As she set a casserole out to thaw, she received a call and didn't recognize the number, but then she saw the name Jason Nash on the caller ID and her breath caught.

She answered the call and heard a lilting female voice. "May I please speak to Emily Knox?"

"This is Emily Knox," Emily answered, barely able to catch her breath and feeling as if her heart was being squeezed by a giant fist. She gulped air, trying to calm.

"Mrs. Knox, this is Becky Nash. I'm Polly's mother. I'm sure you remember us."

"Yes, I do," she said, instantly recalling the discussion with the doctor who'd first told them about the Nash family after the bus accident. "How is Polly?" Emily asked, holding her breath and wondering why she was receiving this call.

"Polly is fine," Becky Nash said. "We'll be passing

through Texas, and we thought we could stop by if you would like to meet our daughter."

For a moment Emily couldn't answer. Tears filled her eyes and she felt a mixture of emotions—dread at revisiting all the pain from those days when Ryan was in the hospital, but also a thrill to get to meet the little girl who had received Ryan's heart. Their Ryan had given part of himself to another child who would have lost her life. Now their Ryan's heart kept Polly Nash alive.

"We'd love to meet her, Mrs. Nash."

"Please, call me Becky. We can come by your house if you'd like. Royal isn't too far from where we'll be on the interstate. I know this is rather short notice, but we changed some plans and now we'll be driving where we can stop by next Tuesday if that is convenient. Would Tuesday afternoon be possible?"

"Yes, that would be perfect. We're at Knox Acres Ranch, just outside town. I can tell you how to get here."

They finished making the arrangements and ended the call. Emily remembered the young mother—a pretty blue-eyed blonde in her early twenties. Jason Nash, her tall brown-haired husband, was an accountant with a big company in Denver. One of the doctors had approached them about the transplant, and later, after they agreed, they met the parents. But Emily and Tom had never met Polly. Now that was going to change on Tuesday afternoon.

She started to call Tom to tell him, but she decided she'd rather tell him in person. And she was curious about the guesthouse. She hadn't been inside since he'd moved there after their separation. She didn't know if he had changed it, spreading out and making a new home for himself. Or maybe he'd just left it the way it was.

She basked in the sunshine as she made the short walk across the yard and wide driveway. The guesthouse was a much smaller, far simpler house than the mansion, with a friendly warmth to it that she'd never felt the large house had. When she arrived, she crossed the porch to the open door. The screen door was closed, so she knocked on that.

"Come in," Tom called.

She stepped inside. "Where are you?" She looked around the living room that looked exactly like it always had after visitors had come and gone. The front room was immaculate and did not appear lived in.

"I'm in my office."

She had no idea where he had made an office, but she followed the sound of his voice and then saw him in the big master bedroom. He was on a ladder in the closet rummaging around on a shelf. Boxes and papers were strewn at his feet.

"I'm glad to see signs of someone living in here since you've been doing so for the past year. But you don't have much in the way of excess anything."

"I don't need much."

"Can you come down from there? I want to talk to you."

He paused and looked at her, and then came down a step and jumped the rest of the way.

He frowned as he faced her. "This must be something serious."

"It is. I need to talk to you."

He held out his hand. "Let's go in the living room and we can sit."

"I don't know that we need to sit to talk," she said, walking back into the front room and turning to face him. "I got a phone call. And I'm worried this might bring up some painful memories for us."

"Who called? This sounds important," he said.

"It is important. It was from Becky Nash."

Ten

Tom's hand stilled. "Why did she call us? Is the little girl all right?" he asked.

"Yes, she's fine. Her mother called because they are driving through Texas and asked if we would like to meet Polly. They are going to stop by here next Tuesday afternoon."

He looked away, his jaws clamped shut while he was silent. Finally he faced her again. "That is a big deal. We're going to meet the little girl who has our son's heart."

Silence stretched between them again, and Emily had a sinking feeling that a lot of their old problems were about to return, ending the fragile friendly truce.

"Would you rather I had told them not to come?"

He flinched and shook his head. "No. You did the

right thing. We should meet her. I just keep thinking that part of Ryan is still a living organ, that there's part of him still here."

"And keeping another child alive. Tom, Ryan has given life to this little girl."

Tom wiped his eyes. "I know that. And that's what we wanted and it's good, but it doesn't make our loss lighter or lessen the hurt of losing Ryan one damn degree. It brings the loss all back in a way. We should meet her, but that doesn't make it easy." He turned his back to her and she knew he wiped his eyes again.

And she knew she couldn't comfort him and he didn't want her to try. He had turned his back on her and was shutting her out of his life.

She hurt more than ever and suspected the last little vestige of her marriage was shattering.

In spite of their time together, the quiet hours spent on Uncle Woody's porch just talking about each other's plans, Emily could tell that this reminder of their loss had thrown them back to the way it used to be. To when they had been estranged and avoided each other.

She knew he didn't want her there, so she walked quietly out of the guesthouse and crossed back to the main house, barely able to see for her tears.

It was definitely over between them. She could tell when Tom turned his back on her that had been a final goodbye.

She had been wrapped in a false sense of happiness when he had lived in the old house with her and helped her get it back in shape. That was over and all the hurt over the bus wreck and loss of their son had returned.

And it would always come back. There would be reminders through life and she and Tom needed to let go and try to rebuild their lives.

She loved Tom and she couldn't imagine ever loving anyone else, but her marriage to him was over. She suspected she would not see him again until the Nashes arrived on Tuesday.

She cried as she walked back to the mansion. But she felt she had known all along the day would come when they would go back to avoiding each other and Tom would sign the divorce papers.

She decided that she would pack and choose what she wanted to have moved to her house in Royal so she could go as soon as the Nashes left.

She entered the empty, silent house, wanting to be back in town and away from so many painful memories here.

She thought of the fun times she and Tom had had over the past days. The evenings they'd spent on the porch, just talking. They had found joy in each other again and she was beginning to have hope. Tom was the most wonderful man she had ever known and she had fallen in love with him all over again. And now she was hurting all over again.

She didn't feel like having dinner and Tom didn't show, so she put the casserole back in the refrigerator and went out to the sprawling patio to sit where she could look at the spring flowers in the yard and the big blue swimming pool with its sparkling fountain. It was a cool March evening and she would rather sit outside.

She would borrow one of the ranch trucks to take

some furniture back with her. Tom wouldn't care what she took or what she left. She doubted whether he would ever live in the main house again, and she didn't want to.

She put her head in her hands to cry. She had lost them both—Ryan and Tom.

She cried quietly as she sat there in the dusky evening, looking at the fountain and feeling numb. She gazed beyond the pool. Silence enveloped her. Occasionally she could hear the wind, a soft sound, the only sound. As if the entire world was at peace. She knew better. It wasn't, and neither was her little corner of it. But the illusion was nice.

"Did you eat dinner?"

She heard Tom's deep voice from the doorway and turned around. He stood in the door with his hands on his hips.

"No. Do you want any?"

"No. I'll stay at the guesthouse tonight."

"I thought you probably would. I'll get my car tomorrow so I can take it back to Royal when I go."

When he didn't say anything else, she finally glanced over her shoulder to see if he stood watching her. She was alone. He had gone, and she wondered if they would ever again be relaxed and compatible the way they had been these past weeks.

Long after dark she went inside and began to gather scrapbooks and small things she wanted to take to Royal. There was nothing to hold her here at the ranch.

She propped up the pillows in her bed and sat against

them on top of the covers to look through the old scrap-books. But they made her sad, so she finally scooted down in bed to go to sleep.

Tom lay awake in the dark. As long as he and Emily were together, there would be reminders of their tragic past, some little moments and some big ones, like the Nashes' visit. Their visit would tear Emily up. It would probably tear him up just as much. He wanted them to come by, but it was going to hurt and be difficult to deal with. It also brought all the memories swarming back, the pain, the fear, the terrible wreck and panic that had consumed him. His inadequacy, his failure to protect the two he loved most—that's what always tore him up.

He couldn't ever forget carrying his son's little body, holding Ryan, which was like holding ice, against his heart, praying for him, unaware of his own injuries until much later. And then the decision to donate Ryan's organs to save another child—to save other parents from going through what they'd suffered.

Tom wiped his eyes. As long as he and Emily were together, they would always have moments when the memories and pain would return full force.

The loss was devastating and it didn't get easier. They had moved on, but the hurt of missing little Ryan…that never changed. Tom knew that if he lived to be one hundred, he would still shed tears over his baby.

The Nashes' upcoming visit complicated the healing process for him. In a way, it was a stark reminder that he had failed Emily when he failed to save Ryan. He had loved her with his whole heart and still loved her in so many ways, but he just didn't know how to make it up to her. Tom was certain Emily would be better off without him in her life.

If they both started with new friends, new homes, new everything—new loves in their lives, even—maybe each day wouldn't be filled with pain and loss and sorrow.

Tuesday would be tough. He dreaded the day, but if he had taken the Nashes' call, he would have done the same thing Emily had and agreed to meet with them. Even though he knew it would be more heartache, he wanted to see the little girl who had Ryan's heart beating in her chest and giving her life.

Just the thought caused a knot in his throat. After Ryan, he had never been able to handle death and dying as well. Maybe it added to his heartache to have Jeremy's death so soon after losing Ryan.

Sleep wasn't going to come easily, probably not at all, but it wouldn't be his first sleepless night. Tom put his hands behind his head and looked out the open window at the stars. The divorce hung over them, and he wanted to go ahead and get it over and done with.

This living together in the same house again was gearing up to cause another big hurt for both of them. He ought to get out and let her go on with her life.

All the basic things were lined up to get done on Emily's old house. Nathan would send someone around to check on her, just like they were doing for Natalie. He and Emily needed to go ahead with their divorce.

Divorce was going to hurt because Emily was part

of his life and it was like cutting into himself, but it would be best for both of them, definitely better for her.

Would seeing Polly Nash tear them both up? Ryan's heart still beat—that was the most amazing thing. Little Polly Nash could live because she had Ryan's heart. They would meet her Tuesday afternoon—and for just a little while part of Ryan would once again be with them, at the only home Ryan had known. Tom stared through the window. It would be another day he would remember as long as he lived. So would Emily.

On Tuesday morning, Tom showered and got dressed in a navy Western-style shirt, jeans and his best black boots. When he was finished, he combed his hair and left the guesthouse.

At noon, he walked over to the mansion and rang the bell. When Emily didn't come to the door, he stepped inside.

"Emily?" he called. He heard her heels as she approached in the hall. Then she entered the room and he couldn't get his breath as he looked at her. Her wavy honey-brown hair fell loosely around her face. She wore little makeup, but had a natural beauty he loved. She wore a sheer pale blue top over a pale blue silk cami and white slacks with high-heeled blue sandals.

"You take my breath away, you look so beautiful."

"Thank you," she said quietly. "I think that should be my line, only substitute 'handsome' for 'beautiful.' You're the one who is dazzling."

"I'm not sure you have ever realized how beautiful I think you are."

"It's nice to hear you say that to me. I won't forget." She smiled, but there was a sad look in her eyes.

"I want to do this, and at the same time, I know it's going to hurt like hell."

"I know," she whispered. "You might as well come in and sit. You're a little early, and they may have trouble finding the ranch."

They walked into the formal living room and she sat in a dark blue wing chair while he went to the window to look out at the drive.

"This week I think we should go ahead with the divorce," Tom said quietly. "I think each of us will be better off. Reminders like today will always bring the pain back, and I just don't think we're equipped to deal with it together."

"I think we're dealing with it okay, Tom. Some things will fade as the years go by."

"We're better off just starting anew." He turned to face her. "You said you don't need me to stay with you in Royal, so I've talked to Nathan and he'll send someone around to check on you."

"Thank you."

"Will you be all right there alone?"

"Yes, I will," she said, smiling, sitting back in the chair and crossing her long legs, which momentarily captured his attention and made him forget everything else.

"I told you I'd deal with the roofers, and I think I can get them out by the first of next week. How's that?"

"It will be fine. Thank you."

He gazed at her, thinking she was being very polite,

which meant she was keeping a tight rein on her feelings. She was probably upset about meeting the Nashes' daughter. He turned back to the window. He needed to get through meeting Polly Nash. Get through the divorce. Maybe then he would find some peace in life.

He saw a car approaching and he doubled his hands into fists. Once again, he asked himself why he hadn't died in place of his son. Emily might not have wanted that, but he did. And why hadn't he died instead of Jeremy, who was within yards of him when he took the enemy fire? Jeremy had had so much to live for.

Frowning, Tom watched the car approach, wondering about those two situations that he had survived. He had better do something useful with his life to make up for the fact that Ryan's and Jeremy's had been cut short.

Emily followed Tom to the front porch and they stood waiting to greet the family as they stepped out of their gray van. A slender woman with straight hair got out as her husband walked around the car to her. He was in tan slacks and a tan knit shirt. He held the door as his daughter stepped out. Polly Nash was a pretty little girl with brown hair and hazel eyes with thick brown lashes—the same coloring as Ryan. She stood politely with her mother and held a wrapped package in her hands.

"Mr. and Mrs. Knox, we're so glad to see you again. This is our daughter, Polly," Becky Nash said by way of greeting.

"Please just call us Tom and Emily," Emily said.

"And you can call us Becky and Jason," Polly's mother replied.

"Come inside," Tom said and held the door.

When they were all in the formal living room, Emily invited them to take a seat. "Thanks for calling us. Are you vacationing?"

"Yes," Jason Nash said. "We're on our way back to Colorado now and thought we'd stop because we were passing so close by."

"Polly has something for you," Becky said and nudged her daughter, who smiled shyly and took the present to Emily.

"Thank you, Polly," Emily said, smiling at the little girl. "How old are you?"

"I'm eight. I'm in the third grade."

"That's great. Third grade is a good year. Tom, come open this with me."

The package was wrapped in light blue paper with a big silver-and-blue ribbon tied in a huge bow. Tom slipped it off the package and Emily carefully undid the pretty wrapping paper. "Did you wrap this, Polly?"

"No, ma'am. Mom did," she said, glancing at her mother, who was smiling.

When they unwrapped the package, there was another in brown mailing paper and tape addressed to a school. Emily handed it to Tom, who took out his pocketknife and carefully cut into the brown paper. When he was done, he pushed the paper away and held up a framed picture of a schoolroom with a picture of a plaque on the wall. The plaque had a picture of Ryan in one corner.

Looking more closely at the plaque, Emily read aloud. "'This Jefferson music room is built, furnished and maintained in loving memory of Ryan Knox of Royal, Texas.'"

"We've done that in your son's memory at Polly's school in Colorado."

"Thank you so much," Emily said. "That is touching and kind of you."

"We want to express our thanks to your son and to you folks in some way that's permanent. You gave our Polly back to us, gave her a chance at life."

"That's a fine memorial," Tom said. "Thank all three of you."

Emily gazed at Ryan's smiling picture. "This is a lovely memorial, and it means so much to Tom and me. Hopefully, we'll get to visit the school and see this," she said, smiling at the Nashes.

Tom turned to Polly. "Do you have a music class?"

"Yes, sir," she answered politely. "I'm learning to play the violin and I take piano lessons. I like my books and I like my piano lessons," she said, smiling.

"She has lots of friends at school, too," Becky added.

"Have you ever been on a ranch?" Tom asked.

Polly shook her head. "No, I haven't."

"Want to see the barn and the horses?"

She looked at her parents. "I think that's a yes," her dad said and stood. "I'll go with you and we'll look a little." He held out his hand and Polly took it. It reminded Emily of how she used to hold Ryan's hand, and she felt a tug on her heart.

Tom walked out with them, sounding friendly and

cheerful, telling Polly about the ranch, but Emily wondered what his cheer was costing him.

"She's a sweet little girl," Becky said. "And I can't say enough how thankful we are—you've given our little girl life," she said, getting tears in her eyes. "That memorial is just a token gesture. We're looking into a college scholarship. Whatever we do, you'll be notified. We wanted to come here to show our gratitude in person."

"We're thrilled that Ryan's heart is giving her life," Emily said.

"I pray for you and your husband every day, and I give thanks that we are blessed to have our little girl. We just owe all of that to you and your husband."

"It's a miracle of science, and I'm thrilled we could help. Polly seems so sweet and bright."

Emily sat and talked to Becky until the others came back, Polly skipping ahead of the men. Emily's heart clutched again as she watched her.

After Polly told her mother about the three horses she had seen, Becky looked over Polly's head at Emily. "We have a lot of miles and should go, but before we do, would you like to feel her heartbeat? We've talked to her about it and she knows where she got her heart and she's happy for you to feel it beating."

Emily stood and crossed the room. "Is it all right if I touch you, Polly?"

Polly smiled and nodded. Emily put her hand on Polly's chest and felt the steady beat of the heart that had given life to her son. For an instant she experienced a renewed tie to her child. Tears filled her eyes.

Emily turned away, wiping at her tears. "Tom," she said. He stood close, and she took his hand and placed it on Polly's small chest.

"That's part of Ryan," he whispered and turned away. Becky wiped her eyes, too.

"We can never tell you what your gift has meant to us except that our Polly wouldn't be here with us today if it hadn't been for your Ryan. We're sorry for your loss. We are so grateful for your gift of life for Polly."

Emily looked into Polly's hazel eyes. "Thank you," she said softly. "Polly, thank you. You share a special tie with our little baby. Thank you." Emily moved away.

She and Tom went out with the Nashes to see them off. Standing on the drive waving as they drove off, Emily knew they would not see each other again.

Without waiting for Tom, she turned and went inside, walking to the kitchen to get a drink of water. She put her head in her hands and cried.

When she felt composed, she went back to the formal living room but found it empty. She walked out to the porch, but Tom was nowhere around. She looked at the guest cottage down the drive and saw no sign of him, but she suspected he was already there and she wouldn't see him again today. She had seen Tom's tears and knew he would be hurting badly.

Once again, she thought about her losses—of her son and her husband, the only man she had ever loved or ever would love. But he was as lost to her as Ryan. Next would come the divorce, and then she didn't know if she would ever see him again.

She felt as if she was losing him for the second time,

but this time, it would be permanent. She went to the bedroom where she was staying.

Soon Tom would be out of her life. She would have to make her own life.

She walked through the house to go upstairs and movement caught her eye. She realized Tom was outside in the back. He was standing on the patio, looking at the pool or the yard or something beyond him. She went out.

"I thought you had gone home."

"Not yet, but I'm going. I wanted to wait until the Nashes were gone." He wiped his eyes. Once again, there was a time she would have gone to him and put her arms around him. Now she knew he really wouldn't want her to do that. The wall was back between them.

He turned around to face her. His eyes were red, and she guessed hers probably were, too. "I think it's time for that divorce. We'll each be better off."

"I know, Tom. It's all right," she said. She looked at his broad shoulders and wondered if he was right. "I'll go back to Uncle Woody's tomorrow. If you can get someone to help me, I'd like to move a few things from here. Can I borrow a pickup?"

"Don't ask stuff like that. Do whatever you damn please. We share this ranch. I'll get two guys to help and you take anything and everything you want. You know how much this house means to me."

That hurt, because this house was where they had spent some wonderful years and it was the only home Ryan had known except Uncle Woody's.

"Thank you for all you did for me in Royal."

"I'll keep up with the window guys, also the floor people and the roofers. The floors should be done in two weeks. I'll check and let you know." He stood looking at her. "I'm going back to the guesthouse. What time do you want the guys here tomorrow?"

"I should be ready at about ten o'clock. I'll take some things. I may want to come back and get some more."

"Sure. Do what you want. Let me know if you need help." He looked at her a long time and turned away, passing her and going inside. She suspected he walked straight through and out the front and was headed to the guest cottage.

She went in, walking to the window to watch, and saw she was right. He walked with that straight back that people in the military develop. With each step he was walking out of her life.

She thought about Ryan's heart beating in Polly's chest. Her baby's heart—still beating, giving life to another child. Longing for Ryan, to hold him again and hear his laughter, swamped Emily. Longing for Tom quickly followed, to have his strong arms around her, his solid reassurance. She put her head in her hands and cried, aware she was losing Tom now even though she still loved him with all her heart. They'd had unhappy moments and she thought their love had crumbled, but she realized that was one more mistake. She loved him and she always would.

When she had calmed down, she locked up and went upstairs to sit on the balcony of the big master bedroom and cried some more. She hurt over both of them and she knew she would continue to hurt.

* * *

The next day she called Tom and didn't get an answer. She selected furniture she wanted and called their foreman, Gus. He already knew she was taking furniture to the house in Royal and he had three guys to help and two pickups and they were ready when she was.

Wondering where Tom was, she told Gus to send the men over. In a short time they were on the drive by the back door. She knew all three—Bix Smith, Ty Green and Marty Holcomb.

She showed them which pieces of furniture to pack up. Tom didn't want anything to do with the house, so she took what she wanted.

She drove her car to Royal behind the two pickups and they spent the morning unloading furniture. The men left before noon, and when she was alone, she looked around, remembering Tom in every room and the happiness she'd had while they worked on the renovations together. The time had been good, but why couldn't life ahead be filled with a lot more good times? They had been through the worst. She stood gazing down the hall, seeing Tom there, smiling, flirting with her, making her laugh. Why were they getting a divorce when they had so much between them that was wonderful and fulfilling?

Thinking about their future, she drove down Main Street, turning on the block where her studio was located. As she stepped out of her car, the enticing smell of baking bread assailed her and she remembered Tom buying two loaves and eating half of one himself that night. She went into the bakery and bought two more loaves. She could always freeze them if she didn't eat them.

She went into her studio to pick up her mail and saw two other proofs of Tom's pictures on her desk. She picked one up and looked at him. "I love you," she whispered.

And that's when it hit her.

"We can't give up what we have," she said. "We're not going to get a divorce, Tom Knox, because life with you is too awesome. It's way too marvelous to give up." She sat there staring at his picture. She didn't want a divorce. They'd had wonderful moments in the past weeks they were together. They had weathered the worst and survived and they still could enjoy each other's company.

She was going back to the ranch to find Tom and tell him she didn't want the divorce. She still had clothes at the ranch, so she didn't have to go home and get anything.

As she drove back to the ranch, she missed Tom and thought about the happiness they'd had together. Their love had moments when it was so great. She also thought about their lovemaking, which had been exciting and bound them together closer than ever. She wasn't ready to give up on their marriage. Not after the time she had spent with him.

But there was still the question of children. She thought about Tom as a father. He needed children in his life. She did, too. He was willing to adopt and he was right—they both would love any child in their lives. Why had she been so opposed to adoption? If she'd only agreed to adopt, this divorce wouldn't be looming in her life. Another big mistake she had made. But mistakes could be fixed sometimes. She hoped it wasn't too late.

As soon as she turned onto the ranch road, she called Tom, but he didn't answer. She didn't see his pickup at the guesthouse when she passed it, so he must be out on the ranch.

She decided to stay at the mansion until she reached him. She tried the rest of the day and that night, but when she still didn't get him at midnight, she wondered if he had stopped taking her calls.

She slept little that night, pacing the floor and thinking about Tom, their past and their future.

By morning she was firmly set in her opinions about their future.

She didn't intend to walk away and lose him, because for the past few weeks, he had acted like a man in love. And she was definitely in love with him. She had fallen in love with him when she was sixteen and she had never stopped loving him.

She had made mistakes that might still cost her the marriage—like being so uptight about getting pregnant. Tom was right and they should just adopt. He was wonderful with any kids he was ever around.

Had he already signed the divorce papers?

It didn't matter. They could marry again. She wasn't giving up, because the days they had spent together had been a reunion for them, binding them together stronger than ever. He thought when they were together, they compounded the hurts. They might sometimes, but they definitely did not compound the bad times often.

Life had rough times, and Tom was tough enough to weather them. And so was she. Together they would do better at getting through them.

She showered, brushing out her long wavy hair and pulling on a red T-shirt, jeans and boots. She left to find him, walking to the guesthouse. He wasn't there, so she had called Gus, who said he hadn't seen Tom but thought he was still on the ranch.

She stood in front of the guesthouse and then she thought about where she might find him. She drove to the most beautiful spot on the ranch, a gradual slope that had a winding, shallow stream along the bottom. There were big oaks planted inside the small area that had a white picket fence around it. It was the plot of land she and Tom had picked out together for the cemetery where Ryan was buried, with a marble angel standing beside the marble headstone and a bank of blooming Texas Lilac Vitex on either side. Tom stood in the shade of one of the oaks with his pickup parked outside the fence.

When he saw her coming, he turned to face her and waited as she came through the gate.

He had on his black Stetson and a black cotton shirt, along with jeans and black boots. He looked wonderful to her.

"I was just about to leave to find you. I figured I'd have to drive to Royal. I thought you went back to town."

"I did, but I came back. I thought I would find you here at the family cemetery. This place holds so much meaning for us."

"It's quiet out here and I can think about Ryan and

about us, the past, the present—these days we've spent together. Think about this miracle of another little child having Ryan's heart that is givng her life."

"I know you used to come out here and just stay for a while."

"For me, it brings up so many good memories. Working on your house together, we added some more good moments."

As he stepped closer, he raised an eyebrow. "Why were you looking for me?"

A breeze tugged at her hair as she faced him.

"Will you come home with me?"

She saw the flare of surprise in his eyes. "I love you, and I don't want a divorce," she said. "Ever since I received the email from Maverick, you have acted like a man in love. We've had a lot of love between us, and I'm not ready to give up on this marriage." She hugged him tightly. "I know I've made mistakes, Tom, but we can work through the problems."

He wrapped his arms around her to kiss her, a kiss that was an answer by itself. Trembling, she clung to him and kissed him back while joy filled her because he would never kiss her this way if he was going to divorce her.

He released her slightly, letting his hands rest on her shoulders again. "Before we go any further, there's something I have to say." His expression was solemn and suddenly she wondered if she had guessed wrong, that his possessive and responsive kiss was goodbye.

Cold fear wrapped around her again. "What is it?"

"Ah, Em, I'm so sorry. I failed you both, you and

Ryan. I couldn't save him. I failed you then in the worst way," Tom said, looking beyond her.

"You didn't fail me. You didn't fail him, either. Don't blame yourself when you are blameless."

"Yes, I did. I should have saved him."

"You couldn't. The doctors said he died from the trauma caused by his injuries in the bus," she said. "You didn't fail me or Ryan, because you did the very best you could. All of Ryan's life, you were an amazing father, and Ryan wanted to be just like you."

"I've always felt I failed you both. I don't know, Em—"

"Well, I know what I want and what I need. Our marriage has been good again—joyous, sexy, productive. We've been best friends and enjoyed each other's company, helped each other. We can do this. I'm not giving up on our marriage," she said, squeezing him tightly as if by holding him she could keep him from doing anything to end their union.

She looked up at him and he brushed her hair from her face to gaze into her eyes.

He stepped back and reached into his jeans pocket, struggling to pull something out. "That's why I was going to town. I wanted to find you and tell you that I don't want the damn divorce. I love you with all my heart and I need you in my life."

Tears of joy filled her eyes as she hugged him. "I love you. We can get through life together. Tom, I love you so."

Wrapping his arms around her, he kissed her again and this time her heart pounded with joy. He leaned away.

"You were always so strong," he said. "Too strong. I didn't think you needed me anymore."

"Yes, I do. I need you desperately. I'm unhappy without you. And I'm complete when we're together. Tom, there will be problems, but we can work through them. I love you. I need you." She looked into his hazel eyes that she loved, eyes that could melt her and at other times give her strength. "There will always be problems. That's life, but we're better at handling them when we're together. I love you and I need you."

"I love you more than you'll ever know and I want to spend my life trying to show you." He released her and held out his hand. "I got this for you after we saw the Nash family."

Surprised, she examined the small velvet box. She couldn't imagine what he was giving her. She looked up at him and he smiled.

"Are you going to see what your present is?"

"Yes," she said, taking the box to open it. Inside was a tangle of a piece of jewelry. She picked it up and gasped as a necklace shook out in her hand. It was a golden heart pendant on a thin gold chain that was covered with diamonds.

"Oh, my heavens, Tom. It's beautiful."

"It's because of Ryan giving life with his heart to little Polly Nash. That holds meaning for both of us. It's a locket."

"Let me see. This is gorgeous—" She gasped when she opened the locket. "Tom, this is wonderful. I'll treasure this always," she said, hugging him again and kissing him longer this time while he held her tightly in his embrace.

She leaned away and held the locket up so they could both look inside at the picture of Ryan smiling into the camera. "You selected this locket for me. You must have changed your mind right after you told me we should go ahead with the divorce."

"It didn't take long. I've spent a year living in the guesthouse alone and then we've had this fantastic time together. No matter what we go through, I want you with me. I thought about it and I've loved you always. You're the only woman for me for the rest of my life. I love you. I'd give my life for you. I've loved you since you ran into my car when we were sixteen. And, Em, you worry so about having my child—"

"We can adopt. You're right. I watched you with the Valentine kids and I played with them and if we adopt, we'll love them like our own. We both would love any child we raised. Whatever you want to do. We can go without kids. There are loads of kids we can help without raising them—through reading programs, starting a ranch camp for kids, playing ball, you know, things you can help with and so can I."

He studied her. "You've got this all figured out, haven't you?"

"I'm desperate. I don't want to lose you, because I love you with all my heart. And you have never failed me, Tom. Never. You couldn't save Ryan. I couldn't save Ryan. The doctors couldn't save him. But you didn't fail me. You tried all you could."

"You're sure?" he asked.

"With all my heart. Please put my locket on me." She handed him the necklace and turned so he could fasten it at the back of her neck. "You really got this since we saw the Nashes?"

"I have a jeweler in Dallas. I sent a text, he sent me pictures of what he had. I picked out this one and told him I wanted it delivered yesterday."

"Oh, my word. Someone from the jewelry store drove this to you?"

"That's right. I didn't want to wait. We've been separated way too long, my love."

She turned to face him. "This is wonderful, Tom, but most of all is knowing you'll be in my life."

"Baby, you're all that I need, and I'll spend the rest of my life making that clear to you. Em, I've thought all this time that you were angry because I failed you—"

"Never. We've both made big mistakes, but we've survived them and some of them we're able to let go and try to forget. They're not part of our lives any longer." She slipped her arms around him. "I'm so happy. I love you with all my heart. I know we'll be all right."

"I know we will. But how the hell do you undo a divorce?"

"I'm leaving that one to you. Oh, how I love you. I'll show you, too. It's time to leave here and go home. Oh, my heavens, we don't have a home," she said, frowning as she looked up at him. "You can't be a rancher and live in Uncle Woody's house in Royal. Neither of us wants to live in the mansion. We're not both living in the guesthouse."

Tom held her with his arms around her waist as he smiled at her. "It's just another problem we'll work out. What do you think about finishing your Royal house? Then that will be our town house and you can still work in town part of the week if you want. And maybe it's time for a redo of ranch house. Or we can demolish it if you want and start over."

"We'll talk about that one—I vote for the redo because we have good memories there. I'll live on the ranch with you and maybe drive into town and keep the studio open by appointment only. But come home with me now," she said. "I've got two new loaves of bread for you in the car. How's that? And maybe some fun in the bedroom?"

"You've got a deal." Laughing, he pulled her into his embrace. "But I don't want to wait to show you how much I've missed you. We're not driving to Royal now. We're going to live in the guesthouse for a little while. I'll tell Gus we're going to Royal and he's in charge, but today, I don't want to drive any farther than our guesthouse. I have plans for us and that bread."

She laughed, looking into his eyes and seeing the happiness mirrored there that she felt.

"Tom, I'm not sure I felt this excited on our wedding day."

"It's a bigger deal now, Em. We know what we lost, what we almost lost and what we have. Our love is the essential part of our lives and we have our memories of Ryan to share. I want to spend every day of the rest of my life trying to show you how much I love you."

His words thrilled her as much as the look in his

eyes. She stood on tiptoe and he leaned closer to kiss her while he embraced her.

Joy poured into her that there wouldn't be any divorce. She loved him—always had and always would. As she returned his kiss, she thought their future was filled with promise and hope.

* * * * *

COMING SOON!

LET'S TALK
Romance

For exclusive extracts, competitions
and special offers, find us online:

- facebook.com/millsandboon
- @MillsandBoon
- @MillsandBoonUK

Get in touch on 01413 063232

For all the latest titles coming soon, visit
millsandboon.co.uk/nextmonth

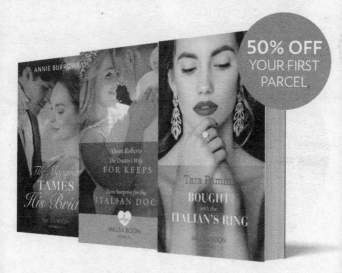